Nicole Murphy has been a primary schoolteacher, bookstore owner, journalist and checkout chick. She grew up reading Tolkien, Lewis and Le Guin; spent her twenties discovering Quick, Lindsey and Deveraux; and lives her love of science fiction and fantasy through her involvement with the Conflux science-fiction conventions. She lives with her husband in Queanbeyan, NSW. Visit her website: nicolermurphy.com

Also by Nicole Murphy

DREAM OF ASARLAI
Secret Ones (Book One)

POWER UNBOUND

NICOLE MURPHY

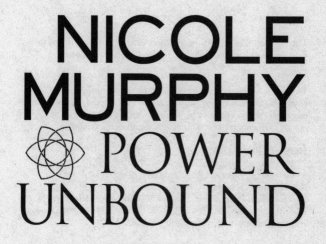

POWER UNBOUND

DREAM OF ASARLAI: BOOK TWO

HARPER
Voyager

Harper*Voyager*
An imprint of HarperCollins*Publishers*

First published in Australia in 2011
by HarperCollins*Publishers* Australia Pty Limited
ABN 36 009 913 517
harpercollins.com.au

HarperCollins*Publishers*
25 Ryde Road, Pymble, Sydney, NSW 2073, Australia
31 View Road, Glenfield, Auckland 0627, New Zealand
A 53, Sector 57, Noida, UP, India
77–85 Fulham Palace Road, London W6 8JB, United Kingdom
2 Bloor Street East, 20th floor, Toronto, Ontario M4W 1A8, Canada
10 East 53rd Street, New York NY 10022, USA

National Library of Australia Cataloguing-in-Publication entry:

Murphy, Nicole R.
    Power unbound / Nicole Murphy.
    ISBN 978 0 7322 9162 4 (pbk.)
    Murphy, Nicole R. Dream of Asarlai ; bk. 2.
A823.4

Cover design by Natalie Winter
Cover image © Studio MPM/Corbis
Author photograph by Cat Sparks
Typeset in Goudy Old Style 10/13pt by Letter Spaced
Printed and bound in Australia by Griffin Press
50gsm Bulky News used by HarperCollins*Publishers* is a natural,
recyclable product made from wood grown in sustainable plantation
forests. The manufacturing processes conform to the environmental
regulations in the country of origin, New Zealand.

5 4 3 2 1   11 12 13 14

To my parents, Gael Scala and Brian Dunkley,
for instilling in me a love of reading,
science fiction and fantasy

and

to my grandmother Kathleen Scala,
who introduced me to the wonderful world of romance.
I'm sorry you're not here to see this.

SHAUNA

Shauna Connell pressed her hands into her armpits to keep herself from grabbing the potion from her fellow student and doing it herself. Star above, but Brian Mochrie was a nervous twit. He came across initially as all arrogant and confident but put him in the spotlight, make him test himself and suddenly he was like a virgin on a first date – shaking with anticipation and fear.

She almost smiled as his trembling hand extended over the beaker, and the dropper he was holding jerked up and down. She glanced sideways to see Asarlai watching him carefully and hoped their teacher realised how undeserving he was.

'*Nervous much?*' she thought at him.

He slid a glare at her from the corner of his eye. He probably wanted to call her every name under the sun, but didn't dare in front of Asarlai.

Despite the fact she and Brian were both members of the League of Purification and dedicated to separating gadda from the pestilence of humanity, she'd never liked him. Brian came from one of the richer families in Sclossin, and didn't understand the value of work, effort and persistence. Everything he wanted had been handed to him from the moment he was born. Shauna thought that made him weak; Shauna was strong.

Brian squeezed the rubber and three drops slipped into the grey emulsion in the beaker. Stillness; Shauna wondered if he had actually failed. Star, let it be so. Then the liquid began to bubble and steam, turning from grey to a purple so dark it seemed black.

As much as she hated Brian, Shauna was pleased to see the potion had worked. The texts had again lived up to their promise.

'It's ready,' Brian said.

Asarlai stood and walked over. Shauna noted the newly grey hair and lines unfamiliar on a face that was well-known to most gadda. She felt a burst of pride that of all the people who could have received this new knowledge, Asarlai had chosen her. She saw something in Shauna that others didn't.

Asarlai bent down, looked at the beaker and sniffed it before she nodded to Brian. 'It looks and smells as it should. Now, see if it works.'

Brian picked up a syringe. Shauna tilted her head to check for the small hair inside the glass vial. Slowly, he drew some of the potion up into the vial. As the purple-black potion touched the hair, he murmured something under his breath. The mixture in the vial bubbled.

'Shauna, bring the animal over,' Asarlai said.

Shauna opened the cage on the bench next to her and grasped the gerbil. It wriggled and screamed, and she gave it a gentle squeeze, sending the message it would not escape. The rodent settled, but it trembled within her grasp.

She took it over and watched calmly as Brian pinched some of its skin and injected the potion. The gerbil screeched and tried to escape, but Shauna held it firm until Brian had emptied the needle. Then she put it back in the cage.

Brian nodded to Asarlai. 'It is done.'

'Give it some time to take effect. You can clean the laboratory.' Their teacher returned to the armchair in the corner of the room.

They started to clean away everything that Brian had used to create the emulsion. As Shauna picked up the beaker with the leftover potion, Asarlai said, 'Don't throw that away. Divide it equally between two containers.'

Shauna felt Brian's questioning gaze on her. She looked at him, shrugged and did as she was told. Whatever Asarlai had planned, it would undoubtedly be for the best.

When everything but the extra liquid had been tidied up, Brian asked, 'Is it time?'

'Try it,' Asarlai said.

Shauna followed Brian over to the cage. He took a deep breath, and she rolled her eyes. Show a bit of gumption, she thought.

He spoke a word. 'Muireadhach.' Irish for lord or master.

For a moment, nothing happened. Then the gerbil began to twitch, and then shake, the small body staggering around the cage. It fell onto its side, shook one last time and then was still.

Shauna almost clapped. She wanted to dance. It was incredible. Amazing. With just one word, the creature had been killed.

'Test it,' Asarlai said.

Brian opened the cage and touched the animal. It didn't react. He poked it harder. Nothing.

'It's dead.' He took a step backward and looked at Shauna.

'It worked,' she whispered, her eyes shining.

'Well done,' Asarlai said. 'However, we need to test it further. I want you each to cut a lock of your hair and put it into one of the beakers.'

Brian looked at Shauna. *'Does she mean to kill us?'*

'Of course not.' Shauna wanted to hit him. *'Why would she do so? She is training us to assist her, has spent more than a month teaching us.'* Shauna walked over to the bench, picked up a knife and hacked a bit off her ponytail. As she went to stand in front of one of the beakers, Asarlai said, 'Wait. At the same time.'

Shauna looked at Brian, who had gone as pale as cream. He was going to refuse. He would show who he truly was, and Shauna would be Asarlai's favourite student. Her right hand. The one she relied on. The one she trusted. The one people would talk about for centuries.

'Brian?' Asarlai's soft voice whispered through the room but Brian shuddered as though she'd yelled at him. 'Will you do as I ask?'

Slowly, he walked over, cut some of his own hair and held it over his beaker. Shauna held hers out and, at the same time, they let go.

As their locks hit the liquid, Asarlai said, 'Cacht.' Slave.

The potions bubbled and then subsided; tendrils of smoke wafted past Shauna's nose.

'Drink it.'

Without hesitation, Shauna picked up the beaker and downed it. The potion had a peppery taste and slid down her throat with more fullness than she expected. It thumped into her stomach and for a terrible moment she thought it would come right back up again.

But she controlled the reaction, turned to Asarlai and said, 'I am worthy.'

The teacher nodded and Shauna felt a thrill. The things they would do.

Brian stared at the beaker for a long while before he finally picked it up and drank it. He put it down, his mouth pulled into a grimace.

'How do you feel?' Asarlai asked.

Brian put his hand to his stomach. 'I feel a little nauseated.' Shauna rolled her eyes and shook her head.

Asarlai nodded. 'You will remain well, unless you betray me. Now, take out your notebooks and write what you have learnt today.'

Shauna bounced over to the notebook, opened it and began to scrawl so fiercely that her pen nib ripped small holes in the page.

She understood why Asarlai had poisoned them – she needed to know they would be loyal to her before she started them on the next, more dangerous path. A path that would lead them all – every gadda alive – to glory.

Shauna was smiling as she wrote.

ONE

Ione Gorton snapped the lid shut on the last plastic container and looked at the results of her morning of effort with satisfaction. There was a large chocolate mud cake — her mother-in-law's favourite — and her father-in-law's preferred potato and pumpkin scones. To keep Jack satisfied on the trip to the farm, she had included a lunchbox of choc-chip cookies and caramel fudge while for Mark there were the ubiquitous currant squares.

She traced her finger over the lid, a half-smile twisting her lips. Every once in a while, she did something that prompted particular memories of Patrick. Currant squares had been her husband's favourite, and as a teenager she'd made them whenever he and Mark went away on a trip together. Her brother always thought she'd made them just for him. She'd confessed the reality to his best friend on their first date.

It had been more than seven years since Patrick's death and still, there were moments where she missed him with a pain that brought tears to her eyes. She brushed her finger over her cheeks and went to find the one person who could always make her feel better.

Jack was sitting on his bedroom floor, surrounded by piles of computer games. His eyes ping-ponged between the two he was holding as Ione walked into the room. He looked at her, his face scrunched up.

'I can't decide,' he said. 'I'm only partway through *Doom 4*, but if I finish it then I'll have nothing to do, but if I start *The Mighty Thor* I might *not* finish it and then I'll have two games to finish, not just one.'

'I'm astounded you're only taking one,' Ione said, moving a pile of games aside to kneel down.

'I'm not.' Jack looked back at the two titles in his hands. 'These are my serious games. I'm taking other games for entertainment.'

Star love him, Ione thought with a smile. She certainly did. 'What other games?'

'Well, I've got my Nintendo DS so I'm taking *Super Mario Galaxy Two* and *WarioWare — DIY* and I'm taking *Rock Band* and the PS3 for Grandpa, 'cause he likes that, you know.'

A suspicion began to dawn on Ione. 'Have you packed?'

'Yep, see?' Jack waved his hand at the large suitcase on his bed.

Ione went over, opened it and stared at the collection of electronic drums, guitars, microphones and games systems. 'Um, Jack ...'

'What?' He didn't look at her, intent on making his decision.

'While I can see that you have your entertainment needs well and truly covered and I congratulate you for being so thorough, I'd like to know what you're going to wear for the next two weeks. You aren't going to have those on day and night, are you?' She pointed to his jeans and jumper.

''Course not.' Jack frowned at her. 'I packed pyjamas.'

Ione looked closer and saw that, indeed, his Godzilla-print flannelette pyjamas had been squashed down the side of the case. 'You need more clothes than this, Jacky-boy.'

'They won't fit.'

'Then you're leaving some of this behind.' She started to pull the instruments out.

'But Mam!' Jack jumped to his feet. 'Grandpa loves *Rock Band*.'

After a hard day in the fields, Paddy Gorton was more likely to want to collapse in front of the television than rock it out on a plastic guitar. That's if Susie would even allow the raucous noise in her house. 'Then your grandfather can get his own. Where are all the clothes I washed for you yesterday?'

'There.' Jack pointed to the floor at the end of his bed. Ione looked and saw a pile of fabric pushed into the corner.

'Patrick Jack Gorton.'

'I'm too little to pack for myself.'

Ione looked at her very intelligent eight-year-old son and snorted. 'Yesterday you said you were too old for me to pack for you. *I wanna do it, Mam, I'm old enough.*' She mimicked his words.

He looked at her with big, solemn blue eyes. Patrick's eyes. 'I'm a kid. I can't be trusted.'

It was hard to be angry with him when all she wanted to do was laugh and hug the stuffing out of him. 'Let's make a deal. You can take *Guitar Hero* and the guitar, but no *Rock Band*; the drums and the microphone are making way for some actual clothes.'

'All right.'

'Now, you go pick that clean stuff up and fold it.'

'You'd do that better than me.'

'You're never going to get better if you don't practise.'

'I love you, Mam.' He fluttered his eyelashes up at her.

She laughed and kissed him. 'Fold. Now.'

Jack turned with a grumble but stopped when a familiar chime rang in the air. Ione watched all his assurance melt and a shifty look appear on his face. Why would Jack be scared of Maggie?

'Stay.' Ione pointed a finger to her son, then went into the loungeroom. On the wall was a button, installed by the previous Sabhamir, that she could use to grant permission to enter. He'd come up with lots of little tricks to get around her lack of power.

Maggie Shaunessy, her best friend, appeared. She was wearing a long red robe. This wasn't a social visit: Maggie was here as the Ceamir, the guardian responsible for overseeing interactions between the gadda and humans.

Ione made an educated guess as to the reason for Maggie's visit. 'What has my son done?'

Maggie rolled her eyes. 'Where is he?'

'Bedroom.' Ione led the way. Jack was standing in the middle of the room, his eyes wide and soft. Trying to butter Maggie up, Ione thought. It didn't work.

Maggie bent down. 'Jack, why did you put that post on the Magic for Kids website about the gadda orders?' she said in a calm voice.

'It wasn't me,' Jack said.

'Yes, it was,' Maggie said.

For a moment, Ione wondered if Jack was going to continue his denials. Then his head slumped forward.

'They were talking shit,' he muttered. 'I had to tell them what real magic was.'

'Jack, how many times have you been told that you don't talk about gadda stuff to humans?'

'Lots,' he muttered, trying to dig a hole in the carpet with the front of his shoe.

Maggie put a hand on his shoulder. 'Mate, I know how hard it can be to keep the secret. Remember, I went to a school where I was the only gadda, and I wanted those kids to know me and like me, and I hated that I couldn't tell them or show them. But buddy, that's what we have to do. Gadda aren't just lucky to have power, we've got a responsibility to look after it.'

Jack looked up at her. 'Are you going to banish me?'

'No. But do it again and I'll send the Heasimir to talk to you.'

Jack's eyes widened and Ione put a hand over her mouth to hide her smile. 'Never again, Maggie, I swear.'

'Good boy. Now, I've fixed the website, so there shouldn't be any damage done. But you aren't to go there again, you hear me? No chatrooms at all, in fact.'

'Yes, Maggie.'

'Good. Now, I'm going to go discuss this with your mother. You need to do something about this bedroom.'

The two women waited until Jack's bedroom door was closed behind them before they began to laugh.

'Great idea, Mags, threatening him with the Heasimir,' Ione said, giggling. The Heasimir was the healer of the gadda and the coldest woman Ione had ever met.

'She has to be of use for something. Now, I believe you should make me some coffee.'

'Sure thing.' Ione led her friend into the kitchen to put the kettle on. 'Rocking the robe, by the way.'

Maggie sighed and her clothing shifted until she was wearing a skirt, jumper and knee-high boots — all red. 'I thought Jack might take me more seriously in the full-on garb.'

'Nice boots.'

'Yeah, I thought they were nice too. Yesterday. When I bought them. When they were black.'

Ione laughed as she pulled the coffee out of the cupboard. There were many things that Maggie had found difficult to deal with since her elevation to the guardianship a month earlier. The fact her wardrobe had become all red was one of the harder ones.

'Be grateful you've got the colouring for it,' Ione said over her shoulder and took a moment to admire Maggie's honey-blonde waves and blue eyes. 'Could be worse, you could be me.' She tapped her own tight red curls.

Maggie snorted as she walked into the kitchen. 'As if you've ever worried about clashing with your hair. God, I'll never forget the electric pink muu-muu.'

'What you'll never forget is how good I made it look,' Ione said as she put the kettle on.

'Yes, damn you. It was a muu-muu, and it was electric pink, and you have red hair, and yet you looked exotic and wonderful and I hated you.'

'Thanks, Mags.' Ione started to put biscuits on the tray, then stopped and looked over her shoulder. 'Is this an I-can-stay-and-pig-out visit or a quick-cuppa-before-I-return-to-saving-the-world visit?'

'Probably the latter.' Maggie leant against the bench, the smile slipping from her face. With it gone, Ione noticed the small lines that surrounded Maggie's eyes and mouth — lines that hadn't been there earlier that year.

Star, had it only been four months since they were flatmates?

'Is everything OK?'

'About as OK as it can be when the most dangerous books on the face of the planet are missing and we don't

11

have a clue where to start looking for them.' Maggie sighed and pushed her hand through her hair. 'Even with Sean Flaherty being as surprisingly helpful as he has been, we've got nothing. Oh, we do know roughly when they were taken, but that's it.'

A chill ran down Ione's spine. The Forbidden Texts were created centuries earlier and, after it became clear that they bent power and people and put the balance of life at risk, they had been kept supposedly safe and secure. So much so that most gadda had forgotten they existed.

But someone had tracked them down and stolen them, and no one really wanted to know what would happen if they weren't recovered.

Maggie herself had experienced the power of the books first-hand — Sean Flaherty had been under the influence of the texts when she had a one-night stand with him. He'd sent a stream of monsters to her family's home in Australia in an effort to bring her back to Sclossin — monsters he shouldn't have been able to create. He'd done that after just one brief touch of the texts.

If the shadows on Maggie's face were any clue, Ione guessed her friend hadn't been getting much sleep in her efforts to help locate the books.

'You'll find them.' Ione walked over and gave Maggie a hug. 'I know it's scary now, but you'll find them and one day, we'll be laughing about this.'

'Oh yes, lots to chortle about so far. Let's see,' Maggie began to tap her fingers to count each event. 'Grandpa was almost paralysed, Mum was knocked unconscious, a human was attacked and, oh yes, Lucas was kidnapped and could have been killed.'

Ione began to tap her own fingers to refute the

blackness of Maggie's thoughts. 'Your grandpa was just hysterically paralysed, and tell me that isn't bloody hilarious for someone who is sixth order and supposedly all-powerful. Your mam finally got to have a rest, which she deserved; the human got a few days off uni which she undoubtedly needed; and as for Lucas, well, you're making it up to him, aren't you?'

Becoming Ceamir was the least of the changes in Maggie's life. She'd found love with Lucas Valeroso, one-time unknown gadda and all-round hottie. If Ione hadn't loved Maggie so much, she'd be annoyed her friend had found him first.

'Bloody oath I am,' Maggie said. 'So hurry up with that coffee, Gorton, 'cause I've got a hot man to return to.'

'Sure, rub it in.' Ione grinned, but looked over when she heard Maggie's gasp.

'I'm sorry.' Maggie moved quickly and flung her arms around her friend's neck. 'I didn't mean that.'

Ione hugged her and laughed. 'I know you didn't. It's OK, Mags. I'm happy that you've got Lucas.'

'And you'll meet someone. I'm sure of it.'

Ione herself wasn't so sure. Not that she steered clear of men – in fact, one of the great things about Jack going to stay with his grandparents regularly was the freedom it gave her to find the occasional partner for a night of fun.

But she was quite sure she'd never meet anyone who could convince her to get fully involved or marry again. She just didn't think any man could make her as happy as Patrick had.

'You know you can always come talk to me about Lucas,' Ione said, changing the subject.

'Thank you. It's good to know you're here.'

'Any time, darlin'. Me for you and you for me, remember?'

There was a knock at the door, followed by Jack's shout. 'He's here. He's here.' The two women turned and watched the little boy barrel past the kitchen and toward the front door.

'And the reason for this excitement is?'

'Mark's taking him up to the farm.'

'What did Jack do to deserve that?'

Ione frowned. 'Can it, Shaunessy.' When Mark and Maggie had first met, they'd got along well and even dated for a while. Then Mark had suddenly adopted an almost obsessive respect for authority which put him at odds with Maggie's eccentricities. Over the years, the relationship had become antagonistic.

'Stay here.' Ione went out into the loungeroom to see her son jumping up and down in front of his uncle.

'When we get there, can we go straight to the creek?' Jack's face was flushed with joy. 'I wanna see if the dam is still there.'

'If there's time before it gets dark, sure,' Mark said.

'Cool. I'll get my things.' Jack spun on his heel and raced back past Ione to his bedroom.

'Hey, Marky Mark.' Ione stretched to plant a kiss on her brother's cheek.

'Io. How are things?'

'Good. Fine. How are things with you?'

'Not bad. Been working hard, so I'm looking forward to the trip.'

'I doubt you'll enjoy it for long. Jack's beside himself and I'm guessing within the hour you'll be regretting taking him.'

'Jack's a good kid. He'll behave.'

Must be wonderful to live in a world of black and white, Ione thought. 'I packed you some food for the train trip. I'll go get it.'

His eyes widened. 'Currant squares?'

Ione laughed. 'Have I ever sent you on a trip without them?'

'Thanks, Io.'

She rolled her eyes at Maggie as she got the containers of food out of the kitchen. By the time she'd returned to the loungeroom, Jack was struggling to pull his suitcase through the doorway.

'Jack, how much clothing did you put in there?'

'All of it. Honest, Mam. I didn't put the drum back or anything.'

'Here, Jacky, let me help you with that.' Mark came forward with a smile to take the suitcase. Ione caught her brother's eye and they shared an affectionate grin.

'I'll just check.' She put the baking down on the lounge and bent to undo the suitcase.

'You really should trust me, Mam. It would be better for our relationship.'

Ione shook her head. Jack had put all his clothes in there, as he'd said. Unfortunately, he hadn't folded them but just stuffed them in.

'Your grandmother is going to think I'm a terrible mother, sending you off with a case looking like this.'

'I'll tell her it's my fault.'

'You bet you will,' Ione said, quickly pulling the clothes out and, with Mark's help, repacking.

They carried the suitcase and the food down to the taxi. Mark had left room in his luggage for Ione's cooking.

'Now, give your mother a hug and then we'll be off,' Mark said.

Jack turned and wrapped his arms around Ione's hips, pushing his face against her stomach. 'Love you, Mam.'

Ione bent and pressed a kiss to the top of his head. 'Love you too, little man. Be good for Uncle Mark, and for Grandpa and Grandma.'

'I will.' There was a flurry of movement, then the taxi sped off.

Ione went back upstairs and, as the door closed behind her, silence fell on the apartment. She took a deep breath against the sudden crush of missing Jack and let it out slowly. She knew it was good for them to have their own time, do their own things, but damn she missed him.

'Oi, Gorton, coffee's getting cold.'

Thanking the universe for a friend who knew exactly what to say when, Ione smiled and she went into the kitchen.

TWO

Muscles straining, teeth clenched, Stephen O'Malley pushed the barbell up from his chest one last time. He held it there, counted to three, and then tilted his arms back. His trainer grabbed the bar and helped him guide it onto the rest above his head.

Stephen sat up and spun his legs around to the side of the bench. He pulled off his gloves and looked at Mike. 'Good?'

'More than good.' Mike leant on the end of the weight. 'Are you sure I can't convince you to come to the body-building championships in Dallas with us? You'd blow them away in the novices, and could probably even take intermediate too. Bit more sculpting and you'll be giving me a run for my money.'

'No.' Stephen stood and held out his hand. 'Thanks for a good session.'

Mike shook it, his eyes running over Stephen. 'It's a waste of all this work, that you look this good and won't use it.'

'I use it. Just not the way you think.' Stephen nodded then made his way through the weight machines toward the men's locker room.

His daily workout in the gym was an important part of a bigger plan, but it wasn't the plan to win the body-building titles that Mike and his friends were chasing. Being physically fit and strong was more about his mental strength than the way he looked. He wanted to be at the peak of his health and fitness, so he could cope with whatever the sixth-order test threw at him.

He knew Mike didn't understand why he was putting in all this effort for seemingly no reward. Unfortunately, Stephen wasn't able to explain that he was a member of a secret magical race and the training was to ensure he was ready to pass one of the most challenging ordeals any living creature could face.

At the edge of the weight machines, he hesitated. In order to reach the locker room, he had to skirt the edges of the aerobics floor.

'Hi, Stephen.' A woman stepped in front of him.

Damn, not quick enough. 'Hi, Mandy.'

She smiled, and then shifted her weight, sticking one hip out and pulling her shoulders back. He knew he was supposed to admire her figure — the lack of fat, the slender arms and waist, the strong thighs, the magnificent and all-too-pert-for-its-size bosom. He admired the work she'd put in to achieve this look, but that was all.

'I was watching you. So sensational.' Her eyes trailed a mental finger over his chest and down to his stomach.

'Thanks.' Then he stepped around her and continued across the gym.

On the other side, another of the gym junkies stopped him. Julia was into body sculpting, and her brief leotard displayed muscles that many men would kill for.

'Great workout today, Stephen. You're getting bigger each time I see you. I'd love to catch up and chat about your routine.' She smiled, her teeth blindingly white.

'Sorry, Julia, another time.' He escaped into the

locker room with a sigh of relief. He quickly showered and changed, not speaking to any of the other men in the room. It was the way he preferred things, being left alone.

He nodded to the girl at the desk as he made his way out to the footpath, where he breathed in deeply the dry, heated air of a Texas summer morning.

He hefted his gym bag onto his shoulder and started the walk home. It was half an hour each way; added to the hour at the gym and the run he took each evening, it was certainly enough to keep him physically fit. He watched what he ate, didn't drink much and made sure he got eight to nine hours' sleep a night, so his health was perfect. The rest of the time was devoted to his studies. Training drills, research, practice, practice, practice. This was what he needed to do to achieve what he dreamt of, and he was so bloody close.

In just over a week, he would be facing the bardria, and the Sabhamir would be testing him for sixth order. If he passed, he would be the second-youngest gadda ever to reach the highest level. The O'Malley name, his name, would be burnt into gadda history.

It will be a hard test, Stephen thought as he strode along the footpath. The bardria couldn't take the risk of anyone saying Stephen O'Malley only passed because the test was easy. The Sabhamir had probably been working on it, researching it as diligently as Stephen had. And he liked the idea that he would be tested to the extreme. Not only would the gadda world know; *he* would know he was one of the best.

Stephen turned from the road onto the path that led to the front door of his apartment block. As he pushed open the door, he wondered if today would be an encounter day or not. I'm about due, he thought, walking up the stairs.

Sure enough, just as he reached the landing between his apartment and that of Sandina Lopez, the old lady's door opened.

'Stephen, so sorry, so sorry, but can you help?'

He smiled at her. He'd been a bit worried when Mrs Lopez had knocked on his door just half an hour after he'd moved in seven years ago, with food and a smile. He'd thought she'd be over constantly, bugging him, interrupting his studies. But Sandina was careful to only grab him when he was out of the apartment, and didn't do that every day.

'What can I do for you, Mrs Lopez?' He put down his gym bag next to his door.

'I drop stove lighter behind stove again. So sorry, Stephen. Please, help?'

'Certainly.' He followed her into her flat. It was, as always, immaculate — swept, mopped, dusted several times a day, he thought. Every available surface held family photographs.

In the kitchen, he moved the gas stove to one side long enough to pull out the lighter. He handed it to Mrs Lopez with a small bow. 'For you.'

'Bless you, Stephen. So strong, such a blessing.' She hugged the lighter to her chest and beamed. 'When you go back home?'

'Tomorrow.'

'This time, you will stay there, I am sure.'

Mrs Lopez considered herself a bit psychic. However, she'd said that every time Stephen went back for a test, and he'd always returned to Austin, so he didn't believe her. 'I'll be back, Mrs Lopez. Have a nice day.' He waved goodbye and left, grabbed his bag and let himself into his own flat.

20

After the family-oriented decorations of Mrs Lopez's apartment, Stephen's appeared bland. In the loungeroom was one large sofa and three huge bookcases crammed with books, old and new. There was no beauty, no softness to the room. He dropped off his sweaty gym clothes in the washing machine on the way to his bedroom.

He pulled the sheets off the bed and put them in the chest by one wall, then lifted the bed so it rested against the window, blocking out the sun and the view into the room. Then he stood in the middle of the room and looked down at the star of gulagh painted on the floor. Six points, one for each of the founding families of the bardria, and the heart in the middle, the symbol of the emotion that drove all gadda.

Stephen pressed his hand against his chest, where an invisible tattoo of the star of gulagh marked him as gadda, different from Mrs Lopez and all those people at the gym. If she were gadda, she'd just move the stove herself with a flick of her wrist.

He closed his eyes and centred himself, blocking out all thoughts, forgetting where he had been, what he had done. Focussing solely on the power within him, refining his control, practising until he could do things that even most gadda only dreamt about. Then he opened his eyes, and he began.

He'd only got partway through creating a lattice of lace from the dust motes that danced in the air when he heard a familiar chime — perfunctory and non-melodic. He sighed, sent a mental reply and stepped out of the circle.

A mauve ball appeared in the air, hovering above the heart. He reached forward and touched it. It peeled back and he heard a soft voice.

'Stephen. It's Blair Callaghan. My apologies if I am disturbing you, but I know the test is in just a few days and I wanted to see what assistance I can offer you.'

Stephen smiled. Blair Callaghan was the head of the gadda school in Sclossin, and had been one of his advisors for the past few years.

'Things are going well. I'm just honing my skills. Otherwise, I feel confident that I've considered every possibility and I'm ready for whatever challenge the Sabhamir chooses to throw at me.'

'Will you be following the same routine as last time? Staying at the hotel and so on?'

Stephen nodded. 'I don't want to make any changes.'

'Understandable. I want you to work at remaining calm, Stephen, and you need to maintain perspective. We all want you to pass this test, but it's not the end of everything if you don't. Few people pass the sixth-order test at their first attempt, no matter how talented they are.'

Stephen nodded, accepting the words but not paying a great deal of attention to them. They didn't apply to him.

'Thank you. Once I arrive in Sclossin, I'll get in touch to organise dinner.'

'I look forward to seeing you, Stephen. I've got some ideas about your life after you've passed the test.'

Stephen smiled as he cut the connection. Life after the test had become a refrain over the past few months and he didn't doubt she was thinking of teaching.

Perhaps teaching would be good, Stephen thought, but right now my focus is on passing the test. He'd worry about the rest later.

THREE

Ione was leaning against the window, watching grey sheets of rain fall on the Sclossin Inn and the bardria building. Despite the cup of hot chocolate in her hand and the warm Australian alpaca-wool jumper she was wearing, she shivered. What a terrible, horrible, miserable day to be out and about. What a great day to be gadda — to be able to just transfer here and there and not have to deal with the weather.

The expected knock on the front door came. Ione opened it to a slightly moist Lucas Valeroso.

'Put the umbrella there, and there's a pot of chocolate on the stove,' she said, pointing first to the corner near the door and then to the kitchen.

'Thanks, Io.' He reached over and rested the wet umbrella against the wall. 'I was just thinking I can't wait until I can transfer and I don't have to walk in the rain.'

'Great minds think alike,' Ione said, following him across the room to the kitchen. 'Except that I'll never be able to transfer, of course.'

'Is this where I pretend sympathy?'

'You've been with Maggie too long. When I first met you, you wouldn't have pretended.'

He grinned. 'When you first met me, I barely knew what transferring was.'

Ione watched him pour a cup of hot chocolate. Lucas was still so overwhelmingly human that it was hard to remember that not only was he gadda, he was already infinitely more powerful and capable than she and was on the fast track to being an extremely proficient oman.

At about the same time Maggie had made her colossal mistake with Sean Flaherty, Lucas had been winning one of the world's most prestigious physics prizes. As a result, he'd got himself a job at Winton University, run by Maggie's grandfather. There, he'd not only found out about the gadda, but had discovered he was one himself.

From that point, it should have been easy, except that his birth father was the murderer Rogan Connor, and Lucas had had to prove he was worthy to be gadda.

Luckily for them all, he had.

He lifted the cup to his mouth, took a sip and sighed. 'Damn, Io, but if you aren't the best cook in the world.'

'Better than Mags, that's for certain. But then, I guess that her cooking ain't the attraction.'

Lucas grinned, his eyes sparkled and Ione remembered Patrick looking like that. 'She's got a few other things to recommend her.'

That sort of happiness should be illegal, she thought, and then shook her head. She turned to get her own drink. She was happy for Lucas and Maggie. Everyone deserved to feel like that.

Star knew she still thought of her moment in the sun.

'So, what exactly is it we're working on, Dr Valeroso?' she said, moving over to switch her computer on.

'Let me see. I believe your exact phrase was "I can't believe that someone of your intelligence can't even use a

24

simple spreadsheet properly".' Lucas joined her. 'The fact that it was working, and I hadn't had time to do anything extra, didn't seem to cut the mustard.'

'Nor should it,' Ione said. 'Bloody genius physicist using *Excel* as a database. Honestly, it's not like *Access* is that hard to use, and there're plenty of programs better again. Now, let's go through exactly what you use it for and see if I can't do you up something more appropriate.'

'For a fee, of course.'

'Of course. Mates rates, however. I know you university types don't make that much money.'

'You are the soul of generosity, Ione Gorton.'

'Did you see how much chocolate I made for you? Don't you be punkin' me, bitch.'

'You know, if you're going to try talking like you're from the hood, you better get the accent down,' said Lucas in his best Bronx drawl.

Well, of course he's good at it, Ione thought. He'd grown up in the notorious neighbourhood after his mother, having been abandoned by Connor, died and left him in the care of a human stepfather. Lucas had grown up with gangs and mob violence and had even done a stint in juvie himself after an ill-conceived carjacking. Luckily, there he'd discovered the structure of science and had turned his life around.

'I've tried. The best I can do American-wise is a Southern belle. Shall I pour you some more julep, Dr Valeroso?' Ione fluttered her eyelashes.

Lucas laughed. 'That's terrible. Vivien Leigh is rolling in her grave.'

'I'm basing myself more on Anna Paquin, actually.'

'Work, Io.' He tapped the table. 'Stop distracting me and work.'

They'd been at it for three solid hours when Maggie's chime rang in the air.

'Can't leave you alone, can she?' Ione said.

Lucas was smiling as he stood and turned to face the middle of the room. Moments later, Maggie was there and they were kissing in a manner that made Ione's heart jump and then clench.

'How are things going?' Maggie said.

'Not bad. We've just about got the basics nutted out. I reckon I can have a working prototype by the end of the week,' Ione said.

'Clever, clever girl.' Maggie kissed her cheek. Then she sniffed. 'Do I smell ...?'

'Stove. Kitchen. Go.' Ione waved her hand.

'So, you think you've got it?' Lucas leant on the back of the chair.

'There are undoubtedly some nuances that we haven't identified, but we're not going to know those until you put the app into practice. But sure, I can build something with this.'

'I do appreciate it, Io.' He squeezed her shoulder.

'There was barely a drop,' Maggie said, coming out of the kitchen. 'Not really worth my effort in licking it clean.'

'Blame Lucas,' Ione said, standing. 'He drank it all.'

'Hmm, no wonder he tasted so chocolatey.' Maggie smiled, a wicked expression that left no doubt about where her mind was going.

'Go home and fornicate, little ones, and have a great time,' Ione said.

Lucas opened his mouth, no doubt to try and soften the obviousness in the room, but Maggie just grinned, blew Ione a kiss, put her hand on Lucas's arm and they were gone.

26

Ione went back over to the window and watched the rain lash the roofs of the town. She pressed her head against the icy cold glass and sighed.

She was lonely. It was hard to admit, but there it was. This was the first time in years that she had spent any real length of time by herself. In the past, when Jack had gone away for holidays, she'd had Maggie for company.

But Maggie was happily ensconced in her suite in the bardria chambers with Lucas. And while Ione was delighted about that, seeing her happiness had Ione yearning for Patrick in a way she hadn't since the months just after his death.

Patrick. Tears started to well in her eyes. She missed his sense of humour, his laughter ringing through the flat. She missed his dedication to making every day special. She missed the tears that filled his eyes whenever he looked at Jack, unable to believe the joy his son brought. Most of all she missed him at night. She'd had lovers in the years since, but none of them had touched her, caressed her, fulfilled her as Patrick had.

She told herself she didn't want them to. Being in love was wonderful, but when it was gone, it hurt too much. She didn't want to go through that again. Or put Jack through that again. He'd missed his father for a while, but his one-year-old mind had quickly forgotten the pain. Better for his sake that neither of them got attached again.

She stood and headed to the bathroom. One thing could get her out of this mood — some red-hot sex. Time to go out and get herself some fun.

FOUR

Stephen heard Mrs Lopez go off to church. He waited ten minutes to be sure she was well out of the way, and then he summoned the Ceamir.

The guardian in charge of human-gadda relations arrived with a wide smile. 'Good morning, Stephen. All ready to make history?'

Stephen smiled. While the thought always came with a dash of guilt, there was no denying that dealing with the new Ceamir was a much more pleasant experience than interactions with her predecessor. Not just because the old guardian had been an ancient, crippled woman and the new was young, vivacious and very attractive.

She was a modern woman, in touch with the reality of life in the human world and what was required for gadda to maintain the secret. The old Ceamir always made him book a flight and come over to Ireland the human way, to make sure nothing could go wrong.

This Ceamir had decided as long as those who counted thought he'd flown to Ireland, there was no need for him to actually do it.

Folding his large body into small airline seats had been torturous, and so he was more than willing to try the new, riskier strategy.

'Ready,' he said.

'You've covered things here?'

Stephen nodded. 'I've told those who know me I'm going out of town for a few days. Mrs Lopez has gone off to mass, so there's no one to notice that I don't get a cab to the airport.'

'Excellent.' She grinned. 'Well then, for the last time before you're qualified to do it for yourself, let me transfer you to Sclossin.'

Stephen picked up his bag and nodded. The Ceamir took his arm and he relaxed, letting the familiar forces of push and pull work on him. Then they stood in the Ceamir's office.

Stephen looked around. 'This is very nice,' he said. The contents of the old Ceamir's office had been very dull — a desk and a few chairs. Now, the desk was a modern light wood, and behind it were some lounges covered in a bright red, black and cream Aztec pattern. In the corner was something that looked suspiciously like a television cabinet.

'Thank you. I hope it will make people feel comfortable and welcome and they'll come to talk to me more. Maybe even the purists.' She pulled a face.

Stephen nodded. Even in Austin, he'd heard about how the tensions between the purists, who wanted gadda separated from humans, and their opponents were rising.

He personally subscribed more to the humanist idea, that gadda should use their power to help humanity, but then he wouldn't have lived in Austin for the past seven years if he didn't like humans.

'Thank you for bringing me over,' he said.

'Not a problem. Just give me a yell if you need anything.'

Stephen headed through the bardria building and, as he passed the bardria restaurant, his steps slowed and he took a peek inside. It was just after lunch in Sclossin, and the room was empty except for staff cleaning up the tables and preparing for the dinner rush.

The room was as elegant as he remembered it from that first meal there with his parents. It had been his thirteenth birthday and he had just become eligible to begin his training.

To celebrate, his parents had taken him to the bardria restaurant. It was the most expensive and most exclusive eatery in Sclossin society, and he had been well aware of what it must have cost his parents to get the booking.

Liam and Elizabeth O'Malley weren't the richest or most powerful of gadda: they were both just second order and his father worked for the bardria as a trainer. But they were optimistic for Stephen. Liam had done everything he could to prepare his son for training without breaking the bardria regulation that anyone under thirteen could not access his or her power. As they prepared for dinner, he had clapped Stephen on the shoulder and declared, 'You'll be the pride of the O'Malley clan, boy.'

They had all donned their best clothes and marched in, shoulders back, heads held high. Stephen had polished his shoes until he could see his reflection in the brassy leather. His father had bought himself a brand-new tie; his mother had been to the hairdresser for a cut and colour. They didn't have a great deal, but they were going all out to make this an important occasion.

The restaurant was incredibly beautiful, with one wall and part of the ceiling made of glass so you looked out onto a garden courtyard or up into the sky. On that night, the roof was open and a soft breeze ran through the room.

Stephen had stood in the doorway and stared. The

room was full of the cream of gadda society, the six old families and their closest allies, all dressed in their finest.

Wonderful smells swept over him, his mouth began to water and as the maître d' showed them to their table he trotted along behind his parents, dreaming of the wonderful meal he was about to eat.

Then he'd become aware of the looks and whispers of the other patrons. By the time the O'Malleys were in their seats, he knew the entire restaurant was looking at them and judging them.

The waiter politely took their order, and then asked if they wanted wine. The O'Malleys had refused, since their budget didn't stretch that far. Stephen heard excited whispering from the table behind him and his spine stiffened. His parents chatted about Stephen's training and how proud they would be when he became first order. Meanwhile, Stephen was becoming more and more aware that they had been found wanting by the social elite.

The meal arrived and it was delicious. They had taken their time in consuming the amazing food, sipping on glasses of water between bites. His parents kept looking around and commenting on the beauty of the room, the beauty of the other gadda.

Stephen's head had begun to ache. The room was unbearably hot; the rich smell of the cooking subsided under the sickly sweetness of the scents worn by the women. To his highly attuned ear, every second word he overheard was about his parents and none of it was flattering.

The waiter had come back to take their dessert order and again, they had refused. This time, Stephen heard a giggle from behind him.

He'd spun around to glare at the people sitting there. His eyes had caught those of a boy about his age. The boy had leant over, whispered something to his sister and they'd both disintegrated into laughter.

Stephen spun back to look at his parents. Fine, let some stuck-up little prick laugh at him. He didn't care.

Then his father opened up his wallet, his mother opened up her purse and they began counting out notes and coins to pay for the meal. Out of the corner of his eye, Stephen could see others watching. A burst of laughter from his right was quickly stifled.

Finally, the O'Malleys gathered the correct amount and handed it to the waiter, who bowed stiffly and took it away. Stephen breathed a sigh of relief, glad this night was almost over.

Then a band had started playing. Within moments, the dance-floor was full of couples. His parents had looked at each other, and his father had smiled at him. 'You don't mind, do you, Steve? One dance?'

"Course not, Dad,' he'd said. His father had taken his mother's hand and led her to the dance-floor.

They had started dancing and, within moments, the other dancers began to return to their seats. By the time the last verse played, his parents were dancing alone, too caught up in the joy of the moment to notice. When the music stopped they had looked around and coloured with embarrassment. They then stumbled to their chairs and sat down.

The next song began and again, the dance-floor was flooded with couples. The message was clear: no one else would dance while the O'Malleys did. His parents hadn't noticed the whispering, the looks, the laughter, but they couldn't fail to notice that. Faces still flushed, they had shepherded Stephen from the room. Not a word was spoken on the walk home or the next day; all three of them had acted as though the night had never occurred.

But Stephen couldn't forget the look on his parents' faces as they left. It hadn't taken him long to realise the only chance they had of being socially acceptable was through him. He had begun his training determined to be successful, to force everyone to accept his family.

He turned away and kept his head down, not looking at anyone or anything until he got to the registration desk of the Sclossin Inn. He put his suitcase down and leant on the desk.

'Stephen. Sorry, have you been waiting long?' Anna walked out of the office with a smile.

'Not at all.'

'This will be the last time, won't it?' she said as she reached forward to touch his hand. Stephen automatically reached for it the human way — it always took him a while to adjust to the gadda greeting of pressing the back of your hands together rather than shaking. It enabled you to feel the other's power without being threatened by it.

'I hope so.'

Anna nodded as she released his grasp. 'I bet you do. Imagine coming all this way, and then failing and having to do it again.' She shook her head. 'You'll be in room six.'

Stephen thanked her, picked up his suitcase, and walked through the lobby and down the hall to his room.

He unpacked, then sat down at the small table and looked at his calendar for the next few days. Even though he knew it by heart, he liked to be sure he hadn't missed anything. All was in order.

Time to go for a walk, he thought, slamming the book shut and standing.

He felt the tap of his feet hitting the floor, and a heartbeat later a loud boom rushed through the room, screaming through his ears and shaking his body.

The floor quaked beneath him, and plaster started to shower from the ceiling onto his head.

Stephen lifted his hands and formed a shield over his head, and then he stilled and waited, wondering if the roof would collapse on him. There was silence, then the sound of people shouting, crying, screaming began.

He pulled the shield tight so it just covered the top of his head, protecting him without being obvious. Then he went over and opened the door.

Two men in suits ran past him, heading toward the back of the hotel. He watched them both dart into a room and slam the door shut. Further down the corridor, at the front of the building, he could see a cloud of dust hovering in the air, blocking the view of the lobby.

Stephen went that way and as he started to walk through the cloud, it settled on his hair, face and body. He put his hand over his nose and mouth, and created another shield to filter the air.

He stepped from the corridor into a scene of devastation. Where once the front wall of the hotel had stood there was now a gaping hole, three metres high and ten wide. Stone, plaster and mortar lay all over the once-pristine red carpet. The windows that had separated the lobby from the restaurant had been blown out, and shards of glass had landed all over the tables and chairs beyond.

'Help me. Help!' A voice screeched from near the restaurant. Stephen started to pick his way over the debris. A man lay on the ground, a massive piece of stone pinning his legs. He looked up at Stephen, tears running down his face. 'Help, please.' He held a hand out.

Stephen walked around and crouched down next to the rock. He pulled on it, and realised that he didn't have enough natural strength to move it. He reached forward, touched the man's arm, and felt for his power. Nothing. He was human.

Stephen was going to have to be subtle. 'Close your eyes in case I disturb some dust.' The man nodded and did as instructed. Stephen grabbed the rock and, as he pulled on it, spread a little push incantation over it. The rock scraped, there was a squeak from the man, and then it was gone.

'Are you badly hurt?' Stephen rubbed his hands over the man's legs.

'I think that one's broken.'

Stephen looked up at the human and noticed he was starting to shake. 'I'm going to take you outside. It will hurt, but I'll be as gentle as possible. You'll be better off.' He bent down to put one arm under the man's thigh, the other around his back.

'Don't,' the man screeched. 'It hurts, it hurts.'

He moved away from him and considered what to do next.

'Need some help, O'Malley?'

Stephen looked over his shoulder to find the Sabhamir, the protector of the gadda, standing there. Dressed all in black, he was a comforting sight. 'This gentleman is injured. I need a hand getting him out of here.'

'Leave him. The building is safe.' The Sabhamir leant over to look at the injured man. 'Medical assistance is on its way, sir.' Then the protector put his hand on Stephen's shoulder. 'Come with me, Stephen.'

Stephen followed the most powerful gadda alive across the ruin of the inn's lobby. He noted Anna was standing over by the reception desk, talking to another woman. They were both covered in dust but appeared unharmed.

The Sabhamir led him outside. A large crowd had gathered, standing in a semicircle a few metres from the front of the hotel. The Firimir, the truthsayer of the gadda, was walking along the circle, talking and keeping people calm.

'Are you hurt?'

Stephen turned to look at the Sabhamir. The third-order gadma, able to kill with a flick of his finger, was looking at Stephen with wide eyes, his concern apparent. 'I'm fine. I was in my room when it happened. Whatever it was that happened.' He looked back over his shoulder and shook his head. He didn't own a television, but you couldn't live in the human world without knowing what a bomb explosion looked like.

'What do you remember?'

He looked back at the Sabhamir. 'Nothing to remember. I was in my room, I'd been unpacking and was about to go out. I heard a boom, and then the room shook and plaster fell on my head. I walked out into the lobby, and there it was.'

The Sabhamir folded his arms across his chest. 'When did you get here?'

'Not sure. Half an hour at most.'

'Notice anything strange?'

'Nothing. It was just as it always is. Anna greeted me nicely, wished me luck with the test and told me about my room. I carried my bag down to my room. There wasn't anyone in the lobby or the restaurant.' It occurred to him the timing of the explosion was good, if such a thing was possible. The lunch crowd had left the restaurant, the human businesspeople who used the hotel would have mostly been at meetings and there wouldn't have been many gadda around. It could have been much worse. 'Anyone badly hurt?'

'Your human friend appears to be the main one. Luckily, the restaurant staff was in the kitchen, so nothing there, and Anna had just popped into the back office, so there wasn't anyone on the reception desk.'

He was right — it had been lucky timing. 'Two men ran past me into their rooms as I was coming out.'

The Sabhamir frowned. 'Could be the perpetrators.'

'Or humans scared of terrorist attack,' a female voice interjected. He and the Sabhamir both turned around to watch the Ceamir walk toward them. 'There have been some instances in the past few years of terrorists setting off bombs, and then going through hotels to find people in their rooms. The poor guys may just be scared for their lives. They won't respond well to anyone unless they're in a police uniform.'

'And just where are we supposed to find one of those around here?' the Sabhamir said.

The Ceamir grinned, looked around for lurking humans and then waved her hand in the air. 'There.'

Stephen looked and saw the Sabhamir's normal black had been replaced with the pale and navy blue uniform of the Irish garda, complete with utility belt and cap. He had to admire the protector's forbearance in not flattening his fellow guardian.

'Suits you,' the Ceamir said.

The Sabhamir narrowed his eyes, and Stephen wondered what mental conversation was unfolding. Then Ireland's newest garda turned and strode back into the ruined building.

'Are you all right?' The Ceamir turned her blue eyes onto Stephen.

'Fine,' he said. Then he looked at the building. 'Is it just me, or does that look a hell of a lot like a bomb went off?'

'It does. Of course, it could be gadda-created, rather than human.'

'But to attack the only building in Sclossin where humans can remain overnight ...' Stephen shook his head.

'I know. I'll have my work cut out over this one, I can tell.' She lifted her head, as if studying something, then nodded. 'Here comes my first client. Take care, Stephen.' Then she hurried over to where the man with the broken leg, now on a stretcher, was being laid down by a couple of gadda.

Stephen crossed his arms over his chest and watched the scene playing out in front of him. It occurred to him just how lucky he was. He could have waited longer to summon the Ceamir. He could have decided to go and have a coffee in the restaurant or have his walk before unpacking.

He shivered.

'Stephen, you are unhurt?'

He turned to look at the Heasimir. Unlike the other two guardians, there wasn't any hint of concern in her expression. 'Yes, Heasimir.'

'Good.' She turned and walked over to the human.

As he shook his head over how the healer of the gadda could be such an unemotional person, another realisation struck him — with damage like this, it appeared that the hotel would have to close down and that meant he had nowhere to stay.

'Shit.'

'Stephen, language.' The Coiremir strode up to stand alongside him. Of all the guardians, she was the one he knew best since she was the teacher. 'I know this is upsetting to you, but please control yourself.'

'Sorry,' he mumbled.

'Such a shame this should happen just a few days out from the test, but I am sure you will do fine.' She patted his arm. 'Why don't you come with me to my office, and I'll get you a cup of tea.'

Without a better idea, he nodded. She took his arm and started to guide him through the crowd and along the road to the bardria building.

Stephen looked up at the imposing two-storey stone edifice and couldn't help but wonder how it would have reacted to the bomb. He doubted much damage would have been done — the bardria building seemed indestructible.

The Coiremir's office was a sparsely furnished space — there was just a desk and a couple of chairs. Most of the space was taken up with bookshelves. She gestured to Stephen to take one chair, then as she sat down on the other side of the desk, a tray carrying tea and biscuits appeared between them.

'I've put a bit of camomile in it to calm your nerves,' the Coiremir said as she poured.

Stephen thought it would take more than camomile, but he obediently took a sip of the tea. Now that he was seated, calmed, away from the scene, he was aware that small tremors were running through his body.

He suspected it was going to be a long time before he felt calm again.

'Now, we need to figure out where you're going to stay,' the Coiremir said. 'It's important to get you settled as soon as possible. I'm guessing you won't want to stay with your parents.'

Stephen shook his head. While he knew his mother would welcome him, he wasn't ready to face his father's accusations. It still hurt that Liam O'Malley had turned against his son two years earlier.

'I might be able to arrange some accommodation here in the bardria building,' she continued. 'But I don't think that's very satisfactory. Who do you know in town?'

Stephen thought about it. Over the years, his dedication to his dream had pretty much destroyed all his childhood friendships, and he'd not had time for many new ones.

One name came to mind. 'Blair Callaghan, perhaps.'

'That would be very suitable. I'll go see Blair now, if that's all right with you.'

'Of course.' She nodded and disappeared. Stephen sagged into his chair and closed his eyes, but quickly opened them when he was faced with a vision of the trapped human, begging for help.

He hoped there would be a solution to this new dilemma soon. He was going to need some quiet time to return his equilibrium and be able to work again.

FIVE

Ione leant out her window and watched the chaos on the street in front of her apartment. She'd been baking when she'd heard the most awful noise. Loud and strong and just like the explosions in the giant-monster movies she loved.

She'd gone over to her window to see what was going on and had been shocked to see smoke rising from the Sclossin Inn. A crowd was gathering in the street in front of it.

The guardians arrived, and she watched and waited as people started to walk out. Her hands clenched the windowsill and she prayed everyone would be OK.

Then she saw a man being carried out of the smoking wreckage of the building and her heart sank. She grabbed her mobile and dialled.

'Lucas Valeroso here.'

'Lucas, it's Io.' She went back over to the window. 'Did you hear about the inn?'

'The bombing? Yeah. Damn, you're just next door. You're all right, aren't you?'

'Fine. The noise scared the shit out of me, but otherwise OK. Unfortunately, it seems someone wasn't as lucky. They've just brought a body out of the building.'

'Fuck. Hang on.' There was a pause, during which Ione guessed he was speaking mentally to Maggie. His words proved she was right. 'Maggie said he's hurt, not dead. Broken leg, it seems. Otherwise, it appears that people have been shaken up a bit but not hurt. Looks like Sclossin might just get off lightly compared with other bombings.'

'Shit.' Ione leant against her windowframe. 'How the hell could this happen? Why would anyone attack the inn?'

'My question, knowing how mad purists can be, is why hasn't anyone attacked the inn before today?'

Ione shuddered. The centuries-long argument over how involved gadda should be with humanity had devolved into a vicious two-way political bunfight.

Purification had been at the heart of what Sean Flaherty had done to Maggie and her family, and if what Ione was now witnessing really was an act of terrorism by some extremists, it seemed the battle was intensifying.

'I can't look any more.' Ione cradled the phone between her ear and shoulder and pulled the window closed, blocking out the sound, although the smell lingered in the room.

'There's a reason I'm not out there looking,' Lucas said.

'Think I'll get stuck into some work.' Ione walked over to her computer.

'Excellent. 'Cause I'm waiting, you know.'

'Slave driver.' Ione pressed the button on her laptop and waited for the whirr of the fans starting and the flickering of the screen. Nothing happened.

'Oh, no.' She pushed the button again.

'What?'

'Either my 'puter's broken or ...' She walked over to flick the light switch. 'Damn, out of power. The explosion must have knocked the building offline.'

'Things are fine here.'

'Shit. It will probably take a day or so for the power to be restored. Longer, maybe, if the bardria decide to avoid calling humans into the town for a while.' And most gadda wouldn't mind. Only she relied on electricity for her job.

'Come stay with us, then.'

'Really?' She leant on the table. 'I won't cramp your style?'

'Not at all.' She could hear the smile in Lucas's voice. 'We don't mind an audience.'

Ione rolled her eyes. 'Just for that, I'll bring my judging cards. See if you can score tens for me.'

'Why do I start these games with you? I know you'll always take it further than I want to go.'

'You'll learn, Valeroso. You'll learn. And I will accept your generous offer, during the day anyway. I'll come back to sleep here, so you don't cramp *my* style.'

'Do you have style, Io?'

'Do you want your program finished, Lucas?'

'You are the most stylish woman I know, Ione Gorton, and I'm anticipating spending many delightful hours with you here in Chez Ceamir.'

Ione was smiling as she hung up and packed her computer. She'd almost forgotten the reason for the new plan until she stepped from the front door of her apartment building and the scent of destruction hit her.

Down here on street level, the sense of horror was almost overwhelming. She could smell something burning. Dust had settled across the road and even on

43

her doorstep, making it look like a foreign scene and not Sclossin at all.

She walked forward slowly, gently pushing her way through the crowd. People moved aside, happy to let someone new come to look. She stopped at the edge of the circle and her jaw dropped open.

Where there had once been a lovely building of wood and stone now stood a shell. A hole ten metres wide had been blasted into the front wall, showering bricks and planks of timber across the road. She could see the staff of the restaurant standing in a group — shivering, clutching each other, covered in dust but otherwise unharmed.

The Sabhamir was talking to the receptionist staff, while Maggie and the Heasimir were bent over the supine figure Ione had seen from her window. Lucas had said he wasn't dead, but he looked close to it.

She reached into her pocket, pulled out her mobile and dialled.

'Hello, Susie Gorton speaking.'

'Susie, it's Ione. Can I talk to Jack, please?'

'Of course.' Ione heard her mother-in-law call for her son. 'Is everything OK? You sound strange.'

'No, it's not.'

'Ione, what is it?'

Ione couldn't bring herself to say the words. 'You'll find out.'

'Here's Jack.' There was a muffled sound.

'Hey, Mam.'

Tears welled in Ione's eyes. 'Hey, Jacky. How are things?'

'Good. Grandpa's going to take me out on the tractor today. He said he might even let me drive it.'

'Be careful.'

'I will. Oh, and Grandma wouldn't let me have a second bowl of ice-cream last night. Can you tell her it's OK?'

The sound of his voice, his concerns over the troubles of childhood, eased Ione's pain. She turned away from the inn and started to make her way back through the crowd. 'It's not. One bowl of ice-cream is ample.'

'But I'm working really hard up here, Mam. You should see. I've got muscles.'

'In which case, you should take care of yourself with healthy food. More vegetables, not more ice-cream.'

'Ice-cream is protein, and protein is good for muscles.'

The little scamp. 'No, Jack. Now, I have to go, so be good for your grandparents and no more demands for extra ice-cream, OK?'

'Yeah, OK.'

'I love you, Jacky.'

'Yeah, love you too, Mam.'

Ione hung up, feeling better.

She walked into the bardria building, putting the fear and mess behind her. The corridors of the building were eerily quiet, and she guessed everyone was outside, either helping or watching.

She walked through Maggie's office almost on auto-pilot, stopping at the door to the apartment and knocking.

Lucas flung it open and put his arms around her for an unrequested but much-needed hug. 'You OK?'

'Fine.' Ione shuddered. 'I'll be better when you get a whiskey into my hand.' She walked past him into the room and stopped when she saw Blair Callaghan sitting there. 'Blair.'

'Ione.' The teacher stood and smiled. 'Bit early in the day for drinking, isn't it?'

'Have you been out there?' Blair shook her head. 'Go out, and then I dare you not to want a drink.' She put her computer down on the floor and slumped onto the lounge.

'Of course.' Blair sat beside her and patted her arm. 'I'm sorry.'

Ione closed her eyes. 'Why would people want to destroy something like that?'

'Sick people,' Lucas said. 'Don't bother trying to understand them, Io, 'cause folks like you and me can't.'

'Belief is a powerful thing,' Blair said. 'More powerful sometimes than right or wrong.'

Ione shuddered. 'Then I hope I never believe in anything.'

'Here, Io.' Ione opened her eyes to find Lucas standing in front of her, holding a glass of amber liquid out to her. She smiled as she took it and the first sip sent a soothing burn down her chest.

'Lucas tells me you're going to be working here for the next few days, since you don't have any electricity,' Blair said. 'Feel free to join us for lessons, if you wish.'

'Stop right there, Blair.' Ione lifted her hand. 'No, I have not passed first order yet, nor do I intend to. The last time I tried, the caelleach actually begged me to never do it again. So I'm afraid the time has come to officially give up on me.'

'What kind of a teacher would I be if I did that?'

'A sane one?'

Blair laughed. 'You may be right. But I can't help thinking that there's something I can crack in you, and if I do, it will make me a better teacher for everyone else.'

'My family thinks I'm already cracked enough, thanks.'

'Is that the only damage to your apartment, that you've lost power?'

Ione sat up, thrown by the sudden change of topic. 'Yes. Why?'

'You could be the solution to a problem, Ione. Have you heard of Stephen O'Malley?'

Ione took a moment to place the name. 'Is that the wunderkind? Going for sixth order at some ridiculous age?'

'That's right. He'll be the second-youngest ever. He was staying at the inn, because he doesn't have any real connections here in Sclossin, and —'

'He was there? When it happened?' Blair nodded. 'Oh, the poor thing.'

'Well, as a result, he now has nowhere to stay. He needs somewhere peaceful and quiet in order to practise. Since you're not going to be home during the day ...'

'Say no more. Of course he can stay at my place. I was planning on going home to sleep, but if he prefers I can stay here with Maggie and Lucas.'

A blankness passed over Blair's face and then she focussed on Ione. 'I just informed the Coiremir. She was hoping you could go speak to her and Stephen.'

'Of course. Will I walk or will you ...' Ione wriggled her fingers in the air.

Blair stood with a smile. 'I'll transfer you over.' She held out her hand and Ione took it.

Ione quite liked transferring — she'd done a lot of it with her insanely powerful family members. She loved that quick sensation of busyness and quietness all at once, and then the tingle in her brain as it adjusted to suddenly moving from one place to another.

The tingle moved to a quiver down her spine as she saw the man sitting in front of the Coiremir's desk. Blond hair was slicked back from an austere-looking face — chiselled jaw, straight nose, wide brow — softened by brilliant blue eyes and surprisingly full lips. He stood, and towered over her — an unusual experience — and his shoulders were so wide that she wondered if they would fit through her door.

There was no other word — the man was an Adonis.

'Ione, this is Stephen O'Malley.' Blair's words barely registered.

She smiled and thanked the fates for landing this in her lap. 'Well, hello.' She held out her hand, her palm facing her chest in the traditional gadda manner.

'Ms Gorton.' He pressed the back of his hand to hers and, even with her tiny power, she could feel the strength of his. 'Thank you for your generous offer.' His voice was a deep rumbling bass, and contained just a hint of American twang to rub against the Irish lilt.

Even his voice was hot.

Ione gave herself a mental shake. She couldn't just stand here and stare at him. 'Not at all. I'm not using the apartment at the moment, and it's the least I can do after what you went through. You poor thing.'

She was surprised by his lack of reaction to her words. 'Thank you.'

'How long can you vacate it, Ione?' the Coiremir asked.

'As long as needed, unless the electricity comes back on and Stephen doesn't mind a roommate.' She certainly wouldn't mind sharing a room with him. Or a bed.

'The test is in a week,' the Coiremir said.

'That's fine.' Ione wished she could tear her eyes from Stephen, but was unable to. By the star, he was beautiful. And he seemed to be having a similar problem with looking away from her.

'Then I'll leave you to take Stephen over and settle him in, if you don't mind.'

Oh, the things she wanted to settle him into. 'Sure. Would you mind transferring me?'

His brow knitted together in a frown. 'Certainly.' He took hold of her hand and Ione tried not to shiver as tendrils of sensation ran through her body.

Wowza.

Moments later, they were standing in her loungeroom. Stephen released her, too quickly for her liking, and looked around. As he turned, the scent of his cologne wafted over her. Her favourite. Was there nothing wrong about him?

'This is very nice.'

'Thank you. Let me show you where you can settle in.' She led him to the spare room.

'Lovely.'

'Again, thank you.' She smiled. 'Now, the hot water and stove are gas, so –' She stopped. 'Hang on, probably shouldn't assume that they're working.' She went into the bathroom and turned on the tap and within moments the water had heated up.

'Good.' She turned it off and spun to find Stephen had followed her into the room. In this small space, his size made her feel both vulnerable and excited. 'No problems with showers or cooking on the stove, although I guess you wouldn't use it. The food in the fridge should be fine for a couple of days, assuming you don't open and close it too much. Unless you'd like me to come over to cook for you?' She flicked her eyelashes a couple of times — nothing too obvious.

'I'm fine.'

Damn, Ione thought. Maybe this attraction was just one way. What a bummer. 'Well then, I'll leave you to your work.'

'Thank you. And I do appreciate this offer. It will help me a great deal.'

'Sure. If you wouldn't mind taking me to the Ceamir's office, that would be swell.'

He frowned. 'You can't transfer there yourself?'

'Nope.' She grinned. She always loved this part. 'No power. No control. Can't even pass first order. Complete failure as a gadda, I'm afraid.' With the right person, this could lead into a conversation of all the things she was good at, followed by some very pleasurable demonstrations.

Unfortunately, it seemed that Stephen O'Malley wasn't going to give her one of those conversations. 'I'm sorry to hear that.'

'Why? It's not your fault.' By now, his brow was so furrowed that Ione was concerned it might stay that way. 'It's cool. I'm glad to do what I can to see a bit of history made. Now, to the Ceamir, my good man.' She held her hand out.

Stephen took it and transferred her to Maggie's office. There, he bowed and instantly disappeared.

Damn, she thought as she went back into the apartment. All that beauty, all that potential, and it was useless. Not one smile. Surely it would be usual to grin politely, say on introducing yourself, something to indicate 'Hi, I'm normal, I'm not gonna bite you'. But no. Apparently, Stephen O'Malley wasn't the smiling type.

Although, considering the day he'd had, that wasn't a surprise. She wasn't sure she'd want to smile much after her hotel had been bombed. Though something told her that this was a fairly normal state of affairs for him.

She let out a long breath. So despite the fact he was

absolutely, sizzlingly gorgeous, he was a dour bloke. Mark for him, mark against.

'So, all sorted?' Lucas said, coming out of the kitchen.

'Indeed.'

'And the superstar of the gadda is ...?'

'Hot. And dull.'

'Maybe you need to try a bit harder, Io.'

'Maybe you need to get back to cooking me dinner, sir.' Ione waggled her finger in Lucas's face. 'Now, where can I set up?'

'Spare room. Use what you need. Did you bring stuff with you to stay?'

'No. Damn. He put me off.'

'Or maybe you forgot to have an excuse to sneak back later.'

'Kitchen, Valeroso. Now.' She picked up her computer and stormed into the spare room with a smile.

After leaving Ione at the Ceamir's apartment, Stephen popped into the room at the inn to get his gear then back to the silent apartment.

He stood in the loungeroom and wondered if this was such a good idea after all. The moment she'd said she didn't have any power, information had started to move around his mind like the pieces of a jigsaw puzzle, and by the time he dropped her off at the Ceamir's office, he'd known who his hostess was.

Ione Gorton was the infamous Ione Hammond. The dath who couldn't pass first order, who'd been a bit of a joke when he'd got to training a couple of years after her first failed attempt.

The dath who, unless he was mistaken, was Mark Hammond's sister.

He frowned. It seemed coincidental, that the woman who was going to save him from this situation was related to one of his great enemies. After all, how could Hammond have planned this?

And he'd all but forgotten Hammond's part in the incident that had re-lit his desire to be the best and forced the wedge between he and his father. His focus had been on Hammond's partner that night – Aaron Lansing.

Eight years after the event, Stephen had distance enough to admit his own part in what had happened. That afternoon, he'd walked into the second-order test cocky and already planning the celebration. After all, he'd been top of his class in first order, thanks in no small part to his determination to pay people back for the snub to his parents.

There was no question in his, or anyone else's, mind that he would pass second order.

He hadn't.

He'd cancelled the party and instead found a quiet corner of the Royal to drink himself into oblivion and forget what he'd done.

He still didn't recall much of that night – at some point, three men had joined him, commiserated with him, helped him drown the humiliation of his failure with countless pints of ale.

He still vividly recalled waking in the park by the river, a crowd of schoolchildren gathered around him.

'Look, he's awake, the big fat eff,' a boy had called out and they'd all started to laugh.

Stephen had sat up and growled. A couple of girls ran off screaming. The rest of the crowd had pulled back a little, but started up a chant. 'Big fat eff, big fat eff.'

It wasn't until he'd got home that he'd realised what

the chant meant. There, tattooed on his right cheek, was a large black letter F. F for failure.

The news had spread quickly around Sclossin, and he'd endured weeks of being pointed to and whispered about and laughed at before the residents moved on to the next source of entertainment.

He'd had to wait twelve months before he could sit the test again. During that time, he'd gone through the very painful treatment of having a power-burnt tattoo removed. He'd also found the three men who were responsible for it and one by one, he'd visited them. He'd looked each in the eye and told them that he knew what they'd done, but he wasn't going to tell the Sabhamir. He'd deal with them himself, when he was ready.

The first, John Scally, had been so terrified to have been found out that he'd burst into tears and thrown himself onto his knees, begging Stephen's forgiveness. The second, Mark Hammond, had apologised profusely and promised never to do anything like it ever again.

Aaron Lansing had also apologised and Stephen had walked away happy.

After passing the test the second time round, Stephen had moved to Austin to focus on passing all the other tests. Five years later, when he'd returned to pass both the third and fourth-order tests on the same day, he'd celebrated by finding each of the three men and reminding them that they still had to pay for what they'd done to him.

The colour that leached from each man's cheeks as he saw Stephen was a joyful thing to see and Stephen had walked away thinking that maybe he didn't need to do any more than that. They'd be waiting, wondering if he'd make good on his promise. Perhaps that was punishment enough.

Until Lansing had gone to see Stephen's parents and had made it all sound as though he were an innocent victim and Stephen was ready to tear his arms from his body. Liam O'Malley knew Aaron Lansing — had trained him for his second order.

He'd believed him over his own son.

Stephen heard a growl and was surprised to realise it was him. He shook his head and looked around Ione's apartment. He'd been so caught up in the memories, he'd forgotten where he was.

Should he stay here? It only took a moment to decide yes. He needed to know what, if anything, Hammond and Lansing were planning.

If they weren't planning anything? Well, he stayed in a comfortable place and got to know a woman he frankly found intriguing. What was the story with her power? And why had her smile been so fetching?

After unpacking, he set about exploring the apartment.

I'm staying here for the next week, he said to himself as he stood in the middle of the loungeroom. I might as well work out where things are.

He was surprised to realise there was a large, flat-screen television in the room and next to it a tower of DVDs. He went over and looked at the titles. *Destroy All Monsters. Invasion of the Astro-Monster. Godzilla. Son of Godzilla. Mothra vs Godzilla.*

Human movies. Very interesting. He looked at the bookshelf: nearly all the books were human too. At the top, novels — mostly crime, it seemed. At the bottom, computer manuals. He crouched down, pulled one off and flicked through it. He knew it was written in English, because he understood the words. He just didn't have a clue what it was actually saying.

So, Ione was into computers. Hence the need for electricity, he thought as he put the book back. He turned and went over to the lounge to look at the photos on the wall there.

One caught his eye and he stopped as he registered what it was. Ione, in a white dress, with her arm around a man in a suit. She was looking at the camera and smiling, while he looked at her with a sense of love and joy that was palpable.

So, Ione was married. It explained why she'd been introduced as Gorton, not Hammond, but otherwise the information didn't sit. No one had mentioned a husband, and he hadn't missed the look of attraction in Ione's eyes.

He kept looking at the photos. The man appeared in a couple of shots cradling a baby. Again, there was that look of adoration, coupled with disbelief. A photo with Ione, her husband and what was undoubtedly their child. But then, the husband was no longer seen. There were lots of shots of Ione with a red-haired boy and even a few of them with the Ceamir.

No wonder Ione had asked to be taken there. Obviously she and the Ceamir were close friends.

So, Ione had a son. Again, there had been no mention of him. Stephen started up the hallway and found a room with *Jack* written on the door. He took a deep breath and opened it just a fraction.

Judging by the mess on the floor, the tousled robot sheet covers and the row of computer games on the table by the door, Stephen would put Jack's age at somewhere around ten. He pulled the door closed.

So not only was Ione giving up her home to him, but she was also making her son sleep elsewhere. Stephen didn't think that could be a good thing. Was Hammond using the boy too?

He wandered back to the loungeroom, considering what he should do, then summoned the Ceamir.

Moments later, she stood in the loungeroom. 'Stephen.' She looked around and blinked. 'OK, I missed this development.'

'Since Ms Gorton can't stay here, she offered it to me for the interim,' Stephen said.

There was a pause and a faraway look on her face. Stephen guessed she was confirming his story. 'Right. So, what can I do for you?'

'I don't want to put Ms Gorton out. Or her son.'

'Oh, you aren't.' The Ceamir waved her hands in the air. 'Io needs electricity — she's a computer programmer — and this place doesn't have it, so she's happy to stay with us. And Jack's on holidays at his grandparents, so he won't even know you're here.'

The more he heard, the more unlikely it seemed this was planned. 'I didn't want to inconvenience her.'

'You won't. Now, while I'm here, I need to grab a few of her things. Lucas just told me Io forgot to get them herself.' The Ceamir waltzed past him and into the only room Stephen hadn't been in yet.

Stephen stood in the middle of the loungeroom, wondering what was still bothering him. Then he swung around and went to the door. 'She wasn't planning on staying at your apartment. She was going to come back here to sleep.'

The Ceamir looked over her shoulder. 'No biggie. Although you're the one missing out, I have to say. The girl can cook.'

'It would be fine if she slept here,' Stephen said.

'I mean, I don't tend to practise in the evening, so she wouldn't be bothering me.'

He didn't like the sudden brilliance of the Ceamir's smile. 'I'll tell her that.' She stood, an armful of clothes clutched to her chest. 'Have a good rest, Stephen, and don't hesitate to call if you need anything.' Then she was gone.

So, there it is, Stephen thought. It looked as though he'd have the apartment to himself during the day and would be sharing the space with Ione at night.

Why did he like the thought of that?

He shook his head. He needed to make sure Hammond wasn't involved before he gave any thought to his very attractive sister.

SIX

Ione stepped from the front door of the bardria building at the exact moment a stray ray of sunshine beamed through the clouds. She closed her eyes and turned her face up to greet the welcome light and warmth. Then the clouds, seemingly incensed by this act of rebellion, closed in and she shivered and pulled the collar of her jacket up around her neck.

I really can't blame the sky for being in such a mood, she thought as she walked down the steps. She wasn't feeling so crash-hot herself, having lost a lot of sleep to memories of the day before. Every time she'd closed her eyes, she'd heard the bang of the explosion and her body had shuddered into wakefulness. She'd try to relax past it, try to settle down, but then it would seem that a whiff of imaginary wind would bring the smell to her and she'd almost gag.

Finally, her body had given way and she'd slept, but she'd woken this morning feeling as though someone had glued her eyes shut and scraped her throat raw.

She stopped at the sight of the ruined inn, and swallowed to catch herself. Material had been spread across the face of the building, hiding the damage. The street had been cleaned, although barriers forced pedestrians off the footpath. There was an eerie sense of shame — as if the building were hiding its face because it couldn't bear anyone to know what had happened.

Ione hunched her shoulders and started to hurry past it. Damn her for forgetting the one bloody book that she needed to work. Otherwise she'd be ensconced in Maggie and Lucas's loungeroom and wouldn't be facing this horror again.

'Ione.'

She stopped and looked around to see who was calling out to her. Across the road was a group of five people and stepping away from them and toward her was Brian Mochrie.

Not for the first time she thought that if he'd just smile properly, he wouldn't be too bad looking. His red hair was a very similar hue to her own so of course she liked it and his green eyes were really quite amazing. But that permanent smirk pulled at lips already a little too thin and made his gaunt face quite unpleasant.

'How wonderful to bump into you like this. You are looking quite well.'

'Good morning, Brian.'

'Terrible, isn't it?' He nodded to the inn behind her.

'Yes.' She and Mochrie were nodding acquaintances at best, so why was he suddenly being so friendly?

'I'm glad I bumped into you today. I've been wondering how you were going. Have you tried out for first order lately?'

He really wanted to have a conversation with her? 'No, I haven't. I've given up on the idea. Not worth the angst, really.'

'That's a shame.' Brian looked sympathetic. 'I can't begin to imagine how difficult it must be, to have such a successful family and not be able to follow in their footsteps.'

'Don't worry about me. I'm planning on living my life vicariously through Jack. He shows a lot of promise.'

'Good, good.' Brian nodded enthusiastically. 'But you shouldn't just give up, Ione. I'm sure it's just a matter of finding the method that works for you. Listen, how about you join me for dinner tonight, and we can talk through a few ideas.'

Ione felt her jaw drop open and quickly slammed it shut. 'Are you asking me out on a date?'

'No.' There was a flicker of disgust over his face and Ione almost asked him why not. 'You see, I'm looking at going for first-order gadma, and I'm thinking of specialising in expanding power. Talking things over with someone like you would really help my understanding.'

Of course it wasn't about helping her. 'Expanding power? I thought there was a finite amount and you couldn't make any more.'

'Well, that's true, but I'm looking at how gadda can add some of the power in nature to their own store, building themselves up, so to speak.'

It was an interesting idea, and the minuscule part of Ione that wished she did have access to her power liked it. But was it worth putting herself through more disappointment? She'd had a pretty peaceful few years since she'd decided it just wasn't going to happen for her.

'No, thanks.' She shook her head. 'I'm happy just the way I am.'

'The offer is open,' Brian said. 'When you change your mind, contact me.'

Ione watched Brian saunter back across the street to his group of friends with a whistle. Shaking her head, she walked to her apartment. She wished people would get over the fact she couldn't use her power. It wasn't an issue for her any more.

She stopped at the door and considered whether she should knock, or try to just sneak in and out without disturbing Stephen. Then she considered the damage that someone about to go for sixth order could do if they were surprised, and decided to announce her presence.

She banged on the door, and then opened it. 'Hello, Stephen?'

He walked out of the spare room and her first reaction was to smile – he really was as hot as she remembered. Then she noted the blackness around his eyes, the slouch of his shoulders, and wondered if maybe he'd had as bad a night as she had. Worse, probably, as he'd been in the inn.

'So, did you sleep well?' She gave him a blazing smile, hoping to relax him into talking.

'The bed was very comfortable, thank you.'

It seemed Stephen should consider a career as a diplomat. Luckily, she had no such qualms. 'I had a shit night. Every time I closed my eyes, I heard it ...' Her voice trailed off as speaking the words brought the horror back.

He stepped forward and she thought she saw a small spark in his eyes. 'You heard it?'

'Heard it, felt it, smelt it.' She shuddered, then tried to smile. 'I can only imagine what it was like for you.'

His shudder matched hers. 'I doubt you can.'

She thought that was probably as close as she would get to a confession about how bad his night had been. She couldn't help but be mad at herself. When Maggie had come back with her clothes and told her that Stephen had said she should feel free to sleep at home, she'd been glad to hear that but had decided to stay with Maggie and Lucas for that one night.

So up until she'd gone to bed, she'd had an evening of laughter and drinking and solving the world's problems while poor Stephen had been here suffering, alone.

'Have you had breakfast yet?'

Stephen shook his head. 'I'm not hungry.'

'I can believe that, but nevertheless you should eat. Do you like omelettes?' She walked past him and into the kitchen.

He came and leant against the doorframe. 'I don't want you to go to any trouble.'

'None at all. Besides, I need to use some of this stuff up before it goes off.' She pulled open the fridge. 'How does mushroom and ham strike you?'

'As delicious.'

'Good. Coffee or tea?'

'Coffee, thanks. I need to wake up.' She looked over her shoulder to see him push his hand through his hair.

'I know the feeling.' She set to work, pulling the ingredients for the omelette together and putting the espresso pot on the stove.

'So, tell me what's involved with preparing for the sixth-order exam. I'm picturing lots of bangs and bumps in the night.'

'Not at all.'

His tone was tight, the words clipped. She looked at him and saw his expression was equally closed. Somehow, she'd managed to upset him.

'Then what is it about?'

'It's all about control. Small, tiny, key movements and pulses of power. No bangs and precious few bumps.'

'Then I don't need to worry about my house being destroyed.' She grinned, and then turned to answer the hissing coffee pot.

'I'll certainly do my best to not destroy it.' This time, he sounded more relaxed.

'I'd appreciate that.' She handed him his coffee. 'I'm sure the neighbours will appreciate it too.' She poured the eggs into the frying pan to start cooking his omelette.

'You work on computers?'

She nodded. 'Try to. Some days are better than others.'

'I didn't know any gadda worked with computers.'

'I have to do something to earn my way, you know.'

'Right. The no power thing.'

She could hear the pity in his tone and it mixed with her irritation with Brian. She turned to face him. 'Yes, the no power thing. Look, I'll be straight with you. I have attempted to pass the first-order exam seven times. I've undergone the training twice. I've had more tutors than you can imagine. None of it matters. I'm never going to pass. It's just not in me to do it. And I don't mind about that. There are lots of things I can do that no sixth-order dath or oman can do, and I bet they aren't concerned about that. So why should I be concerned they can do things that I can't?'

Stephen looked at her, his eyes wide. Glad to have shocked him, Ione continued as she finished off his omelette. 'I know there are people who consider themselves above me, but I don't like any of them, so I don't have anything to do with them. They can sit in their ivory towers, worried about appearances. I'd rather sit with my friends, have a laugh, have a few drinks and live. Wouldn't you?'

For a moment, she thought he wouldn't respond. Eventually, he shrugged his shoulders. 'Each to their own, I guess.'

'Exactly. Now, here you go. Better eat up before it gets cold.' She held the plate out to him. He took it, turned and walked into the loungeroom, obviously still mulling over her words.

Ione started to crack eggs for her own omelette, thinking that keeping a man like Stephen on edge was probably a very good idea.

Stephen sat down at the table and stared at the glistening pile of eggs, with mushrooms and cheese oozing out the middle. Despite his earlier contention that he wasn't hungry, the moment the smell of the cooking had reached him he'd begun to drool.

He picked up a knife and fork, cut a piece off and put it in his mouth. The taste danced across his tongue with explosions of delight. How, in just a few short minutes, had she created this? And with not a bit of power involved.

Another mouthful and another. He hadn't had dinner the night before either — when he'd gone into the kitchen to make something, he'd caught sight of the ruined inn next door and it had robbed him of his appetite. Ione came out and sat opposite him. 'Like it?'

He swallowed the mouthful more quickly than he wanted to so he could respond. 'It's amazing. You're a remarkable cook. How do you do it without any power?'

'The same way humans do. Maggie came from a very human-intensive place, and while she can't cook to save herself, her grandfather is a whizz and took great delight in teaching me.' Ione took a mouthful and her eyes glittered. 'Damn, I am good, aren't I?'

Stephen was about to answer when a deep, sonorous chime sounded. The Sabhamir.

'You know, sometimes I think he knows when I'm cooking,' Ione said. She walked over and hit a button on the wall. The Sabhamir appeared.

'Ione. Stephen.' The protector nodded his head to each of them. 'I hope I'm not interrupting.'

'No, you just hope you've arrived in time for breakfast.'

Stephen opened his mouth to warn Ione not to antagonise the gadma, but to his surprise, the Sabhamir grinned. 'Well, if you're inviting me, I guess I can stick around.'

Ione snorted and headed back into the kitchen. 'Won't be long,' she said over her shoulder.

'I've made it a rule of my life to never turn down food made by Ione Gorton,' the Sabhamir said. 'Now, I came over to make sure you're coping, and to talk to you further about yesterday.'

Just like that, the sense of peace and happiness that Ione had managed to instil was gone, and Stephen had to fight not to be overwhelmed by shame and failure. He'd been disgusted when he'd woken himself from the nightmare with a scream and then burst into tears. This morning had been one of the worst practice sessions he'd ever had, and he'd been extremely grateful for Ione's interruption.

Stephen thought about lying to the Sabhamir and saying he was fine. Then he looked at the other man and realised his hesitation had already spoken for him.

'It's not been a good morning.'

The Sabhamir nodded. 'Give it time and don't push it. I don't doubt that you want to be prepared for the test, but I'm also sure that you arrived here in Sclossin ready. Taking a bit of time to get over what happened at the hotel shouldn't hurt you.'

Stephen could see the logic in his words. Unfortunately, his mind was shouting at him to keep practising, to never stop. 'I'll try.'

The Sabhamir just looked at him and Stephen knew the protector didn't believe him, but wasn't going to say so. 'Good. Now, I'm sorry about this, but I'd like to scry you.'

Stephen nodded. Scrying enabled you to look through the memories of another person, to see the small details that he or she might not have noticed consciously. 'Of course.'

The Sabhamir walked over and put his hands on either side of Stephen's face. Stephen felt his senses numb until all he was aware of was the beating of his heart and the swirl of blood through his veins.

Then pictures began to play through his mind. He saw himself transfer to the Ceamir's office and walk through the bardria building. The Sabhamir slowed his memory down to focus on the faces that Stephen saw in the street as he walked to the inn but not everyone there was recognisable. Memories were notoriously inaccurate and incomprehensible.

Stephen watched Anna serve him, watched the movement as he walked to his room. He saw the words of his calendar.

Then — the explosion. Deep. Short and sharp, but very deep. The sound punched through him, like it was moving through the air. Then the building shook, and flakes of plaster from the ceiling started to fall on Stephen's head.

He shuddered, and felt a pulse of warm energy move over him, calming him. He tried to keep himself distanced as he watched himself make a shield, open the door and see the two humans run past and go into a room at the back of the hotel.

The memory faded as the Sabhamir himself appeared.

The guardian removed his hands from Stephen's face and pulled a chair out to sit down in front of him.

'Thank you,' the Sabhamir said. 'I'm sorry to make you relive those memories.'

'What do you think is going on?'

'Breakfast is served. Luckily, I had enough for three.' As Ione came out of the kitchen, carrying a tray loaded with a plate of omelette and a pot of steaming coffee, she narrowed her eyes at the Sabhamir.

'Here, let me help you.' The Sabhamir stepped forward and took the tray.

'I'll just get the knives, forks and mugs.' Ione turned to the kitchen.

'Done.' The Sabhamir looked at the table and not only was his place set, but the meal was served.

'Thank you.' Ione bowed her head with a queenly grace. 'Some flowers would be nice.'

A wave of a slender hand, and a vase of bright orange and yellow flowers appeared in the centre of the table. Ione smiled, leant forward and smelt them.

'Gerberas,' she said. 'My favourite.'

'A thank you to a gracious hostess,' the Sabhamir said.

'Keep giving me flowers, and I might keep inviting you.'

The two of them continued to banter in an easy fashion as they began to eat. Stephen was quite stunned by it all. It had never occurred to him to treat the Sabhamir with anything but the utmost respect. This friendliness made the protector seem not just a powerful gadma but a man who had feelings as well.

'So, how are things at the inn?' Ione said.

The Sabhamir shrugged. 'Not a lot to say at the moment. The inn's going to take a couple of days to repair.

No one was seriously hurt.' He looked at Stephen. 'The man you found had a broken leg. We transferred him to the hospital at Carrick-on-Shannon and he's resting comfortably. The two men you saw running up the corridor were, as the Ceamir suspected, hiding in case the bombers came looking for them. They were shocked, but otherwise unharmed and left as soon as they could. We've had to deal with a lot of media interest from the human world, but the Ceamir is handling things admirably.'

'I'll tell her you said so,' Ione said. 'So, do you have any suspects?'

The Sabhamir took a mouthful of omelette. 'Yet again, a masterpiece, Ione.' It was clear from his tone that he was done discussing the bombing.

When the meal was over, the Sabhamir stood to leave, but he stopped and looked at Stephen. 'Have you done a ceremony of welcoming yet?'

Stephen shook his head. The ceremony was traditionally used when a gadda went to stay with another for an extended visit.

'Might help settle the nerves, to feel you belong in this house.' Then the protector was gone.

Stephen looked at Ione. 'What do you think?'

'You know more about power than I do. Do you think it would help you?'

'It could.'

'Would it hurt?'

'No.'

She nodded as she stood and started to collect the dishes. 'Then I think you should do it.'

'You'd need to be part of it as well.'

'Sure. Do you want to do it now, or when I come back tonight?'

'Now.' Stephen surged to his feet. For some reason, this made him feel he was doing something positive to deal with the explosion, rather than just waiting for it to stop bothering him.

'OK. My star is in the middle of the loungeroom. I'll leave you to organise the room while I do the dishes.' She carried the remains of the meal into the kitchen.

Stephen turned and walked into the middle of the room. Usually, you could feel a star of gulagh the moment you stood on it, even if it was covered in carpet. However, Ione's star had such a shallow resonance, he really had to concentrate to locate it. That makes sense, he thought as he started to move her furniture around to pull the carpet back and reveal the star. She wouldn't use it, so its power would have dulled. Hopefully, he'd be able to fire it up again.

The star of gulagh was a faint outline on the wooden floorboards. Stephen crouched down, put a finger to one of the points and fed a tiny amount of power into it. The line started to sparkle, and the shimmer travelled away from his finger and down into the star.

He went around to each point and by the time he was done the star was starting to hum.

Ione came back into the room, carrying a white box wrapped with string. She stopped and smiled.

'I'd forgotten how pretty it is,' she said. Then she lifted the box to draw his attention. 'If memory serves me correctly, because we don't have access to soil we have to use something of great value to the homeowner.'

'That's right.' Stephen wondered what Ione's thing of value would be.

'I'll need you to put this on the heart and set the star alight,' Ione said as she went over to the dining table, put the box down and started to open it. 'I know I should be doing so, but the last Sabhamir taught me an incantation you can use in my stead.' She lifted something from the box and turned to face Stephen.

'What is that?' Stephen looked at the bundle of white material in her hands.

'My wedding dress. Be careful, please.' She extended her arms.

Stephen looked from the dress up into her face, and saw it was blank. He wanted to ask her where her husband was, but now wasn't the time. He nodded and took the dress from her. 'Expert care will be taken.'

'Thank you. Now, the words to the incantation are: "I stand in Ione's stead, I speak with Ione's voice, I have the power to wield her star and do so with a free choice". Feed your power into the dress as you say it, then place it on the heart and it should work.'

Stephen did as she said, although he couldn't see how it could work. The words didn't have any real power.

But then he felt something flutter through his hands, and a picture of a young, laughing, happy Ione grew in his mind. The words might not have power, but the dress had a lot.

He set the dress on the heart, stepped back to one point of the star and felt a flush of heat move up his body as the star came to life.

Ione stood on the point opposite him, and extended her hand. Stephen put his on top.

Ione spoke first. 'In the name of all the Gorton, past, present and future, I welcome Stephen O'Malley to my home, the place of my heart. May it bring him peace.'

Then they crouched down together, until Stephen's hand pressed Ione's onto the dress.

He felt a sensation of contentment and humour that he was sure he would forever recognise as Ione melt into his bones. I couldn't have found a better place to stay, Stephen thought as they stood. Already, he felt better.

Then they changed their hands, so Stephen's was on the bottom.

'I thank the Gortons, through the voice of Ione Gorton, for the welcome to this, the place of her heart. I hope to bring peace to this household.'

Again, they crouched and this time, Ione's hand pressed his down. As his palm met the soft silk of her wedding dress, he tried to send her a sense of his gratitude for looking after him. Unfortunately, without being able to feel her power, he didn't know if she received it or not.

They stood and walked in a circle — three times clockwise, three times widdershins. Then, together, they lifted their hands, pulling them back around behind them until they rested by their sides.

'There, how was that?' Ione smiled.

'Wonderful.' Stephen smiled at her. 'Thank you.'

She bowed her head. 'My pleasure.' She went over to the dining table, picked up the box and came back to the star with it. 'Can you put the dress back, with the words: "I relinquish this back to Ione's care"?' Stephen did as she asked. 'Now, I'll head back to Maggie and Lucas's to work and leave you to your practice, but I'll be back to cook dinner. Does six sound good?'

'Perfect.'

Only after she had gone did Stephen realise he hadn't even thought to ask her about her brother. Well, he'd have time tonight to find out if he needed to worry about her or if he was free to enjoy her company.

He was whistling as he went to practise.

SEVEN

The afternoon proved much more successful and, when he heard Ione come into the apartment, Stephen felt that he was getting back on track.

He left his bedroom and found her in the kitchen, humming as she pulled containers out of the freezer. She looked at him with a smile, and he found himself smiling back before he had considered it.

'Wow. That's better.' She nodded.

'What's better?'

'You. Smiling. You should do it more often; you've got a killer smile.'

'Um, thanks.' He watched her empty the containers into a large pot on the stove.

'Now, I must apologise,' she said as she went back to the fridge. 'Normally I'd make some bread to serve with the stew, but without electricity I can't operate the bread maker. You'll have to make do with regular shop bread, which just isn't good enough in my opinion. But at least you're getting old stew, which is a million times better than when I make it fresh.'

'Sounds fine. I'm not sure I've ever seen a gadda kitchen with so many things in it.'

'I know. My family takes great delight in buying me things. They don't even know what half of them are for, but any time they see something new in a human kitchen store, they have to get it for me. Hell, half the time I don't know what it is. But I love cooking, and I appreciate the thought.'

'So you really do like cooking?'

'Absolutely. When you've had a bad day, nothing gets rid of your frustration like pounding a piece of meat into submission. And it's good thinking stuff as well — I've come up with lots of solutions for problems while stirring a cake.'

As she moved around the kitchen, putting the meal together, Stephen considered that this was actually quite a relaxing thing to do — watching someone cook, as opposed to the wrist-flick employed by most gadda.

'And what about you? What do you do to relax in between practising and testing?'

'Walk. Go to the gym.'

'Watch telly?'

He shook his head. 'I read human newspapers, because I find them fascinating, but there's something too passive about television.'

'Ah, that's 'cause you're not watching the right things or with the right people. That shall be my mission while you're here — to convert you. Now, please don't tell me that you never drink alcohol.'

He smiled. He couldn't help it — just being with her made him want to smile. 'In moderation. Getting drunk and achieving sixth order before the age of twenty-six don't mix.'

'I hope today you're prepared to be moderate.' She walked toward him. He stepped aside to give her space to leave the room, but still he caught a whiff of her perfume as she went past and was surprised at how his stomach clenched.

73

'Not today,' he said. 'I like to keep clean in the week leading up to the test. But don't let me stop you.'

'Certainly won't.' Ione went over to the cupboard near the dining table and opened it. Stephen almost whistled at the display of bottles there. 'Sure I can't change your mind for a Connemara Peated Single Malt from Cooley's, aged twelve years, distilled using traditional processes?' She showed him the bottle, then poured herself a glass.

'Not tonight, thanks.'

She took a sip and sighed. 'Life, my friend, rarely gets better than this.'

'So that's the best thing in your life, a glass of whiskey?'

'Of course not. But this moment, this first sip, is very, very fine. Right up there with a first kiss.' There was a momentary flash of heat in her eyes. 'You haven't been stingy with yourself in that area, have you?'

There was a sudden intimacy about the moment — a man and a woman, standing in a loungeroom, talking — that threw him. 'No.'

'I'm pleased to hear that.' She lifted the glass, as if toasting him, and then sauntered past him and into the kitchen with a swing of the hips that momentarily hypnotised him.

Boy, he hoped she wasn't caught up in some scheme of her brother's.

'I'm serving up, if you can set the table,' she called from the kitchen. 'Everything's in the cupboard below the alcohol.'

He opened the door and saw tablecloths, napkins and placemats in a variety of matching colours. He chose a navy and white set and put them on the table, with the Sabhamir's flowers as the centrepiece.

Ione smiled as she came out, carrying the tray with two steaming bowls on it. 'My favourite,' she said as she put the tray down. 'A great choice.'

The smell of the stew made him realise he was starving. He sat down, liking the sturdiness of the wooden chair. He picked up a fork and speared a piece of meat from the stew, then lifted it to his lips. The meat was so tender it fell apart in his mouth, the gravy slowly dribbling down his throat. It was, he decided, the most amazing mouthful of food he'd ever had.

Next, he speared a large chunk of potato and mashed it against his palate before swallowing it. It just got better and better. Carrot next, then a forkful of peas. The warmth of the stew spread through his body, the taste dancing on his tongue.

Ione reached over to give him a slice of bread. Stephen grabbed it, tore off a chunk and dunked the bread in the stew before stuffing it in his mouth. Fresh bread and spicy stew sauce. Was there anything better?

'Didn't you have lunch?' Ione sat down and took a piece of bread. She was more delicate, but she dunked the bread and popped it in her mouth as well.

Stephen chewed as quickly as he could and swallowed. 'This is incredible. What is it?'

'Hammond Stew and, before you ask, no, I can't give the recipe to you. It would be worth more than my life. The only way to get it is to marry one of us.'

'Worth it just to get your hands on this.' He took another mouthful of the stew.

'Glad to hear I've got something to offer,' she said. Stephen lifted his head, expecting to see a hurt expression on her face, but she winked at him before taking a mouthful herself.

'So, we've established that apart from your focus on achieving sixth order as early as possible, you like to exercise, you don't watch television, you don't drink much, but you haven't kept yourself from all the fun in life.' Her eyes sparkled. 'What else should I know about Stephen O'Malley?'

'He's rapidly becoming addicted to your cooking.'

'Glad to hear it. So where do you normally live, if not in Sclossin?'

'Austin, Texas.'

She frowned. 'Not a lot of gadda there, I wouldn't have thought.'

'Just the one — my mentor, Hannah Wilson. She likes the challenge of trying to live the life of a powerful gadda within the restrictions of a large human city.'

'And do you like it?'

'I'm looking forward to returning to Sclossin.'

'Then why leave?'

Her honest curiosity took the sting from the question. 'I wanted to be away from distractions.'

She accepted the answer, and it gave him the opportunity to ask his own questions. 'The Ceamir said your son is with his grandparents.'

Ione nodded. 'They have a farm in County Clare. I send him there as often as possible, so he doesn't lose touch with his father's heritage.'

'His father is?' Stephen hoped the question sounded casual enough.

'Dead.'

He almost choked on the piece of meat he was chewing. Ione flew around the table and began to thump his back.

'Sorry,' she said. 'I know that wasn't the answer you

76

expected, but I don't like doing the expected. It was mean of me to shock you like that.'

He managed to swallow the mouthful and collect himself. 'That's OK. I shouldn't have asked.'

'Of course you should have. You handled my wedding dress. You've probably looked at the photos on the wall. You must have questions.' She gave his back one more thump, followed by a swirl of her fingers across his shoulders that felt less medicinal and more sensual in purpose. Then she went back around to sit down again.

'Patrick and I married when I was nineteen and he was twenty-three,' she said. 'He was my brother's best friend and I had my eye on him from the moment I first noticed boys. I set out to seduce him once I turned sixteen and succeeded very nicely. Jack was born a year after we married and we were blissfully happy, until a year later when Patrick was hit by a car while we were visiting his parents.'

She spoke calmly, but he noted the darkness growing in her eyes. 'I'm sorry to hear that.'

'Thank you.' She took a deep breath. 'So, now you know everything about me. Widow, unable to access my pitiful share of power — pretty sad case, really.'

Except that she sat opposite him, her calm and inner happiness radiating. 'Not sad at all.' She rewarded his words with a smile that set his heart thumping.

It took him a moment to realise she'd given him an opening to mention Mark. 'You've got a brother?'

She nodded. 'I do. One older, often a pain in the arse, brother. He's up at the farm with Jack.'

'A pain in the arse why?'

'Ah, if you have to ask that, you obviously don't have any siblings.' Ione grinned.

77

Stephen shook his head. A one-child family was the norm for the gadda, and childless couples were more common than many of them wished. The low fertility rate of the gadda was a constant source of concern. 'Enlighten me.'

'Well, as all older brothers do, he can tend to be a little too interested in my life. Mark and I don't agree on a lot of things — he's a real stickler for the rules, and I tend to be a bit more forgiving of people's eccentricities, so we often fight. But all in all, he's a good man.'

That description of her brother surprised him, even as she confirmed it was Mark Hammond. A stickler for the rules? 'How did you end up so different from each other?'

Ione frowned. 'Actually, that's a really good question, and I don't have an answer for it. Mark had been a bit of a wild child, and then about seven years ago he suddenly straightened himself up. I guess it was realising he was an uncle; he had to do right by Jack.'

Or maybe it was coming face to face with the horrible thing he'd done. 'So are you and he close?'

Ione put her fork down and looked at him seriously. 'No, not really,' she said. 'Even when we do get together, it's always because of Jack. That's quite sad, isn't it? We used to be really tight.'

He looked at her and felt certain she was telling the truth. She wasn't close to her brother and that meant his being here had nothing to do with the past.

He was free to consider what the present could be.

As the light dimmed, Stephen considered what would happen. Last night, he'd just taken himself off to bed, but after the terrible night he'd had, it didn't seem that tempting an idea. Luckily, after dinner, Ione decided that it was time for the television conversion to begin.

'Come, sit,' she said, patting the lounge next to her. 'Sorry about just watching it on the laptop, but without electricity we can't use my television, and we've got to do something tonight.'

Stephen wasn't going to refuse the invitation to sit next to her. Her scent wrapped around him, making him think of things summery and pretty.

'Now, I'm about to introduce you to the greatest daikaiju of all,' Ione said, leaning over and switching the computer on.

'Daikaiju?'

'Giant monster. Invented by the Japanese, but luckily other cultures of the world realised how awesome they were and created their own versions.' As she spoke, the computer jumped to life and there appeared a creature unlike anything Stephen had ever seen.

A giant multi-snake-headed centaur lifted its foot and stamped it down on a plywood house, smashing it. Then there was footage of people running away and screaming and then a word flashed across the screen: *Fatharr*.

'What is that?' He stared fascinated as the creature lumbered around, lifted one of its snake heads and roared like a lion. Actually, only two of the heads were really snakes — the ones on the side. The middle head, which was larger and on a longer neck, was more like a lizard's, except for the large, round golden eyes. The three necks and heads were scaled, but as they joined and thickened into the torso and curved under the horse's body, they merged into skin and fur. Sparks lit up from the hoofs as they crashed into the ground.

'Fatharr. In my mind the greatest of all daikaiju, defender of the environment and all-round bodacious dude.'

'I don't think that answers my question.'

'Fatharr is, as you can see, part horse and part snake, with three heads 'cause that's cool. He came from a polluted swampland and seeks to destroy all who would threaten the environment. Most daikaiju eiga have strong political themes, you know.'

'Daikaiju what?' Stephen was sure he'd never had a more confusing conversation.

'Eiga. Film, movies. There are a lot of giant monsters better known than Fatharr —'

An image popped into his mind. 'Like Godzilla?' Stephen was glad he could finally contribute something.

'Gojira, actually.' Ione grinned. 'I love Fatharr because he ups the absurdity factor and has a weird sense of humour. I'm sure he laughs when he gets a particularly bad bad-guy. Oh, like this one. Go, Fatharr.'

Stephen watched the two slimmer snake heads swoop down in a manner that more resembled the swoosh of an arm than anything else and take the hat off an officious-looking young man. Fatharr's middle head tipped back and the roar did sound like a laugh. 'Is it just me, or does Fatharr look like a couple of guys in a rubber suit?'

'Hush. I won't have you say a thing against Fatharr or any other daikaiju. If you won't watch it seriously, go to bed. Hit him, Fatharr!'

'Bit hard to sleep with you yelling.'

'Then put up. Yes!' Ione jumped off the lounge with a yell as Fatharr flattened the car and sent the man running.

So Stephen found himself watching his first ever giant-monster movie, and despite the small screen and muffled sound, loving it. From time to time, he looked at Ione. Her face was lit up with joy, her eyes were sparkling, her cheeks were rosy.

He was disappointed when the movie ended, and Ione stood and yawned. 'Well, that's me for the night. I'll see you in the morning.' She stumbled into her bedroom and closed the door.

Stephen sat on the lounge, considered how different his life had become in the past couple of days, and was amazed that he liked it.

EIGHT

Ione's eyes were open and she was sitting up in bed before it registered she'd been woken by a cry. Her first thought was *Jack*, and she swung her legs over the side to go to him. Then she remembered Jack wasn't here. So what had woken her?

A deep, loud moan reached her, and she shivered. Stephen. A nightmare? Some side effect of his training, or perhaps the bombing? Ione stuck a knuckle in her mouth and gently bit down as she considered what to do. Would it be OK to go into his room and wake him, attempt to comfort him? Or should she just let him be?

Another cry, and Ione was on her feet and marching to her bedroom door. There was no way she could ignore someone in pain.

At his bedroom door, years of living with powerful gadda had her hesitate as she reached for the handle. She took a deep breath, flung open the door so it slammed against the wall, screamed, 'Stephen!' at the top of her lungs and then jumped back out of the doorway to avoid any blast that might come.

There was no instant reaction, so she peeked around the corner. Stephen was sitting up, his hands extended, looking around. His eyes were wide and his nostrils flaring.

'Sorry.' Ione stepped into the room, seeing he was

under control. 'I hate waking people like that, but I hate being hit by power more. You were having a nightmare.'

His hands fell onto the quilt and his eyes became shadowed. 'I'm sorry I woke you.'

She sat down on the bed, her hip next to his thigh. This close to him, his size was overwhelming. 'Do you want to talk about it?'

He took a deep breath and the air shuddered out of his mouth. 'If I had arrived at the inn later, I would probably have been in reception when —'

She put her hand on his. 'But you weren't.'

'Tell my dreams that.'

'I am.' He frowned at her. 'Well, the technique always seemed to work on Jack. Every time he had a nightmare about a monster under his bed, I'd shoo it away and then he'd sleep happily.'

'I'm not sure my monster will shoo that easily.' But there was a slight creasing of his lips and Ione thought he was already feeling better.

'When Jack's monster wouldn't shoo, Maggie bought him a stuffed dragon and said it would fight the monster away and that did the trick. I could get that for you to sleep with.'

'I'm surprised it wasn't a stuffed Fatharr.' He shook his head. 'Actually, as fun as the movie was, I'm not sure it helped.'

Ione thought about the destruction the monster had wreaked. 'Shit. I'm sorry.'

'Not your fault,' Stephen said. 'I didn't think it either at the time.'

'Tomorrow night, we'll watch a Bollywood film. I dare you to have a nightmare after a couple of hours of Indian dancing and romance.'

He grimaced. 'You think that's the solution?'

'They're so happy.'

'I'm not really a musical kind of guy.'

'I bet you haven't seen the right musical.'

'Another thing to convert me to?'

Ione laughed. 'Indeed. And how's this for conversion? I think what we need is a hot toddy.'

He nodded. 'Sounds good.'

Ione stood. 'Then one hot toddy it will be.'

She went out into the kitchen and put the milk on the stove to warm. Then she chewed on her fingernails, wondering what to do. How could she help Stephen to overcome the trauma?

Her first thought was to ask the Heasimir, but she banished that. Apart from the fact she just didn't like the guardian, she felt sure that Stephen wouldn't appreciate her knowing about his night terrors.

Inspiration struck. She looked at the clock and calculated the time in eastern Australia, and then went into the loungeroom to make the call. It rang a few times before being answered.

'Hello, Siobhan speaking.'

Ione grinned. Maggie's mum wasn't just a fourth-order dath, she was a human doctor. She'd know how to help Stephen. 'Siobhan, it's Ione.'

'Well, hello, Miss Io. What are you doing calling at your time of the night? Is it Maggie?'

Ione heard the rapidly rising panic in Siobhan's voice. 'No, Maggie's fine. I don't know if you heard about the accident at the inn yesterday.'

'I did. Apparently there was a human injured and a couple of them badly spooked, but otherwise no one was hurt. Thank the star. If it had been at dinner time ...'

'One of the gadda who was staying at the hotel has come to stay with me. Stephen O'Malley, going for his sixth order. He's been having nightmares, so he's obviously traumatised. I was hoping you'd tell me how to help him.'

'Has he spoken about it?'

'Yes. Kind of. He knows I was affected by it as well, so he's opening up to me.'

'Good. It's important that he talk and not deny that it happened. What you can do is provide him with a comfortable environment, try to eliminate as much stress as possible and make sure he knows that he can talk to you if he feels he needs to. What's his health like? How old is he?'

'I think he's pretty healthy. Young, mid-twenties, obviously works out and managed to put away a fair bit of Hammond Stew at dinner.'

'Mid-twenties? And he's going for sixth order? Oh, yes, now I recall. From what I've heard, he's an impressive young man.'

In a lot of ways, Ione thought, allowing her mind to drift mentally to Stephen's hair-roughened chest. She'd not really noticed it when she was in his room, but a part of her brain had taken note and was now replaying the very nice image for her pleasure.

Then she wondered if it was just his chest that was bare and heat flooded her face. 'Right, thanks for that, Siobhan.' She put down the phone and went back into the kitchen.

The milk was ready, so she poured two cups, added a bit of brandy and then took one into Stephen. He was lying so still that for a moment she thought he'd gone back to sleep, but then an eye popped open.

'Thanks.' He sat up and reached for the cup. Ione handed it over, and tried to ignore the tingle that whizzed up her arm as their fingers touched.

'Pleasure.' She kept her eyes resolutely on his face. She wasn't going to look at his semi-naked body. Perhaps even fully naked …

'Here's to good sleep, pleasant dreams and health and happiness for all.' She lifted the cup in a toast.

'Indeed.' He tilted the cup at her, and then took a sip. 'Perfect.'

A part of her wanted to sit back down and keep talking to him, but now that she was so aware of his body she wasn't sure she'd be content with just talking.

She considered trying to seduce Stephen and decided against it. He wasn't just a hot man she'd picked up. He was someone she was quickly coming to like, and that put a whole new complexion on things.

'I'll leave you to relax and get back to sleep,' she said. 'But any time you need to talk about it, I'm here.'

He looked at her for a moment, and then nodded. 'Thank you. And again, I'm sorry for waking you.'

'Not a problem.' Ione turned and walked back to her bedroom. She closed the door, leant back against it and sighed, cradling the warm drink in her hands. Thank goodness she'd made herself one as well. It was going to take her some time to get over the sight of Stephen and back to sleep.

'So, I take it things are going well with the man of the moment?'

Ione stuck her tongue out at her friend as she closed the door to the Ceamir's office behind her. It seemed the best response to Maggie's comment.

'Oh, come on, Io. You have to tell me. How can I live my life vicariously through you if you won't give me details?'

'Why do you want to live your life vicariously through me? Sick of Lucas already, are you? 'Cause if you are, I'll happily take him off your hands.'

'Keep your hands offa my bloke.' Maggie growled. 'And I'm referring to the life of someone without responsibility who can just do what she likes when she likes it.'

Ione stopped and looked at Maggie and realised the cheerfully rude question had been a performance. 'What's wrong?'

'Been a bad night.' Maggie ran her hand through her hair. 'News of the bombing got out and I've been dealing with news organisations from all over the world about our apparent terrorist attack.'

Ione reached across the desk and put her hand on Maggie's. 'I'm sure you've done a brilliant job.'

'I have. They all believe it was just a gas leak and it's become yesterday's news, thank goodness.'

'But it wasn't just a gas leak, was it?'

'No. It's abundantly clear that power caused that damage.'

Ione felt her stomach drop away. 'Gadda did it? But why would they attack the inn?' Then she remembered some of the events of the past couple of months. 'Purists.'

Maggie nodded. 'That's the most obvious assumption. We've even got suspects – the League of Purification that Sean was part of. Unfortunately, the bardria is locked over whether the guardians have the power to call them in for questioning when there isn't any evidence that they did it.'

The current council was split evenly along the political lines of purist and humanist. Ione could see that the purists would want to keep their own safe.

'Can't the caelleach break the deadlock? He's on the humanist side, right?'

'Except he's worried about it looking like persecution, so he's put it back on us to find evidence. Poor Hampton's going mad, trying to work out how it was done.'

Ione thought about how normal the Sabhamir had seemed yesterday and wondered how he was able to go about his duties with such calm.

'And in the meantime, there's pressure building over the texts,' Maggie continued. 'The bardria are getting more and more touchy over the lack of information we have, and there've just been no further clues to help us.'

Ione squeezed her hand. 'You'll think of something. I'm sure of it.'

Maggie smiled wanly. 'Thanks, Io. Well, I guess I'd better get back to it.'

Ione went into the apartment and knocked on Lucas's door. She heard some shuffling inside before it was flung open.

'Morning, Io.'

'Morning. Just checking to see if there's anything you've thought of before I knuckle down to it.'

Lucas frowned and looked over his shoulder. Ione peeped and saw there was a mound of wiring on top of a steel platform in the middle of the room. 'Ah, I see your mind has been otherwise occupied.'

Lucas flushed. 'Sorry, Io. Got an idea and got caught up with it.'

'That's fine. I'll just get to work and if you think of anything, come see me.' She went into the spare room, turned on her computer and was soon lost in the world of databases.

The day passed quickly – Lucas didn't come to see

her, obviously swept back into his experiment — as she ploughed along with her work, taking breaks from time to time to eat or refresh herself.

At five-thirty, she turned off the computer and gathered her things. She interrupted Lucas to tell him she was done for the day and then she headed not to her apartment, but to the shops.

She bought a couple of thick, juicy steaks and some vegetables and apples, and then made her way back home. While she thought the food in the fridge was probably still OK, she wanted to cook something fresh and wholesome for Stephen.

She smiled at herself. The last time she'd planned and cooked a meal for a man, Patrick had been alive. She'd forgotten how much fun it was — anticipating their enjoyment and how they might repay you after.

Did she want to sleep with Stephen? Her steps slowed. Physically, the answer was an undoubted yes. Under different circumstances, she wouldn't hesitate to do whatever it took to get him naked. Exploring that body would redefine fun.

But she was dealing with these circumstances, and they were that she liked Stephen. There was a friendship building between the two of them and she didn't want to ruin it. Then there was the fact that she still thought the best thing for Jack was for her to keep her relationships as casual as possible.

Besides, Stephen hadn't really shown any inclination for her. She thought she'd seen a bit of heat in his eyes from time to time, but it was hard to know if it was for real.

No, she told herself as she let herself into the apartment, the smartest thing would be to look and not touch.

Then he stepped from his room and her breath caught and she wondered if she'd be able to refrain from touching.

'Evening.' She smiled. 'I got us some steaks for dinner. I hope you like a big slab of meat.'

'Love it.' He smiled back and she felt her knees shake. He really did have a knock-out smile. 'I'm just in the middle of a test, so do you mind if I leave you to it? I should be done in twenty minutes.'

'That's perfect.' He nodded and went back into his room and Ione let out a sigh.

What a bummer that such a powerful attraction would come to naught.

She was taking her frustration out on the steak when there was a knock on the door. Ione put down the meat tenderiser and wiped her hands on her apron as she went over to open it.

Brian Mochrie stood at the door, smiling, holding a large bunch of flowers. 'Ione. I realised that you live near the inn and I came over to make sure you were all right.'

Ione looked at the flowers, then at Brian. This show of concern was disconcerting. 'I'm fine, thank you, Brian.'

'It must have terrified you, hearing that noise and wondering what was going on and not being able to protect yourself.' He looked over her shoulder into the flat as he spoke. 'I thought I could set up a shield for you and Jack. Unless you've decided you want to work with me on improving your power so you can do it yourself?'

Ione frowned. Was he really going to use the scare of the bombing of the inn to convince her to work with him? 'I don't think I need protecting; and if I do have a problem, I can summon the Sabhamir.'

'Ah, but what if he's busy elsewhere? What if you'd needed him yesterday, for example? He couldn't have left the inn to come to your aid.'

What he said was true, and the fact he'd brought it up made her more uncomfortable. 'Nevertheless —'

Brian stepped forward, and Ione scrambled backward to avoid contact. 'You and Jack deserve to be safe, Ione. Let me help you.' And he thrust the flowers into her face.

The scent wrapped soft tendrils around Ione's head and as she took it in, she felt warmth and energy rush through her system.

'Ione?'

She spun around to look at Stephen, who'd come to stand behind her with a stealth she hadn't expected from a man his size. Her nostrils flared as a bolt of lust hit her hard. Her nipples tightened as though he were already suckling on them and she felt a flush of moisture between her legs.

She tried to shake the sudden desire away, wondering why the attraction was escaping her control.

'Are you all right?'

'Ione.' Brian's voice sounded higher than it had.

She turned back to face him. 'Brian, thank you for coming to check on me but as you can see, I am fine. Goodbye.'

'The flowers.' He pushed them at her again.

'Fine.' She took them. 'Goodbye.'

He looked from her to Stephen, his face set. Then he shook his head, turned and stormed away. Ione lifted her hand and sent a muttered push incantation after him. She couldn't cast it in any meaningful way, but saying the words always helped relieve tension.

She turned back to Stephen and this time she shook her head. Normally arousal like this took some very pleasurable time to build. It shouldn't just appear.

She needed some space between them, to calm whatever this reaction was. 'I need to put these in water.' She walked around him into the kitchen.

He followed her. 'Are you all right?'

'Fine.' She filled up a vase and put the flowers in it. While she wasn't looking at him, her arousal started to settle, but then she turned and looked at him and bam!

'Do you mind if we have dinner a bit late? It's going to take longer than I thought.'

'Sure.' He smiled and Ione felt her heart flutter. 'Call me when it's ready.' He turned and walked away.

Ione gave a sigh of relief. Then she leant against the counter and frowned. Why had she had such an intense reaction to Stephen? And how the hell was she supposed to keep her hands off him if she wanted him this badly?

NINE

Stephen walked into his bedroom and sat down on the bed, pondering what had just happened.

He'd heard someone at the door and had come out in case it was his family, finally catching up with him. Instead, a strange man had been at the door with a bouquet of flowers. Stephen's first thought was that Ione had a suitor, and he'd been surprised that he didn't like the idea. But something about the way he was looking at Ione made Stephen realise this was less a suitor and more a nuisance.

She'd turned to look at him and there had been a sudden heat in her gaze that ruffled Stephen's power. He knew she was attracted to him, but the strength and warmth of the lust in her eyes had made his entire body tingle.

He shook his head to clear his thoughts. While he liked being attracted to Ione, he couldn't let it distract him from his priority – passing the test. He reached to grab the glass he was using for his latest control exercise but fumbled, and it slipped from his grasp and crashed down onto the floor. Splinters went flying, and a piece of glass lodged itself in the side of his foot.

'Fuck!' He lifted his injured foot, placing it on his other knee to look at it.

His door slammed open and Ione appeared with wide eyes. 'Are you OK?'

He grinned, feeling like a complete idiot. 'I dropped a glass, and it's cut my foot.'

She looked down at his foot and colour drained from her face. 'Star above. Can you transfer to the bathroom? I've got some stuff there.' She turned to walk down the hallway.

Stephen concentrated and within a second was standing in the middle of the bathroom. He sat down on the toilet and propped his injured foot up on the bath. It wasn't a large piece of glass, but it bloody well hurt.

Ione came in and bent over to inspect the damage. 'If I pull it out, how much healing can you manage?'

'All of it.'

She looked at him, then shook her head. 'Of course you can,' she muttered. 'You aren't Jack.' She reached down, grabbed the glass fragment between her fingernails and pulled. It came out smoothly, and Stephen sent a quick pulse of power into his foot, closing the blood vessels and sealing the skin.

'There, none the worse for wear,' he announced.

Ione bent over his foot and poked at the blood that pooled where the wound had been. 'You don't appear to have bled too much.'

'Nothing that a good hearty meal can't fix,' Stephen said cheerfully.

She looked at him and then shook her head. 'Food can fix anything for men, can't it?'

'Goes a long way.' He grinned. 'Especially a hunking big bit of steak.'

'Just let me clean up the glass in your room and —'

'Allow me.' He swished his hand. 'There, done.'

She frowned, then turned and marched from the

bathroom. Stephen grabbed a washer, cleaned the blood from his foot and followed her. He found her in the doorway to his room, staring at where moments before a shattered glass had lain.

She smiled at him. 'From time to time, I get reminded just how much easier life is if you can use your power.'

Shit, Stephen thought. He'd reminded her of her lack. 'Ione, I'm sorry. I didn't mean to —'

She put her hand up and he stopped. 'This is the last time I'm going to say this, Stephen. I don't have a problem not having access to my puny power. I don't begrudge you for the gifts and talents and hard work that have got you to where you are. I will, however, begrudge you severely if I don't have a whiskey in my hand inside a minute.'

'A minute?' A glass appeared in the air, golden liquor over a mound of ice.

She took hold of it, sipped and grinned. 'The Connemara. You remembered. Say, when you've finished the test, you don't want to hire yourself out as a home help, do you? I could get used to this.'

'Depends. What's the going rate for a home help around here?' He leant against the wall and noted a red flush that climbed her cheeks. Just like that, the attraction that he'd managed to push below his attention sprang up again.

'Bed and board. What more do you want?' She turned and walked into the kitchen.

'I don't know. I'll think about it while I'm setting the table and let you know over dinner.' He went out into the loungeroom and began to make up the dining table for a nice meal. He was looking forward to this dinner and spending some time with Ione.

The longer he was here, the more he liked Ione. Her positive outlook on life was refreshing after the obsession he'd forced on himself. And there were hidden depths to her, mysteries that were surprising for someone so upfront. For example, what had been the story with that guy?

Maybe it would be worth sticking around in Sclossin for a while after he passed the test. He actually found himself whistling while he finished the table.

They were soon sitting down and tucking into a thick steak with salad and potato.

'So, what do you have to do to prepare for the test?'

Stephen wondered if she was really interested, or if she just wanted to reassure him that she really was comfortable with the differences in their power. 'Mainly it's ensuring that my control is exact.'

'I guess you have to know all the skills and activities as well, so you can choose any of them if you have to.'

There was no mistaking the spark of interest in her eyes. Ione really did want to know. 'The moment I passed fifth order, I got a list of all the sixth-order tasks for the last three hundred years. I've tested myself against every one of them, so I know I can do it.'

'Which one do you think they will choose for you?'

'They always do something a bit different, so I can't get fixated on any one idea or activity.'

Ione nodded. 'I think that's my problem with the first-order exam. I know the bloody thing so well, I get fixated on the bits I know I can't do. I reckon if I could sit for second order, I'd romp it in.'

Stephen put his knife and fork down and clasped his hands together. He was fascinated by the idea of not passing first order. 'You said you've tried seven times. Exactly what's happened?'

'Well, each time it's a little different. I always have problems with altering my appearance; I just can't make it do what it's supposed to. But sometimes my beasts run amok, sometimes my concoctions explode and on one, glorious occasion, I transferred my book onto the chairman's head.' She laughed. 'I had no idea someone could look exasperated and pitiful at the same time.'

'You said you did the training twice. That didn't help?'

She shook her head with a cheerful grin. 'I think I just got worse. And the tutors ended up confusing me. Oh well, that's life, as they say.' She took another mouthful of food and as she chewed, a serious expression crossed her face. 'A question for you – do you think it's possible to increase someone's store of power?'

'Not by natural means, no.' He sought for some examples from the past. 'The only time I've come across it in my research was during the time that the Forbidden Texts were being used.'

'Really?'

Stephen nodded. 'It seems that one of the things they worked out during that time was some way to increase people's store of power. However, your body adjusts to the natural amount of power you have as you grow up. Taking in too much, or not having enough, can be dangerous. There aren't a lot of details from that time, but I do know that everyone who survived did so with their natural power levels intact.'

'See, now that's interesting. Brian met me in the street a few days ago and claimed that he was investigating a way for a person's natural amount of power to be increased by taking power from other living things. He said it was part of his studies to take first-order gadma. He wants me to be his guinea pig.'

'Brian?'

'The guy who was here earlier. Brian Mochrie. He seems quite intent on convincing me to be part of his experiments.'

'Don't do it.' Stephen shook his head. 'That sort of experimentation is dangerous.'

'That was the feeling I had. I'm glad to have it confirmed. Should Brian ask me again, I'll make it damn clear that I've got no interest in helping him.' Ione frowned. 'Should we tell the Sabhamir?'

'I guess so. He'd want to keep an eye on Brian, in case he goes ahead with the experiments.'

'Can you tell him? I can't do the whole mind-talk thing.'

Stephen nodded, and got in touch with the guardian. *Sabhamir? I've just been talking with Ione, and she's got some concerns about Brian Mochrie. Apparently he's been asking her to help him with some experiments to increase her power.*

The protector's voice was strong in Stephen's mind. *'Has he done anything to her?'*

Stephen posed the question and Ione shook her head. *'She says no. It seems he hasn't done anything yet, was just sounding her out.'*

'Thank you. I'll keep an eye on him.'

'I'd say the Brian Mochrie problem is over,' Stephen said.

Ione smiled. 'Thank you. I'm glad you're here.'

'So am I.'

Ione closed the bedroom door behind her and breathed a sigh of relief. So, she'd done it. She'd eaten an entire meal and then watched an entire movie — not Bollywood, one of the Austin Powers films instead — without tearing Stephen's clothes off his body. Good for her.

That intense lust for him hadn't gone away. Watching him eat — the glitter in his eyes as he tasted the food, the soft sighs of enjoyment — had been a sensual experience that did nothing to take the edge off her craving. Then it had taken all the self-control she could muster to stop herself leaning on him on the lounge. She had to curl up against its side and press her hands down between the cushions so she wouldn't reach for him.

Especially when she'd seen him smile and laugh. The man had a smile that could light up all of Sclossin.

The payoff for that had been the continuing growth of their friendship. There was a lot to admire and like in the man.

She went over to her bed, and bent to smell the flowers Brian had brought. They were beautiful, and she was determined not to let her dislike of him stop her enjoyment of them.

As she drew in the scent, images came to her mind of her and Stephen. She was intimately aware of her bed next to her, the mattress touching her thigh. It was a large, substantial piece of furniture, and would well handle her and Stephen moving on it —

No. She thumped her fists against her thighs. She wasn't going to think about being with him. She wasn't going to think about what it would mean to have all his formidable concentration focussed on her. She wasn't going to think about running her hands through her thick hair and pressing herself against him —

'Argh!' she screamed and threw herself onto the bed. Why couldn't she get those thoughts out of her head?

There was a knock at the door. 'Ione, are you all right?'

Shit. She lifted her head. 'Fine. Just stubbed my toe on the bed. It's stopped hurting now.'

'OK, but if you need my help, let me know,' he called back, then she heard him walk into his bedroom.

Where he would be getting ready for bed no doubt. Did he sleep naked, slipping his body between her soft sheets, draping them over his —

'Stop it, Ione, stop it, stop it, stop it.' She grabbed the quilt and pushed her face into it. But her mind wouldn't stop.

What sort of lover would Stephen be? She stilled, considering the thought. Would he like to take his time, slowly and deliberately learning every part of her body? A thrill ran through her and she smiled. She'd like that. There again, she'd also like it if he proved to be aggressive and insatiable, thrusting into her again and again until she fainted from the pleasure. A tingle grew between her legs. Perhaps, if she was really lucky, he was able to both give and take, driving her crazy with desire.

No, she had to stop this, she really did. She jumped up, tore off her clothes except for her knickers and crawled into bed, curling into a ball as she always did. She tucked her hands under her chin and closed her eyes. She was tired, but her mind was full of visions of being with Stephen. The visions taunted her, refusing to allow her body to relax. The throbbing between her legs increased.

She rolled onto her other side and thumped the pillow. This was ridiculous. She had a lot of work to do and she needed to get to sleep. She banished the thoughts from her mind and tried to settle her breathing, seeking the calm she needed to sleep.

But her body had other ideas. Every twitch of her body made her arms rub against her erect and sensitive nipples and her underpants pushed deliciously against her.

She lay on her back and clenched her fists. She was

going to stop this and stop it now. She closed her eyes and began to count her breathing. Slowly, her body began to relax.

She might have made it if she hadn't suddenly heard the shower go on. Stephen. He was just on the other side of the wall, completely naked, water cascading over his body.

She groaned. She had to do something or she'd never get to sleep. For a moment, she toyed with the idea of joining him in the shower, then discarded that. That left her only one option.

Her hand snuck down her body and into her pants. She gave a sigh of relief as her finger gently touched her clitoris. As she began to pleasure herself, she pictured herself with Stephen, his hand upon her. It gave her an intense shock of delight and she gasped aloud, her back arching.

Slowly, the tension built and her fantasies about Stephen became more explicit. She could feel him touching her, feel his mouth caressing her, feel him press slowly into her while she panted and moaned; she was in heaven. Good thing she was never going to do anything with him, she told herself as her hips bucked and her back arched, because in reality he could never be this good.

She began to sweat, her breath coming out in quick pants. She could feel herself reaching the pinnacle and clutched at it while she imagined feeling this way with Stephen moving within her, thrusting into her again and again until she was almost sobbing with the need for relief. She briefly thought she had never been so turned on in her life and then her orgasm came upon her, causing her to cry aloud as waves of pleasure washed over her. On and on, until she let out a final shout and her body relaxed against the bed.

Sweat dripped from her forehead and her body shook. She turned onto her side, curling up and squeezing her thighs together, trying to keep the last little shivers going for as long as possible. She fell asleep with a smile on her face.

Stephen leant against the wall, his fists clenched, his body rigid. He'd been walking back to his room, his nostrils still full of Ione's bewitching perfume after the shower, visions in his head of watching her stretch her sleek, sexy body as she put the perfume on.

Then he heard Ione moaning. Thinking she was having a nightmare, he had reached for her doorhandle, ready to wake her and comfort her if necessary. Then there came the sexiest gasp he'd ever heard and he realised what she was doing. His first thought was that he shouldn't stay and listen to such a personal moment. But his legs refused to respond to ethics.

He'd pictured her, her body straining, her face shining as her pleasure built, until he was sporting an erection like none he'd ever known.

She'd cried out and Stephen's body had bucked in response. As her orgasm went on, his breathing had become harsher. Finally, silence had settled over the flat.

Stephen waited to hear more. It crossed his mind that if she were still horny, it was his manly duty to go in and give her a hand. He grinned. Who was he kidding? He wanted her. He wanted to hear those sexy gasps in his ears. He wanted her to cry out like that because of him.

There was still no sound, and Stephen decided she must have fallen asleep. An orgasm like that would exhaust the fittest of people. So he wasn't going to get a chance to be her knight in shining armour tonight.

He looked down at himself and grimaced. In the meantime, he needed to have another shower. A very cold one, if he was going to get any sleep tonight. He turned and headed back to the bathroom.

TEN

Stephen woke up the next morning feeling as though his head were stuffed with cotton wool. He'd slept very badly. The cold shower had had little effect but he couldn't bring himself to relieve the problem as Ione had; he didn't want to do it by himself. He wanted to be with Ione.

He lay in the bed, looked up at the ceiling and wondered what to do. For six years, he'd avoided any meaningful romantic entanglement and now, just two days before the sixth-order exam, he was facing the greatest temptation of his life. Should he give into this urge, hope he would get Ione out of his system and then focus back on his preparation? He shook his head. That wouldn't be fair to Ione, and he didn't want to hurt her.

The only thing he could do was to try and forget it. He got out of bed and stretched. Then he began working on his exercises for the morning.

When he went out to get himself breakfast, he was surprised by a burst of light in the kitchen and a constant hum that played at his ears.

The electricity was back on. Ione could come back here to work, if she wanted.

She could be here. All day. Distracting him ...

He heard the bedroom door open and Ione came out. Today, she was dressed in a patchwork jacket and a straight black skirt. It was, he thought, the most conservative outfit he'd seen her in. Until he looked down and saw she'd added joggers and black and white check stockings.

She looked at him, blushed and her eyes skidded away, and Stephen had a horrible thought – what if she'd heard him in the hallway? What if she knew he'd been listening to her?

She frowned, and then looked around the kitchen. 'The electricity's back on.'

'Sure is. You can move back in here again, if you want.'

'I don't want to disturb you.' The way she was avoiding looking at him confirmed his fears – she had heard him.

'Let's get what's really going on out in the open. I know you're embarrassed about me hearing you last night, but you shouldn't be.'

Slowly, her head came up and her face was flushed bright red. She looked him directly in the eyes and he saw surprise there and also a hint of questioning. 'You heard me?'

He nodded. 'I'm sorry, Ione. I know I shouldn't have listened to something so personal, but I couldn't stop myself.'

'Why?' Then her eyes widened and she shook her head vigorously. 'Don't worry about that. I need to get to work –'

Stephen grabbed hold of her shoulders, forcing her to stay there and face him. 'Why what, Ione? Why couldn't I stop myself from listening to you? Because that was without a doubt the sexiest thing I've ever heard. It was wrong, I know, but I wanted to hear. And see and feel too, for that matter.'

She shook her head until he thought her brain must be rattling around. 'No. No, no, no.'

And there was his answer. She didn't want him. He dropped his hands, touching her suddenly painful. 'I'll go and pack. This is your home, you should be free to work here.' He turned and walked into his bedroom. With a flick of his wrist, his suitcase flipped from under the bed onto the covers. The drawers slid open and his clothes flew into the case.

All the time he cursed himself. How could he have been so stupid, to take a chance like that? He knew what worked for him — keeping his focus on the tests, not letting anyone or anything distract him.

Not even incredibly sexy women he'd give anything to be with.

Lesson learnt, he thought.

Ione watched Stephen disappear into his bedroom and told herself it was the right thing. But a mantra was repeating itself in her head: *he wants me, he wants me*. It overpowered her and she realised she was being an idiot. She liked Stephen. She wanted him. He wanted her. That was enough.

She walked down the hallway and into his room. He was packing, his clothes flying from the drawers to his suitcase. 'Stephen.'

He looked up and she saw the tightness in his expression, the lack of interest. For a moment, she hesitated. Was she wrong? Then her normal self-confidence reasserted itself. She had never judged a man's desire wrong yet. She walked across the room, wrapped her arms around Stephen's neck and pressed herself against him. He felt even better than Ione had dreamt. His body was so large and warm and hard that she felt surprisingly small and feminine. She lifted her head and pressed her lips to his.

He didn't hesitate. He put one hand behind her head to hold her mouth to his and pressed his other hand to her back, moving her closer to him. He nibbled on her lips, sucked her lower lip into his mouth, then delved into her mouth with his tongue. Heat rushed through Ione, followed by shivers of pleasure. She reached up to push her hand through his thick hair and clamped his mouth to hers, while one of her legs wrapped around his knee, fusing their bodies together.

His hand moved from her head to clasp her bottom and push her against him, and she was aware of the thickness of his erection pushing against her stomach. She moaned and rubbed herself against him, smiling as she heard his answering moan. Star above, but she wanted him.

They kissed until she began to feel dizzy, then he pulled away. He stretched out to knock the suitcase off the bed then laid her on it, pressing his body to hers. Ione wriggled against him and delighted in his gasp.

'You feel even better than I thought you would,' she said, pressing a kiss to the skin just below his ear. 'Taste better too.'

'You're the one who tastes good,' he muttered and then they were kissing again.

She welcomed the thrust of his tongue into her mouth, thought about the thrust of another part of him into her and liquid heat lit up her veins. Desperate to feel him, she reached down and started to tug his shirt from the waistband of his jeans.

'Gotta – get – clothes – off,' she panted between deep kisses.

'Like this?' Their clothes were gone, and she gasped as his hair-roughened skin rubbed over her body.

'Oh, exactly like that.' She ran her hand over the straining muscles of his back and cupped his buttocks, pressing him harder against her. 'That's exactly what I wanted.'

'Tell me what to do, Ione,' he gasped in her ear. 'Tell me how to please you.'

'I'll do better than tell you,' she said, pushing at his shoulders. 'Roll over and I'll show you.'

He flopped onto his back, and Ione crawled on top of him, straddling his hips. She looked down at his prone body and smiled.

'Boy, have I been looking forward to this,' she said as she swept her hand over his chest, 'from the moment I saw you in the Coiremir's office.'

She leant forward and pressed kisses along his jaw and down his neck. Her fingers pushed through the crisp hairs that covered his chest, taking time to explore the softer, smoother skin of his nipples.

She began pressing kisses to his chest, enjoying the hardness and breadth of him. Her tongue flashed across the top of his nipples, drawing them up then sucking on them. The salty tang of his sweat on her tongue enthralled her.

Ione worked her way down his chest, learning the shape and taste of every muscle. She took her time learning the curve of his bellybutton, diving her tongue into the dip.

He moaned, his hips jerking underneath her, his power fluttering against hers. For her to be feeling it, he must be really turned on.

Ione smiled. She couldn't believe how much she was enjoying this. He had barely touched her and yet she was sure she had never been readier for a man. And did she have something to be ready for.

She sat up, straddling his thighs. She looked down at him. His chest was rising and falling with his deep breaths, his face was flushed and his dark eyes burnt with a passion she'd never seen before. His musky scent wrapped around her, calling to her. 'I'm going to make your every fantasy come true,' she whispered.

'You've made a good start.' He reached for her, to pull her back down to him, but she shied away.

'Ah, ah, ah.' She waved her finger at him. 'Now, I'm sure that I wanted to get you into bed first, therefore I get to be in charge. But don't worry,' she added as she trailed her finger from his bellybutton to the head of his penis, 'you'll find I'm a very generous boss.'

She flicked her eyes to his penis and sighed. He was magnificent, thick and long. Ione slowly drew her finger across the head of his cock and then down to his balls, spreading her hand to cup them. Stephen groaned and she looked up to see his eyes closed, his mouth open.

She smiled, then she bent down and pressed her mouth to the tip of his penis. He gasped and his body shook, almost tossing her off.

She lapped her tongue around the head of his cock, dragging the tip through the slit and tasting the liquid evidence of his arousal. She loved this — tasting, touching, watching a man's body react and knowing that she was making him feel this way. It almost turned her on more than being touched herself.

She sat up straight again, and wriggled forward until her warm wetness was pushed against Stephen's erection. He was looking at her intently, his jaw tense and a tiny pulse in his throat beating quickly.

She shifted her hips and then rolled them forward, pressing her clitoris against the ridge of his penis. Her breath caught in her throat as the exquisite sensation rippled through her.

'I hope you know how utterly beautiful you are,' she said as she started to tease herself with him, slowly building the small tremors of pleasure. Her legs trembled. 'Just looking at you like this is enough to make me hot.'

His hands wrapped around her thighs. 'You're the beautiful one.' His eyes skimmed up her body, from where his penis was pressed between her legs to her erect nipples.

She leant forward, he lifted his head and then he was suckling her and Ione felt her womb clench with delight. She rubbed her throbbing nub against his hardness and began to pant.

His mouth was incredible. He flicked his tongue across her nipple, each stroke causing a corresponding tingle in her clitoris. Then he pressed his lips down and sucked hard. Ione's back arched as delight streaked through her.

He moved his mouth to her other breast, giving it the same attention until Ione decided she'd had enough. She pulled back and lifted her hips to position herself over him.

Stephen looked down, then back up at her. 'Ione, wait.'

Ione grinned. 'Not on your life, boyo. It's already been too long.' And she began to sink down onto him.

He pushed her open, spreading her as she couldn't remember being spread before. She lifted herself and began pushing down again. At this rate, she was going to come before she had even begun.

She looked at Stephen, who had again closed his eyes. She smiled. He must think he was dying and going to heaven. Well, best get him there. She pushed down, hard. He was within her, her buttocks pressing against the tops of his thighs.

Ione took a moment to get used to the thrilling, shocking sensation of being so stretched she wasn't sure where she stopped and Stephen began. Then she began to move, up and down, slowly, feeling her juices wetting him, making him slick.

Stephen's hands moved to her hips and he began to guide her. She followed his lead, more concerned about pleasing him than her own pleasure.

Slowly, the movement sped up and with it tension rose within her. She began to pant, her focus narrowing to where her body joined to his and the pleasure shooting from there.

She slid up and down, faster and harder, feeling him press deeper into her until she thought he would break into her soul. So close, so very close. Then she felt him stiffen, heard him call out, felt him begin to empty himself within her. It was enough to send her crashing over the edge, her orgasm taking her and shaking her to the core.

She fell onto his chest, panting. Stephen's arms wrapped around her, holding her against the thud of his heart. Ione lay there and wondered if she would ever know a more perfect contentment. This had turned out to be a very, very good idea.

Stephen slid a hand down to the middle of her back and spoke the words that killed his sperm. Ione hoped she'd feel the tingle of his power inside her — that had been so good it deserved a magical outcome. Of course, she felt nothing.

'I've got a question.' Stephen panted the words out between deep breaths.

'I shudder to think what it is.'

'Isn't bossiness supposed to be a bad thing?'

Ione smiled. 'Depends on who's doing the bossing and what they're bossing about.'

'Feel free to boss me in bed any time.'

Ione wanted to laugh. The thought that he was so willing to do this again made her giddy. He probably had a lot of abstinence to make up for.

'So, why have you been so obsessed with passing sixth order so quickly?'

'Really? That's the conversation you want to have right now?' He swept his hand down her back, caressing her buttocks.

Ione shivered. 'I thought you might want some time to recover before we get onto what I really want to converse about.'

'Not me, but I understand that things start to slow down with age ...'

Ione gasped, lifted her head and then laughed at the delight in Stephen's eyes. 'You *do* have a sense of humour.'

'Well, sure.' He shifted her body so she could feel that he wasn't joking this time — he didn't require any recovery.

'Just answer that one question, then we'll play. Why the obsession?'

A shadow passed over his eyes and Ione wondered if she might regret pushing for the answer. 'It happened on my thirteenth birthday. My folks took me to the bardria restaurant as a treat. They were so happy to be there, laughing and dancing. But the people treated them like shit. Laughed at them, refused to dance when Mam and Dad danced, looked down at them. It broke Mam's and Dad's hearts, ruined what was supposed to be the best night of their lives. So I decided to make sure that no one would ever look down on the O'Malleys again.'

'And so you decided to become one of the most

powerful gadda in history.' Ione smiled tenderly. 'Your parents must be so proud of you.'

His frown deepened and now she was sure this had been the wrong thing to talk about. 'I can't wait until I take my parents back to the bardria restaurant and everyone crowds around to congratulate them for having such a wonderful son. Then it will all be worthwhile.'

Ione leant forward and pressed a soft kiss to his lips. 'You are a truly remarkable person, Stephen O'Malley. Not because of what you've done, but why you've done it.'

His eyes glistened. 'Thank you.'

That's enough deep and meaningful for now, she thought. 'OK, conversation over. I think it's time you show me this recovery of yours.'

He put one large hand on her waist and held her close while he rolled over, pushing her deep into the mattress with his weight. Then he lifted his torso, resting on his elbows while pressing his hips against hers.

'Here's a game I want to play,' he murmured while he rocked against her. 'You're the boss, and I have to do as I'm told.'

'Ah.' Ione pulled her legs apart and wrapped them around his waist. Stephen's eyes darkened as his penis was surrounded by her wet warmth again. 'Luckily for you, that's one of my favourite games and you're in a very good position to start.'

'Really?' He looked down at where their bodies were so close to joining.

'Oh, yes.' Ione tilted her hips. Stephen shifted and then was pressing into her, slowly, shock on his face as he felt how ready she still was for him.

'See, I told you,' she murmured, lifting her head to lick his throat. 'Just do what I say, and you'll be fine.'

ELEVEN

Ione lay on Stephen's chest, her chin cupped in her hands, watching him sleep. In sleep his face relaxed, the lines of responsibility and dedication gone. Instead, his youth and his goodness shone through.

She grimaced. God, listen to her. One good — no, great — morning of sex and she was turning him into some sort of saint. That wasn't a good sign.

She got up, careful not to wake him, and pulled her clothes back on. Then she went out into the loungeroom and looked at the clock. Time to think about lunch. Actually, more like dinner. Her stomach agreed, growling at her.

She went into the kitchen and began to pull things out of the cupboards to make a chocolate pudding. She could think things through while she cooked, and chocolate pudding always made her feel better.

She'd told herself that it would be just sex, and that's what it was going to be. Stephen would leave once he'd passed the test, and then Jack would be back and it would all be over. She wasn't to get too attached to him.

Not that she'd want to, she told herself as she started to stir the mixture. He was an obsessive personality, and if one of those took hold of the wrong obsession it could be difficult. And he had no plans beyond what would happen in two days, and she didn't particularly want to deal with a man hanging around the apartment and moping because he had no sense of direction or ambition. And the size of him; he'd eat her out of house and home.

Except that if *she* became his obsession — no, that would be bad, because she had never had time for men and their jealousies.

She banged her fist against her head. Get with the program, Ione, she told herself. You are not allowed to fall in love with the man. You're not. You've got Jack to worry about.

Ah, now that worked. Jack, who she wanted to protect for as long as possible. If she did get involved with Stephen, and he stuck around for a while but then it ended, poor Jack would be the one who really suffered.

That's it, she said to herself, nodding her head as she spooned the mixture into a baking dish. For Jack's sake, there would be nothing more between her and Stephen except some red-hot sex. When he passed his test she'd congratulate him, wave him goodbye and then forget about him.

There was a knock on the front door, and Ione's head whipped around. Damn it. She stood still with the bowl in her hand, wondering whether the interruption would go away if she didn't respond. Another knock, a pause, then some continuous thumping.

Nope. Whoever it was would stand there until she answered, that was clear. With a sigh, she put the bowl down and went over to the door, wiping her hands on her apron. She pulled it open, ready to snipe, but was instead almost bowled over by a small figure.

'Mam.'

'Jack.' Ione crashed down onto one knee in order to hug her boy to her chest. She looked up into her brother's face. 'Mark? Is everything OK?'

'Paddy's sick, Susie's looking after him and I decided to give them a break from Jack. What happened to the inn?'

'No one quite knows yet.' She stood and pressed a kiss to her brother's face. 'It was horrible, Mark. I'm never going to forget that sound.' She hugged Jack closer to her, ignoring his complaining wiggles.

'Mam, Mam.' Jack pulled on her sleeve, drawing her attention. 'Grandpa is sick and Grandma was too busy to look after me. But she said I could probably go back before school starts again. Can I?'

'We'll see,' Ione said, smiling at his bright and earnest face. Jack started to shift his weight from side to side, signalling the beginning of the release of pent-up energy from sitting on the train most of the day. 'Now, take your bag into your room, unpack and put your washing in the basket.'

'Can I play my computer game? Grandma wouldn't let me; she said I have to spend time outside.' He wrinkled his nose in disgust.

'Unpack first.'

He skipped down the hall. Mark stepped forward and put his hands on her shoulders. 'You weren't hurt in the blast?'

'No, really, I'm fine. It scared me, but that's all. How's Paddy?'

'Really sick. It was quite sudden too. Susie thought maybe food poisoning, but none of the rest of us got sick. I hope it's nothing major.' Mark pushed his hand through his hair.

'It was probably the stress of dealing with Jack.'

'Maybe. Apparently your son has developed an allergy to utensils. Has to eat with his hands.'

'Ugh. Well, I'll deal with —' Ione stopped as she heard a door open. She paled as she remembered Stephen's presence in the apartment. She stood and spun around, but not in time to stop him.

Stephen stepped into the loungeroom and Ione felt a twin spurt of gratitude and sadness that he'd put clothes on. She looked at his face and was surprised to see a flash of hatred cross his strong features.

Then his expression went as calm as it had been when they'd first met. 'I thought I heard someone.'

Mark grabbed her arm and Ione squeaked as pain rocked through her shoulder. She wrenched from his grasp and turned to him. 'Mark, stop it.'

Mark wasn't looking at her. His focus was on Stephen. 'O'Malley.'

'Hammond.'

Ione looked over her shoulder and saw a smile flicker on Stephen's face. 'You two know each other?'

'What's he doing here?' Mark's voice growled in her ear. She turned back to her brother and saw his face was red, his lips tight and his eyes wide.

Yep, they knew each other and not in a good way. 'Stephen was in the inn when it was bombed. He needed somewhere to stay.'

Mark's eyes narrowed. 'I bet he did,' he snarled.

Stephen's response was forestalled by Jack, who came running down the hallway. He skidded to a stop next to Stephen and then craned his neck up to look at him.

'Wow, you're big.'

'Jack, come here.' Mark's command cracked across the room. Jack continued to stare up at Stephen with fascination.

'How'd you get so big? Power?'

'Jack, here. Now!' Mark's voice rang with panic and now Ione felt scared. Why was he so worried about Stephen?

'Jack, come here,' she said. Jack looked at her, sighed and padded over. Mark grabbed him and pulled the little boy behind his body.

'What are you doing here, O'Malley?'

'It's just a coincidence, Hammond.'

'Bullshit. This is part of your plan, isn't it?'

'Right, that's enough.' Ione stepped between them and turned to face Mark and Jack. 'Jacky, you get to have an hour of television.'

Jack looked around his uncle's legs and she hated the fear she saw in his eyes. 'Is everything OK?'

'It's fine, little man.' She kissed his forehead. 'I just need to chat with Uncle Mark, so you watch the television.'

Jack walked slowly over to the lounge, his eyes flicking from Mark to Stephen and back.

Ione turned to her houseguest. 'Can you give us some privacy please?'

'Sure.' Stephen went into his room, closing the door.

'You. In the kitchen. Now.' She marched into the room, her heart thudding and her legs shaking. She got to the sink, spun around and hissed at her brother, 'What the fuck is going on?'

'You tell me,' he hissed back. 'How the hell did O'Malley end up here?'

'I told you — he was in the inn when it was attacked and he needed somewhere to stay. The electricity was cut and I couldn't work here, so it seemed an ideal solution.

I worked at Maggie and Lucas's, he practised here. How do you know him?'

Mark pressed his lips together so firmly the skin around them went white. 'I'd rather not –'

'No. No way, Mark Hammond. You're not going to scream at my little boy and scare him and not explain it to me. You're spilling, and you're spilling now.'

He closed his eyes and his shoulders slumped. 'I didn't want you to ever know this.'

'Know what?'

When his eyes opened, they were wide with a plea for understanding. 'Remember about eight years ago, there was that story of the bloke who was found passed out in the park with a big F tattooed on his cheek?'

Ione nodded. It had happened just a few days before Jack was born. Then the subtext of what Mark was saying hit her. 'Are you saying Stephen did that?'

He shook his head. 'No. Stephen was the victim. I was the one who did it.'

Ione leant back and grabbed the sink behind her. 'What?'

'I was pissed off, because it was meant to be a night with the boys, but Patrick cried off 'cause he was scared of missing Jack's birth. And I got drunk, really drunk, and me and Aaron and John went looking for someone to take our frustrations out on. I don't really remember what happened next, but about eight months later, there was a knock on the door. I opened it and there was O'Malley, with some of the tattoo still on his face, and then it started to come back to me. He'd just failed second order and was drunk himself, and we thought his complaining so funny and how ridiculous that he couldn't pass second order, so we –'

He stopped but he didn't need to go on. 'You kept feeding him drinks until he passed out, tattooed an F for failure on his cheek and left him in the park so he'd be humiliated.' Star, no wonder she'd seen the hate on Stephen's face when he looked at Mark. Right now, she hated her brother too.

'We were drunk ourselves, and I was upset.'

'Upset? Because Patrick couldn't join you? If my memory serves correctly, you'd been planning that night for ages and Patrick told you time and again he wasn't going to leave me in the last few days of the pregnancy, but you went ahead and organised it anyway. Whereas if you'd waited until the day after Jack was born, when I was still in bed and Patrick was ready to celebrate ...' She shook her head.

'He was my best friend,' Mark hissed. 'I had every right to expect to be able to socialise with him.'

'He was about to become a father for the first time and was scared stiff, but you didn't care about that, did you?' Ione shot back.

'You mean you wouldn't let him go. It was pathetic, the way you'd hang around and try to keep him away from his mates.'

'I never —' Ione heard her voice rise and stopped. She wasn't going to yell at Mark in front of Jack. 'You're wrong.'

'Am I? I don't think so. And I'll tell you something else — if you've got any brains at all, you'll tell O'Malley to go find somewhere else to stay. He's only here to get at me. He swore he would.'

'Get out,' Ione snarled. 'Get out and don't bother coming back until you're ready to apologise.'

'I'm giving you two hours to get rid of him, Io, or I'm

120

coming to take Jack away. I won't leave my nephew in danger.' Mark turned on his heel and stormed out of the flat, slamming the front door behind him.

Ione put her hand to her forehead and sighed.

'Mam?'

She looked up. Jack's tiny face poked around the door to the kitchen. He was so pale, every little freckle stood out.

'Come here, little man.' She crouched down and opened her arms. Jack ran to her, almost knocking her over.

'Why is Uncle Mark so mad at the man?' he whispered.

'I don't know, cushla.' She hugged him to her. His trembles cut into her heart. 'But you're OK.' She pressed a kiss to the top of Jack's head and hoped she was right.

Stephen's first reaction when he walked into his room was to smile. Damn, but the look on his enemies' faces, when they saw him and remembered what they'd done, was absolutely priceless.

Then he realised that all this probably meant the end of he and Ione. Hammond would convince her that he was the victim, and she wouldn't want to see him again.

He slumped down onto his bed. Maybe when Ione had asked him why he was so obsessed with passing sixth order he should have told her the whole story, not just the initial impetus of the night in the restaurant.

Maybe if he'd gone into detail of how he'd felt when he'd woken in the park and been taunted by those kids, maybe she'd be on his side and not Hammond's. But his thoughts wouldn't end on that story. They'd keep going to his threats against the perpetrators. To the first time he went to see them after passing third and fourth order.

To when he'd returned to his parents' place after celebrating — not drunk but pleasurably fogged — and bumped into Aaron Lansing, leaving.

Lansing had looked at him with a smile before hurrying past and a lot of Stephen's good mood had dissipated as he walked in the door.

'Stephen.' Liam O'Malley had appeared in the loungeroom door. Liam was tall and blond, but without the bulk his son had developed. 'Can I speak with you please?'

'Sure.' Stephen strolled into the room and collapsed onto the lounge. 'What's up?'

'I want to know why you threatened Aaron Lansing.'

The room started to spin and Stephen wondered if he'd drunk more than he thought. 'I beg your pardon?'

'Why did you threaten Aaron Lansing? He's terrified, Stephen, came here begging me to stop you. Why?'

Stephen started to laugh. Then he realised his father wasn't in on the joke. 'It's fine, Dad. Lansing's running scared but he deserves to.'

Liam frowned. 'He deserves to be so terrified that he can't keep any food down?'

Now it was Stephen's turn to frown. Lansing hadn't seemed that scared to him. Scally had, but not Lansing. 'A guilty conscience will do that to a guy, I guess.'

'Guilt over what?'

'He was one of the men who tattooed me.'

To Stephen's amazement, Liam shook his head. 'No. I know Aaron. He wouldn't do that.'

Stephen sat up, the fogginess of the alcohol pushed aside. 'He did do it. He admitted it to me.'

'Then why hasn't he been charged by the Sabhamir?'

'I'm not dobbing them in to the Sabhamir. They humiliated me. I'll deal with it myself. When I'm ready.'

'I don't believe it.'

'Believe it, Dad.'

'No.' Liam shook his head. 'You're mistaken, Stephen.'

'I'm not.'

'Yes, you are.'

'So what? You're going to believe Aaron Lansing and not me?'

'Aaron Lansing wouldn't do that,' Liam said.

And so it had begun. Over the years, that simple disagreement had turned into a fighting arena for Stephen and Liam, until it had become easier for them not to meet.

Stephen bowed his head. He couldn't tell Ione half the story and not consider the other half, and he didn't want to think about how his relationship with his father had been destroyed by Lansing's lies.

There was a knock at the door and Stephen sucked his breath in between his teeth. He forced it out slowly, trying to remain calm. He stood and readied himself to face Ione's revulsion toward him. 'Come in.'

She opened the door and he was surprised by how soft her eyes were. 'Can we talk?'

'Of course.'

'Out here. Jack's in his bedroom.' She turned and walked into the loungeroom. Stephen followed.

She faced him and he was stunned by her smile. 'Mark told me what he did to you. I'm so sorry.'

Hammond had told the truth? 'Thank you.'

She shook her head. 'I just can't understand how he could have done that. I thought he was a good man ...'

Stephen's body went tight. This was going to be like his father, he thought. Ione would believe Hammond, not him.

She looked at him and there were tears in her eyes. 'I don't know how you haven't killed him for it. I want to.'

She believed him. Star above.

'You didn't dob him in to the Sabhamir?'

Ah, so Hammond hadn't told the whole story. 'I decided to handle it myself. I found your brother and his friends and told them all I'd deal with them when I was ready. Then I focussed on getting to sixth order so I could.'

Her lips twitched. 'No wonder he practically shit himself when he saw you here.'

'Between you and me, I don't think I'm going to take it any further than that. Every time they see me, they lose it. I think feeling like that for more than seven years is punishment enough. But I'd appreciate if you don't tell him until after the test.'

Ione laughed. 'Ah, Stephen O'Malley, that is truly Machiavellian of you.'

'Machia-what?'

'Devious. Mean. Perfect. If you like, I can turn the screws a bit, pretend that you do have something planned, make Mark sweat.'

'You'd do that?'

She pulled a face. 'Let's just say that I'm not feeling particularly charitable toward my brother at the moment and leave it at that.'

He looked at her — glowing, ready to support him to the end — and something inside him melted. 'You are remarkable.'

'Thank you.' Then her lips twisted. 'Unfortunately, my support for your nefarious plans isn't the end of this little problem. There's the fact that Jack's back.'

Inside, things started to get cold again. 'Jack.'

She nodded. 'Jack changes things. He's my first priority, and I can't risk him.'

In all the ways he'd thought of Ione, he'd never thought of her as a mother. Yet it was obviously something that had never been far from her mind. 'Of course.'

'I'm sorry, he was supposed to be at his grandparents' until after you passed the test.'

He'd only known her a few days, so why did leaving here feel so bloody terrible? 'I'm glad you assume I'll pass it.'

'Of course you will, and you'll go down in history as one of the most remarkable gadda ever.' She took a deep breath. 'But really, it isn't your achievements that make you remarkable. It's who you are. Remember that?'

His hands itched to reach for her, he wanted nothing more than to kiss the lips that said such wonderful things. But he knew that wasn't a good idea. The leave-taking was hard enough. 'Thank you, Ione.' There were so many things to say, so many things to ask, and he didn't have the right to ask any of them. 'Well, I'll get my things and go.'

He returned to his room, grabbed his bag and walked back into the loungeroom. Ione hadn't moved. Her hands were clenched so tightly in front of her that her knuckles were white.

She nodded. 'Good luck.'

He half hoped she would fling herself at him, give him one last kiss. But she stayed put.

Stephen contacted the Coiremir and transferred to her office, trying to convince himself that he was fine with just that small taste of bliss.

TWELVE

Ione closed the door, and leant against it with a sigh. She knew she was doing the right thing, letting Stephen go like that, not encouraging any sort of hope for a future.

But damn, it had been one of the hardest things she'd ever done.

Ione started to head to Jack's bedroom to check on him, but stopped at the sound of Maggie's chime. Frowning, Ione granted admittance. Moments later, Maggie stood in the middle of her loungeroom.

'Ione.' She nodded her head. 'Is Jack here?'

Ione frowned. 'He's playing in his bedroom.'

'I'm sorry, but I need to speak to him. Can you get him?'

'Sure.' Ione went down the hallway to Jack's room, wondering if Jack had somehow managed to get his hands on a computer and post more secrets of the gadda online. His happiness at being told Maggie wanted to see him seemed to suggest he hadn't done anything to be guilty about.

He almost skipped out into the loungeroom. 'Hey, Maggie. I had to come home early 'cause Grandpa got sick.'

'I know, sport. That's kinda what I want to talk to you about. Your grandma said you and your grandpa went to see Evelyn Scott yesterday and she gave you some lollies.'

Jack nodded. 'She always does.'

'Did you eat any?'

He shook his head. 'She said I had to share them with Mam. But I gave Grandpa one, 'cause he said he really wanted one. Is that OK?' He looked at Ione, who nodded.

'Of course, buddy.' Then Ione looked at Maggie and saw relief sweep across her friend's face.

'I'm sorry, Jacky, but I need those lollies. Turns out there was something wrong with them. That's why your Grandpa is sick, and Miss Scott is too.'

'Really? You're sure? Miss Scott gives me good lollies.'

'I'll get you some more, I promise,' Maggie said. 'Come on, show me where they are.' Maggie took the little boy's hand and led him down to his bedroom.

Ione sat on her lounge and rubbed her hands together. Had Jack really not tasted the lollies? She'd hate for him to get whatever Paddy and Evelyn Scott had.

Maggie came back with a brown paper bag in her hand. 'He's back playing games,' she said. 'I'm sorry, Io.'

'Hey, anything that saves Jack and me from getting sick is welcome,' Ione said, standing. 'Are Paddy and Evelyn going to be OK?'

'Fine. It'll take time but they'll be fine.' Maggie's smile was weary. 'Thanks, Io. Much appreciated.' She came over to give Ione a kiss and pulled back seconds after contact with a frown on her face. 'Are you sure you didn't have any of the lollies?'

'I didn't know Jack had any. Why?'

Maggie didn't respond. Instead, she turned around to face the middle of the room and then the Sabhamir was standing there.

'You got them?' he said.

Maggie nodded. 'I did, and Jack and Ione say they didn't have any. Jack feels fine, but Io ...'

The Sabhamir moved forward. 'Hand, please, Ione.'

Ione lifted her hand to him without thinking. 'What's going on?'

He touched her and frowned. 'You didn't have any of the lollies?'

Ione felt something cold shimmer over her skin. 'No. What can you feel?'

He ignored her question and went back to stand in the middle of the room. He turned in a slow circle, stopping when he faced the hall. Then he strode forward.

Maggie dashed after him and Ione followed. She was shocked to see them walk into her bedroom.

The Sabhamir was standing on the other side of her bed, Brian's bouquet in his hands. 'Where did you get this?'

'Brian Mochrie. He gave them to me yesterday. Stephen told you about the experiments he wanted to do.'

The Sabhamir nodded as he bent his head to sniff the flowers. His eyes widened and his nostrils flared. He closed his eyes, shook his head, then looked at Ione. 'I'm sorry to have to ask a really personal question, Ione, but have you had sex with anyone since you got the flowers?'

'Yes, this morning.'

'With Brian Mochrie?'

'No, Stephen O'Malley. Would you please tell me what's going on?'

'It would seem that Mochrie has used the Forbidden Texts to try and get you to sleep with him, Ione. I've got to go. Maggie, you explain.' He disappeared.

'What the fuck?' Ione spun around to glare at Maggie.

Maggie took Ione's hand and led her into the loungeroom. 'You carry the darkness of the Forbidden Texts, Ione. I could feel that someone's been using them on you. I called the Sabhamir, 'cause I thought it might be the lollies, but —'

'Hang on, Paddy and Evelyn were poisoned with the texts? And Jack could have been next?' Ione's knees began to shake.

Maggie pushed her down onto the lounge. 'I'm getting you a drink,' she said, moving over to the bar. 'Yes, someone gave Evelyn lollies with twisted power within them, and she reacted very badly to it. But before she got sick, she shared some with Jack and others as well, who also got sick. Thank the star she told him to share with you and that this time he actually did as he was told.' Maggie brought a whiskey back to Ione.

Ione tipped her head back and drained the glass. 'And now I've been touched by them?'

Maggie sat down next to her. 'Via the flowers.'

'That means ...'

'Brian Mochrie has been using the texts. Undoubtedly those experiments he was talking about doing on you would incorporate their teachings.'

Ione shuddered. She flopped back against the lounge and closed her eyes, trying not to think about how close both she and Jack had come to real danger.

'Ione, I've summoned the Garramir.' As Maggie spoke, Ione felt a shift in the air. She opened her eyes and a short, balding man in a bright green Hawaiian shirt and cargo pants stood in front of her.

'Hello.' He smiled and his friendliness immediately put Ione at ease. 'So, what's been going on here?'

'Ione has a touch of darkness that needs to be neutralised,' Maggie said.

'Sure, sure.' He came over and put his hand on Ione's shoulder. 'Bah, barely enough to worry me over. There, all done. You'll be sweet, Ms Ione.' His eyes twinkled and Ione felt as though things really would be fine.

'Thank you.'

'Not a problem. If you feel unwell tomorrow, give me a yell and I'll come check you out, but I'm sure you'll be fine. Now, if you'll excuse me, the Sabhamir needs me.' He nodded to Maggie, and was gone.

Maggie leant over to look Ione in the eye. 'Io, I have to go. Is there someone you want with you?'

Stephen was the first person that sprang to mind. 'No, I'll be fine.'

'I'll put a lock over the house, so no one can get to you without me knowing. Io.' Maggie touched her hand. 'I'm so sorry this has happened to you.'

'It's OK, Mags.' Ione patted Maggie's hand. 'Luckily, nothing really did happen.'

Ione sat on the lounge after Maggie left and stared at the floor. So Brian had concocted some sort of spell to make her want him, only it had backfired and made her crazy for Stephen instead.

She winced. Everything that had happened in the past twenty-four hours — her overwhelming lust for him, her decision to throw caution to the wind and have him regardless — had been powered by a spell. Not by a real desire for Stephen.

He'd been used, by her and by Brian's flowers. She was going to have to find him and apologise.

Stephen wandered through the corridors of the bardria building, wondering what to do with himself. The Coiremir had organised a room to stay in until the test was over, but he didn't want to practise or sleep. What he really wanted, of course, was to be with Ione, but that wasn't an option now either.

He stepped outside in the cool of the darkening day. He stretched his shoulders and used the steps to warm up his legs and calves. Then he started to run.

He went down Bardria Avenue to the main street then along the path, ignoring the parkland between him and the river. The shops were dark but light, music and warmth spilt out of the door of the Royal, the oldest and most popular pub in Sclossin.

Stephen ignored the siren call and kept his focus on keeping his rhythm, breathing deeply, maintaining the run for as long as possible. Sweat built on his body and he began to feel constricted within his clothing.

As the road reached the end of town, he turned and headed back to the bardria building. He estimated it was about four kilometres each way – he should probably run for longer as he'd not really exercised for a few days, but it would do.

As he was passing the Royal, the door opened and two men stumbled out onto the footpath. One was trying to keep the other upright, but it was clear to Stephen both of them had drunk a great deal.

A spear of light from the closing door ran across the men's faces and Stephen shuddered to a halt. Aaron Lansing.

Lansing looked up and swore. 'Damn, don't tell me it's that time again.'

Stephen smiled. 'Shall we dance, Aaron? I'll remind you of what I promised to do, you'll go run to my father with another tale, he'll yell at me and it won't change a damn thing.'

Aaron's eyes wavered in their focus. 'Go to hell, O'Malley.'

'Not me, Lansing.'

'Have we got a problem?'

Stephen looked past Aaron and his companion, and saw the Sabhamir appear out of the gathering darkness. With his dark hair and darker clothing, he looked for a moment like a disembodied head.

Stephen looked at Lansing and lifted an eyebrow. While Aaron might consider him no threat, the protector was another matter.

'No, no, Sabhamir.' Aaron tried to turn around, stumbled, and his friend almost went down.

'Good. Stephen, I need to speak to you.'

'Of course.'

'Watcha done now, O'Malley?' Aaron's voice rang with glee.

Stephen leant closer. 'You'll see,' he whispered and watched the colour drain from Lansing's face. He touched the Sabhamir's shoulder and transferred with the guardian to his office with a smile.

The Sabhamir's office was quite a normal-looking room — desk, chair, lounges for people to sit on and chat. It suited the man himself, who was never obvious about the power he wielded.

'I'm afraid I need to test you, Stephen. It seems that Brian Mochrie did something with the flowers he gave to Ione and I need to make sure you haven't been tainted by it.'

'Of course.' Stephen put his hand out. The guardian took hold and after a moment nodded.

'All is well,' he said, then folded his arms across his chest. 'You appear not to have been affected by the flowers; however we need to be careful. I'm afraid we'll have to postpone the test a few days.'

'What?'

'I'm sorry, Stephen.'

'What the hell could he have done to the flowers that would stop me from taking the test?'

'I'm not at liberty to say.'

Stephen took a deep breath to control himself. He wasn't being banned from taking the test, it was just being postponed. 'I would prefer to know.'

'I understand. I hope one day I can tell you. Now, you told me Brian had asked Ione to meet with him with a view to helping him with experiments.'

It took Stephen a moment to realise what the Sabhamir was referring to. 'Did he start experimenting by giving her the flowers?' Rage flooded through him. 'Is she all right?'

'She's fine. The Garramir is with her now, making sure of that. Thank you, Stephen.' The dismissal was clear.

Stephen walked out of the office, stunned by the sudden turn of events.

He stood in the middle of the corridor, his fists clenched. Star, if he had Mochrie there with him ...

Mochrie put Ione at risk. Star knew the damage he could have done.

Damn, but he wished he could go to her, hold her, comfort her. She must have been terrified when she was told. He thumped his fists against his thighs.

'Star burn you, Brian Mochrie. If you've hurt her ...'

Stephen sighed. He didn't have the right to be angry on Ione's behalf. He didn't have the responsibility to protect her.

He stomped back to his room, knowing he'd get no sleep that night.

ASARLAI

'*He what?*' Asarlai leant forward, not wanting to believe what she'd just heard.

'*I don't have the details,*' Lachy Ackland sent. '*After I overheard Stephen O'Malley in the corridor, I asked around and it seems clear that the Sabhamir has Brian. I thought I should tell you straight away, in case it's to do with our studies.*'

'*How did you happen to be there?*'

'*I was with my friend Aaron when the Sabhamir came to get O'Malley. I thought maybe I'd overhear something, so I dumped Aaron and loitered outside the Sabhamir's office.*'

'*Thank you.*' She broke the mental communication and swore. She didn't doubt for a moment that it was to do with the texts, or that Brian Mochrie had been unable to resist the temptation to use them for his own ends.

She pictured his laboratory and transferred. It was a bloody mess — half-filled beakers, open containers, powder spilt on the floor. She shook her head, wondering why Brian would be so careless with something so powerful.

A sweep of her hand, and the laboratory was restored to rights. Then she began to search, knowing that at any moment the Sabhamir could come here searching for his own evidence.

Luckily, she had some extra knowledge on where to look. She found Brian's notebook, where he'd been copying the texts for his own study, in a hidden compartment built into his desk. A compartment that she'd directed all her apprentices to create.

Holding it, she sent out tendrils of power to sense any extra darkness. It was in the equipment but not in any of the other books. Satisfied that she had all the information Brian had, she transferred to a spot in the countryside outside of Sclossin. From there she went to the intran room of the bardria building, then walked around the corner to the outtran room. The rooms provided a safe spot for ordinary gadda to come to the bardria and the outran room also gave an extra boost to a transfer to get them home. She had to wait for a couple of people to transfer in front of her but she didn't mind — if people saw her here right now, they'd be less likely to connect her to a cover-up at Brian's laboratory. And the more people who were transferring in and out of the building, the harder her trail would be to follow.

From there, she transferred to her laboratory. She sat down and began to flick through Brian's notebook.

She looked through all her apprentice's notebooks after each session with them, so she knew what they were recording from the texts. However, after Brian's last session notes were pages of questions and diagrams. He had taken the basic gadda conjuration of an aphrodisiac and had worked out ways in which to combine some of his learning about the texts to increase its potency, so that it would work even with someone you weren't attracted to.

Clever, she thought, looking through it. What a waste of talent. If only he'd brought this to her, instead of using it for his own means. She continued reading his notes, and realised that he'd fixated on the League of Purification's dislike of Ione Gorton and her human career.

Make her more gadda, she won't have to do it, he'd written. *Increase her power. Make her want to work with me.*

Asarlai shook her head, then mentally connected with Brian. She could hear the response to her call whizzing through his mind — terror, concern, fear. She spoke one word.

'*Cacht.*'

His thoughts stopped, he focussed on the word and she heard a whispered, '*No.*' She cut herself off from him. She thought being connected to someone while they died could be dangerous.

Ione Hammond Gorton is an interesting choice for Mochrie's experiment, Asarlai thought. She had a son, so her bloodlines were already passed on. More, with her lack of power, her loss wouldn't rob the gadda of anything they would need in the new order.

She connected with the rest of her apprentices. '*I want to see you, now.*'

It took a couple of minutes for all five to appear. She tapped Brian's notebook against her chin and let the silence settle around them. She hoped they recognised what she was holding. She looked at Lachy and saw his eyes darken — he should be suspecting what she was about to say.

'Brian Mochrie is dead.'

Faces paled, Shauna gasped. 'How?'

'I killed him.' She watched understanding dawn across their faces. She knew they were all thinking of the potion.

'Brian stupidly used what I've been teaching you for his own ends. He made a mistake, and the Sabhamir found out and arrested him. He had become a liability, and so I got rid of him.'

The five apprentices were all pale and each shivered

to a varying degree. Asarlai watched them with a sense of satisfaction.

Killing Brian was a shame, but in the end she thought it would probably make her relationship with these apprentices clearer. They'd be even more willing to please her, knowing what she could do to them.

She leant back in her chair and lightly drummed her fingers on its velvet-covered arm. 'Tell me what you have learnt from his mistake,' she said softly.

'To not do anything without your permission,' Shauna said.

'To put the goals of the texts before our own personal agenda,' said Shauna's and Brian's rival, Ellen Pearce, with a smile of glee. As a member of the Anti-Human League, she was undoubtedly delighted to see her rival group fail.

'To act with stealth and keep our identity shielded,' said Glen Flaherty, a member of the great Flaherty clan and someone devoted to ensuring the glory of the gadda.

'Good.' Asarlai nodded. 'Now, you are all going to have to be very careful for a time. The guardians will be scouring Brian's life, and will undoubtedly find you, Shauna. They may also locate the rest of you. Do not do anything with the texts, do not practise any skills until I contact you. Make sure your notebooks are well hidden. Brian's foolishness means we will have to delay our plans for a while, to ensure we do not draw attention to ourselves before we are ready. Do you understand?'

'Yes, Asarlai,' they chorused.

After they had gone, Asarlai got up and stretched her legs. Dealing with arrogant young fools like Mochrie was putting quite a strain on her. She couldn't believe how tired she'd been feeling lately.

Her own experiments were going well. She'd seen how easy it was to spread the impact of the texts through the gadda — the parcel she'd arranged to have delivered to Evelyn Scott nominally from a niece had been distributed around half a dozen families. The only ones who hadn't tried the lollies were Jack and Ione Gorton. Everyone else was still in the healing wing of the bardria. She wondered if the Heasimir had found and neutralised the true terror of the sweets, and not just stopped at ridding people of their symptoms. Time would tell whether the guardians fully appreciated what they were dealing with.

There was a knock at the front door. Asarlai stood and walked out of the laboratory, closing the door behind her. Then she went through her loungeroom and threw the front door open.

Kimberley Gaines, a teacher at the gadda school, smiled at her. 'Evening,' she said brightly. 'May the star bless you and all your endeavours.'

'Evening, Kimberley. You're the first one here.'

'Excellent. I wanted to ask you about the task we set for homework at the last meeting.' Kimberley walked in with a smile on her face.

Asarlai closed the door and watched her visitor settle herself on the lounge. Kimberley was one of several teachers who were working on developing their own power past the usual skills for their level. All the men and women involved said they did so in order to learn and thus be better teachers. Asarlai didn't doubt for a moment it was all about self-gratification.

She hadn't chosen any apprentices from this group — none of them were suitable for that — but she had other plans, particularly for Kimberley.

'Of course,' Asarlai said with a smile. 'How can I help you?'

THIRTEEN

Ione was woken from a deep sleep by Jack, bouncing on her bed.

'Mam, Mam, can I have pancakes for breakfast?'

Groggily, she pulled him to her, holding him still. He happily curled up against her, hugging her back. She tried to conceive of what she would have done if Jack had been hurt by the texts, and shuddered. It was too terrible a thought.

'Yes to pancakes, but I've still got some work to do, so you have to promise to go and play quietly in your room this morning. If you're good, we'll go to the park this afternoon.'

'Yay!' Jack jumped out of bed, full of boundless energy and seemingly unconcerned with having had his holiday cut short and his lollies taken away.

Ione sighed as she pulled herself out of the bed. She'd not got to sleep until late, her thoughts full of fear. This morning, she felt like just staying in bed and sleeping, but the responsibilities of motherhood precluded that.

After breakfast, she made sure Jack dressed, cleaned his teeth and brushed his hair, while he complained throughout. Then she left him in his room with his computer games and went into the loungeroom. She stood and stared at her computer. She should get to work, hopefully lose herself in the demands of coding.

But she had something else to do first. She reached for the phone, wishing she could do the mind-talk most other gadda took for granted.

Maggie picked up on the third ring. 'Hey, Io. How are things?'

'Fine. Jack and I are both OK. Seems the texts weren't able to do their worst to us.'

'Good.' Ione could hear the worry and the exhaustion in Maggie's voice. 'Now, what can I do for you?'

'Can you get a message to Stephen? I need to explain to him about the flowers and apologise.'

'Sure. I'll tell him to pop over and see you.' Maggie hung up before Ione could say she'd prefer to do it on the phone.

Ione put down the receiver with a sigh. She didn't want to see Stephen in the flesh — it was all too embarrassing. She sat down on her lounge, twisting her fingers together. Maybe it wasn't too late to call Maggie again, and get her to —

A deep tone rang in the air, and Ione jumped. She stood, and pressed her clammy hands to her thighs. Then she gave permission to enter.

Her first thought was that, even without the flowers, she still considered him good enough to eat. Then she noted that his face was pale and there were dark circles around his eyes, and guessed he hadn't slept very well either.

'Ione.' He started to reach for her then stopped and dropped his hands awkwardly down by his side. 'I'm glad you asked to see me. I wanted to come when I heard but ...'

She nodded. 'I wondered if the Sabhamir had told you. Stephen, I'm so sorry.'

'Sorry for what? It's not your fault that Brian Mochrie was a dick.'

'It isn't fair that you got used in that way.'

He frowned. 'What way? What are you talking about?'

'What did the Sabhamir tell you?'

'That Mochrie had put something in the flowers and it had impacted on you. They tested me to make sure I was all right because, well ...' He grinned sheepishly.

So he hadn't been told it was about sex. 'It wasn't just something, Stephen. Those flowers were the world's most potent aphrodisiac.'

She waited, and knew from the bleakness that entered his eyes the moment he made sense of her words. Damn, she hated hurting him.

'I see. So the only reason that you slept with me is because of the flowers.' His tone was flat, his voice quiet.

'No, not the only reason.' Ione shook her head violently. 'I wanted you the moment I saw you. It's just that if it wasn't for the flowers, nothing would have happened and we wouldn't be ... in this mess, I guess.'

His lips twisted. 'That's as good a word as any to use to describe it, I guess.'

It was clear that he didn't believe her, and she couldn't leave him thinking that it had just been the flowers that caused the incredible time they'd had together. So she stepped closer, pressing her body to his and wrapping her arms around his waist. She heard his breath catch in his throat and wished she had better control of her power, so she could feel him properly.

'Let me make this clear, Stephen O'Malley. Were it not for the fact that my eight-year-old son is just metres away, I'd take you into my bedroom now and prove to you it wasn't just the flowers. You are one hell of a sexy man.'

'It's only Jack stopping you?'

'Always has been. Otherwise I would have jumped your bones the moment we met. Well, not quite the moment we met, because the Coiremir's office ain't the place for that, but the moment we were alone.'

He smiled and a spasm of lust raced through her. Lust that had nothing to do with any stupid power and everything to do with how much she'd enjoyed being with him and her desire to do it again. Even if it wasn't the right thing to do. With regret, she unwrapped her arms from him and stepped back. 'I think we'd be safer not to talk about that any more. With or without the flowers, I'm a single mother and I have Jack to think about.'

He nodded. 'I understand.'

Part of her wished he didn't. She wanted him to yell, to rant and rave about how unfair it was, to call her names for using him. If he got angry, he'd get over her faster.

He nodded his head. 'Thank you for explaining, I appreciate it. Take care.' Then he was gone.

Ione sat down on the lounge and wiped away a tear. It was the right thing to do. It was.

Stephen lay on the bed, his hands behind his head. He was mentally tracing patterns on the ceiling above him. It was the only thing he could think of to stop himself going completely barmy.

After Ione had explained the truth of what had happened the day before, he'd thrown himself into his exercises, perfecting his control. The power reacted to his every demand instantly and with precision, and he hadn't put a foot wrong.

But there was only so long even he could concentrate on practice. Normally, he'd go exercise or read, but he didn't have the enthusiasm for those things. It had taken all his discipline to just complete today's routine.

He turned his attention to seeing how many geometric patterns he could make from the dots on the ceiling. He was in the middle of creating a dodecagon when someone knocked on his door.

He breathed a sigh of relief and jumped up to answer, hoping whoever it was would stay for a while. He flung the door open and saw the caelleach of the bardria smiling at him.

'Good evening, Stephen.' Horatio Cormac nodded his head. 'If you're not too busy, I was hoping you'd join me for dinner.'

Stephen took a deep breath so he could answer calmly. 'I'd be delighted.' He stepped into the corridor and pulled the door shut behind him.

He expected to be led down to the bardria's refectory but instead found himself being hustled into the restaurant. He stopped in the doorway and looked around. It was quiet tonight but the few meals that were being eaten were obviously part of important meetings.

Stephen looked down at his jeans, jumper and runners then looked at Cormac. 'I don't think I'm quite dressed for such finery.'

Cormac leant close. 'The secret is to act like you are, even if you aren't.' He stood straight, pulled back his shoulders and marched in as if he owned the place.

Which, Stephen thought, he does — technically. Still, it was a good example to follow. So he pulled his own shoulders back, lifted his head high and followed Cormac to a table near the open fire, admiring as he did so the caelleach's unerring ability to negotiate the tables and chairs despite his blindness. As he sat down, Stephen looked at the dance-floor in the centre of the room, and the image of his parents' humiliation flashed into his mind. It still hurt, that they could have been treated that way.

Cormac signalled to the waiter, who came over. 'A nice bottle of Chardonnay will go down well, don't you think?'

Stephen swung his attention to the caelleach and then realised the meaning of his question. 'I don't drink much alcohol.'

'Probably very wise of you.' Cormac smiled up at the waiter. 'I'll have a glass of the house Chardonnay and Stephen will have ...?'

'Orange juice, thank you.'

The waiter nodded and walked away. Cormac turned his attention to Stephen and, for a moment, Stephen had the impression his soul was being weighed. Amazing the caelleach could do that when his eyes couldn't focus and he appeared to be blankly staring into space. Then the older man nodded. 'I've always wanted to tell you how impressed I have been by your dedication. I'll never forget the day you passed third order and immediately asked to be tested for fourth. And you passed without a whimper. I was terrified you were going to ask for fifth and sixth order that day, and we wouldn't be able to come up with anything suitably taxing.'

Stephen couldn't help but return the smile. It was comforting to know that someone as distinguished as the caelleach of the bardria experienced moments of discomfiture. 'Can I assume from that you've spent the past year coming up with a really difficult sixth-order test?'

'I'll admit we've given it more thought than usual.'

'I just hope you haven't made it impossible.'

'The Sabhamir assures me that it is sufficiently difficult to test you without being impossible for a sixth order to accomplish.'

Stephen nodded. 'That is all I ask, sir.'

The waiter returned with their drinks and took their orders. Stephen found himself drawn to the meal he'd had twelve years earlier — steak in pepper sauce — and, after a moment of indecision, ordered it. He looked down into his orange juice, trying to decide exactly how he felt. Fact was, he'd expected his first meal in the restaurant to be a moment of triumph. It wasn't that; nor was it awkward. In fact, sitting here and chatting with the caelleach felt quite comfortable.

'So, has Brian Mochrie been charged with what he did to Ione yet?' Stephen sipped on his drink.

'No, unfortunately.' The caelleach scowled. 'We won't get to charge him at all. Whoever was training him had something implanted in him and, a few moments before we were to start questioning him, he died. Bloody inconvenient.'

Damn. 'Did you mind-read to see who he was working with?'

'No. He died too soon after we took him into custody.' Cormac shook his head. 'There's so much we need to know, and so little that we actually can find out.' Then he looked over Stephen's shoulder. 'Is that your father coming over here?'

Stephen turned and noted his father's approach. Then he turned back to the caelleach. 'How did you know that?'

'Your father has a very distinctive walk.'

This didn't answer the question of how the caelleach was able to hear it in the noise of the restaurant. Stephen silently swore to never underestimate the oman.

'Caelleach.' Liam O'Malley stopped by the table and bowed his head to Cormac. Then he turned to Stephen. 'Stephen.'

'Father.' Stephen bowed his head respectfully while he tried to gauge his father's mood. Liam's back was stiff, his face drawn. It did not bode well.

'Liam, good to see you,' Cormac said. 'Won't you join us for dinner?'

'Thank you, but I cannot. My wife has food waiting for me.' He looked at Stephen. 'I was hoping to have a word with my son, if you don't mind.'

'Of course not. I need to go and speak to Eva Harris.' The caelleach stood and gracefully made his way across the room.

Liam took the vacated seat and Stephen forced himself to look up into his father's eyes. They glittered with the harshness of diamonds. 'Your mother has been worried sick about you. Didn't it occur to you to let us know that you were all right?'

Stephen felt the squeeze in his heart and realised his father was right — he should have known his parents would hear about the hotel and think he would be there. It would have been simple to reassure them he wasn't hurt. Shame they didn't have the type of relationship where he felt comfortable doing that.

'As you can see, I am fine.'

'So I'd heard. From someone else.'

Ah, so Aaron had gone running to dob on him. 'Get it over and done with.'

Liam frowned. 'I don't like how flippant you've become over this, Stephen.'

'I don't like that you won't believe me.'

Liam looked around. Stephen knew his father wanted

146

to scream his frustration, but was hampered by their public surrounds. He felt the same. 'I want to believe you,' his father growled. 'It's just so bloody unbelievable.'

'And it's too much for you to trust me, right?'

'If you're the victim in this, why do you keep hunting Aaron out to taunt him?'

'To remind him he hasn't paid for it.'

'He swears he didn't do it.'

Stephen leant back in his chair. 'Really? Is he prepared to have the Firimir vouch for that? Because I am.'

Liam blinked, and then surged forward. 'You would let the truthsayer read your mind to prove you're telling the truth?'

Stephen nodded. Having the Firimir touch your mind was something most gadda tried to avoid, not wanting the unassuming man to know their innermost secrets. 'I would. I have nothing to hide.'

Liam stood. 'I'll talk to him about it.' He walked away and for the first time in years, Stephen thought that maybe there was hope he and his father could reconcile.

The caelleach slid into his chair and smiled. 'So, I hope you're hungry. I've overheard the kitchen staff are quite excited to have Stephen O'Malley here and are preparing their finest.'

The rest of the night passed in talking about Stephen's life in America. The steak arrived and was as mouth-watering as memory had made it. As the night waned, people began to come over to give their regards to the caelleach. Stephen was amazed when a couple turned to him as well.

'Such a pleasure to meet you, O'Malley. You're a credit to the gadda. Not too surprising, however. O'Malleys always were good people.' The old woman who said this nodded her head as if she were speaking a universal truth.

'Thank you.' Stephen watched her sweep from the room with wide eyes. As the oldest living Hallaran, she was one of the matriarchs of gadda society. A smile crept over his mouth as he took another mouthful of food. It appeared he'd achieved that original aim — making the O'Malley name noteworthy.

There was just passing sixth order now, and then the beginning of the rest of his life.

FOURTEEN

Stephen was flicking through the *Sclossin News* and finishing his coffee when someone slammed down into the seat opposite him.

He ignored whoever it was. While it might have been polite to ask him beforehand, the refectory was the place for bardria employees and visitors to grab a quick meal, and was always busy. You grabbed a seat where you could.

'Stay away from my sister.'

Oh, great, Stephen thought. He lowered the paper and looked at Mark Hammond. The other man's eyes were red and ringed with dark shadows.

'I beg your pardon?'

'Look.' Hammond leant closer. 'You've got a right to be mad at me: what I did was wrong. Do what you feel you need to me, but leave Ione and Jack out of it. They've done nothing to you.'

Stephen stared at Mark. This matched Ione's description of her brother, and it made Stephen wonder if his part in the attack was an aberration, or if he'd since changed his ways, or if indeed it was all an act to try and ward off Stephen's revenge.

'I'm not interested in hurting innocents, Hammond. I only go after people who deserve it.'

Mark winced. 'So you'll leave Ione and Jack alone?'

'Whatever I have planned, I can assure you that your sister and nephew won't be hurt by it.'

Mark slumped in the chair. 'Thank you,' he said in a gravelly voice. 'I know that you mean that.'

'Good.' Stephen picked up the paper to resume reading, ignoring Mark's departure. The *Sclossin News* was always an entertaining read. It had been devised by humanists after some humans visiting the town commented on the lack of a local paper. The journalists went to extraordinary lengths to be accurate while keeping the truth of the gadda a secret. The gadda were referred to as the Church of Sclossin, and things such as order tests became ceremonies. The guardians were ministers of the church with special responsibilities and the bardria the priesthood.

It was to Stephen's mind quite pointless — any gadda could get this information through their power so the attention to detail was wasted. The journalists could have written complete fiction and the humans wouldn't have known. That might also make the paper more appealing to the gadda as a whole — it didn't sell well and burnt piles were often found around the town.

'Stephen.' He moved the paper and watched his father sit down. 'I've spoken to Aaron.'

'Let me guess.' Stephen folded the paper up. 'He won't undergo the mind-read. He says he shouldn't have to prove what he's saying is right, that he should be believed because he's a good man.'

Liam frowned. 'Do you understand how difficult this is for me? I want to believe you —'

'Then do it.' Stephen stood up. 'Or don't do it. This has been going on for so long that it doesn't matter to me any more. Excuse me.' He tucked the paper under his arm and transferred into his room.

He shook his head. He couldn't see why he should have to prove that he was right if Aaron didn't have to. Either his father believed Aaron or believed Stephen.

It was that simple. It was that hurtful.

After two days, Ione had to admit that she was fooling herself if she thought she could just forget about Stephen O'Malley. Only once before had she found herself this tied up with a man after sleeping with him just once, and she'd married that one.

So she did the only thing a girl could do in this dilemma — she grabbed a bottle of whiskey, dropped Jack at her parents' place and headed to the bardria building.

She marched through Maggie's office and banged on the door to the apartment. There was a pop and a red message ball appeared next to her head.

'Hi, I'm afraid I'm not available at the moment, but if you'll just sit and wait, I'll be with you as soon as possible.' Maggie's voice sounded very chipper.

'Hurry up, Mags,' Ione shouted at the door.

She heard a faint sound, like someone scrambling around, and then footsteps. The door swung open and Maggie frowned at her.

Ione looked over the dishevelled clothing, the wild hair and guessed why Maggie had been unavailable. 'Whoops, sorry. Continue, I'll just wait here until you're done.' She waved the bottle of whiskey at the lounge.

'Thanks.' Maggie closed the door and Ione grinned. She walked over and sat on the lounge, reefed the cork out of the bottle and took a generous swig. It burnt down her throat, settling in her stomach and immediately giving her a sense of calm.

She leant back on the chair and allowed her thoughts to wander; and knowing what Maggie was doing in her apartment meant those thoughts arrived quickly at their chosen destination.

She liked sex. She wasn't afraid to admit it. Her self-imposed famine while she had Jack often had her itching for some good loving. Perhaps that was why she'd always been so quick to find a playmate when he was gone.

She would prefer to have sex on tap, but then she'd always thought it wouldn't be a good idea to risk Jack's heart.

Who was she kidding? It was *her* heart she hadn't wanted to risk and, by picking up any old Joe, rooting his brains out and then getting rid of him, she'd managed to get her kicks and keep her heart safe.

Then Stephen had come along, and circumstances had meant she got to know him, to like him, to care for him before she got him to the bedroom.

She took another swig of whiskey. So now, the question — did she risk her world, Jack's world, for the chance of something better with Stephen? True, she'd been lonely, but she and Jack had been safe from real hurt. Safety was good. Safety was what being a mother was about.

But so was teaching your child, and didn't Jack need to be exposed to as many life experiences as possible while he was still within her protection and love? Would he be capable of having good relationships, being a husband and father, if he never saw that in his own home?

Was this actually the right thing to do for Jack?

Was it the right thing to do for her?

'Damn it, why can't this be easier?' she shouted at the ceiling.

There was a noise, and the door opened. 'This better be good, mood-killer,' Maggie said.

'Have a drink, stop your whining and tell me whether I should let myself fall in love or not.' Ione thrust the bottle into Maggie's hands as she pushed past into the apartment. 'Hi, Lucas. Sorry for the interruption, I won't be long and you can get back to business.'

She smiled as red rushed up his cheeks. He put his hand to his head and tried to push his hair back into place; an act ruined by the fact he had his T-shirt on inside out.

'I'll just be in my lab.' He turned and almost ran from the room, and Ione stifled her laughter as she turned to look at Maggie.

'Fall in love with who? Ooooh, you don't mean our yummy sixth-order wannabe, do you? Isn't he a bit young for you?'

Ione frowned. 'Just a couple of years, Mags. It's not like he's in school.'

'Cradle-snatcher.' Maggie drank from the bottle and grimaced. 'You know, I'm starting to suspect that part of being a guardian is that alcohol no longer affects you. Makes sense; you don't want a drunk Sabhamir.'

'Then stop wasting my bloody good whiskey.' Ione took possession of her bottle. 'Now, should I hook up with him or not?'

'Why not? If you like him and all.'

'Hello, single mother.' Ione stabbed her own chest with her finger, then grimaced. 'Ow.'

'If Jack meets him and likes him, that's not an issue, is it?'

Ione sighed. 'If Jack gets too attached, and then it doesn't work out, and Jack's heart is broken —'

'You mean if *you* get too attached, and then it doesn't work out, and *your* heart is broken.'

'Bitch.' Ione thumped down on the lounge. 'Seriously, Mags. I've been playing this around in my head for days now, and it's driving me mad.'

'OK. Serious it is.' Maggie sat down next to her. 'First, let me tell you from a bit of personal experience that a happy parent is way better than a miserable parent. Maybe if Mum had found someone else, she wouldn't have been so anti-Dad and I wouldn't have spent most of my life hating my own father. And if Jack does get attached, but it doesn't work out, well it's not going to be the end of the world. He'll go back to the life he had before, a life that's comfortable, so he'll be fine. So, put Jack out of the equation. It's down to you and Stephen. How do you feel about him?'

'I like him. I mean, really like him. He's amazing. Smart, and dedicated, and when he smiles, it's incredible. And as for the sex —'

'Uh-huh.' Maggie held her hand up. 'Do not talk about sex with me at the moment.'

'Then I'll just smile smugly and move on.' Ione did just that. 'On the other hand, he has been almost obsessive with his push to sixth order, and now that's almost over, maybe he'll be too unsettled for a relationship.'

'Or maybe a relationship is just what he needs to keep him grounded until he works out what to do with the rest of his life.'

'Assuming he *wants* a relationship.'

'OK, I'll tell you what I'm hearing. You're falling for him. You're already more than a little in love with him, but you're scared. Now, answer this question — if you don't try this, if you don't give Stephen a go, how do you think you'll feel in a year? Five years? Ten years?'

'I don't know.'

'That's right. You won't know. You'll always wonder. Is that what you want?' Maggie leant over and patted Ione's hand. 'Take it from me. Life's too short. You don't know what will happen or how. So take what you can, while you can. Be happy.'

And just like that, it all became clear. 'Thank you.' Ione pressed a kiss to Maggie's cheek. 'Do you know where Stephen is?'

'Hang on.' Maggie's expression went blank, then she nodded. 'The healers' wing.'

'No.' Ione bounded to her feet. 'How badly is he hurt?'

'Well, that reaction alone is your answer,' Maggie said, standing. 'He's not hurt, he's talking to Madge about some control issues. I've asked Madge to send him to my office and he should be there now.' She nodded to the door.

Ione spun around and realised just a few steps and a door stood between her and a life-altering moment. 'Right.'

'You know, I've generally found that walking and opening doors gets you into rooms a lot faster than just staring.'

Ione swung her arm out and felt it connect with Maggie's forearm with a satisfying thud. 'Shut up, Shaunessy.' She closed her eyes, took a deep breath in, released it and then stepped forward.

Stephen was standing in the middle of the room and swung around to face her as she came through the door. 'Ione.' His eyes moved over her and she felt heat pour through her body. 'Is everything all right?'

'Not yet, but it soon will be.' She walked forward, not stopping until she had wrapped her arms around his neck and pressed herself against his body. 'Now it's all right.' She smiled up at him.

He frowned even as he put his arms around her waist and held her tight. 'I thought ...'

'I know. So did I. Then I thought some more and realised all that thinking is stupid. This is right.'

'Jack?'

'If you think you can put up with him, I'm sure he'll adore you.'

He smiled, and her heart skipped a beat. 'Almost as much as I do his mother, I hope.'

That deserved a reward, and luckily a kiss was a good thing for them both. So Ione pushed aside her fears, and decided to focus on brilliant possibilities.

Ione put the flowers on the table, stepped back and tilted her head. Then she reached forward, turned the vase a little and stepped back again. Still not right. She moved the flowers closer to one end of the table. Then the other. Then she swapped them for the candles on top of the alcohol cabinet. Then she put the flowers back.

She wrung her hands, unsure what to do. What if Jack didn't like Stephen? After all, their first meeting hadn't gone that well. What if, after taking this step, it all died before it could really begin?

Well, at least the step would be taken, she told herself. And if she took this step, then maybe she could take others. Maybe if it didn't work with Stephen, there would be someone else who *would* fit into her little family.

Except she didn't want anyone else.

The request for admittance shocked her and she let out a little squeak. Then she pulled the lacy top she was wearing firmly down around her kilt-enclosed hips and touched the wall.

Stephen looked fantastic. He'd slicked his hair back

from his forehead, bringing the sharp angles of his face into relief. The woollen jumper clung to the muscles in his chest, and Ione wished she had the time and privacy to rip it from his body.

'Hey.' He smiled, and she saw nerves in the twist of his lips. 'How are you?'

'Nervous.'

'Me too.'

Ione took a quick glance down the hall, then planted a hasty kiss on Stephen's lips. 'I'm sure you'll make me feel better later.'

'I'll certainly try to.'

Ione was smiling as she called for Jack. He ran into the room and stopped, staring solemnly up at Stephen. When she'd told him Stephen was coming for dinner, she'd assured him that he didn't have to worry about anything. Obviously, he didn't quite believe her.

'Jack, this is Stephen. Stephen, Jack.'

'Hello.'

'Hi, Jack.'

They stood in awkward silence for a moment. Ione wasn't used to having to fill in for her son's conversational lapses. 'Jack, did you know Stephen's going for sixth order in a couple of days?'

That got him started. 'Sixth order? You're too young,' Jack said with the wisdom of children.

'That's what people tell me.'

'Let me feel.' Jack held out his hand. Stephen touched the back of his to the little boy's and Jack whistled. 'Wow, you feel as powerful as Maggie.'

'That's a good sign,' Stephen said.

'Are you really going for sixth order? Can you show me the Tranton? My friend John said it's impossible,

157

but I said that a sixth order can do it. Can you do it?' Jack's eyes narrowed and Ione realised he wasn't ready to believe.

'I'm not sixth order yet, Jack.' The little boy's face fell. 'However, I can show you part of the Tranton.'

'Cool.' Jack went over to the lounge and sat down, ready for the show.

Ione went into the kitchen, figuring she was safe to leave them in each other's company for a while. By the time she came out with a pot of soup for starters, Jack was standing on the lounge, mirroring Stephen's moves as tiny sparks of light danced between Stephen's hands.

'Make 'em blue, Stephen. Now black. Now green. Now all the colours.' He clapped his hands, laughing with delight.

'Dinner time,' Ione said. 'Jack, go wash your hands.'

'But Mam!'

'Now.'

Grumbling, he went down the hallway. Ione walked over and wrapped her arms around Stephen. 'Sounds like it's going well.'

'He's a great kid, Ione.'

'Of course he is. Look at his mother.' She started to kiss him but pulled back when she heard Jack dash out of the bathroom. She wasn't ready to be that demonstrative in front of her son yet.

The meal was as successful as Ione had dreamt. Jack didn't stop talking, questioning Stephen about power and his own development. For someone who'd had minimal contact with children, Stephen handled the little boy well, answering his questions calmly and without patronising him.

Afterward, they started to watch a Godzilla movie,

and Ione felt tears in her eyes when she saw Jack fall asleep on Stephen's lap.

She paused the movie. 'I'll take him to bed,' she whispered, leaning close to pick him up.

'I'll do it.' Stephen stood as though Jack's weight meant little to him. Ione led the way to Jack's bedroom, pulled the quilt back and watched Stephen lay Jack down gently. She covered her son up, kissed his forehead and then they crept outside, Ione turning off the light and closing the door.

'Is he going to stay asleep?' Stephen whispered.

'Probably.'

'Good.' Then he pulled her close and kissed her, and Ione pressed herself against him and gave herself up to the glory of his touch.

A band was playing – light, happy music – and people were dancing and there were laughter and smiles. Despite the fact he'd never really danced before, and could be a little uncoordinated, Stephen was whizzing Ione around the dance-floor like he was Fred Astaire.

At times their feet weren't touching the ground and the music and the happiness carried them instead. His heart was swelling until he thought it would burst through his chest and fill the entire room with contentment.

Then the band struck a discordant note, and the dancing stopped. He and Ione dropped to the ground as the room started to go dark.

The note turned into a deep yet melodious tone that sent shivers through his body. Blackness enveloped him so he couldn't see Ione. Then he couldn't feel her, and his entire body went cold.

Something touched his shoulder and, with a shout, he sat up and opened his eyes.

The Sabhamir was standing by the side of the bed, looking down at him. 'We need to talk,' the protector said, and then he turned and strode out of the room.

Stephen blinked a couple of times as the last vestiges of the dream wafted away. Then he felt Ione sit up and lean her head against his shoulder.

'What is it?'

Stephen kissed her forehead. 'The Sabhamir's here. He wants to talk to me.'

'What about?'

'I don't know. Nothing, I'm sure.' Stephen kissed her again. 'Go back to sleep.' He got out of bed and, in the dark, found his pants and pulled them on.

He heard Ione doing the same, and thought about telling her to stay in bed but decided he'd rather have her by his side. He took her hand and led her into the loungeroom.

The Sabhamir stood in the middle of the room, his arms crossed over his chest. Under the blazing lights, his normally well-groomed black hair was in some places plastered to his head, in others sticking out like an obelisk. There were dark rings around his eyes and his entire body hummed with tension.

With him was a smaller man in a navy blue robe. His face was round and smooth, his balding head rising above a mass of tight blond curls. He looked unassuming enough — except he was wearing the robe of the Firimir, the truthsayer of the gadda.

'What is it?' Ione spoke first. 'What do you want?'

'Ione.' The Sabhamir bowed his head. 'My apologies for interrupting your sleep. Stephen, I'm sorry, but we need to do a mind-read of the events around the bombing. Now.'

Stephen shivered, and he felt Ione step closer to him. A mind-read would allow the Firimir to go deeper into Stephen's memories than the earlier scrying had and see not just what he remembered, but every piece of information that had entered his brain, both visual and auditory. It was generally considered safe, but there was risk of damage to the mind. 'The test is tomorrow. Can't it wait?'

The Sabhamir shook his head. 'I'm sorry, but the situation with Brian Mochrie has inflamed the bardria. I've held them off as long as I can. We will take every care.'

'But there's no guarantee.' Stephen closed his eyes, and took a deep breath. Could he voluntarily do something that might destroy his chance of passing?

He felt a tug on his hand, and turned to look at Ione. She lifted herself up on her toes and kissed him. 'You don't need the test to be amazing,' she said. 'But you do need to do this in order to be able to live with yourself.'

She was right. He really couldn't say no to something that could help the gadda. He leant down and kissed her back, then looked at the Sabhamir. 'All right.'

The Sabhamir's clenched hands relaxed. 'Thank you, Stephen. If you could take a seat, we'll begin.' A flick of the wrist, and one of Ione's dining chairs shot across the room and stopped in front of the guardians.

Stephen sat down, his back to the gadma. He gave Ione a wink, hoping that the act might also convince him there was nothing to worry about. Then he closed his eyes and started through his meditation sequence until he was relaxed.

Even so, he jumped a little when he felt the Firimir's hands take hold of his head, one on each side. '*Calm,*' the

Firimir's voice said into his head. '*Don't fight me: open up, show me everything and there's little chance of danger.*'

Stephen went back in his memories to his arrival at the inn. Stephen was there again, walking from the bardria building, looking around the town and taking note of changes. Except he wasn't just seeing what he'd noted — other things were there now, people and items that he didn't remember seeing.

Every face, every stone in the street, every crack in the pavement, every brick in the building was examined and noted as he moved so slowly he seemed to be making his way through water.

The Firimir's doing this, he thought. He's looking at everything I saw, whether I consciously noted it or not.

'*Don't think, Stephen. Be quiet.*'

Stephen quietened his thoughts. Now was not the time to be interrupting the guardian. Instead, he watched the events play out before him slowly, carefully. Every step he took was examined, every face that passed anywhere within sight studied.

Even when he got into the room and was sitting at the table the memory passed slowly. When the explosion came, it wasn't a shock — the sound, the sensation built evenly so Stephen knew it was coming before it fully hit.

The dredging of Stephen's thoughts didn't finish until he was in the Coiremir's office. The Firimir let go of Stephen's head, and the sudden rush of thoughts and information from then until the present screamed through his mind with a force that was painful. He winced, and thought that maybe he'd let out a little moan.

'Do you have any painkillers, Ione?' He heard the Sabhamir's voice as if through a fog.

'What have you done to him?'

'He's got a headache, a common side effect of mind-reads. We can't use power to heal it; it's too soon to do anything to his mind. Painkillers?'

'If you've hurt him, I'll hurt you,' Stephen heard Ione say, then she left the room.

Stephen opened his eyes, but the light that poured in was like a dagger in his brain. He closed them again with a moan. 'Did you find what you needed?' he croaked. Star, he'd never known pain like this.

There was a pause before the Sabhamir spoke. 'We don't know yet. Once Ione gives you the painkillers, go back to sleep. You should be fine in the morning. I'll come over around ten to make sure there's no damage done before the test.' Stephen felt a shift in the air; the guardians were gone.

Fuck.

'Here.' He heard Ione come back in. She lifted his hand and put a couple of tablets onto his palm. 'I'll get you some water.'

'Thanks.'

He sat quietly, his eyes remaining closed, as he listened to her move around the kitchen. She soon returned, and put a glass of water into his other hand.

He took the tablets, and then held the glass out to her. She rushed away, and then came back, stood behind him and put her fingers on his temples.

'Does this help?' She started to massage in tiny circles on his skin.

'Yes.'

'Is it that bad?'

'Yes.'

'Did they at least get what they wanted?'

'I don't know.' He leant his head back against her chest and relaxed. That helped to soothe some of the pain.

'Next time I see him, I'll give him what for.'

Stephen smiled. 'He was just doing his job, Ione. They both were.'

She shifted, and he felt her lips press against his forehead. 'You are a good man, Stephen O'Malley.'

Stephen thought that if he was getting to be a good man, it was because of Ione.

'Come on, back to bed.' Ione tugged his hand. 'Sleep will help.'

He stood and followed her, something tugging at his memory, something he needed to consider. He was sitting on the bed when he realised.

'I can't stay,' he whispered. 'Jack.' They'd agreed he wasn't going to stay the night.

'I'm not letting you go back to that room by yourself when you feel like this,' Ione said. 'I'll deal with Jack; you rest.'

Stephen wasn't going to argue with her. He lay down, she turned off the light and the instant darkness relieved some of the pain. Ione curled up against his side and whether it was her presence or the pills, eventually the pain subsided and he fell asleep.

Stephen slept in until just after nine the next morning, late enough for Ione to take Jack to her mother's for the day and thus save them all an awkward morning encounter. He was tucking into bacon and eggs for breakfast when the Sabhamir appeared.

'Good morning.' He inclined his head at the guardian. The headache was gone, but the memory of the pain was one he'd live with for some time.

'How are you feeling?' Stephen fancied he might be hearing guilt in the guardian's voice.

'Better, thank you.'

'Your power?'

Stephen frowned. 'I haven't tested it yet.' He put his knife down, flexed his hand, then stretched out his fingers. He focussed on a tiny crumb of toast on the side of the plate. At his command, the crumb lifted in the air. He swung it back and forth across the plate a few times before he put it down. 'Seems fine.'

'Let me see.' The Sabhamir beckoned. Stephen stood and went over to the guardian. The Sabhamir put his hands on either side of Stephen's face and he tried not to shiver from the remembrance of the night before.

'I'll try to take your power, you try to hold onto it.'

Stephen nodded, reached inside and grasped his power. He felt the force of the Sabhamir surround him, penetrate him, grab hold of the power and try to reef it away. After tugging for a few seconds, the Sabhamir's power disappeared.

'Good.' The Sabhamir smiled, but his mouth twisted a little as a show of understanding. 'I'm glad you're all right. I'll tell the caelleach you'll be right to take the test at midday.'

Stephen folded his arms over his chest. 'You didn't tell me what you found.'

'We're not yet sure. I'll tell you when we are.' The Sabhamir was gone before Stephen was able to finalise his thought that the guardian was lying. They hadn't found a damn thing.

A door in the hallway flung open and Ione appeared. She was dressed in a purple paisley cardigan over a black and orange check dress.

'Where did he go?' She looked around. 'Don't tell me I missed him.'

'Sorry.' Stephen went over and kissed her. 'If it's any consolation, I don't think he's particularly happy with himself either.'

'No, it's not. But he can wait.' Then she smiled at him. 'Is everything all right? Is the test going ahead?'

'It is.'

'Yay!' She flung her arms around his neck and smooched kisses on his cheek. 'Just a few hours and you'll be sixth order and we'll have to celebrate.'

Stephen pulled her tight against him and felt an instant flare in his power. He couldn't get over how his desire for her was always there, ready to flood to the surface at the first opportunity.

He pushed it aside. Time enough for that later. Right now, he had to achieve his life's ambition, and pass the sixth-order test.

FIFTEEN

At midday, the bardria chime rang. Stephen took a deep breath and slowly let it out. Then he turned to Ione. 'Ready?'

She smiled. 'Absolutely.' She turned off the television and stood, then held out her hand. Stephen took it and pushed himself off the lounge. Then, with an arm wrapped around her, he transported them to the bardria building and they walked from the intran room to the chamber.

The entire bardria was present, along with all the bardria guard. The guardians stood to one side. The Ceamir grinned, and flashed a thumbs-up at Ione. The rest of the guardians stood with either their hands behind their backs or, in the case of the Sabhamir, crossed over his chest and without any smiles. Hannah Wilson was there, as were Stephen's parents. After greeting everyone and introducing Ione to his parents, Stephen stepped forward to face the bardria.

The caelleach stood. 'Are you Stephen Rove O'Malley?'

Stephen nodded his head. 'I am.'

'Why are you standing before the bardria of the gadda?'

'I come to take the sixth-order test.'

'Are you prepared to accept any and all consequences of this test?'

Stephen nodded. Death was not unheard of. 'I am.'

'Then, Stephen Rove O'Malley, this is your test. You are to take the twenty chrysalises you see before you and call the butterflies forth into maturity. You are to create a filigree, a patchwork and a French lace pattern with the butterflies. You are then to meld the twenty butterflies into one large butterfly and send it to the medical unit where Madge will paint a white stripe on one wing. You will then bring it back, break the butterfly back into twenty separate butterflies and then return each to its own chrysalis, ensuring all go back to whatever level of maturity they currently possess. Do you want me to repeat the task?'

'No.' It was very similar to a task used a hundred and twenty years ago and Stephen had practised it. He had no doubt he would be successful. He stepped up to the bardria table and, one by one, touched the chrysalises to ascertain their maturity. Then he closed his eyes, reached for his power and began.

Stephen opened his eyes and laid a finger on the first chrysalis. It shivered, then slowly split open and a mature butterfly, beautifully coloured in iridescent blue and purple, crawled onto the table. It shook its wings and then flew into the air, hovering over Stephen's head. One by one, he transformed the remaining chrysalises until twenty butterflies of unwavering beauty flew in circles around his head.

Then he sent his power out to the butterflies, entering their simple psyches and directing them. Slowly, they fluttered into the air and formed the first pattern, remaining in that shape for two minutes. Then he faultlessly moved them into the second pattern and after two minutes into the third. He also held that for two minutes, then he drew the butterflies down into a mob in front of him.

Now came the delicate part. He needed to meld the butterflies together without upsetting them or losing any one of the twenty individual psyches. He took time melding their minds together until they thought as one, reacted as one. Then he brought their bodies together and shaped them, adapted them, until in front of him flew one large butterfly, about the size of a dinner plate.

He could feel the touch of the twenty individual psyches and knew they were still healthy and happy. Then he focussed on the medical centre and sent the creature there. It shimmered in front of him and he had a moment of concern, then it disappeared.

He kept his breathing calm and even, his attention focussed on the butterflies' psyches. After two minutes, he pulled the large butterfly back. A large white stripe was painted down one wing. He turned the butterfly around, to ensure everyone in the room saw the stripe. Then he began to separate it, physically at first, then all the little psyches detached one by one. Finally, all twenty butterflies were separate entities. Then he put them back in their chrysalises, taking time between each to remember the next one's state of maturity and ensure it got there. When the last chrysalis closed over he sent his power drifting over them all, ensuring they had not been unduly stressed by the task. Then he opened his eyes and smiled at the caelleach. 'I am done,' he said.

The Sabhamir and the Heasimir moved forward to check the chrysalises, then nodded to the caelleach. A cheer rose up from the crowd behind him and Stephen relaxed. He had done it.

The caelleach stood, his hands clasped in front of him. That was when Stephen realised Cormac wasn't smiling. Stephen frowned. What was going on?

'Stephen Rove O'Malley, it is my duty to inform you that you did not satisfactorily complete all the elements of the task.'

Stephen's heart began to thud. 'What?'

Sadness entered the caelleach's expression. 'You were asked to do a filigree pattern and you did a fotenuit. I'm sorry, but you have failed the sixth-order test. You may take the test again in twelve months.'

Blood roared through Stephen, stopping any other piece of information from entering. He'd failed. After everything he'd done, he had failed.

He felt a touch on his arm and knew instinctively it was Ione's. Just as instinctively, he shied away and then transferred to his apartment in Austin.

He paced up and down the loungeroom. He'd failed. Because he'd used the wrong pattern. Fotenuit. That had been the pattern in the nineteenth-century test. He was such an idiot.

There was a bang on the door. 'Hello? You in there? I hear you. I am calling police.'

Shit. Mrs Lopez. He couldn't let her know he was here, couldn't let humans know what he was. He formed a picture in his mind of a desolate plain nearby, closed his eyes and transferred.

The bright Texas sun glared into his eyes and he flung his arm up over his face. He'd forgotten how intense the sunlight was here compared with Ireland. He turned and stumbled through the long, yellow grass to a misshapen tree that stood alone on the flat plain. Within its shadow, he took his hand from his eyes and looked around.

In the distance, yellow-hazed hills rose, cutting off any possible view of nearby towns. Far off, he saw the glint of an oil well. Otherwise, there was no sign of habitation. He was completely, utterly alone.

He slumped onto the ground. Good. He needed to be alone, to figure out what had gone wrong.

He looked down at his hands, resting on his knees. He'd failed. How could he have been so stupid? One tiny mistake and all his dreams were crushed. *Don't be stupid*, a small voice said inside him. *They aren't crushed, simply postponed.* He ignored the wise words because they did not suit the pain that was ripping through his heart.

A tingle rippled over his skin and he looked up to see the Sabhamir appear. The gadma looked around, his disdain for the surroundings obvious. Then he began marching toward Stephen.

Stephen scrambled to his feet, knowing he needed every advantage he could gain.

The Sabhamir stopped a metre away from him and nodded. 'Stephen.'

'Sabhamir.' Words threatened to tumble from his mouth but he stalled them. He wanted to know what the Sabhamir was thinking.

'Ione is very concerned about you. As are the caelleach and your parents.'

Ione. The word cut through him. He should have been sharing his triumph with her. He couldn't bear to share his defeat. 'I'm fine.'

'If you say so.' The Sabhamir's tone made it obvious that he didn't agree. 'I can understand that you need some time alone. After you've calmed down, contact me to come and fetch you.'

Stephen took a deep breath and then a bitter laugh exploded from him. 'Yes, that's right. It doesn't matter that I have the ability to transfer from country to country. I'm not sixth order so I'm not allowed to use it. Tell me, will I be censured for my disobedience? Banished, perhaps?'

The Sabhamir frowned. 'The bardria will no doubt make allowances for your emotional state.'

'How considerate of them.'

The Sabhamir shook his head. 'You have experienced great disappointment and must deal with that, but it does not give you permission to do as you will.'

'Fine. Just leave me alone.'

The Sabhamir nodded. 'As you wish.' Then he disappeared.

Stephen sat down. His head bent to rest on his knees. He became still and waited for the pain to pass.

SIXTEEN

'What do you mean he wants to be left alone?' Ione knew she was screaming. She also knew yelling at the Sabhamir wouldn't achieve anything, except probably damage to herself when he finally lost his temper. But from the moment she had realised Stephen was gone, she hadn't been able to control her emotions.

'Stephen needs some time to adjust to what has happened.' The Sabhamir spoke quietly and Ione saw the understanding in his gaze. That made her feel worse about yelling at him but still she didn't stop.

'Why can't he adjust to it with us? We want to help him, right?' She looked over her shoulder at Stephen's parents and his mentor, Hannah Wilson.

Elizabeth stepped forward and put a hand on Ione's shoulder. Considering Stephen had said he was unable to stay with his parents, she'd been surprised by how warm and friendly Liam and Elizabeth O'Malley were. 'Stephen is used to handling things on his own. Give him some space and after a while he'll realise he wants our comfort. Then he'll come to us.'

'What if he doesn't?' Ione twisted her hands together. 'What if he blames himself and tears himself apart over it? He needs to know that it's OK, that we still care.'

Maggie came over and put her hand on Ione's. 'I'm going to take you home,' she said. 'Our place. You'll be here in the bardria building, so you'll hear about Stephen sooner, and Lucas and I can look after you.'

Ione looked at her friend and nodded, unable to think. That Stephen would react so badly and abandon them — abandon her — had frozen her mind.

She was vaguely aware of Maggie transferring her to the apartment, of being guided to a chair and of a glass being put in her hand. She took a sip and the fiery liquid that rushed through her body shook her from the fog she was in. She looked first at Maggie, sitting next to her, then Lucas sitting across from her.

'How could he do that?' she whispered. 'How could he just leave?'

'Sometimes you're feeling so much you can't deal with anyone else,' Lucas said. 'I did much the same thing when Maggie told me about my father.'

Ione clung to this lifeline. 'But once things calm down, you come back to the ones you love, right?'

'Eventually.' Lucas looked at Maggie with a grimace, and Ione realised that he had planned to never see Maggie again.

'I'm sure Stephen's mother is right, and he just needs a bit of space.' Maggie patted Ione's hand. 'I bet he'll be back here in the morning, planning his next assault on the test.'

Ione stared at the drink and hoped that Maggie was right. Then she looked at her friend. 'Can you go get Jack for me? He's at Mam and Dad's.'

'Sure.' Maggie smiled and disappeared. Ione leant against the back of the lounge and took another sip of the alcohol. A hug from Jack was just what she needed right now.

Then Lucas bounded to his feet. 'Io, we have to go to the healers' wing.'

She almost spilt the drink as she lurched forward. 'Stephen?'

'No, Jack.' Lucas grabbed her hand and pulled her up. 'Maggie said there's something wrong with him and she's taken him straight there. Come on.'

Ione wanted to scream. Her brain wanted to explode at this news of danger to Jack following Stephen's failure so closely. She couldn't react at all, though, and so allowed Lucas to drag her at a burning pace through the halls of the bardria building.

When they got to the door of the room where Jack had been taken, Ione finally let out the scream. Her son was lying on the bed, and his stillness was terrifying. His skin was flushed and beads of sweat dotted his forehead. The Heasimir and Madge Florrie, head of the bardria healers, were bent over him. At the foot of his bed stood Maggie, the Sabhamir and the Garramir.

'Star above.' Ione rushed forward. Maggie stepped in front of her. 'Let me pass.'

'Io, you need to give them room to work,' Maggie took her arm and pulled her away.

'I don't understand. What is this? What's happening?'

'It's the lollies, Io. When he gave me the lollies, he managed to sneak a couple away and he ate them this morning.'

Ione began to shake so severely she was glad for Lucas's arms coming around her to hold her up. 'The texts?'

'We've put him under a stillness resolution, which will hopefully stop the worst of the poison.'

Poison. The texts. Death. Ione closed her eyes as the room spun around her.

When she regained control of herself, she was sitting in a chair in the corner. Lucas stood next to her, holding her hand. The Sabhamir was crouched in front of her, the Garramir standing behind him.

'Be at peace, Ione,' the Sabhamir said. 'The worst of the illness has already been dealt with.'

She looked into his dark eyes, heard his calm voice and some of her terror ebbed away. 'He's going to be OK?'

'The touch of texts has been neutralised,' the Garramir said. 'We're just taking away the symptoms now. He'll need to stay overnight, but he's not been anywhere near as affected as the others were. He'll be fine.'

Lucas squeezed her hand. 'There you are, Io. He's going to be fine.'

Where she had been full of fear, she was now overwhelmed with relief. With what had happened to Stephen, it was too much. Ione burst into tears.

Stephen was sitting beneath his tree, his legs curled up to his chest, when the Sabhamir appeared. He'd been here for hours and hadn't been able to push past the disappointment. He kept reliving the test, again and again, unable to believe he'd made such a simple error. He'd explored around the area and found a collection of small insects. Then he'd done the test himself, again and again, over and over, ensuring he created the right pattern, until he could do it with his eyes closed.

When the light had drained from the sky, he'd let the bugs go and had retreated to his position under the tree. The sky was almost completely dark when the outline of a man appeared in front of him. Stephen didn't need any more light to recognise the Sabhamir.

He got to his feet and bowed. 'I'm not ready to go back.'

'Have you eaten?'

Stephen's stomach growled. 'I'm not hungry.'

'As you say. Your parents are very worried about you.' Stephen snorted. 'You underestimate them, Stephen.'

'Is there anything else?'

'I thought you might be interested to know that Jack Gorton is in the healers' wing.'

'What?'

'A shame Ione doesn't have someone to support her during this time.'

The mention of Ione's name hit Stephen like a blow to the stomach. Should he go to her? Would she want him to, after his failure? 'Is she all right?'

'As well as can be expected, for a mother who thought she was going to lose her son.'

Her son. The most important person in the world to her. 'I hope he recovers soon.'

Stephen could feel a pulse in the Sabhamir's power, and knew the gadma was not happy. 'You want to stay?'

'I do.'

'Then I will leave you in peace.' With that, he was gone.

Stephen went back under his tree and sat against it. He leant his head back against the bark, giving it a quick blast of his power so it smoothed out.

Jack was sick. He barely knew the little boy, so why did that thought scare him so much? And thinking of how Ione would be feeling, watching Jack, hoping he wouldn't die ...

He wished he could go to her. He wished he could hold her and tell her everything would be OK. He couldn't. She was right — Jack had to be her first, her only priority. She didn't need to deal with an idiot failure as well.

He closed his eyes and wiped his mind of all thoughts, taking deep breaths to relax. However, there was one thought he couldn't get rid of and, as he fell asleep, it was with Ione's smile alight in his mind.

SEVENTEEN

The next day, Jack was sitting in the bed in the healers' wing and begging to be allowed home.

'I'm bored,' he said. 'There's nothing to do here.'

'The resilience of youth,' Madge said. 'All the adults are still unwell, days after they ate the sweets, and here's Jack ready to bounce home less than twenty-four hours later.'

'I wonder if it's because his power is not yet awakened,' the Heasimir said.

'Can I take him home?' Ione said. 'If he stays in bed and rests, and I promise to call you if anything changes?'

The two healers looked at each other. 'I'm not sure ...' Madge said.

'They can stay with us,' Lucas said. He and Maggie had taken the vigil with Ione through the night – although Maggie had been called away a couple of times.

'That sounds satisfactory,' the Heasimir said.

'Keep a close eye on him for the next few days, Ione,' Madge said.

The Heasimir transferred Ione and Jack to Maggie and Lucas's apartment, and stayed until Jack was settled into the spare bedroom. Once she was convinced of his comfort, she left and Ione finally had time alone with her son.

She sat down on the bed, reached forward and took the game from Jack's hands. 'We need to talk.'

'I'm sick, cough, cough.'

'Can it, you little scam artist. Why, when Maggie said those lollies made people sick, did you decide to keep some and eat them anyway?'

''Cause I'm just a kid and I don't know better?'

'Where the hell did you hear that?'

'Madge said so.'

'Well, it's crap, no disrespect to Madge. You knew it was the wrong thing to do.'

'Yes.'

'Are you ever going to try a trick like that again?'

'No, Mam.'

She reached forward and hugged him. 'You scared me, Jack. Scared me good.'

'Sorry, Mam.'

'Now, you're going to rest until lunch.'

'Can I have my computer games?'

'No, you can have a nap or you can just lie here and think about how stupid you were.'

'Wasn't almost dying punishment enough?'

'No.' Ione stood. 'Rest.'

She walked to the loungeroom and flopped down on the lounge, sighing. Moments later, Maggie appeared.

'So, how is he?'

'He'll be driving us all batty by mid-afternoon. He's going to be fine. Me, I'll never recover the ten years he just ripped from my life.'

Maggie squeezed her hands in front of her and Ione realised her friend was nervous. Then Maggie burst out, 'I'm so sorry. This is all my fault.'

'How do you figure that?'

'I know eight-year-olds. I should have realised Jack hadn't given me the whole stash.'

Ione held out her hand, Maggie sat down next to her and the two women hugged. 'So should I. I guess we'll have to both be more suspicious of the little bugger in future.'

Maggie nodded. 'Do you want me to go get some things for him?'

'Yes, thanks. Me too.' Ione grimaced. 'And thank you for putting the two of us up. I don't think I could –'

'Say no more. You know Lucas and I love having you here. Party time.' She grinned and disappeared.

Lucas pushed the door to the apartment open and sauntered in. 'So, how is he?'

'Fine. I'll just go check on him, if you can scare us up some coffee, maybe some breakfast. I don't know about you, but I'm suddenly starving.'

'Sounds like a plan.' Lucas went into the kitchen.

Jack was asleep, and Ione spent some time tucking him in and looking at him. So close, it had been so close.

When she went back out, Maggie and Lucas were sitting at the dining table. Lucas was pouring coffee while Maggie opened a container of baking she'd obviously snaffled from Ione's apartment.

'So,' Maggie said, breaking apart an Anzac biscuit and popping it into her mouth, 'I note that Stephen hasn't come racing back to support you.'

Ione thumped down onto a chair. 'Not sure I want to talk about that, Mags.'

'When he does come back, I hope you give him a hell of a time before you jump his bones.'

'If he comes back.' Sitting by Jack's bed overnight, Ione had had a lot of time to think, and with the thoughts had come a growing anger. She could understand Stephen's disappointment, but running away never solved anything. It spoke of an immaturity that had her doubting whether pursuing a relationship with him was a good idea.

'Less talk of bozos and more happy chat, please,' she said.

'Not sure I can provide that,' Maggie said. 'The fucking texts are really starting to give me the shits, and then I'm still dealing with fall-out from the bombing of the inn.'

'Lucas?'

'I could bore you solid with my latest test results.'

'You two really do have to go get a life.' Ione took a sip of coffee and sighed.

She had her little boy, and he was on his way back to full health. She had friends and family who loved and supported her. She had a job she found challenging and satisfying.

She didn't need anything else.

Stephen twisted his body so every part was within the meagre shade the tree offered. After a day and a half in the desert, his skin was red-raw from the sun and he had decided enough damage had been done. The pain kept his mind from his disappointment, almost as well as his hunger and thirst did.

As the sun slowly descended and the shadow of the tree lengthened, thoughts began to bloom in Stephen's mind. One pattern. One stupid pattern. He'd done everything asked of him, shown all the control and inventiveness demanded of a sixth-order oman, and one wrong pattern had robbed him. He was sixth order in all but name.

What had gone wrong? What had made him make such a fundamental error when he never made mistakes? What had gone so wrong?

His preparation had been — hampered. He saw that easily enough. And then he'd gone to stay with Ione, and he'd spent little time on practice, in between missing her or loving her. He'd given Ione his heart and soul, and in doing so, robbed himself of his sixth-order qualification.

He'd known she'd be trouble the moment he laid eyes on her. No, that had been nice. What had been the clear warning was realising she was Mark Hammond's sister.

He swore, wondering why it had taken him so long to realise. He'd convinced himself that Ione wasn't part of any plans that Hammond had to stop him, but he'd been wrong.

It couldn't just be coincidence that it was Ione that he'd stayed with. Or that she'd come back to him when he'd got away.

Shit, even Hammond's display in the refectory had probably been a performance, designed to weaken any suspicions he might have of Ione so he'd go back and the plot wouldn't be ruined.

She and her brother had set him up to fail.

Well, he had just learnt a valuable lesson. Luckily he had another chance. And this time, he wasn't going to fail.

First, he would go back to Sclossin and get the sunburn dealt with. Then he would go home to Austin and study and practise until he was finely honed, like Usain Bolt ready for the hundred-metre final at the Olympics. He would be sixth order.

Then he would make Ione Hammond Gorton and her brother pay for this further humiliation. He was smiling as he summoned the Sabhamir.

Within seconds, the gadma appeared. He frowned at Stephen. 'Do I need to take you to the healers?'

183

Stephen nodded. 'Thank you.'

The Sabhamir put his hand on Stephen's shoulder and they transferred.

They appeared in a small, white room with a hospital bed and screen. Moments later the door opened and Madge came in.

'Star save us, Stephen O'Malley, what foolishness is this?'

'Necessary.' He didn't want to explain his motives to anyone. He just wanted to be out of here.

The air swirled and the Heasimir appeared. She looked Stephen up and down and nodded. 'It appears painful, but I can deal with it.'

Stephen raised an eyebrow but said nothing. The Heasimir stepped forward, raised her hands and moved them gently over his burnt skin. He felt warmth spread through his body. Then she stepped back and nodded again. 'You need to avoid harsh sunlight for a time, but you will heal well.'

'Thank you, Heasimir.' He turned to the Sabhamir. 'And thank you, Sabhamir.'

'Where are you going now?' The Sabhamir folded his arms across his chest.

'Austin to continue my training. I've got twelve months to ensure I don't make another foolish error.'

The Sabhamir frowned. 'There isn't anyone in Sclossin you need to see?'

'No. I'd appreciate it if you could take me straight home.'

An aura of darkness fell over the Sabhamir and Stephen realised the other man was barely holding onto his fury. What did he have to be angry about?

'Very well.' The guardian put his hand on Stephen's

shoulder and then they were standing in Stephen's apartment. The Sabhamir released him and stepped backward.

'I didn't take you for a coward, O'Malley.'

Stephen frowned. 'I don't understand —'

'If you're going to dump a woman, have the guts to do it to her face.' Then he was gone.

Stephen snorted. It was easy for the Sabhamir to see Ione as the wounded party in all this. He didn't realise she and her brother were probably celebrating right now.

He went to the window and looked out. It was now mid-morning, plenty of time for him to draw up a schedule and decide how to attack the next year before lunch time.

He sat down at his dining table and brought paper and pen flying from the kitchen over to him. Then he started to make notes.

A ping sounded. He turned and swore at the sight of the lilac message ball. He went over and activated it.

'I'm fine, Mother.'

'Stephen.' Her voice shook. 'Are you sure? The Sabhamir said you'd been badly sunburnt.'

'The Heasimir dealt with it.'

'Oh.' There was a pause. 'Stephen, please come home. Your father and I —'

'Mam, don't insult my intelligence. I know he doesn't care a jot about me.'

'Stephen, that's not true.' Her voice started to break. 'Please, if the two of you could just talk, not fight, just listen to each other, I'm sure —'

He hated that this was hurting her so much, but there was nothing he could do. 'He doesn't believe me, Mam. Am I supposed to listen to him call me a liar and not react to that?'

'It's not that he thinks you're a liar, Stephen. He can't understand how this is happening. Please, come home.'

'Sorry, Mam. I love you.' He touched the ball and the message winkled out. He closed his eyes and breathed deeply to fight back the tears. He was so sick of the arguments, so tired of how his family had been torn apart.

But he couldn't just forget that his father hadn't trusted him. He didn't know what to do.

He turned back to the table, hoping that pouring himself into his studies would wipe the sadness from his mind.

Ione was sitting in an armchair in Maggie and Lucas's loungeroom, her laptop perched on her lap, deep in solving a programming error, when Maggie walked in from her office, followed by the Sabhamir.

Maggie looked as though she wanted to hit something, hard. The Sabhamir was calmer but still visibly angry.

'All right, what's up?' Ione closed her computer and put it on the table beside her.

'We've finally heard from dickwad,' Maggie said.

Ione rolled her eyes and looked at the Sabhamir. 'Would you like to tell me what Stephen had to say?'

'Not a lot, actually. I've taken him back to Austin and he's started working on his studies.'

Although it only confirmed what she'd already been thinking, Ione was surprised at how shattering the words were. 'Right. I see.'

'I'm sorry, Ione.'

Star, his sympathy made it harder. 'Thank you, Sabhamir.' She nodded at him, hoping he'd take the hint.

'Any time.' He disappeared and Ione breathed a sigh

of relief that at least one man in her life had some sort of decency.

'Right, here's what I'm thinking.' Maggie started marching up and down the loungeroom. 'I'm thinking we go over there and I hold him down while you kick him in the nuts.'

Despite the pain, a smile pulled at Ione's lips. 'Won't that get you into trouble?'

'The caelleach would be happy if something did. I'm sure he's just waiting to see what I do next, so I might as well meet his expectations.'

Kicking Stephen wasn't Ione's idea of a good time. In fact, she didn't particularly want to face him at all.

'I can't believe he's just slunk away like this and couldn't even bring himself to send you a message to say sorry.' Maggie's fists opened and closed. 'I think we should say he can't do the sixth-order exam again because he's a coward and we don't want his type.'

Ione leant back in the chair. Watching Maggie's rising fury was much more to her liking than giving into her own despair. 'Maybe you can do a retroactive stripping of the orders?'

'Cowardly little dickwad,' Maggie snarled. 'He's not a man; he's just a scared, pathetic little boy.'

Maggie's words matched her own growing thought that Stephen wasn't mature enough to have a real relationship. She however was; and that meant facing the tough parts as well.

She stood. 'Take me to Stephen.'

Maggie spun around, her eyes shining. 'We gonna get him?'

'I'm going to make him tell me why he's breaking things off.'

Maggie crinkled her nose. 'That sounds a bit tame.'

Ione smiled. 'I'll make sure it won't be. Tell Lucas he's on Jack duty and let's go.'

Maggie's face went blank and then she nodded. 'Stephen's given permission for me to come over. Come on.' She took Ione's hand and they transferred to Stephen's apartment.

He was standing near the dining table and he took a step backward when he saw her. 'Ione.' Then his eyes narrowed. 'So, you had to come and gloat, did you?'

Ione looked at Maggie and saw she didn't understand Stephen's words either. 'Gloat over what?'

'Over what you and Mark did to me. Clever. Very clever, I'll give you that, but you won't succeed. I will pass sixth order.'

Ione shook her head. 'Stephen, you're not making any sense.'

'You can cut the act,' Stephen said. 'I know you probably don't want the Ceamir to know what you're capable of, but I don't have any qualms.' He looked at Maggie. 'Your friend here, and her brother, set me up to fail the test.'

'What?'

Stephen nodded. 'I've got a bone to pick with Mark Hammond, and he's determined to get to me first and he convinced Ione to help him.'

Ione put all the disjointed information together. 'You think Mark asked me to seduce you and put you off the test because he's scared of what you'll do to him about the tattoo.'

'What tattoo?' Maggie looked from one to the other. 'What the hell are you talking about?'

Stephen snarled and Ione knew she was right. 'That's not true.' She rushed forward. Stephen started to back away and she stopped, not wanting to frighten him. 'Stephen, it's not true. I haven't spoken to Mark since the day he dropped Jack back. Everything that's happened has been because I wanted it to, not because of Mark.'

'Then why did you do it? Why did you distract me so I'd fail the test?'

In the face of his stubbornness, Ione's temper began to fracture. 'I didn't distract you so you'd fail the test. If I distracted you at all, it's because I couldn't keep my hands off you. Might I point out that in the week before the test you were in a bombing, then almost poisoned by the Forbidden Texts and then had your mind read by the Firimir, leaving you with a stonking great headache? Why not blame one of those events instead of me? Or better still, why not accept the responsibility for it yourself? You did the test, you made the mistake, and you failed it.'

By the end of her speech, her heart was pounding, her chest heaving and her body shivered with anger. Stephen looked at her with contempt, and it didn't bother her at all.

Damn, it was over.

'Get out,' Stephen said.

'With pleasure.' Ione turned, held her hand out to Maggie and then they were back in the loungeroom in Sclossin.

'Io, I'm so sorry.' Maggie wrapped her arms around her friend. 'He's a complete and utter dick.'

'He sure is.' Ione squeezed her tight and then let her go. 'And so not worth any more of my consideration. What do you say you and I drown my sorrows in the appropriate manner tonight? Lucas can look after Jack, right?'

'Sure he can,' Maggie said. 'Assuming I have the night off. It's been a while since we were at Kitty's. The night I slept with Sean, in fact.'

'Back to the scene of the crime, hey?'

'At least this time I know that when I go to bed with a man tonight, he'll make sure I come. Multiple times.'

Ione winced. 'I really don't want the details of yours and Lucas's sex life.'

'You sure? 'Cause it's good.'

Ione laughed and gave Maggie a hug. 'Love you, Shaunessy.'

'You too, Gorton.'

Stephen slammed down onto his chair, anger flushing out of him to be replaced by disbelief and despair.

He knew Ione was right. Her words had punched past the anger that had been supporting him and had lit the truth within.

Blaming her was the easy option, because she was there. Blaming the bombers — less easy, because star knew who they were. Blaming Brian Mochrie and those bloody flowers — impossible: Mochrie was dead.

Blaming himself? He shuddered. The fact was, he hadn't failed the test because he wasn't ready, or because he was stressed or traumatised or too focussed on Ione.

He'd failed the test because he'd been too confident. Just like he had been with second order.

It was his fault.

And because of his stupidity in trying to find any answer but the real one, he'd destroyed any chance he had with Ione.

What a complete and utter cock-up.

EIGHTEEN

Stephen was midway through his control exercises when the Sabhámir asked for admittance. With a sigh, he gave permission and by the time he walked into his loungeroom, the guardian was waiting for him.

'Stephen. I've just heard something interesting from the Ceamir.'

Star, Stephen thought. Were the guardians going to punish him for what he did to Ione? 'What was that?'

'Something about Mark Hammond and a tattoo and that you thought Ione had set you up to fail the test because of it. She wasn't entirely sure, but then I remembered the incident in the park.'

Damn. As the whole thing had taken place during the time of the last Sabhamir, Stephen had thought this one would know nothing of it. 'What about it?'

'Do you know who did that to you?'

Double, triple damn. He considered lying, but then thought about the consequences if he were caught. 'Yes.'

'How long have you known?'

'Since before I actually passed second order.'

'Why didn't you tell the Sabhamir?'

'Because I wanted to deal with it myself.' He hoped that might still be the case.

A small smile from the guardian and Stephen knew his plans for revenge were over. 'Who were they? Apart from Mark Hammond, of course.'

'Aaron Lansing and John Scally.' Stephen was surprised by the sense of relief. This was no longer his problem. The Sabhamir would take them before the bardria, they would be punished and whatever happened didn't affect him.

'Do they know that you know?'

'Yes. I went and saw them and told them I'd make them pay when I was ready. Every time I go back to Sclossin for a test, I track them down and remind them.'

The corner of the Sabhamir's mouth twitched. 'That's very cold-blooded of you.'

Stephen shrugged. 'There's a human saying — revenge is a dish best served cold.'

'I can understand your need for revenge. What they did to you was reprehensible.' Stephen nodded. 'However, their punishment is now the responsibility of the Sabhamir. You are not to approach any of them any more.'

'If they approach me?'

'You summon me, immediately.'

'Will you take them before the bardria?'

'I will.'

'I'll be ready to testify.'

The Sabhamir nodded and left. Stephen went back to his practice, a smile on his face. It felt good to no longer have to worry about it.

An hour later, he was again taken from his work, this time by a chime he hadn't heard in his apartment for a number of years.

He went into the loungeroom and stared at the beige message ball. Should he answer his father or not? He pictured the hurt on his mother's face if he didn't and sighed.

'Yes, Father?'

'Stephen.' There was a strange hesitancy in Liam's voice. 'How are you?'

It was the most civil opening to a conversation they'd had for some time. 'I'm fine. Feeling good, working hard.'

'Good. I'm glad.' They both fell silent but the ball stayed in the air, telling Stephen his father hadn't signed off yet.

'The Sabhamir was just here.'

Stephen frowned. 'Why?'

'To arrest Aaron.'

'Lansing was there?'

'He's in training for his third-order exam, and I've been working with him.'

Stephen nodded. Liam O'Malley was a well-regarded trainer for gadda going for the middle orders. He would have liked to have worked with his father himself, except for the breakdown in their relationship. 'Right.'

Another pause. 'Stephen, when the Sabhamir arrived Aaron was so surprised to see him that he pretty much confessed. I'm sorry.'

Stephen should be feeling an overwhelming rush of satisfaction right now, but all he could feel was sadness. 'So am I.'

'I wanted to believe you, son, I truly did. None of it made sense, either that you would do it or Aaron. But then you didn't deny threatening him, and you moved away and became so distant, and Aaron was so convincing ...' Liam's voice dropped away.

Stephen didn't know what to say. Part of him was delighted by the apology and wanted to just fall back into communion with his father. The other part was still hurting and wanted his father to hurt as well.

'Stephen?'

Stephen opened his mouth, as much to see what the response was himself as anything, but an unseen force hit him in the chest. He stumbled backward and fell onto his lounge.

Power. It surrounded him, held him still and then, to his horror, started to insinuate itself into him.

'Sabhamir!' he shouted. 'Fuck. Someone, anyone, help me.' He strained with every bit of power he had to hold the invading force at bay.

'Stephen? What's wrong?' His father's voice was a distant echo.

The air shifted, and the Heasimir appeared. She frowned at him, then put her hand on his shoulder.

'Stephen, what —' She stopped; her eyes widened and then started to shine with the sudden welling of tears. 'All will be well. Remain calm. The Firimir will explain what is happening.'

Within moments, the Firimir appeared and the Heasimir was gone.

The Firimir put his hand to Stephen's forehead.

'Don't fight it,' he murmured.

'Maybe I wouldn't if I knew what it was,' Stephen panted.

'Stephen, I'm sorry to have to tell you this, but the Coiremir is dead,' the Firimir said.

Stephen stared up at the guardian, aghast. 'Dead?' But he'd seen her, just a few days before at the test, and she'd looked fine ...

'I need to take you to the bardria building. Agreed?'

Stephen nodded. The gadma took his hand and next

thing Stephen knew they were in the Sabhamir's office. The Firimir gestured for Stephen to take a seat in front of the Sabhamir's desk, which he did gratefully. Behind the guardian, the Garramir and Ceamir appeared. The human–gadda liaison was crying, and her fellow guardian was comforting her.

The Firimir began to speak and Stephen turned his attention to the truthsayer. 'Stephen, you have been chosen to be the new Coiremir. That is the force you are feeling — the spirit of the teacher of the gadda, come to its new home. Don't fight it, let it in. You can still say no, and pass it on if you choose not to accept.'

'Me?' Stephen squeaked. The shock of the news was enough to weaken his resolve and the power flowed in, surrounding his own and then starting to meld with it.

He heard the Ceamir mutter something into the Garramir's chest, and didn't doubt it was along the lines that he wasn't good enough. He completely agreed.

'Are you sure?' he asked the Firimir.

'The spirit of the guardian knows the one best suited to take on the task,' the truthsayer of the gadda said. 'And I must say that I agree with the choice. You have a knowledge of the power, how it does and doesn't work, that few have. You have dedicated your life thus far to education and learning. I cannot think of anyone better suited to overseeing the development of power in others.'

'Fuck,' Stephen whispered.

The Sabhamir and Heasimir returned. Both their shoulders were hunched over. The Heasimir's face was bent down to the carpet, the curtain of white hair hiding her expression. The Sabhamir's eyes were gleaming with unshed tears, while his face was white and his jaw clenched.

'Well?' the Ceamir demanded.

The Sabhamir shook his head and she started to cry again. He walked over and put his hand on Stephen's shoulder. 'How are you?'

'OK, I think.'

The other man nodded. His entire body drooped under a dark shadow. 'Has Owen explained to you what is happening?'

'Just that the Coiremir is dead, and it seems I've been chosen as her replacement.'

The Sabhamir nodded. 'The guardians will support the choice. If you accept, we'll take the vote to the bardria, who should have no objections. We can have you sworn in tonight.'

Stephen's head began to swim. 'That soon?'

'We don't have time to waste. This is not the right moment for the gadda to be short a guardian. Understand, Stephen, this won't be a temporary appointment. If you accept the mantle, you will be Coiremir until you die, and unfortunately it seems that might not be as far in the future as you would wish.' The Sabhamir pushed his hand through his dark hair.

'I don't understand. I mean, I know there are inherent dangers to being a guardian, but that's not all, is it?'

'No. Stephen, the Forbidden Texts have been stolen.'

'What?'

'They were taken from the bardria building a few months ago, and we've been searching for them ever since.' The Sabhamir extended an arm to gesture to the rest of the guardians. 'The Coiremir has been killed by whoever has the Forbidden Texts. It would seem that somehow she stumbled upon this person, because Wilma would never have gone in to face him or her alone. Both the Heasimir and I have tried to follow the trail of the essence that the killer left behind, but the texts have made that too difficult.'

'Are there any clues about the person's identity there?' the Garramir asked. Stephen stared at them, trying to make sense of the conversation going on above his head.

The Sabhamir shook his head. 'It is a laboratory, but it's in a shed in the middle of a field, with no residence apparent. There's nothing in the laboratory except the equipment — not even the normal books or notes. It would seem it was used solely to work from the texts, and whoever killed the Coiremir took them when escaping.'

'Deeds,' the Firimir, Owen, said. 'There must be a record of who owns the land. That could be a clue.'

'And the fact Wilma went there alone also tells us a great deal,' the Heasimir said. 'You're right, Hampton, she wouldn't knowingly face this person without us. So it must be someone she didn't suspect, but someone she knew well enough to be in their laboratory with them.' As she spoke, she lifted a shaking hand to ensure her hair was still in place. Stephen was stunned to see the usually unflappable Heasimir upset.

The Firimir turned to Stephen. 'There is something we can try, if you don't mind. A newly released spirit carries with it the memories and feelings of the person it has left. If you let me do a mind-read, the spirit of the Coiremir might tell us who Wilma went to see.'

Stephen didn't hesitate. 'Absolutely.'

Owen smiled, then put his hands on both sides of Stephen's head. 'Relax,' he murmured.

Stephen felt fogginess slip over him, until he couldn't hear, see or feel anything. It was as though he were floating in a cloud, his only anchor Owen's hands. Then he began to feel things. At first he thought it was his own emotions, but then he realised there was a tinge to them that was different.

The fog disappeared and he was forced back into the real world as Owen released his head. The Firimir looked at him thoughtfully.

'No memories, no pictures, but there was a deep sense of betrayal.'

'Not disappointment or fear?' the Heasimir said.

Owen shook his head. 'No, it's betrayal. Bone-deep betrayal. Whoever the person was, Wilma took it as a personal affront that they were the one with the Forbidden Texts.'

'So a family member, perhaps,' the Sabhamir, Hampton, mused. 'Someone Wilma cared about.'

'I didn't know she was that close to her family,' the Garramir said.

Stephen thought back on the Coiremir, a person he'd known well, and it became clear to him. 'A teacher.' All the guardians looked at him. 'The Firimir —'

'Owen.'

'— Owen said that I'd been dedicated to education and learning, but that was nothing compared with the Coiremir. It was everything to her, and the most important people in her life, in the world in her eyes, were her teachers and trainers.'

'That would make sense.' Hampton began to pace up and down the room. 'Whoever learnt of the Forbidden Texts needed to be someone with both an interest in history and the skills to research it, which applies to most teachers.'

'And it would explain why Sean Flaherty had no

198

memory of who had the books when he touched them,' Owen said. 'Teachers would be below his concern.'

'So now we know that it's a woman, probably a teacher, who was in the bardria building on 31 January.' Hampton's pacing began to increase in speed.

'And someone who has had a recent relationship or connection with Brian Mochrie,' the Ceamir said. Stephen paled. He connected Ione's mention of the Forbidden Texts with the flowers.

'And someone who has visions of grandeur for the gadda.'

'Before we get carried away,' the Heasimir said, 'Stephen hasn't confirmed whether he will accept the position of Coiremir.'

Stephen looked at the faces around him, and realised he didn't have much choice. The power within him was already insinuating itself, filling him with strength and desire and an overwhelming sense of this being right. For that, and for the sake of the gadda, there was only one answer.

'I will.'

NINETEEN

Ione looked at herself in the mirror and smiled. Damn, but she looked hot tonight. The look was fairly conservative for her — a fitted black woollen dress over leopard-print tights and black wedges — but it showed off her slim figure and the bright paleness of her skin to perfection. Add some chunky gold jewellery and a slash of red lipstick and she was ready to put Stephen O'Malley behind her and rediscover the male population of Sclossin.

She looked over her shoulder at her sleeping son. He'd tried to tell her he was fine, but the fact he was asleep before his official bedtime revealed the truth of his health.

She went out into the loungeroom to make herself a cocktail to start the night and wait for Maggie. Lucas came out of his laboratory and whistled.

'Nice, Io. Very nice.'

She pouted. 'Nice enough to dump Maggie for?'

'Sorry, Io, ain't nothing in the world good enough to achieve that.'

'Well, your loss.' She took a sip of the margarita and sighed. 'So, how long before the object of your affections joins us?'

'Hang on.' Lucas's face went blank, a sign that he was speaking with Maggie mentally. 'Oh, fuck.'

'What is it?'

'Io, the Coiremir has died. Seems she stumbled on whoever has the Forbidden Texts.'

Ione gasped and lifted her free hand to her mouth. The tears came quickly. She'd got to know the Coiremir well during the years when she and her family had struggled to have her achieve first order. She hadn't been a particularly friendly or effusive character, but she had been patient and kind and absolutely dedicated in her efforts to help Ione.

With each passing week, the impact of the Forbidden Texts was getting more and more out of control.

'No,' she whispered.

'Shit, she was a good teacher,' Lucas said. 'The sacrifices she was willing to make to help me ...' His voice trailed off.

Now there was no one to help the special cases of the gadda. People like her and Lucas. And Stephen. He'd undoubtedly known her well too.

'Oh, now there's a development.'

'What's a development? What's she telling you?'

'Io, you won't believe who the next Coiremir is.'

Even though she asked, somehow she knew. Thinking of Stephen had brought him clearly to mind, and so she wasn't surprised when Lucas said his name.

So, no sixth order for Stephen O'Malley. Instead, he was to become a guardian of the gadda.

'That's not fair,' she muttered. 'He doesn't deserve it.'

'I'm not sure I'd call having a guardianship something that someone deserves. Except maybe the Heasimir.'

She couldn't continue the conversation any longer. The knowledge that the Coiremir was dead, the idea that Stephen would step into the role, was making her feel ill.

She went over and sat at the dining table, putting the margarita down. The idea of a night of fun had lost its appeal.

'Needless to say, Io, tonight's adventure is off.'

She looked up at Lucas and saw the tightness of his jaw that spoke of strong emotions being withheld. 'Spill, Valeroso.'

'It's just things like this remind me that Maggie's in a dangerous position, and that every time she leaves –' He clenched his hands, and then smiled at her wanly. 'You know, I think you're going to end up grateful that Stephen O'Malley dumped you like he did. The life of a partner of a guardian sucks.'

He walked from the room and Ione wanted to go and try to comfort him, but her mind was still processing the news.

He'll be here, she thought. In Sclossin. No going back to America. No choosing to live anywhere else for Stephen O'Malley. He'd be in the bardria building. She'd probably see him, hear of him, all the time.

How the hell was she supposed to live with that? She pulled the underside of her lip between her front teeth and softly gnawed on it while she tried to think of a solution. The sudden ring of her mobile phone shocked her and she bit down on the delicate skin. Yelping and cursing, she fished the phone out of the bag hanging on the back of one of the dining chairs and stabbed at the green button.

'What?'

'Don't answer the phone like that.' Her brother's irate voice came down the line.

'Fuck, what do you want?' Ione turned and headed to the kitchen to get some ice for her wounded mouth.

'I heard about Jack. Thanks for contacting me yourself, sis.'

Ione put a lump of ice into her mouth. 'Well, excuse me for having been a bit busy.'

'Are you eating?'

Ione spat the ice into her hand as she started to walk back to the loungeroom. 'No, you douche bag. I bit the inside of my mouth when you called and I'm sucking on some ice.' She slurped the ice back into her mouth.

'Oh, sorry.'

'So you should be.'

There was a pause. 'So, is Jack OK?'

'Fine.' Ione closed her eyes. 'Driving me mad.'

'I've got an idea. Why don't we go up to Paddy and Susie's place? I was talking to Susie last night and she said that Paddy was feeling much better and they hoped they could see Jack before school went back. And you know you love it at the farm.'

Love's a strong word, Ione thought. She'd loved going up there with Patrick, but that was because he was so enamoured with the place and she was seeing it through his eyes. She herself was more city-girl than country-lass.

Still, it was a very good idea, if only because it got her out of Sclossin so she didn't have to see Stephen for a while. 'Let's do it.'

'Great. I'll book the train tickets, and pick you and Jack up at about nine tomorrow morning.'

Ione hung up, feeling better now that she had a plan.

She picked up the phone again and lifted her hand to punch in her parents' number, but stopped when a deep, sonorous chime echoed through the apartment.

She spun around and watched a purple message ball appear in the middle of the room. She frowned, wondering why they'd be receiving an official message from the bardria. Lucas walked out, his face blank. He reached forward and touched the ball. It peeled back and disappeared, and the caelleach's voice rang out in a sombre tone.

'My fellow gadda, it is with great sadness that I must report the death of the Coiremir, the teacher of the gadda. Once known as Wilma Halliday, she was killed in an accident in her laboratory. We mourn her, and thank her for her selfless dedication to educating all gadda and helping us achieve everything we wanted to be. A new Coiremir has been chosen, and will be sworn in tonight. I'm sure you join with me in wishing him all the best in his new role.'

There was a repeat of the dark chime, signalling the message was over.

She and Lucas exchanged a brief glance before he went back into his laboratory.

Ione stared at the space where the ball had hung. They'd lied about the cause of death, and kept hidden the identity of the new Coiremir — something that hadn't happened when Maggie had taken over as Ceamir.

The bardria didn't want anyone knowing that the Forbidden Texts had claimed a guardian, but did want people to know there was a new one. She guessed that was because Stephen would need to begin his tasks straight away, and the bardria wanted to give people warning that the next time they saw a brown-robed figure, it wouldn't be the familiar middle-aged woman.

But why keep the role of the Forbidden Texts secret?

She closed her eyes. She couldn't think any more. Grief and anger were combining with the events of the last few days, and a wave of exhaustion washed over her.

She dragged her feet across the loungeroom, down the hall and into her bedroom. She flung herself onto her bed, lying on her stomach and burying her face in the pillow.

The Coiremir was dead. The effects of the Forbidden Texts were getting worse. Stephen was going to be living in Sclossin.

Life sucked.

Stephen paced up and down the loungeroom of the Coiremir. It was easy to walk a good route – the Coiremir's apartment was even more sparsely furnished than his place in Austin. This room had just one lounge and a coffee table in front of it. The only sign it had ever really been inhabited at all was the book on educational theory that sat on the table.

As in most gadda kitchens the cupboards and drawers were empty, but so too was the refrigerator. The last Coiremir either bought food as she needed it or ate out a lot, Stephen decided. In the bedroom was a double bed and a cupboard.

The laboratory was clearly the only place that the murdered Coiremir had spent any time, but even it was clean and orderly and held nothing but the most considered of texts and materials.

Only in the bathroom was there any sign of personality in the presence of a bottle of hair dye.

It wasn't the lack of furnishings that had Stephen pacing. His parents were on their way, being brought to him by the Sabhamir.

The door to the office which linked his apartment to the main building opened, and Liam and Elizabeth walked in. His mother took one look at him and burst into tears.

'No.' She rushed over and flung her arms around his waist, pressing her face to his chest. 'No.'

Stephen frowned at his father, who gave a shrug. 'Your mother is —'

'*We are*,' Elizabeth snapped out.

'We are concerned about this, Stephen. Being a guardian isn't an easy thing.'

'Why can't you be normal?' Elizabeth wailed. 'Why can't you just be normal, and have a wife, and have kids?'

Stephen wrapped his arms around his mother and pressed his lips to the top of her head. 'It wasn't my choice.'

'But you can say no.' Elizabeth pulled back to look up at him. 'You must be able to say no. You can't be forced to do this, can you? Can he?' She spun around to glare at the Sabhamir, who stood in the office doorway behind Liam.

'Stephen is free to choose,' the guardian said calmly.

'There.' His mother swung back to him, her face lit up with triumph. 'Tell them no. Tell them they have to find someone else. And come home with me.'

Stephen kissed his mother's forehead. 'There isn't anyone else,' he said softly. 'It's just me.'

Elizabeth began to sob again, and Liam came forward to take her into his arms. He looked at his son.

'Stephen.'

With what was happening to him, what he was about to face, the fight didn't seem important any more.

'It's OK. We're OK.'

Liam held his hand out. Stephen pressed his against it and felt his father shaking.

'I want to know you've considered this carefully, that you're not being railroaded or blinded by the glamour.

Tell me that you understand the risks, the responsibilities, and that you believe you're capable of it,' said Liam.

Stephen nodded. 'I do.'

Liam smiled. 'I always knew you were remarkable, but this time you've surprised even me.'

'So much for wanting to be sixth order, right?' Stephen said.

There was a twinkle in Liam's eye as he said, 'Well, at least you don't have to face the prospect of failing that test again.'

Stephen shook his head. Elizabeth moaned, 'How can you joke about this?' She reached out to grab Stephen's hand. 'Promise me you'll be careful. That you won't take any unnecessary risks. Promise me.'

'I promise.' Stephen squeezed her hand.

'And if anything happens to him, I'm blaming you.' She stabbed a finger in the direction of the Sabhamir.

'I would be disappointed if you didn't,' the protector replied. 'I'll leave you all to talk but not for too long. Stephen needs some time to get ready. There will be coffee for you in the refectory.'

The Sabhamir walked out, closing the door to the office behind him.

'I'd offer you some coffee or something myself, but there doesn't seem to be much in the way of food and drink here,' Stephen said.

Elizabeth took a deep breath in, then scowled at him. 'You need to sort things out with your father. I won't have you taking this risk when things are still bad between the two of you.'

'Don't worry, Mam. Dad's apologised. I've accepted. We've both made mistakes, but we'll trust each other more fully in the future.'

'Absolutely.' Liam nodded vigorously. 'I have to say, I'm glad you're going to be in Sclossin permanently, son. I'd like the chance for us to get to know each other again.'

Stephen thought that was good, although he wondered how long it would take to repair the damage that had been done.

'There.' Elizabeth clapped her hands while tears started down her cheeks. 'That's all I need to be happy, for my boys to be friends.'

It was worth putting his feelings aside, to see that happiness on his mother's face.

Her next words, however, gave the lie to her previous ones. 'That Ione is a nice girl.'

'Oh, Mam.'

'Well, she is. She was so worried when you left. I think she's quite taken with you.'

'Not any more she's not,' Stephen mumbled.

'Why? What did you do?'

'I was a complete idiot, Mam. Let's leave it at that.'

'Well, never underestimate the power of a good apology.'

His mother kissed him; his father shook his hand in the human manner, a peace offering. Then they left him to get ready.

Stephen sat down on the loungechair and stared at the carpet between his feet.

He had to admit, his mother's plea for him to have a normal life, with a wife and children, sounded appealing. Especially if the wife was Ione. But none of that was possible.

He had to make the best of the life he was living.

The Firimir's chime sounded, and Stephen signalled him to enter.

'I've come to talk you through the ceremony and make sure you're ready,' the truthsayer said. Then he frowned. 'What's upset you?'

Stephen stared at him. 'Don't tell me you can actually read minds.'

Owen grinned. 'No. But don't tell anyone, I like to keep them on their toes. What I do is read bodies. You're slouched over, your face is pale and you've knotted your hands so tightly your knuckles are white: classic signs of upset. Plus, Hampton told me about your mother's reaction.'

Stephen returned the smile. 'You should have kept that last bit secret. Leave me a little in awe of you.'

Owen shrugged. 'You'll find we guardians try not to keep secrets from each other. Except for Sarah. You'll also find our current Heasimir is the exception to almost every rule.'

'Can't see the Ceamir confiding in me any time soon, either. I'm not her favourite person.'

'She'll come round. Maggie's emotional, but then aren't we all? Now, the ceremony. Pretty standard to start with — I'll mind-speak the oath to you. Then while you're standing in the centre of the star, we'll start it up. Be warned: it's going to be at full power, and a lot of people find it very overwhelming. How did you go the first time you stood in a live star?'

Stephen thought back to his first-order graduation, when he officially became gadda and was marked with the invisible tattoo of the star of gulagh on his chest. 'It felt good. Awesome in the true sense of the word, and a little scary, but welcoming too.'

'Then you'll do fine. I like to warn people, because some don't like living stars. Although can I ask you not to

209

pretend that it *is* concerning you? Apparently Kenyon —
the Garramir — rattled and shook so much that some of
the councillors ran screaming from the room.'

'Best behaviour, I promise.'

'Good. Now, while you're in the star, something will
appear to you, a type of food or drink. You need to ingest
it. Then the star will flare once and, when it's gone, you'll
be the Coiremir. Any questions?' Stephen shook his head.
'Good. Then I suggest that you spend the next few hours
meditating and preparing yourself mentally. Your life is
about to change in ways you can't even begin to imagine.'
Owen nodded, and was gone.

Stephen forced himself to relax. There was no point
hankering after Ione. He had to get ready to become a
guardian.

He closed his eyes, reached for his power and began
to meditate.

TWENTY

As he walked into the bardria chamber, Stephen thought he'd never seen it look more beautiful. All the furniture had been removed and the room was lit only by the moonlight that shone through the glass ceiling. Beneath the silver streams, the star of gulagh inlaid in the floor shimmered like a jewel.

At five of the points of the star stood the other guardians. All looked at him calmly, even the Ceamir. It appeared that here at least she would be courteous.

He became aware of movement in the shadows that lined the walls and looked around. All the members of the bardria stood there, along with his parents. Elizabeth managed a weak smile, and Stephen felt much better.

With his head high, he walked forward until he stood at the sixth point of the star. The silence that descended was like a shroud over them. When Owen began to speak, his voice cracked through the air.

'Stephen O'Malley, step forward.'

Stephen took a deep breath, released it and walked to stand in front of the Firimir. Owen put his hands on either side of Stephen's face and the same dullness fell over him. Then he said aloud the words Owen spoke into his mind.

'I, Stephen O'Malley, accept the role and responsibility of Coiremir. I commit myself fully to the guardianship of the gadda, in particular to ensuring every gadda reaches his or her full potential and has every opportunity to grow and learn. My first priority will always be the safety and welfare of the gadda, and I will abandon all other pursuits in the face of any trouble or threat. I commit to serve the bardria of the gadda, and all dath, oman and gadma with diligence and pride. This is my oath and my vow and may my life be sacrificed should I break it.'

Every word seared onto his soul as he spoke; he really would die if he broke the vow.

Once it was done, the star flared to life. Hot and cold; windy and still; wet and dry; happy and sad: the power of the star was all things, all at once. Stephen closed his eyes and opened himself to it.

Then he felt a change. He opened his eyes and saw a piece of meat in front of him. It was raw, the flesh dotted with flecks of every colour imaginable, while a rich red liquid dripped from it.

He took hold of it and swallowed it whole, and it softly slid down his throat, sweet and sour. As he swallowed it, he was aware of images, smells and sounds. Each disappeared before he could fully recognise it, and yet he knew he was learning every one of them.

Then his throat constricted and choked off the air and the wonder of the star. He could feel blackness there: squeezing, filling, bulging.

With one hand he reached for his throat while mentally he tried to grab hold of his power — but the blackness had cut him off. His heart thudded, his chest tried to expand and pain flashed through his lungs as they burnt from lack of oxygen.

A black flash speared through the brightness of the star and appeared before him as a hand. Stephen reached up to try and hold it off, but it lunged at his throat and wrapped itself around his neck.

I'm dying.

Then the blockage was gone. He collapsed, gulping air into his heaving chest. The light of the star flared, and then went out.

He was the Coiremir, but he didn't care about that. All he could think about was that he'd almost died.

The Sabhamir knelt in front of him. 'Stephen, are you all right?'

Two hands rested on his shoulder. 'He's fine. The darkness is gone,' the Heasimir said.

'What was that?' Stephen croaked through a throat that felt as though it had been turned inside out.

'Don't talk, rest,' the Heasimir said.

'The spirit of the Coiremir must have been infected by the Forbidden Texts and reacted badly to the ingestion,' the Sabhamir said, pushing his hand through his hair. 'I should have realised it would happen. I'm sorry, Stephen.'

'Don't be ridiculous, Hampton,' the Garramir snorted. 'How are you supposed to know that?'

'It's the Forbidden Texts. I should expect anything.'

'What the hell is going on here?' The caelleach's voice broke into the conversation.

'I'll take Stephen to the healers' wing,' the Heasimir said. A blink of the eye, and he was slumped on the floor of a hospital room.

'To bed.' The Heasimir released him and stood. 'You're fine, but a bit of rest will do you the world of good.'

Stephen wasn't going to argue. He felt sore and tired, and was already wondering if he'd done the right thing.

Perhaps he should have listened to his mother. Then he moaned when he realised she would have seen that.

'Check that my mother's OK,' he croaked as he stumbled to his feet and over to the bed.

He'd never been happier to lie down than he was to sink his head onto that pillow. He closed his eyes, and was asleep before he had time to thank the Heasimir for her care.

When he woke the next morning, Stephen was very foggy. He sat up, his brain feeling like someone was squeezing and releasing it like clay. Gingerly, he swung his legs over the side of the bed and considered whether he was willing to try standing up.

'Ah, Coiremir.' Madge bustled into the room. 'How are you feeling?'

'Crap.' His voice scraped up his throat with razor blades.

'Not a surprise, not a surprise. The Heasimir will be here in a moment to see what she can do. In the meantime, do you feel up to visitors?'

'Is he awake?' Stephen heard his mother shout in the corridor, her voice squeaking.

'Better let her in,' he said, flopping back against the pillows.

Elizabeth stopped in the doorway and gasped, then rushed forward. 'Stephen, you're OK.'

'In a manner of speaking.' He managed a wan smile.

Liam followed behind her. 'And that manner of speaking is?'

'He'll be fine. He's just got a few symptoms from the texts, but we'll deal with those,' Madge said.

'The Forbidden Texts.' Elizabeth squeezed Stephen's hand. 'I can't believe that they've been stolen, that someone's using them. Did you know that before you took this role?'

'Yes.'

She thumped his arm. 'Stephen O'Malley, you chose to go after this danger?'

'Mam, please.'

'Well, you can't say no now, but I'm going to make sure that you stay safe. None of this staying in the bardria — you'll be living with your father and me, and you'll be home for breakfast and dinner every day, and —'

'I think the boy needs to rest, Elizabeth.' Liam put his arm around his wife. To his son, he said mentally, *'I'll calm her down. I understand that staying with us isn't an option.'*

'Thanks.'

'I will say one thing, though. This is going to be a dangerous life you live. You don't have time for regrets. I'd get working on that apology to Ione right away.' Liam smiled and guided Elizabeth out of the room.

The Heasimir came in and stood next to the bed. She put her hand on Stephen's forehead and nodded. 'The darkness of the texts is gone. I'll relieve your symptoms and you will be fit to resume duties.'

As she spoke, the thudding of his head decreased and his vision became clear. She removed her hand and Stephen stood up.

'Thank —' He frowned. 'My throat?'

The Heasimir put her hand on his neck and her brow creased. 'This is a damage I cannot fix with power, Stephen. You'll have to wait for it to heal naturally.'

'Anything I can do to aid that?'

'Madge will help you.' The Heasimir disappeared. Stephen looked at Madge and the old healer shook her head.

'She knows her gadda healing like no one I've ever known, but nothing beyond that,' Madge said. 'Come, I'll give you a soothing draught that you can make up with hot water. I'd keep the talking to a minimum as well, if I were you.'

Stephen wasn't sure that would be possible — he had a hell of a lot of explaining to do to Ione. He followed Madge and watched her make up the drink for him. When he took a swig, it was sweet and smooth and, even without talking, he could feel that his throat was better. He took another batch of the medicine for later, thanked her silently and then transferred to his apartment.

It was the cleanest, fastest transfer he'd ever experienced. He stared around the unfurnished flat, amazed at how quickly his power was developing.

He was walking from the room when the Sabhamir — he guessed he'd have to get used to calling him Hampton — signalled he wanted to come over. Stephen told him yes and turned as the other man appeared in the middle of the loungeroom.

'Stephen. Sarah told me you were up and about. I'd like to test your power before you start using it too much.'

'Of course.' Stephen took a deep breath and prepared himself.

There was quite a tussle before his power was finally wrenched from him. Hampton quickly put it back and patted Stephen on his shoulder. 'How do you feel?'

'Fine.'

'Good. We need to meet with you, to get you up to speed with what's been going on. The sooner we get you involved in the search, the better.'

'If I can have the time to do one thing first ...?' Hampton frowned. 'I want to apologise to Ione.'

'Ah.' Hampton nodded. 'We'll meet in an hour, then.' He disappeared.

Stephen looked down at the brown robe he was wearing and considered changing. Then he shook his head. The sooner Ione saw him like this, understood everything, the better. If he was going to have any chance with her, there could be nothing hidden.

TWENTY-ONE

'Jack, hurry up! Uncle Mark will be here soon.' As she shouted at her son, Ione spun around and took a mental note of the items in the loungeroom. Her suitcase, all packed — check. Her computer and power cord — check. Jack's suitcase, packed — check. Her handbag, with wallet and mobile phone — check.

'Mam, can I take *Rock Bard* this time?' Jack's voice spilt out of his bedroom. They'd come back to the apartment this morning to prepare for the trip to Paddy and Susie's. Jack was back to his usual hyperactive self.

'No.'

'Oh, but —'

'Do you want me to ban all your games?'

'No.'

'Then hurry up.' Ione picked up her handbag. She was starting to get excited about this. It had been ages since she'd left Sclossin, and it would be nice to go somewhere she'd be looked after.

The tone that sounded shocked her, and sent a frisson of excitement down her spine. Shit. Stephen.

He shouldn't be able to affect her like that.

She briefly considered ignoring his request, but decided that was pointless. As the Coiremir, he could just barge his way in.

She gave permission and stood back, steeling her heart against him. But she couldn't stop her eyes wandering over him the moment he appeared, drinking in his face, his body, his robe.

His rich brown robe. The robe of the Coiremir. The robe that suited him.

Damn.

'Hello, Ione.' He smiled.

She gritted her teeth against the warmth of that expression. 'Coiremir. What can I do for you?'

'Nothing. I've come to apologise.'

She frowned. His voice sounded scratchy; was he sick? She hated that she noticed, and that she cared. 'Fine. You've apologised. Goodbye.'

His mouth twisted. 'I deserve that. I know I've been stupid, and reckless, and selfish, and moronic, and ridiculous. But I want you to know that I regret it. I regret being such a loser, I regret the pain it's brought everyone, especially you, and most of all I regret that it lost me any chance of happiness with you.'

She hadn't known that she wanted to hear the words until he said them. They bloomed in her heart and she realised she'd been fooling herself. She wasn't over Stephen O'Malley.

'I'm going to spend the rest of my life regretting that.'

And he wasn't over her either. She didn't know what to do — laugh, cry, launch herself into his arms.

'Stephen.'

Jack ran into the room and threw himself at Stephen's legs, wrapping his arms around his thighs. Stephen smiled down at him and ruffled his hair.

'Hello, buddy.'

Jack looked up and frowned. 'You sound funny.'

'Sore throat.'

'Mam makes me a honey drink when I've got a sore throat.'

'You're a lucky boy.' Stephen quickly glanced at Ione, and her knees almost buckled from the warmth and tenderness she saw there.

'Why are you wearing that?' Jack drew his attention back.

'I'm the Coiremir now.'

'Really?' Jack's eyes lit up. 'Cool. Can you get me into training early?'

Stephen laughed, and Ione's heart clenched. 'Sorry, Jack. You're going to have to wait until you're thirteen, like everyone else.'

'Bum.'

Stephen looked at Ione, and there was enough desire in his gaze to set her on fire.

'I don't deserve it,' he said. 'I don't deserve you. But if there's any chance that you could forgive me, I promise I'll spend the rest of eternity making you happy.'

Then he stepped out of Jack's grasp, nodded and disappeared.

Shit, Ione thought as she stumbled over to a dining chair and sat down. He still wants me. I still want him.

What the hell do I do?

'Mam, Mam, isn't that cool? I know the Coiremir. When I go to training, the other kids will have to be scared of me, right?'

There was a knock on the door. Ione sat as if glued to the chair, and watched Jack fly over to open it.

The danger occurred to her moments after he let Mark in.

'Hey, Uncle Mark, guess what? Stephen's the Coiremir, isn't that cool? He's got a brown robe and everything.'

Mark narrowed his eyes as he looked at Ione. 'He was here?'

'I don't want to hear it, Mark.' Ione surged to her feet. The holiday was still a good idea; she needed time and space to think. 'Let's go.' She grabbed Jack's hand and began to drag him toward the door.

'But I haven't finished packing my games yet,' Jack wailed.

'Tough titties,' Ione replied. 'You had your chance, and you blew it.'

'So did O'Malley.'

Ione refused to respond to Mark's growl. She stormed out of the apartment, leaving her brother to collect her luggage, determined that somehow, by the end of this holiday, she would have her life back on track.

Stephen stood in his office and, slowly, a smile grew across his face. If he wasn't very much mistaken, his apology had blown Ione Hammond Gorton's disgust with him right out the window.

There was hope.

'*Stephen.*' Hampton's voice popped into his mind. '*Meeting now.*' A picture of an office — desk, chairs, bookcase, lounges — appeared.

His first official duty as Coiremir. Stephen sent his affirmation, and then transferred.

He was the last of the guardians to arrive. The Sabhamir was leaning against his desk; the rest were sitting on the two lounges that faced each other. The only available spot was next to the Ceamir.

Stephen nodded to her as he sat. She nodded back graciously. Still behaving, he thought to himself.

'Thank you for coming,' Hampton said. 'We need to work out exactly where we're up to in our search for the Forbidden Texts, fill Stephen in on anything he doesn't know, and work out the plan from here. But first things first — here within the guardian relationship, we use our first names. So you can call me Hampton. This is Owen, Kenyon, Sarah and Maggie.' The Firimir, Garramir and Heasimir nodded their heads as Hampton named them. The Ceamir — Maggie — didn't respond.

'Stephen, how about you recap what you do know, so we can fill in the gaps and get the whole picture.' Hampton leant against his desk and folded his arms across his chest.

'Good idea,' Stephen said. 'OK, from the beginning, I gather from what was said yesterday that you know when the texts went missing and that they were taken by a woman. How do you know that?'

'Good question.' Hampton flashed a quick glance at the Ceamir.

Maggie sighed. 'I know, my story.' Stephen turned to face her. 'The first person we found who had contact with the Forbidden Texts was Sean Flaherty. Sean exhibited a sudden increase in his powers a few months ago, being able to do things like transferring people and creating and sending high-level monsters — stuff that someone of his ability shouldn't be able to do. When it was realised what he was doing, he was confronted, but he swore that there was an innocent reason for the change.'

Kenyon snorted, and Maggie flicked a quick glare at him before returning to the story. 'Testing found a darkness in him that was only known in association with the Forbidden Texts. He remembered being here in the bardria chambers on 31 January, and picking up some books that an older woman dropped, but he didn't pay any attention to who it was, so we couldn't see the identity of the woman. And we left it too late to get permission for a proper mind-read — he was stripped of his powers as punishment. We're sure that was all the contact he had with the books. So, that's how we know.'

Stephen was quite sure from Kenyon's reaction that Maggie hadn't told him the full story, but it seemed to him that she'd told him enough.

'So that's all the clues you've had until — what, Brian Mochrie?'

'There've been some minor instances of the balance of power being disrupted in a few places without any explanation,' said Kenyon. 'I was able to rectify the balance easily, found some hints of the darkness of the texts. However, none of the areas gave up any clues about the identity of the person wielding the books or where they now are.'

Stephen looked at Kenyon. 'Where were those areas?'

'Near Galway Bay, down at Carrigaholt, Haresmead in Wexford and south of Dungloe in Donegal.'

'Dungloe.' Hampton stood straight and walked slowly down the middle of the room toward the door. Then he stopped and spun around. 'Isn't that where Wilma was killed?'

The colour flooded out of Kenyon's face. 'Yes. Damn, why didn't I search it?'

'Because it belongs to humans, and you aren't allowed to search human properties,' Owen cut in. 'You wouldn't have paid any attention to it.'

'Clever of our friend, to use human properties to hide what she's doing from us,' Maggie said.

'I should probably go back to the other locations and check out human properties that might be suitable for gadda needs,' Kenyon said.

'Not a bad idea,' Hampton said, striding back to his position against his desk. 'Anything else, Stephen?'

Here was the time for his big unanswered question. 'What did you get from the mind-read of me?'

'Clues we needed, but which haven't taken us as far as we wanted,' Hampton said. 'From what we saw, I worked out they'd used an extremely strong power punch. It could only have caused that damage if created by either a high-order gadma or a whole lot of people working together, and at a very close distance. I worked out they'd hidden in the front yard of a house across the road from the inn and I've collected essence, but the yard is planted with crab apples and so it's hard to refine the essences enough to identify how many and who they were.'

Stephen nodded. Crab apples had something of a natural resistance to power. As a result, they were a popular plant for the gardens of gadda, providing privacy and a modicum of security.

'We're pretty sure it's a group called the League of Purification. We've got no evidence, but it seems they may have been doing some pretty radical things in the name of the purist movement.'

'Why blow up the inn?' Stephen shook his head.

'Well, we know the purists hate the idea there is somewhere in Sclossin for humans to stay, even if it is well controlled. If you wanted to separate from humans, getting rid of the inn would be a good start,' Maggie said.

'Are they using the texts?'

'We don't think so,' Hampton said. 'We can't decide if it's coincidental or not that this group has risen at the same time the texts were stolen.'

'You can't decide,' Maggie said. 'I'm convinced it's not, and we just have to work out what the connection is.'

'The person who has the texts, perhaps,' Stephen said. 'Maybe they're just part of the plan, whatever it is.'

'Star, we don't want this to get more complicated,' Owen said.

'Did you get anything from Brian Mochrie before he died?'

Hampton shook his head. 'We'd barely started questioning him when he began to shake and dribble and then he fell down, dead. I've never seen anything like it. We do know that Brian was an extremely committed purist and never left Sclossin if he could help it, so it's not a bad assumption that the work he did with his teacher was done here.'

'And we're back to *teacher* again,' Stephen said. 'So what we've got now is an older female teacher, who was in the bardria building on 31 January, and may have links to one or more of the sites that Kenyon was talking about.'

'Which is where my idea comes in,' Hampton said. 'I would imagine that one of the first things a new Coiremir has to do is meet with the teachers and find out what's going on, how things are, what students are where and so on. Now, the smart thing would be to call one big meeting, but I think that we can come up with a good enough excuse to meet a few of them individually.'

Stephen quickly saw where he was going. 'The older, female teachers. I want to talk to them first, to get advice, being a young man not long out of school myself.'

'Exactly.' Hampton grinned. 'And if you get an excuse to touch each one of them, you'll be able to feel any darkness in them.'

'Exactly how many teachers are we talking about?'

'Can't be that many,' Hampton said.

Maggie snorted. 'Oh, please,' she said. 'For starters, there are easily twice as many women as men in the teaching ranks. And secondly, all we've got from Sean is an older woman. Knowing him, that could mean anyone from thirty upward. I'm afraid we're talking dozens of gadda.'

Stephen saw the horror on Hampton's face, and didn't doubt his expression was the same.

'Now, I suggest you start with those who are based in Sclossin, since they're the most likely to have been in contact with Brian Mochrie,' Maggie said.

'I'll get started on the search of the sites of imbalance,' Kenyon said and disappeared.

'I think I'll go have brunch,' Owen said, standing.

Stephen stared at him.

'Brunch?' Maggie gasped.

'Keep my ear to the ground, see what I can pick up. We said once that this is a person probably with delusions of grandeur. I'll see if I can work out which teachers are thought of that way.' And he sauntered out of the room.

'I'll go talk to the Mochrie family, see if there was anyone Brian talked about being with more often than usual.' The Sabhamir was gone.

Stephen looked at the other two guardians. The Heasimir nodded, and then disappeared.

'Talkative, isn't she?' Stephen looked at the Ceamir, only to find her glaring at him.

'I'll work with you, but don't expect me to be nice to you.' Then she too was gone.

Stephen sighed, then shook his head. He had a lot of work to do, and the sooner he started, the sooner he would be done. So he transferred to the office of the Coiremir, and started looking for contact details for the teachers and trainers to see who he should interview first.

TWENTY-TWO

Ione sat on the porch of Paddy and Susie's farmhouse, a whiskey in her hand, and looked back on one of the most exhausting and hellish days of her life.

The train trip had been torturous. Jack was so excited by the news about Stephen and going back to his grandparents that he swung from overenthusiastic chatter to bursting into tears over the slightest provocation. After two hours, he'd finally fallen asleep with his head on Ione's lap and she'd thought that maybe she'd finally get some peace and quiet to think.

But that was just the signal for Mark to begin.

'Are you still seeing him?'

Ione lifted her chin and regarded Mark in what she hoped was a regal manner. 'That is none of your business.'

'Shit, Ione. He's just using you.'

Ione was proud she maintained her composure. 'I am capable of making my own decisions, thank you.'

'So you'd put Jack at risk for sex?'

Ione gasped, the calm demeanour falling away. She leant toward Mark as much as Jack's head would allow. 'I would never put my son before sex,' she hissed. 'How dare you say I would?'

'He's bad news, Io.'

'I'd say, all things considered, *you're* the bad news. You're the one who defaced him and left him to be publicly humiliated.'

Mark blushed. 'I'm sorry I did it. I've turned my life around since then.'

Ione sat straight. 'Is that why you started the Mark Is The Arbiter Of All Rules campaign?'

'I learnt a lesson, Ione, and I'm determined not to make any more mistakes like that,' he said quietly.

'And why you and Maggie broke up.' He winced. 'So it was Stephen who scared you onto the path of all-consuming right.'

'I don't trust him, Io. Every time he's come to Sclossin, he's made a point of finding me and threatening me. It can't just be coincidence that he found you on the eve of him passing sixth order and having all the power to do what he wants to me.'

'Are you saying that he blew up the inn, then organised for Blair to be in Lucas's apartment when I got there and for her to ask if he could stay at my place?'

Mark lifted his chin and Ione was miffed that he could pull off regal. 'I don't care about the how, Ione. I'm interested in the why and in keeping you and Jack safe. Particularly Jack.'

'You're stark raving bonkers. You know that, don't you?'

Mark frowned. 'I will do what I have to in order to protect Patrick's son.' He had turned away and stared out the train window, leaving Ione to silently seethe.

'Beautiful night, isn't it?' Susie stepped out of the house. Ione smiled up at her mother-in-law. Every time she looked at Susie, her heart skipped a beat. Patrick had been the image of his mother.

'Right now, I can't imagine why I don't come up here more often,' Ione said.

Susie laughed as she sat down, nursing a whiskey just like Ione. 'Because you know this feeling only lasts a few days, and then you're hankering to get back to the city, and your family and friends. We know this isn't the life for you, Io.'

'And yet you supported your only child in marrying a citified girl.'

'Well, you made Patrick happy, and that's what mattered.' Susie patted her hand. 'Although we did have nefarious plans to convince you to love this place enough to come up here and take over when we couldn't run it any more.'

'Really? How nefarious?'

'We actually looked into getting satellite connections so you could work up here. Believe me, that salesman bugged us for months, so we suffered for our belief in you.'

Ione burst out laughing. 'I'm surprised Paddy didn't try to build one himself.'

'How do you know I didn't?' Paddy said as he came out, his favoured evening drink of warm milk in his scarred, tanned hand. His face was still pale and his shoulders bent more than usual, but otherwise he was recovered from his sudden illness. 'And I didn't just try, Miss Ione, I succeeded.'

'Until you realised what you'd actually built was a giant convex mirror that nearly burnt the shed down,' Susie added.

Ione laughed harder. 'I may not always miss the farm, but I do miss the two of you.'

'And we miss you.' Paddy sat down on the other side of Ione, stretched his legs out and sighed with satisfaction.

'So, I hear you have a new boyfriend.'

Ione spat out the mouthful she'd just taken over her knees. *Damn you, Mark.* 'Actually, no.'

Susie frowned. 'Mark said he saw him at the apartment when he dropped Jack off. Seems to think he's quite unsuitable.'

Ione wished it was her brother's neck she was squeezing, not the whiskey glass. 'Actually, he's very suitable. But we're not together.'

Susie leant forward. 'Is that why you're here? Are you escaping a broken heart?'

'More a confused one.' Susie and Paddy looked at each other then frowned at her. 'I thought it was broken, only just before we left to come here he came to apologise for this stupid thing he did and now I'm not sure any more.' Oh star, why was she having this conversation with Patrick's parents? 'It's nothing. Don't worry about it. Jack and I are just fine on our own.'

Susie put her hand on Ione's arm. 'Ione, sweetheart, it's OK. We both know that one day, you're going to fall in love with someone else. That's the way it should be. We just want it to be the right person, for your sake and Jack's.'

'Who is this young man?' Paddy said.

'It's the new Coiremir.' Mark walked onto the verandah. 'Once known as Stephen O'Malley; and he's not to be trusted.'

'Mark, you can't speak that way about a guardian,' Susie said.

'Guardianship doesn't change a person's personality,' Mark said as he sat down. 'I've had personal dealings with Stephen O'Malley, and I tell you he's overly emotional and holds grudges for a long, long time.'

'A grudge he deserves to hold,' Ione muttered. Susie looked at her but she kept quiet. It wasn't for her to tell the Gortons what Mark was really like. He'd become something of a replacement for Patrick and she wouldn't take that from them.

'Well, I can't see how his being the Coiremir makes him untrustworthy, and the vow would keep him from hurting anyone,' Susie said. 'On the other hand, he is a guardian. He's probably not in a position to have a relationship.'

'Why not?' Ione said. 'Maggie and Lucas are managing.'

'That's different,' Mark said. 'She's just the Ceamir, and he's not even really gadda.'

Ione almost choked on her outrage. 'What do you mean, just the Ceamir? And Lucas *is* gadda.'

'Come on, Ione, everyone knows the Ceamir is the least of all the guardians. I mean, dealing with humans — that's no big deal. It's not like she's the Sabhamir, or the Heasimir, or the Coiremir, responsible for the education of all the gadda. She's got time to do the happy, happy home thing, and he doesn't know what his life should be and so he'd just live with it. But you *do* realise, and O'Malley wouldn't have time for you. Or more to the point, if he did make time, he wouldn't be a good Coiremir.'

There was a part of Ione that knew Mark was making a good point. Both Maggie and Lucas had spoken about the sacrifices they had to make because of Maggie's role. But she sure as hell wasn't going to admit that her brother was right.

'You don't know Stephen if you think he'd be incapable of being both a good Coiremir and a good partner. He's remarkable.'

'You see?' Mark looked at Susie and Paddy. 'I told you.'

The Gortons exchanged a quick glance. 'Come on, Mark, let me walk you through my latest plans,' Paddy said, standing.

Mark glared at Ione but got up and followed the older man back into the house. Susie patted Ione's arm.

'I know he's wrong to say that about Maggie and her boyfriend, and I wish that girl every happiness,' Susie said. 'But he is right to say that being with a guardian is just too hard, Ione. There's a reason that all of them bar Maggie are single at the moment. And consider poor Aisling Rourke and how she went mad and then committed suicide after the Sabhamir was killed. Think of what that did to her son — becoming Sabhamir himself and then losing his mother. You don't want to put yourself or Jack in that position.'

'I guess not.' Ione chewed at the inside of her cheek wondering what the answer was. The sound of her phone ringing jarred. She reached into her pocket and looked at the display before answering.

'Bit late, isn't it, Shaunessy?' She looked at Susie and mouthed to her, 'Maggie.' Susie nodded and smiled. Both the Gortons loved Maggie for the support she'd given Ione.

'Where are you?' Maggie said.

'Up at the farm.'

'You didn't tell me you were going.'

'Didn't know I had to pass my every move by you, Mags.'

Maggie snorted. 'Don't be stupid. I just wanted to call in for cake and chatter.'

'You can come up to the farm, if you like.' As she said it, she looked at Susie, who nodded. 'Susie said that's fine.'

'I'll go get another drink and chair.' Susie went inside.

'On my way.' Maggie hung up and seconds later was walking out of the house, carrying a chair and rolling her eyes at Susie, who was following her with a whiskey.

'I know it could be worse, but all red all the time?' Maggie said as she put the chair down.

'All she does is complain about the colour thing,' Ione said.

'You'd complain too if you no longer had the opportunity to do one of your fabulous ensembles.' Maggie nodded at Ione's current clothing selection — a short flared red skirt over polka-dot leggings with an Ireland rugby jersey. 'So, what's with the sudden decision to come up here?'

Ione shrugged. 'Just wanted a break. You know.'

Susie shook her head. 'You can tell Maggie, Ione. Don't be worried about talking in front of me.' She looked at Maggie. 'She's confused over what to do about the Coiremir.'

'Surely not,' Maggie said with a frown. 'I thought that was all sorted and we'd agreed that he is a friggin' jerk.'

Ione sighed. 'Except today he apologised.'

'He did? Damn, why didn't you tell me? I've been treating him like persona non grata all day. So, does that mean it's back on?'

Ione looked at Susie, and her mother-in-law sighed. 'I can see that you're not going to talk openly with Maggie while I'm here. Just don't make any hasty decisions.' She kissed Ione's cheek and went inside.

'Right.' Maggie leant forward. 'What's the story, Gorton? Is he forgiven and are you back on or not?'

'Does it matter either way? It's not the only consideration. We were just talking about how hard it would be for Jack if it didn't work out.'

'I thought we'd already decided it wouldn't be such a problem for him,' Maggie said. 'He'd be losing a step-in parent, not his real one, so not such a big deal.'

'That was before Stephen was a guardian and so perhaps not such a good bargain for a kid.'

'So now the fact he's a guardian is a point against the relationship?' Maggie growled.

'I thought you were anti-Stephen.'

'I'm whatever you want me to be. You want me to be anti and I'll give him chills he'll never forget. You want me to be for him and he won't go into any situation alone. But his being a guardian can't be the reason for the decision.'

'Paddy and Susie, and indeed Mark, have a point. Being with a guardian isn't easy. You say it often enough.'

'You'll have to ask Lucas, not me.' Maggie slumped in her chair.

'And if I did? What would he say?'

'He'd say it's worth it.' She sighed. 'It is hard, Io, but you can make it work. Lucas and I do. Not always happily, but it's working. If we can do it, then you and Stephen can try.'

'And you really don't want to know Mark's answer to that.' Ione took another sip, trying to hide her smile as she waited for her friend's inevitable reaction.

Maggie's eyes narrowed. 'What don't I want to know?'

'Oh, that the Ceamir isn't a real guardian.' Ione grinned over her glass.

Maggie sputtered. 'Not a real guardian? Not a real guardian?' She reached out sideways, her hand wide. Then she clenched her fist, as if grabbing hold of something, and pulled her arm back to her side.

Ione gasped as Mark appeared. He stumbled and fell

to his knees in front of Maggie, her hand gripping the neck of his T-shirt.

'Not a real guardian, heh?' Maggie snarled.

Ione stared at her friend, her mouth gaping open. Maggie was wielding power in ways Ione had never witnessed before. Ione was struck by what Maggie now was. She was a guardian. She was powerful. She was dangerous.

'What?' Mark gasped up at the Ceamir, his face pale with shock.

'I hear you think I'm not a real guardian.' Maggie leant over and almost spat the words into his face.

Ione stepped forward, wondering if she should intervene, if she even could. Then a calm voice said, 'Something up?'

She looked over Maggie's shoulder to see the Sabhamir standing near the front door and breathed a sigh of relief. Paddy and Susie appeared behind him, gaping at the picture Maggie and Mark were presenting.

Maggie lifted her head. 'Nothing major. Just making sure that Mr Hammond here understands that I really am a guardian.'

'I dare say he has the message now.'

'Fuck, yes,' Mark stammered, staring up at Maggie. 'You're definitely a guardian.'

'Well, now that's settled, I'll pop back home,' the Sabhamir said. He winked at Ione, and then disappeared.

Maggie looked down at Mark and shook her head. 'If I ever hear that you're giving Ione a hard time for loving a guardian, I'm gonna come back here and bury your nose between your arse-cheeks. Comprende?'

Mark nodded viciously, then he disappeared. Maggie looked at Paddy and Susie, and the two of them went silently back inside. Maggie gave her head a shake, then lifted her whiskey to her mouth.

'There, I think that problem's solved,' she said.

Ione sank down onto the chair. 'Mags, do you know what you just did? And you summoned the Sabhamir? What was he going to do, hold Mark for you?'

Maggie winced. 'Sorry about that. The others are a little worried 'cause Stephen and I are inexperienced, so they've put a tag on us. If either one of us gets a bit antsy, one of the big guns will come immediately, just in case.'

Ione closed her eyes. The threat to Maggie, to Stephen, became suddenly clear. 'Fuck.'

Then she opened her eyes and lifted her glass toward Maggie. 'You are not to die. Or Stephen. I don't want either of you to die. Especially Stephen.'

'We're trying to avoid it, Io. Believe me, there've been enough close shaves already.'

'What do you mean?'

Maggie looked at her, as if making a decision. Then she leant forward. 'You need to know that he's fine.'

'Stephen?'

'Something happened during the ceremony. It seems that somehow the Forbidden Texts touched the spirit of the Coiremir and reacted badly to the star. It was close, but Ha — the Sabhamir got to Stephen in time.'

Ione could hear her heart thudding. Her whole body shook with the rhythm. 'Stephen almost died?'

'He got a bit of a shock, but he's fine.'

Slowly, as if the air was thick, Ione flopped against the back of the chair, her chest heaving. He'd almost died. Stephen had almost died.

Thoughts scattered and then reconfigured into one

bright, beaming message — she loved him. She didn't want to lose him.

Ione surged to her feet. 'Take me to him. Now.'

Maggie didn't argue. She stood, put her hand on Ione's shoulder and they transferred.

They were in a very plain, very boring office. Boring except for the sight of Stephen, walking around the desk toward them. Maggie gave her shoulder a squeeze and disappeared.

'Ione?'

Ione flew to him, threw her arms around his neck and burst into tears.

Despite the emotional turmoil, feeling Stephen's arms wrap around her and hold her tight against his body was wonderful.

'Ione, sweetheart, it's OK. Whatever it is, we can handle it.'

His attempt to make her feel better, not knowing what the problem was, was like candy to her soul. She pulled back and looked up at him. He smiled that heartbreakingly beautiful smile.

'You almost died,' she whispered. 'You almost died and I wouldn't have had the chance to tell you that I love you.'

He squeezed her tight. 'I'm all right.'

She sighed. 'You certainly feel it.'

He kissed her, and it was like finding a soft place to land and the most exciting ride at the same time. Ione moaned and lifted one hand to the back of his head to hold his lips to hers.

He picked her up and carried her over to his chair. Ione curled up on his lap and Stephen rested his cheek against the top of her head.

'I will never leave you again.' Stephen's voice rumbled through her. 'I swear.'

Ione looked up at him with a smile. 'You can't promise that.' She pressed a light kiss to his lips. 'I know full well that people leave, regardless of what you or they want. Just promise that should you need to walk away, you'll come face me first.'

'I will.'

She rested against his chest again. 'Good.'

'Can you stay?'

'No. I need to go back to the farm, get Jack, explain things. Then we need to pack up our apartment to come live here.'

'Ah, so you're assuming you're going to move in?'

Ione hit his chest. 'I know the danger the guardians are facing. We need to spend every moment we can together, because we don't know when it will end.'

Stephen squeezed her, silently agreeing. Ione closed her eyes and thanked the star for taking such good care of her.

TWENTY-THREE

Ione was barely awake when Mark stormed into her room. She sat up and rubbed her eyes. 'What?'

'Where were you last night?' He loomed over her. 'We got this message from Maggie, saying that you'd had to go back to help with some case, and then I see you return in the moonlight with him.'

Way to ruin one of the best nights of my life, Mark. 'So?'

'You were with him, weren't you? Couldn't keep away from him. You're an oversexed bitch.'

'Excuse me.' Susie's quiet voice drifted in from the doorway. 'I just wanted to point out that Jack's awake, and he can probably hear you, so perhaps you want to have this conversation elsewhere.'

Mark leant over. 'Every day, you prove more and more that you're unfit to be Jack's mother.' Then he turned and stormed out of the room.

'Hey!' Ione jumped out of the bed. 'Are you threatening me?'

'Ione, hush.' Susie came into the room. 'You'll upset Jack.'

'Did you hear him? He's gone mad.'

'I'll deal with Mark,' Susie said. She sat down on the bed and patted the cover. 'So, you've decided to try things out with the Coiremir, have you?'

Ione slumped down next to her. 'I love him, Susie.'

'Then I'm sure it will be fine. Ione, just promise me one thing. Regardless of what happens, Paddy and I will still see Jack.'

'Susie! Of course you will. You're his grandparents. Any time, anywhere, if you need him or he needs you, then you'll be there for each other. I couldn't break that even if I wanted to, and I don't.'

Susie smiled. 'I'm pleased to hear that. I must admit, there's a part of me that hoped you'd stay single, so that we'd never have to worry about losing touch with Jack.'

'It won't happen. Single, married, in a harem. I swear it.'

'Let's not do a harem, shall we?' Ione grinned and Susie laughed. 'Now, change of subject. Blair called in last night, after you left. She hoped you'd call over to see her today. Apparently she's been hearing a lot from Lucas Valeroso about computers and she wanted to discuss it with you.'

Ione did a quick mental calculation and decided she had time to do it before she went back to Sclossin the following day. She also decided not to tell the Gortons or Mark that she and Jack were returning just yet. The less explaining she had to do, the better.

'I'll go see her after lunch.'

Blair's home was one of those picturesque little cottages that always seemed to Ione to be right out of a fairy tale — climbing roses all over the walls, rambling garden and a chicken sitting on the roof.

Her old teacher was delighted to see her.

'Ione, I was so pleased when Susie told me yesterday you were here. A wonderful surprise.'

'Blair.' Ione reached forward and shook her teacher's hand. As she always did when she met Blair, she tried to feel the gadma's power; Ione felt bad about being Blair's failure. As always, she felt nothing. 'We only just came up yesterday. Sudden decision.'

'How unlike you to be spontaneous,' Blair said with a smile, and Ione grimaced.

'You know me too well. I think that means we've spent too much time together over the years.'

As Blair led her into the loungeroom, she said, 'So was there anything in particular behind your sudden decision?'

Ione decided not to tell anyone about her and Stephen yet. Not until they'd worked out the details. 'Yes and no. Is it just me, or can life be unfairly complicated sometimes?'

'It's not just you. What's complicating your life? Something to do with those computers of yours?'

'I wish. Computers can be frustrating and annoying, but generally there's an answer, even if it's a cheat. But people ...' Ione sighed.

'Ah. Romance.' Blair nodded. 'Life is certainly easier without it, although perhaps not as rich. I can see that taking chances, living life, makes you a better person than you would be if you didn't.'

Ione looked at her. 'That's very philosophical of you.'

'Something about being with you makes me philosophical.'

Ione laughed. 'That's generally not the effect I have on people.'

'Maybe you don't frustrate them the way you do me.'

Ione patted her arm. 'For your own sake, Blair, give it up.'

'Perhaps you're right, Ione. So, I've been thinking about those computers of yours, and that maybe I should get, what is it, conflicted with the interweb?'

Ione tried hard not to laugh. Blair was making an effort. 'Connected to the internet. I think it's always a good idea.' As she spoke, she bent down and pulled her laptop out of its bag. She opened the computer and turned it on. 'OK, first thing you need to know is that computers run on electricity. Have you got power hooked up here?'

Blair shook her head. 'Totally gadda here.'

'That's fine. I've got my battery charged up at the moment so I don't need to plug it in, but if you want to use a computer, you're going to have to get a human in to wire your house for electricity.'

'What is that?' Blair leant over her shoulder and stared at the picture on the screen.

Ione looked at her wallpaper and laughed. It was a still shot from the Fatharr movie that she and Stephen had watched together. 'That, Blair, is the mighty Fatharr. He's a daikaiju, a giant monster. Fictional and very cool. He likes to stomp around the place and destroy polluters and vandals, flatten them with just a step.'

'Fascinating.' Blair tipped her head to one side. 'Humans believe in these things?'

'No, but they enjoy being entertained by them. Movies, books, cartoons, that sort of thing. Now, the internet. In order to be on the internet, you need to have a modem. This is a mobile one.'

For the next half an hour, Ione took Blair through the practicalities of getting online, and showed her examples of the types of training websites and courses that were run.

Blair finally shook her head. 'I'm really not sure I'd be able to do this myself,' she said.

'I can give you lessons. Or if you like just come over and check stuff out on mine.' Ione shut the computer down.

'I would like that. Thank you, Ione. More coffee?' Blair stood.

'Yes, please. Where did you get that blend from? I love it.'

'Just made it up out of some leftovers,' Blair said as she walked into the kitchen. 'Can't remember what quantities of what, so I won't be able to make it again. Enjoy it while it lasts.'

'Certainly will.' Ione put her computer away in her case, and then leant back against the lounge.

Blair brought the coffee out and poured Ione a new cup before refreshing her own cup of tea. As she sat down, a chime rang in the air and a chill went down Ione's spine – Stephen's chime.

A brown message ball popped into the air, hovering above the coffee table. Blair stood and touched it.

'Good afternoon, Blair.' Even though the words weren't addressed to her, Ione felt warmth pool in her stomach and spread through her body at the sound of his voice. 'No doubt you've heard that I'm spending my first days as Coiremir speaking to some of our more experienced teachers, to gain some advice as to the directions required in educating the gadda. I'm hoping you'll be able to come and see me on Friday, say around two? Let me know if there are any problems.' The ball shimmered, then peeled back onto itself and disappeared.

'That's clever of him,' Blair said, sitting down and picking up her cup of tea. 'Get the teachers onside from day one. He's a canny operator, that Stephen O'Malley.'

Ione opened her mouth to agree, and then at the last moment recalled that most gadda weren't supposed to know that he was the Coiremir. 'I'm astounded. That really was him, wasn't it? He really is the Coiremir.'

Blair looked at her. 'You didn't know?' Ione shook her head. 'I'm surprised. I'd heard that you and Stephen were quite close.'

'We had a fight.'

'Ah.' Blair nodded. 'When you said that you came up here because of romantic problems, I wondered if it involved our new Coiremir.'

Ione shook her head. 'Can't hide anything from you, can I?' She leant forward. 'What do you think of the question of guardians having relationships?'

'Hmm.' Blair tapped her chin. 'I've been working quite closely with Lucas, you know, and, while he doesn't talk about it, I can see that there are good and bad days.'

'But there are in all relationships, don't you think?'

'True, but I'd imagine they'd be worse with a guardian, especially knowing you can never be first in their life. Not many people could handle that.'

'True.' Was she mad, to want to make things work with Stephen?

Blair patted her hand. 'He'd be awfully busy at the moment, Ione. However you feel, I'd give him time to settle in before you start broaching the possibility of a relationship with him. That is, assuming whatever you fought about can be rectified.'

Ione nodded, but she finished her coffee and left Blair's home with a heavy heart. She did have a point – Stephen was incredibly busy. Not just with being the new Coiremir but probably with helping to locate the Forbidden Texts.

Fretting, wondering, she wandered back to the farm.

***

Stephen's first interview was with Angela Roy. She was a wizened old woman who had been teaching before his parents were born. She was the oldest of the teachers in Sclossin, and Stephen had decided to start with her not because he suspected her but because he thought he might get valuable clues from her.

'Coiremir. Greetings.' She nodded, then held out her hands. Stephen walked over and pressed the back of his hands to hers in the traditional gadda greeting.

As their skin connected, he felt the swirl of her power, and quickly ascertained it contained none of the darkness he was looking for.

Stephen got none of the clues he was hoping for from Angela, nor from any of the other ten teachers he interviewed that day. As he closed the door on the last, he leant his head against the wood, breathing in the quiet and solitude.

He looked at his watch – 8.30. No wonder his stomach was growling: he hadn't eaten properly for more than twelve hours. And really, he told himself as he started to walk across the office toward his apartment, I should have known that I wouldn't be able to keep them all to half an hour. Some of them were retired, and lonely, and desperate for someone to listen to them.

At least they'd kept him from missing Ione too much.

His hand was reaching for the doorhandle when the Sabhamir's chime rang. Then he heard Hampton's voice in his head. '*Stephen, I need you now.*'

Stephen locked onto Hampton's voice, and transferred. He found himself standing in the middle of a field with the other guardians. In front of them was a large green mound that appeared to be a pile of leaves.

The mound shifted, and Stephen realised it was alive.

'What is that?'

'That, I think, is a leftover of the work of the Forbidden Texts,' Hampton said. 'Under there is the shed where Wilma was killed. We're just waiting on Kenyon to get the power under control, and then we need to kill it.'

Stephen looked over to his left. The Garramir stood at one corner of the mound, both his hands extended toward it. His brow was shining with sweat and his lips were trembling.

'This is the third such problem we've dealt with tonight,' Hampton continued. 'All in this area. This seems to me an indication that this is where our antagonist is operating.'

'Unless they want you to think that, so you won't look in the right place,' Maggie chimed in.

Hampton shook his head. 'Cop shows,' he said to Stephen.

'But it's a fair call, right, Stephen?'

He looked at Maggie and nodded. 'It's certainly the type of thing I'd think of doing.'

'There.' She almost glowed with triumph.

'Done.' Kenyon walked over, tremors in his hands and shoulders. 'That was the most powerful one yet, but I guess if this is where she was doing most of the work, it's to be expected.'

'OK,' Hampton said. 'Stephen, I need to borrow some power.'

Stephen nodded, and put his hand on Hampton's shoulder. He took hold of his power and started to feed it to the Sabhamir in a steady stream. At the same time, he felt for and began to pull the energy from the grass beneath his feet into him. He concentrated to ensure the energy coming in had time to meld with his power before he fed it through to Hampton. Maintaining a natural amount of power was all-important for balance.

Hampton raised his hand and a black stream of light shot out and slammed into the plant. It shuddered, and Stephen fancied he heard a scream, although there was silence. Tendrils roiled and vines lashed out toward them. The other guardians dealt with them, burning them into ash as they approached, while Hampton focussed his attack on the base of the plant.

There was a violent shuddering, and then the plant exploded, bits flying through the air. All the guardians ducked, their backs turned.

When Stephen looked again, the shed was clearly visible. The remnants of the plant lay all over the ground.

'Clean that up,' Hampton said as he strode over to the shed door. After a quick glance at his fellow guardians, Stephen followed the Sabhamir. This was the place the last Coiremir had been killed — maybe he would pick something up.

Inside was very dark, so Hampton lifted his hand above his head and a light ball appeared. It was dim, and just barely lit the corners of the shed.

'Don't want humans to see any more than they may already have,' he said as he stepped inside. 'Maggie's going to have a job to do round here over the next couple of days.'

Stephen followed him in. The shed was completely bare of anything that might label it gadda. There were no furnishings, no books, no jars of elements or tools for mixing potions. There wasn't even a star on the floor.

'Are you sure this is the place?' Stephen stopped in the middle of the room and looked around. There was shelving on the wall to his left, and two windows — one next to the door, the other on the far wall. Even the human owners hadn't been there for some time.

'Stay still and feel,' Hampton said. 'You'll know.'

Stephen closed his eyes, took hold of his power and centred himself. Then he tried to open his senses to what was around him.

It was cold in the shed — to be expected with the sun gone down. Except then he realised it was a little too cold for a summer night, and from there he could follow it down to a shimmer of something not right in the floorboards. Once he became aware of it, the shed reeked of false and dark emotions and of power out of place.

'She wasn't here for too long, because the imprint isn't strong enough, but she was definitely here,' Stephen said.

'And definitely cleared out, but still managed to leave that nasty little surprise to bloom,' Hampton said. He bent and touched the floorboards. 'It's only a little weaker than it was when I found Wilma. There's a staying power to the Forbidden Texts.'

Stephen heard a movement behind him and turned to see the Heasimir silhouetted in the doorway. The moonlight glistened in her white-blonde hair.

'We've dealt with the refuse, but you need to take care of the root.'

'Thank you.' Hampton walked out, and Stephen moved to the doorway to watch him crouch down next to a stump at the corner of the shed. The Sabhamir put his hand on the stump and shuddered, then he closed his eyes. There was a pause, during which Stephen questioned if anything was happening. Then the stump popped up, the roots retracting into it. It became a ball of blackness in the Sabhamir's pale hand.

Hampton stood and held the ball up in front of his hand. 'I'll take this back to my lab to study,' he said. 'Kenyon, call me if you find anything else.' Then he was gone.

Kenyon stretched and yawned. 'I'm going for a walk around, make sure the power is back in balance,' he said.

'I'll come with you,' Owen said, and the Garramir and Firimir walked together into the darkness.

Stephen felt the Heasimir disappear from beside him, leaving him and the Ceamir alone. He remembered what Hampton had said.

'Do you need a hand in dealing with the humans? I have some experience.'

Maggie shook her head. 'Thanks, but I can handle it myself. Besides, no doubt Io will be wanting another booty call tonight.' She winked.

Stephen blushed and waved, the sore throat an excuse not to respond verbally.

He transferred back to his apartment and sat down on the lounge. He was tired. He was beat from the long day and the battle with that dark plant. Nevertheless, if Ione wanted him, he'd be there. He wondered how long it would take for his obsession with her body to wear off.

He was still wondering when he fell asleep.

TWENTY-FOUR

Ione woke up and lay on the bed, staring at the dappled sunlight that sprayed over the floor through the lace curtains. She was exhausted. After she'd got back from Blair's the afternoon before, she'd come across Mark and Jack together. She hadn't liked the smirk on her brother's face, and had spent the rest of the day keeping Jack away from him so her little boy wouldn't be impacted by Mark's poison.

As she'd tucked Jack into bed, she'd decided not to tell him they were going back to Sclossin the next day, nor that they'd have a new home when they got there. She wanted him to sleep well, so he'd not be too disruptive on the train.

Once alone in her bed, she'd considered contacting Stephen and spending some time with him, but decided against it. The less she rubbed Paddy's and Susie's faces in her new relationship, the easier it would be for them to adapt to it and realise they had nothing to fear.

Now, in the still and quiet of the dawn, the doubts that Jack's happy voice had chased away came flooding back.

What if Jack didn't cope? He was an absolute deal-breaker: if he was unhappy she'd have to go through the heartbreak of leaving Stephen.

What if Stephen didn't cope? What if this current mess of happiness drizzled into a puddle of hatred?

What if she didn't cope? Actually, she could probably get some mileage out of people's sympathies for a while ...

She got up and dressed in jeans and jumper, slid her feet into her boots, put her mobile phone into her pocket and went outside.

The air was still and the sounds of the morning danced through her ears — animals and insects preparing for the hard work of living that came with the dawn.

She traipsed past the shed and across the field toward the stream that ran along the bottom of the Gortons' farm. There, under the trees and with the babbling brook whispering in her ear, she remembered the last time she'd been here.

It had been during her first visit to the farm after Jack's birth. Motherhood was proving to be more of a strain than she'd imagined, and Patrick had been quick to whisk her away from her crying three-month-old when they arrived here.

'Mam can look after Jack, and you need some Pat time,' he'd said, taking her hand and drawing her out of the house.

Here by the stream, she'd pressed her head against his shoulder and cried.

'Why can't I do this?' she'd wailed. 'I'm such a failure. I can't do first order, now I can't be a mother.'

'Baby, you're new at this. We both are. It makes sense that it will take us a while to get the hang of it. Personally, I think the fact we've not killed Jack yet is something to be proud of.' Patrick had rubbed her back and she could hear the smile in his voice.

'Yesterday, I almost did. I almost dropped him. What kind of mother almost drops her son?'

'A klutz?' Ione gasped. 'Io, baby, it's scary. Bloody scary. There's this little boy, and for the next while, you and I are all that stands between him and certain death. But you know what? It is you and me. Together. There's nothing we can't do together. You aren't alone.'

'Thank the star,' she'd sighed. 'I don't know what I'd do without you.'

'I know what you can do with me, and I don't think we should waste this precious time alone, do you, Mrs Gorton?' He'd bent his head to kiss her neck and Ione had agreed that it would be a shame to waste good baby-gone time.

Ione walked away from the spot with a soft smile. Thankfully, Patrick had waited until they'd got Jack past the certain-death zone and she'd perfected motherhood before he died and left her. And she'd been lucky to have Maggie there to step in and help her, so she wasn't alone.

Nor was she now, she realised. There was someone else — another adult — with whom she could discuss things and make decisions.

With a smile, she grabbed out her phone.

'Fuck, Io, do you know what time it is?'

'Morning, Mags.' Ione pushed her way under a willow. 'Can you let Stephen know I need to see him?'

'What am I, your bloody social secretary?'

'Please, Maggie. I'll love you forever!'

'Crap,' Maggie said and the phone went dead.

Ione stopped on a flat place by the creek and waited.

Seconds later Stephen appeared and Ione ran her eyes over him, amazed at how quickly her body could switch from calm to aroused. 'I didn't get to say this the other night, but that works on you.'

Stephen looked down at the robe and winced. 'I'd much rather be in civvies, but thought I'd better look the part at the beginning.'

'I'd much rather you were naked.'

His smile was wide and wicked and set fire to her. 'That can be arranged.'

We can sort out the problems later, Ione thought and she threw herself at him. Stephen caught her up in his arms and immediately they were kissing.

But just for a second. To her amazement, and disappointment, Stephen pulled away. He stepped back, his hands on her shoulders. He was frowning.

'What?'

'Ione, I want you to stay calm,' he said.

That just scared her all the more. 'Stephen!'

'What is it?' came another voice.

Ione screamed and spun around to face the Sabhamir. 'Touch her,' Stephen said.

'Would someone please –' Ione stopped as the Sabhamir lifted a hand and put his finger on her forehead.

He looked down at her. 'Ione, you need to come back to Sclossin with us.'

Before Ione had a chance to reply, the world wavered before her eyes. Within the space of a heartbeat, she went from standing on the bank of the river to standing in the middle of a laboratory.

Ione looked around, astounded. She'd never seen a lab like it. It was a mess of books, liquids, powders, glass jars, metal implements, swatches of material, two rows of specimens in some opaque liquid, and something bubbling and popping on top of a flame. Pieces of paper covered every remaining surface.

'What is this?'

'My lab.' She looked at the Sabhamir and he winced. 'Haven't had many chances to clean up lately.'

A bench pressed up against all four walls, and above it were shelves to the ceiling. Despite that, the room didn't feel crowded — it was at least as large as her loungeroom, perhaps even bigger.

It was, Ione decided, exactly what she would have imagined the laboratory of a Sabhamir to look like.

'Take a seat.' The Sabhamir gestured to the armchair that sat near the end of the room to her left. Ione flumped down onto it. Stephen grabbed a wooden chair, sat down next to her and took her hand.

'I'm sorry we had to bring you here so suddenly, and sorry for scaring you. But there's something we need to tell you, Ione,' Stephen said.

Her curiosity about the lab disappeared with his words. 'Then tell me.' She gripped his hand as hard as she could.

'There's something happening to your power. Somehow, the Forbidden Texts are working on you, and so far your power has almost doubled since the last time I touched you.'

She stared at him. She turned her head to look at the Sabhamir, who nodded, then looked back at Stephen. Then she realised her mouth was open and snapped it shut.

'What?' she finally whispered.

'I can feel that your power has increased,' Stephen said. 'And I can feel darkness.'

'Oh, star.' Ione pressed her free hand to her chest, glad to feel her heart beating as it should. 'The texts?' They nodded. 'Am I going to die?'

'No,' Stephen said.

'We need to investigate, Ione,' the Sabhamir said.

Ione looked from one to the other and saw that while the Sabhamir was being sensible about her chances, Stephen was reacting emotionally. He didn't want her to die.

That was nice.

'What do you think will happen? What is happening?'

The Sabhamir leant against the tabletop and folded his arms across his chest. 'The obvious answer would be that it's a reaction to what Mochrie did to you.'

'Except why is it suddenly starting now? Why didn't anyone feel it before this?' Stephen said. 'I didn't feel the slightest hint of it. I felt her power just a couple of days ago and it hadn't changed at all.'

'Did you now?' the Sabhamir said.

'Very intimately,' Ione said with a grin.

The Sabhamir's lips twisted. 'So, the apology worked then.'

Ione looked at Stephen and saw he was blushing. She kissed his cheek. That was also very nice.

'You're right,' the Sabhamir continued. 'Her power after the darkness from the flowers was neutralised felt as it always has. So logically, it can't be the poison in the flowers causing this.' He surged forward, standing straight again. 'Which means —'

'Ione's had contact with the Forbidden Texts since.' Stephen's expression grew dark.

'But how? How is that possible?' Ione said.

'When you don't know who has them, or who they've taught the contents to, it becomes very possible.' The Sabhamir's lips tightened. 'I need you to tell me every person you've had contact with since the poison in the flowers was neutralised.'

Ione felt her face screwing up as she struggled to bring to mind everyone she'd spoken to since that time. 'Well, there was you, Maggie, Jack, the Garramir. Then there's everyone who was here when Stephen was tested, and —'

'Damn.' The Sabhamir spun around and stormed to the far end of the room and back again. 'This is as bad as with Flaherty. Too many possibilities.'

'Maybe we don't have to go as far back,' Stephen said. 'I mean, I got a pretty good taste of Ione's power just two nights ago.' Ione looked at him and saw he was blushing again. 'There was no darkness in her power then. So I think it's safe to assume that this change has happened since.'

The Sabhamir shook his head. 'I don't like it. I don't like to assume anything about the texts.'

'Let's start here — we could find the answer in this small sample and if not, then we can move our focus out.'

The Sabhamir tapped his finger against his chin for a moment, then nodded. 'All right. Who have you seen since you last saw Stephen?'

'Well, Jack, Mark, Paddy, Susie and Blair Callaghan.'

The Sabhamir surged forward again. 'Blair Callaghan?'

Ione frowned. 'Yes. She has a property next to the Gortons', remember? I had afternoon tea with her yesterday. She's interested in computers.'

The Sabhamir spun round to face Stephen. 'She's a middle-aged female teacher.'

'Fuck,' Stephen said.

Ione hit his arm. 'What is it? You can't possibly think that Blair has the texts. She's a teacher, she'd never do anything like that.'

'Just considering all eventualities, Ione,' the Sabhamir said, once again all smooth calmness. 'Thank you for that; I'll investigate those ideas. In the meantime, we need to keep you safe in case this continues to develop. I think we need to put you under the stillness resolution.'

Ione remembered seeing Jack's small, perfectly still body and shivered.

'It's the safest option, Ione.' As the Sabhamir spoke, the Heasimir appeared.

'What are the other options?'

'Well,' the Sabhamir scratched his chin, 'if we put you in a safe place, and barred you from contact with any gadda, that might be OK.'

'Then do that. But I'm not going to be stuck on a bed, unable to move.'

The Sabhamir's mouth twisted, and Ione felt momentary sympathy. This must be a wretched time for him. But then it was gone.

'She can stay with me,' Stephen said. The Sabhamir frowned. 'You know that no one enters the apartment of a guardian without permission. I can put locks on it to stop Ione leaving. And if somehow her power is developing, then she's going to need help in controlling it, and that's my job.'

The Sabhamir frowned again. 'She needs to avoid getting overemotional, to keep the power safe.'

Ione saw the brilliant chance of spending time with Stephen slipping away. 'I won't get overemotional. I promise.'

'Right.'

'I swear. Stephen and I will behave, won't we?' She appealed to him.

'I will.'

She poked her tongue out at him, then looked at the Sabhamir. 'Please? I'm sure I'll be safe with Stephen. I don't feel like I can be anywhere else.'

With a shake of his head, the Sabhamir said, 'All right. But I'm locking her powers, and the moment she gets out of control —'

'I'll hold her in place so you can still her.' Stephen looked at Ione. 'Deal?'

'Deal.' Win, Ione thought as she stood and allowed the Sabhamir to put a lock on her power, which bothered her not at all — she hadn't really felt her power before anyway. The apartment would be prison, of a sort, but a prison with Stephen as the gaoler had definite possibilities. Even if they did have to behave.

She almost changed her mind when she saw the apartment. She stared aghast at the minimalist furnishings.

'How can you live here?' She spun around. 'There's no comfort, no personality, no — furniture.'

'Kinda low on my list of priorities at the moment,' he said and Ione put her hand to her mouth.

'Star, of course it is.' She rushed over and put her hands on his chest. 'I wasn't judging you.'

'I should hope not.'

The heat of his chest radiated into her palms, and she pressed them a little more firmly into him, remembering the hard ridges of his muscles. She looked up, wondering if she could recommence what they had begun by the river. But Stephen shook his head, and then pressed a kiss to her forehead.

'I'm sorry, Ione, but we promised to behave, so those thoughts are going to have to wait.'

'Well, if you can promise me that we'll definitely revisit them, then I guess I can wait.' She was sure all her desire was shining from her eyes.

He groaned and closed his. 'Stop it, Io.'

Being with him, being able to touch him, was the

most enticing drug she'd ever known. But there was just one more thing before she would be completely satisfied.

'We are going to make this work, aren't we? You and me, I mean.'

He smiled and pulled her close to him. 'We are.' Then he kissed her and, even though her power couldn't react, it well and truly ranked in one of the top five kisses of her life.

Then he released her. 'I hate to leave you, but I have work to do.'

And so this early she was getting a lesson on living with a guardian. 'I know. I understand. Just as long as you make it up to me later.' She fluttered her eyelashes at him.

'Shit,' he muttered and then he was gone, obviously removing himself from temptation.

Ione looked around and grimaced. OK, so apparently she was in danger from the Forbidden Texts, again, and as a result was imprisoned and unable to see her family or friends. Ione flopped down on the lounge and wondered when it would end.

She quickly pulled herself back together. First things first. She pulled her mobile out of her pocket and dialled.

'Hello, Susie speaking.'

'Susie, it's Ione.'

'Ione? Where are you? Aren't you in bed?'

'No. Susie, something's happened. I've come back to Sclossin. The thing that happened to Paddy and the others? Well, it seems to have happened to me.'

Susie gasped. 'Ione, no. How is that possible? Are you all right?'

'I feel fine, but something strange is happening to my power. Until it can be worked out, I'm staying in the

Coiremir's apartment. I'm sorry to ask this, but can you please look after Jack for me until we've got this sorted?'

'Of course.'

'I'm so, so sorry about this, Susie. I know it's an imposition.'

'No imposition, Ione. Keep us in touch with how things are going.'

At least one thing was working out, Ione thought as she hung up.

Stephen appeared in the Sabhamir's office to find all the other guardians there.

'You can't think that of Blair!' Maggie was saying. Stephen sat down next to her. 'She just wouldn't do it. She's a good woman, a dedicated teacher.' She swung around to face Stephen. 'You must know her well, Stephen. You must see that she wouldn't do this. And how's Io? Is she OK?'

'She's fine. A bit worried, but taking it in her stride. And I agree it's hard to imagine Blair taking the Forbidden Texts, but she does fit all the criteria.'

'Not all,' Maggie shot back. 'We agreed that the person who took the texts must be some sort of megalomaniac, after world domination, and that's not Blair.'

Owen's voice broke in. He was staring down at the floor. 'She is very dedicated to learning and there are different techniques and knowledge in the texts. And she has been quite vocal over the years about her determination to get Ione past first order. Maybe she came across the texts and was tempted.' Then he looked up and around, as if surprised to see them there. 'Well, that's a possibility.'

'More than a possibility,' Hampton said from his customary position, leaning on his desk. 'Sounds damn good, and it might just be the lead we're looking for. Stephen, have you interviewed her yet?'

Stephen shook his head. 'I sent an invite to her for tomorrow at two. I haven't heard anything back, so I assume that's fine.'

'But if she has been experimenting on Ione, and then realises that Ione has vanished, she might decide that we suspect and not come,' Kenyon said. 'Maybe you should go see her now.'

'She won't have time to hide the evidence,' Maggie said.

'Good point.' Hampton stood straight and opened his mouth. Stephen leant forward, ready for the instructions. But instead of talking, the Sabhamir suddenly frowned and looked at Maggie. 'We've got problems up in Donegal. Matthew Maguire has just reported what seems to him to be a magical fire, and he said there are humans involved.'

'Damn.' Maggie stood. 'I'll go to Matthew's place and check it out. Will report soon.' She disappeared.

'Do you still want me to go see Blair?' Stephen said.

'Yes. No. Wait until Maggie reports what is happening at Matthew's, and we'll see if we need you or not.' Hampton started to pace from one side of the room to the other.

'Interesting that all these problems have been happening around Donegal, and now our main suspect lives on the other side of the country,' Sarah drawled.

'It wouldn't be that hard for someone with the Forbidden Texts to be doing things from a distance,' Kenyon said.

Hampton stopped pacing and held up his hand. Silence descended on the room. Stephen watched the Sabhamir's eyes gaze into the distance and guessed he was talking to Maggie. After a moment, he nodded and then turned to face the guardians.

'OK, here's the story. A field down the road from Matthew's place caught fire about half an hour ago. He's been watching it, concerned, but was sure the humans would respond and put it out. They did respond, quickly, but they can't get it out. That was when he realised it's not a conventional fire. There are about a dozen human firefighters there, plus some locals, and Maggie said the media's just turned up.'

'Damn,' Owen said.

'We've got no choice but to go up there, stop that fire and take the memories from the humans. So I'll need all of you.' Then he nodded at Stephen and Sarah. 'No robes.'

Stephen stood, his hands shaking as he changed his brown robe into brown trousers, jumper and shirt. Going up against that conjured plant was one thing, but this was scarier. Humans, he well knew, were unpredictable and this situation had enormous potential for disaster for the gadda.

They all transferred into Matthew's loungeroom. He was standing by the front door, pointing.

'The Ceamir's already out there,' he said.

Hampton led them out; Stephen found himself walking between Kenyon and Owen, the Heasimir behind them. Up ahead, he could see a small woman with blonde hair and red clothes chatting to another woman who was holding something under the first woman's nose. There was a cameraman filming them both.

The Ceamir was on television.

As they approached, he could see that Maggie was already taking care of this situation. 'So as you can see, the new firefighting apparatus that we're testing here today is proving less than effective. It's a severe disappointment, because we had great hopes for this. Our scientists have been working for years on refining this use of un-oxygenated flame-retardant liquid or UFRL, as we call it. Unfortunately, we're just going to have to resort to old-fashioned water for the time being. I do hope that this camera is working, because this is fascinating stuff.'

As he passed her, Stephen saw Maggie give him a quick wink and he was quite sure that when they returned to the studio, the journalist would find the film was blank and there would be no footage.

Maggie had also given them the manner by which to fight the fire without detection — put power into the water that the firemen were using. He mentally sent the message to the Sabhamir and Hampton changed his direction slightly to stop next to the water tanker. He leant on it almost nonchalantly and appeared to focus his attention on the fire.

The Heasimir was unable to look as comfortable in wielding her power, so Kenyon and Owen both went to stand with her on the far side of the truck to shield her from human eyes. Stephen went over to Hampton and stood just a little behind him so he could place his hand on Hampton's back, his feet on the soil at the edge of the road, and lend him power without anyone seeing.

Over Hampton's shoulder, Stephen could see the firemen in the field. They were yelling, and occasional plumes of water would shoot in the air as they debated how best to put out a fire that didn't seem to react to the water at all. The liquid was just moving through the flames as though they weren't there, but the heat said they were.

Stephen then focussed on the flames. He tilted his head a little, looking for a sign that they were anything but real. But they looked, and felt, and smelt, exactly like a typical blaze — except that water had no impact on it.

'The sooner we get this out, the better,' he muttered. Hampton grunted and didn't take his eyes from the fire.

Stephen saw the sudden difference in the water — it darkened as the power of the guardians mixed with it.

'Make it clear,' he hissed.

'Fuck.'

He could feel Hampton's back tighten, the muscles clenching as he fought to make the power not only work but clear as well.

'Clear,' Stephen shouted, leaning back a little to look at the other three guardians behind the truck. Then he spoke mentally. *'The water is colouring; it needs to be clear.'*

Owen nodded, and he knew he'd been understood. He leant forward again, and looked at the water, holding his breath. He mentally counted, *one, two, three,* waiting, hoping.

Then it looked like normal water again and at the same time the firefighters in the field cheered and he could see it was beginning to work. The fire was going out.

Steam rose in great plumes, overwhelming the black smoke and helping to smother the flames. The minutes ticked over, and Stephen was sure they were going to win.

'You folk there. Get away from the tanker.'

Stephen looked up to see a man in a fire uniform storming toward them. His face was flushed and his moustache twitched as though it were alive.

'Maggie. We need you,' he told the Ceamir.

'Didn't you hear me? I said get away from the tanker.'

264

The man bustled up to Hampton, spittle flying from his mouth.

Hampton stood straight, but kept a hand on the tanker. 'Sorry. Just watching.'

'You can get over there and watch.' The man thrust his thumb toward Matthew Maguire's house. 'Just get out of our way. Go on, move.'

'*He's not noticed the others,*' Stephen told Hampton. '*They can keep working.*'

'*Just do as he says,*' Maggie said. '*Keep him happy, try to draw him away from the tanker.*'

'So, what's the story?' Hampton said casually, stepping away from the machine.

'Don't know. Someone musta flicked a cigarette out of their car. Go and stand over there and stay out of our way.'

'Sure, fine, sorry.' Hampton nodded to Stephen and they walked over to the other side of the road.

The man turned and watched them walk with a frown, then spun back around and marched to the edge of the field to shout instructions to the firefighters.

'*So, how are we going?*' Hampton said.

'*The water still looks good from here,*' Stephen said.

'*We've increased our power a bit, but I'm guessing it's going to take longer than it would have with you two,*' Owen said.

'*Maybe we can make our way back,*' Hampton said and he took a few steps forward.

As if he had eyes in the back of his head, the man turned and glared at him. Hampton smiled and stepped back next to Stephen. '*No, can't move. Maggie, how are things going there?*'

'*Peachy keen. Thank the star I actually pay attention to Lucas when he's talking about his experiments. I'm dazzling them with scientific mumbo-jumbo.*'

Time wore on, and Stephen put his hands behind his back so he could clench them without the humans noticing. What would happen first — discovery of the remaining guardians, or the extinguishing of the fire?

It was the fire. The humans in the field began to move forward at a rapid pace, and the flames drizzled away. Thick black smoke poured up from one small section in the middle of the paddock.

'All done?' the man yelled.

'All done, boss.'

'Then start packing up.' He turned to look at the people standing around him. 'Now, would someone like to explain what the hell happened here?'

Maggie walked past Stephen and Hampton and up to the frazzled man, her hand extended and a bright smile on her face.

'Hi, yes, I would. Maggie Shaunessy, from Winton University in Australia. Hi, fellas. Sorry about this, but we couldn't tell you about the experiment, in case it caused you to change your methods.' Then she launched into a story that contained so many scientific terms that Stephen thought she might as well be speaking Spanish.

Certainly the controller seemed to think she was, staring at her as though he thought her quite demented. But that expression softened a bit with a few tosses of Maggie's blonde curls.

Stephen shook his head. Funny how a pretty woman could get away with anything with some men.

The other five guardians regrouped by the side of the road, and watched Maggie calmly and neatly turn all the firefighters' thoughts from the weirdness of the fire to anger at being the unwitting dupes for a bunch of scientists. Not all of them were willing to be charmed by her looks, and from those men she copped quite a bit of abuse. But she smiled, and remained calm, and eventually they all left, angry and confused but no longer thinking along lines that could have them guessing the fire was other than normal.

'So, how did I do?' Maggie sauntered across the road toward them, swinging her hips and waving goodbye to the firefighters.

Hampton shook his head. 'You are a bloody marvel, Mags.'

'Damn sure Patricia wouldn't have been able to do that,' Owen said, his eyes shining.

Stephen thought about the ancient woman who had been the Ceamir a few months earlier and agreed wholeheartedly with Owen.

'Was all that flirting really necessary?' Sarah said.

Maggie shrugged. 'Much as I would like everyone to think of my brains first, it is a simple fact of life that I have been blessed with looks that turn heads. You might like to consider using yours when necessary.'

Sarah snorted and started across the road toward the field.

'I'm saying that you're attractive,' Maggie yelled after her, then added under her breath, 'you frigid cow.'

'Mags.' Hampton shook his head and then followed the Heasimir.

'Don't worry, Maggie, we like the theory.' Owen clapped her on the shoulder, grinned and then set off after the other guardians.

Maggie looked at Stephen. 'Would you refrain from using your strength, if it was the right thing to do?'

'Not at all. Nor my looks either.' He winked at her, hoping the joke would ease the tension.

'What looks?'

'Thank you, Maggie. Thank you.' He bowed his head to her.

'Well, don't want you getting too full of yourself. Can do your ego in, suddenly becoming a guardian. Believe me. Actually, believe Lucas. Apparently I've become unbearable.'

Stephen grinned. 'Become?'

Her eyes narrowed. 'Don't you start. Just 'cause you've sorted things out with Ione, don't think you can start on me.'

A cough drew their attention to the fact Kenyon was still with them. He was smiling.

'Less arguing, children, more investigating the evil fire,' he said, pointing at the field.

Stephen was smiling as he walked over. He was glad that even under these circumstances, the guardians found time to be themselves.

Hampton was crouched next to the burnt crops, touching the ground.

'Darkness.' He looked around. 'Some poor farmer's going to have a hard time getting this field back to rights.'

'They'll think it was the chemicals in UFRL,' Maggie said.

'Is there some way we can recompense them?' Stephen said.

'A sudden surprise win in a lottery,' Maggie said. 'Remember that ticket you bought all those years ago, we finally found you, blah, blah, blah. I'll handle it.'

'Kenyon, can you look after restoring the balance of power here?'

'Sure can.' Kenyon knelt down and pressed his hands against the ground.

'Right. Stephen, no point to you going to see Blair now. Unless she pulls out of tomorrow's appointment, keep it.' Stephen nodded. 'OK, I suggest we all go home and rest, 'cause star knows when we'll have to face something created by the texts again.'

Leaving Kenyon behind, they all walked back to Matthew Maguire's house. They thanked him for letting them know what was happening, and then transferred.

As he returned to his office, Stephen realised that he was going home to Ione. He was smiling as he stepped into the apartment. Then he stopped and stared.

It was transformed. There was a bright, floral sheet flowing over the lounge, hiding the drab brownness. The coffee table had been pulled across the room, and another sheet laid across it, folded and placed at an angle so some of the wood was still visible. On the floor around it were piles of towels and blankets, obviously functioning as seating. Between the lounge and what was now a dining table was a rug.

With just a few simple things, Ione had turned the lifeless space into a home.

He went in search of her. As he walked into the bedroom, he stopped at the sight of the bed, the only piece of his own furniture here. Ione had remade it, and put some blankets over it, making it a very inviting object.

He heard whistling from the ensuite, and went over. Ione was scrubbing the shower, her arm energetically moving across the surface as she began to sing a song he recognised from human radio.

He leant against the doorframe and smiled. Leaving her each time he was summoned was going to be hard, but coming home to her was going to be fantastic.

She turned and gasped, then frowned. 'You scared me. How the hell does someone as big as you move that quietly?'

Stephen stood straight and walked forward, stepping into the shower. Ione squeaked and backed up against the wall, but her eyes were shining.

'I thought you liked how big I am,' Stephen said, pressing his body to hers and pinning her against the wall.

Ione dropped the sponge and wrapped her arms around his neck. 'I love it,' she said and then she reached up to kiss him.

Perfect, Stephen thought as he opened his mouth to hers. This, right now, was perfect.

TWENTY-FIVE

Ione was just starting to get into the kiss when Stephen pulled away. She pouted up at him. 'No fair.'

'Sorry.' He grimaced. 'Hampton's just reminded me that we promised you wouldn't get overexcited.'

'Spoilsport.' Then the meaning of his words struck her. 'Fuck, he isn't going to know every time —'

'No, and he didn't know now. Just sent me a gentle reminder with incredibly good timing.' Stephen kissed her forehead and put his arm around her and led her through the bedroom into the loungeroom. 'The apartment looks good.'

'As good as it can with the paucity of materials I have to work with. We'll need to move my stuff over if we're going to live here with any sort of comfort.'

'After dinner,' Stephen said. 'I've ordered something to be delivered from the restaurant. How are you feeling?'

Just like that, the thoughts that Ione had spent all that time pushing away flooded back into her mind. She shuddered. 'Fine. I've been waiting for the Heasimir to appear to check me out, and I'm glad she hasn't.'

Stephen smiled. 'Shouldn't have mentioned that.' He walked her to the side of the room, leaving space in the middle. Ione hoped she managed to hide her grimace as the Heasimir appeared. With her white-blonde hair and red lips, she was objectively a beautiful woman. But subjectively, Ione saw nothing attractive about her.

'Ms Gorton, I want to see how you are reacting to the lock, and whether the extra power is making you ill. Come here, please.'

Ione toyed with the idea of tightening her grip on Stephen's hand and refusing. But she stepped forward and stopped in front of the healer.

The Heasimir lifted her hand and pressed her palm against Ione's forehead. It rested there for a moment, then moved over the top of Ione's heart. Ione watched the other woman closely, looking for a sign of what she was thinking on the perfectly pale face. There was nothing.

The Heasimir took a step backward and nodded to Stephen. 'She is well.'

'Good. I assume you'll do regular checkups.'

'I'll be in tomorrow,' the Heasimir said, and then disappeared.

Stephen rolled his shoulders, straightened his back and then looked at Ione. 'Nice girl,' he said.

'Do you think anyone likes her?' Ione walked over and pressed herself to Stephen's side. He wrapped his arm around her waist to hold her against him. It felt natural and right.

'I don't think she cares,' he said, leaning down to press his face against Ione's hair.

Ione closed her eyes and relaxed against him. As scary as this situation was, being with Stephen made it bearable.

'Does Jack know what's going on?'

Ione nodded. 'I rang Susie, my mother-in-law, and told her.' She pulled back a little to look up at him. Mentioning Susie had reminded her that there were things they hadn't talked about yet. 'You do know what you're getting yourself in for, right? That I come as part of a package, and that Jack and I will be in constant touch with my husband's family.'

Stephen pushed a curl behind her ear. 'I like Jack.'

'You won't when he's being a pain in the arse about going to bed, or when he gets sick, or when he refuses to do his homework and we get into a fight.'

There was a pause before he spoke. 'What are you saying?'

'I want to know you understand exactly what this means. You're getting an instant family. Just a few weeks ago, you weren't even picturing having a girlfriend, and you've just become a guardian. It's a lot.'

'You want to know I've thought about this.' Ione nodded. 'I admit, I haven't. I've been focussed on how fantastic it is to be with you.' He kissed her forehead. 'But you're right, there is more than that. Jack does need to be considered. Can you give me some time to work out what I think and then we talk?'

'Sure.' Ione snuggled back against him.

The Garramir's chime rang and Stephen gave him the all-clear. He appeared with a grin.

'Ione, sorry to bother you on your first night of reunion with Stevo here, but I'm afraid I need to give you a check over.'

'Why do they call you the gardener?' Ione said as he came forward. 'You don't seem to have anything to do with plants.'

The Garramir winced. 'Crap, isn't it? I've tried to think of another name, but all I can come up with is the Scale of the Gadda, you know, balance and all that. But then I thought about people calling me the Scale and I just shuddered.'

Ione stood still as he put his hands on her shoulders. 'So what is it you do?' she asked.

'It's my task to ensure the power remains in balance. Lack of balance is bad. When there's too much of something where it shouldn't be, and not enough where it should, then things happen that shouldn't. It is kinda like gardening, in that you're trying to keep nature in balance, but nothing to do with plants.'

'The Equaliser? You know, keeping the power in balance.'

'Yes!' Kenyon's face almost split in two, his smile was so sudden and brilliant. 'The Equaliser.'

'Makes you sound like a superhero,' Stephen said.

'Works for me.' The Garramir stepped back, releasing Ione. 'Now, that's interesting. All your power feels perfectly natural to me, Ione.'

'What does that mean?'

'Stephen and Hampton tell me that your power has at least doubled. I would have expected to be able to tell the difference between your natural power and the extra stuff because it should be straining you, but I can't. It's as if you didn't have the right amount of power before, and now you do and your body doesn't have any problems with it.'

'Does that mean we won't be able to separate or remove it if we have to?' Stephen said.

'That's exactly what it means.' The Garramir looked at Ione. 'I rather suspect that if we tried to take this extra power from you, your body would react as if it was a permanent power loss, and you would be weakened and maybe even ...'

'Die.' The word struck Ione hard. 'So this power could kill me, being forbidden, but taking it from me could also kill me.'

Stephen pulled her against him and squeezed her tight. 'We're not going to let that happen.'

'We will certainly do our best,' the Garramir said. 'I think you're quite well, and safe for the time being. I think keeping the lock on is a good idea, but otherwise it's pretty much a wait-and-see proposition at the moment. We may not be able to solve this until we find the texts and work out how it was done and therefore how to undo it.'

'Then what are the two of you doing standing here? Go find those texts!' Stephen and the Garramir looked at each other, then at Ione. She sighed. 'Too early for jokes?'

'Way too early.' Stephen kissed her forehead. 'But thank you for trying.'

'I'll come check on you daily,' the Garramir said. 'In the meantime, the slightest thing — headache, weakness, pain, whatever — you call the Heasimir. Understand?' Ione nodded. 'Good. Now, I'll leave you two to your reunion.' He grinned, and was gone.

'I think I like him.'

'They're all good,' Stephen said, resting his cheek against the top of her head. 'Except the Heasimir.'

'Well, five out of six ain't bad.'

'I'm sorry we don't have more answers for you. Or that you can't have Jack with you.'

Ione closed her eyes. 'I don't want to die,' she whispered.

She waited for Stephen's pledge that she wouldn't and was scared that this time, he said nothing.

ASARLAI

Asarlai sat in her chair, breathing shallowly. Every bone, every muscle, every cell in her body ached if she moved too much. She felt as if she were caving in, shrinking.

She knew that wasn't the case — a quick look in the mirror assured her that while she looked tired and old, she was still whole. But she felt the empty space within her, and couldn't understand why her body wasn't being sucked into the midnight chasm.

It was gone. Her power was gone. She had first noticed that it was sluggish and somehow low the night that the plant exploded. Yesterday, the panic had built as simple tasks, such as cleaning the dishes or sending a message ball, had become harder and harder.

She'd woken this morning and looked inside herself. Her entire body had quaked as she realised how little was left. She'd reached forward; there had been a tearing and a rushing, and she'd grabbed frantically, pulling on her power, then watched it run through her fingers and disappear.

She tried to throw herself into that infinite blackness, to follow her power and wrestle it back from wherever it had gone, but her body remained firmly planted in reality.

In a mad rush she'd run into her laboratory, torn open the texts and searched every page for information that she knew wasn't there. The texts taught how to increase someone's power, or take it completely away. They didn't say anything about creating power in something lacking it entirely.

Her power was gone, and she didn't know where it was or how to get it back.

As she sat, the ache ebbed away. She took a chance on a deep breath, and her lungs moved as easily as they always had. She lifted her hand and placed it gently on the arm of the chair. She shifted forward and pushed herself to her feet.

She could move freely, without pain. She was even starting to lose the sense of the emptiness where her power should be.

Star above, she was becoming human.

She shuddered. The timing could not be worse. She was meeting Stephen O'Malley today — he'd know something was wrong the moment he touched her and found she had no power. If he came here, and felt the power of the texts ...

Well, she'd been wanting a test for her apprentices. Now was the time. She triggered the summoning stone she used and, by the time the apprentices arrived, Asarlai was sitting in her chair, feeling calm and excited about what she was going to do.

'The time is approaching for the final phases of the plan to be put into action,' she said. 'In order to decide who will perform which task, I require you all to undertake a test. As you can feel, this place hums with the power of the texts. I want to see what you can do to nullify it.'

Grace, Glen and Ellen immediately turned to each other and began to discuss ideas. Lachy frowned and looked around him — floor, ceiling, walls, bookshelves, table — searching for inspiration.

Shauna nodded. 'If you don't mind, Asarlai, I've been practising something in my own laboratory, in order to hide the work I have been doing. I'd like to try my idea on a room here in your home and see what you think.'

Asarlai smiled. 'Of course, Shauna. Try the spare bedroom — it would be the least power-ridden of any space in the house.'

Shauna swept out of the room and after watching the others for a moment, Asarlai followed. She was sure they would come to her before they began work and in the meantime, she was interested to see what Shauna had come up with.

The young woman stood at the door of the spare room and tilted her head as she looked around. She glanced over her shoulder. 'I've found something human that's helpful in this circumstance.' She reached into her pocket and pulled out a clear bag. 'It's plastic, and there's something about the way it's made that means it can trap power.'

Asarlai noted the information. 'Show me what you do, Shauna.'

Shauna put her hands out in front of her and circled them in front of the doorway. Asarlai heard the words and realised she was sealing the room. Then Shauna put the plastic bag against the seal and spoke the words of a conjuration from the texts that combined the usual gadda asphyxiation with suction. As Asarlai watched, something grey started to fill the bag.

Shauna's face flushed, and she looked as though she were going to be sick, but she held the bag steady against the seal until it was full. Then she closed the open end and pulled it away, removing the seal.

She stepped inside the room and nodded. 'It has worked well, Asarlai.'

Asarlai stood at the door and nodded. It felt clean to her, but then she wasn't feeling power any more. Even the delicious darkness of the texts was gone.

'Well done, Shauna. That seems a very effective solution. Do you have enough bags to clean my bedroom and the kitchen?'

'I do at home.'

'Then get them. I am very happy with you, Shauna. Very happy.' The apprentice was smiling as she transferred.

'Asarlai.' She turned around to see Grace, Ellen and Glen walking toward her.

'We believe that we have a solution,' Ellen said. 'The power-strip conjuration from the texts talks about having others spliced to it. If we combined it with a simple cleaning incantation ...'

Asarlai nodded. 'An intriguing idea. Try it on the loungeroom and see how it works.'

It worked beautifully. With Shauna taking care of the kitchen and bedroom, that left just the laundry and laboratory.

Asarlai had the trio clean the laundry, while she went down to see what Lachy had devised. He was still standing in the middle of the laboratory, staring at the star painted on the floor.

He looked up when she walked in, his face flushed. 'Asarlai, I am sure that if you just give me a moment —'

'Go and help Shauna and then all five of you must clear this laboratory.'

Lachy nodded and ran upstairs. Asarlai walked over to the bench and gently traced a fingertip over the nearest book.

So close, and yet so far.

She wrapped the texts up, first in silk and then in leather, and put them inside a wooden box. She'd just completed this when her apprentices came in.

'The rest of the house is clean, Asarlai,' Shauna said.

'Good. This room will be the hardest and must be the cleanest of all. No power is to be left behind. Understand?'

They nodded. Asarlai picked up the box and went through the house and outside. At the back, pressed into a corner of the stone wall that enclosed the garden, was a small shed. She put the box in there, and closed and locked the door. It was only a temporary resting place, and should be safe enough.

She was sitting in the loungeroom when the apprentices came up. They were all smiling, their faces flushed.

'It's as though this house is human,' Ellen said.

'Well done. Now, I know that you, Grace and Glen worked together but I must know — who was the true originator of the idea?'

The three of them looked at each other. Asarlai saw Grace raise her brows and so knew the answer before Ellen spoke. 'It was Grace who put the discussion together and came up with the combination we used.'

'Well done, Grace. And to you, Shauna. I am impressed by your initiative. Now, in order for me to put the last piece of the plan in place, I need to move the texts and that means I need a diversion.'

'What do you want us to do for you, Asarlai?' Lachy said, eager to make up for his recent failure.

'Something big. Something that threatens all of Sclossin, yet is within the capabilities of the guardians. Something that is not easily defeated, and will require hours of time and even weaken them.'

'Another bombing?' Glen said.

TWENTY-SIX

Stephen woke up and had a moment of disconnection as he tried to figure out what was different. Then he smiled and tightened his arms around Ione, who was still fast asleep, her back pressed against his chest.

He lifted his nose to press it more firmly into her hair and took a deep breath. She smelt wonderful — earthy and sweet.

Despite the terror of the situation she faced, last night with Ione was both the nicest and the most frustrating of his life. She'd managed to put the worst of her fears aside to chat with him about his first few days as the Coiremir. He took his lead from her, and they didn't talk about them, or her increased power, or the future.

When bedtime approached, Stephen had begun to feel awkward. There wasn't another bed in the apartment, but could he ask Ione to sleep with him when they couldn't indulge in the pleasure he was sure they both wanted?

Then Ione had placed a hand on the centre of his chest and smiled up at him. 'I know it is probably a bit too much to ask, but I want to sleep with you, even if we can't have sex. I just need to be held.'

What man could refuse a request like that from the woman he loved?

So they'd got ready and climbed into the bed and Stephen had taken Ione in his arms, shifting his body so his inevitable erection hadn't been too obvious.

It had been a long while until they slept. Neither had spoken; they'd just taken comfort in the simple act of being together.

Lying with her now, Stephen decided that this moment was worth the frustration of the night before. Waking up next to Ione, knowing that she was now sleeping peacefully because of the comfort he had given her, made him feel fantastic.

Unfortunately, it wasn't a feeling he could indulge for too long. He had work to do — the first teacher would be arriving for the new day of interviews in an hour. So he kissed Ione's temple, and stayed still as she mumbled and wriggled in a way that did nothing to soothe the whole new erection he'd woken up with, and then settled back down into a deep slumber.

He went through the first five interviews of the day with little thought, barely aware of what anyone said. His brain was split between worrying about Ione and rising tension over interviewing Blair Callaghan. Their number one suspect. The woman who may have put Ione's life at risk.

He let the fifth interviewee out of his office then walked around it slowly, clenching and unclenching his fists, hoping the movement would dissipate his concern. Even knowing that all the guardians were currently sitting in their offices, ready to come to his aid, he was nervous. After all, if they were right, this woman had killed the last Coiremir — someone much more experienced and skilled than him.

He started forward, covering the space from the

middle of the room to the door to the apartment in just three steps. He threw it open and stepped inside.

'Ione!'

He heard a scramble, and the door to his laboratory opened. 'Stephen.' She rushed over to him, her hands stretched out. 'What's wrong?'

Stephen crushed her against his chest, pressing his cheek against her head. He allowed her warmth to seep into him and give him some comfort.

'I have to see her now,' he said.

Ione wrapped her arms around his waist. 'It's fine. I'm sure it will be fine.'

'I'm not.'

She squeezed him. 'Tell you what, how about you take over my job, and I'll take over yours?'

That didn't sound too bad an offer to him. He lifted his head and looked down at her. 'What is your job exactly?'

'I write database applications for dickheads. Except Lucas, of course.'

Stephen blinked, and then laughed. He hugged her tight and kissed the top of her head. 'Thank you.'

'Now, go meet Blair, realise it isn't her, then find and kick the correct bastard's arse.' Ione reached up and pressed her lips to his. Stephen was debating whether he had time to deepen the kiss when he heard a chime from his office.

'What's that?' He released Ione, turned and walked to the door. A message ball hovered just above his desk. He walked over and touched it.

A woman's voice echoed through the room. 'Coiremir, this is Shauna Connell, on behalf of Blair Callaghan. I'm sorry to say that Blair isn't feeling well today, and so is not capable of transferring to see you. She was hoping you'd be able to come out to the farm instead.'

'Shit.' Stephen mentally contacted the guardians, and told them what Blair wanted.

'*Do it,*' Hampton replied. '*We'll still be ready and able to assist in seconds, and you might get more of a read of her from her home.*'

'*Or she might have set a trap,*' Maggie said.

'*Unless she kills him instantly, and herself and Shauna, we'll get there in time,*' Hampton said.

'OK, I'll go,' Stephen told them. He turned around and smiled at Ione, who stood in the doorway.

'I hope you're right about her.' As he spoke, he sent a request for entry to Blair's home.

'I am,' Ione said as his permission was received. Stephen walked over, gave her one quick kiss, and then transferred.

He found himself standing in a plain yet pleasant loungeroom. The furniture was either dark wood or cream wool, and the walls were white, with exposed wooden beams. He stood on a cream-coloured rug on a dark wooden floor. There were flowers in vases on the windowsill, and a lacy white runner down the middle of the coffee table.

He turned at a noise behind him and saw Shauna step out of another room, carrying a tea tray. Her eyes were bloodshot, and her skin pale.

'Apologies for the late notice, Coiremir.' Shauna put the tray on the coffee table and nodded. 'I have been telling Blair all morning to contact you, but she was sure she would be better.'

'Not at all. If it suits, I can make another appointment.'

'Please, don't listen to her, Coiremir.' Blair stepped into the loungeroom. She was ashen, and Stephen noted an air of frailty about her that he had never seen before. 'I am perfectly capable of speaking with you. I have some interesting theories that I wish to discuss.' She sat down and nodded at Shauna. 'Please pour, dear.'

Shauna sat next to Blair and began to pour, leaving Stephen no choice but to sit opposite them.

'How do you take yours?' Shauna asked.

'White and one.' Stephen leant back and watched Blair. She seemed entirely herself, other than the air of illness. Maybe he and Hampton had it all wrong.

When Shauna handed the tea over, Stephen sniffed the cup first, just in case, then took a sip. It certainly tasted like tea, and his power wasn't reacting to any concealed danger.

'So, what have you learnt so far from your interviews?' Blair said.

'Differing views. People seem to be in two camps. They either think the system works pretty well as it is, or believe that some element of more formal education is required after first order. Pretty much all of those believe second order should also be undertaken through formal lessons, but then it diverges.'

Blair nodded as she leant back in her seat and sipped on her tea. 'I can see arguments for both sides,' she said.

From there, they slipped into a good half-hour of discussion of formal versus free-form education, and whether they needed to be more flexible in terms of people's needs. As they spoke, Stephen tried to keep sounding intelligent while he sent tendrils of power out along the floor to see if he could find some hint of darkness in the house. He found none, and what power he did feel was so muted that he guessed Blair mustn't spend much time here.

Then his attention was snapped back to her fully when she mentioned Ione.

'Take either Ione Gorton or Lucas Valeroso, who I believe you know,' Blair said. 'Neither of them fit the normal pattern of learning, yet there're not really systems in place to help them achieve their potential.'

Stephen thought of the change in Ione's potential and almost shuddered. Still, he was glad Blair had brought her up. 'Ione's always struck me as being quite happy with where she is,' he said.

Blair shook her head. 'She may have given up, but I haven't,' she said. 'I refuse to admit such an intelligent, capable person can't pass first order and one day, I will find a way.' Blair put her cup down. 'I'm sorry, but my headache seems to be worsening. Would you mind if we put the rest of this off to another time?'

'Of course not.' Stephen put his cup down and stood. 'I'm sorry you aren't well, I was enjoying our talk.' He held his hand out and almost held his breath. What would he feel?

At that moment, he felt something move against him. Ione had broken the lock on the apartment and opened the door to someone.

'*Maggie?*'

'*Yes?*'

'*Can you check on Io? I think something's wrong.*'

'*Not a problem.*'

By the time he focussed on Blair, she had stood and Shauna was standing in between them.

'Thank you, Coiremir.' Blair nodded as she leant on Shauna. 'I look forward to working with you.' Then she allowed Shauna to guide her out of the room.

Stephen stared at the door, wondering if it meant

anything that Shauna had all but blocked Blair from his touch. Then he heard Maggie's voice.

'Stephen, all is OK here. It's just Mark come to call.'

Stephen thought Ione probably wouldn't call a visit from her brother OK, but it meant he was able to transfer directly to Hampton's office. The Sabhamir was sitting at his desk.

'Well?'

Stephen sat down facing him. 'It all seemed fine. I could feel no darkness in the house. In fact, any discernible power was so muted, I'd say she doesn't spend much time there. And she was normal enough; she brought up Ione and her health herself.'

Hampton frowned. 'I thought Blair was quite fond of the cottage, and went up there regularly.'

'It didn't feel like it.'

Hampton started to drum his fingers on his desk. 'You didn't feel any darkness when you touched her?'

Stephen sat up straight. 'I didn't touch her. I put my hand out, but she ignored it. Tottered away on Shauna Connell's arm like a little old woman. You know, she has been looking pretty sick lately. Maybe she is just ill.'

'So you're saying it's not her?'

'I'm saying I found no evidence it is her. Maybe we need to try to catch her out. Maybe like Maggie said, she had enough time to hide the evidence. Maybe it's not her at all and she's just sick.'

Hampton shook his head. 'Shame you didn't touch her. I'd like to barge in and grab her myself, but if she turned out to be fine and reported me ...' He shook his head. 'I'll talk to Sarah. Since Blair's unwell, she can't object to a visit from the Heasimir. In the meantime, you need to keep up your interviews, so if Blair is watching it seems like you don't suspect anything. And —' He stopped and at the same time, Ione's voice rocketed through Stephen's head.

'*Stephen?*' The panic in her tone was clear.

Seconds later, Maggie spoke. '*Stephen, Hampton, I need you here now.*'

Both men stood and transferred to Stephen's office.

'Here.' Stephen turned in the direction of Maggie's voice and was stunned to see a hole in the wall next to his office door. It offered a clear view to the corridor beyond. On the floor, leaning against the far wall, was Mark Hammond, his eyes closed and his head slumped. Maggie was crouched beside him. Between them and the hole was a spread of debris.

Stephen spun around and saw Ione leaning against the door to the apartment, pallid and trembling. 'Ione, what is it? What happened to your brother?'

She looked up at him, eyes bright with tears.

'I think I killed him,' she whispered.

Ione sat on the lounge, her arms wrapped around her waist, shivering. She was aware of Stephen's arm around her shoulder and of Maggie's knee pressed against her thigh, but she couldn't hear what they were saying, or look at them.

Instead, her mind was focussed on the events of the last half-hour.

She'd been sitting in Stephen's laboratory (the only room with a desk), working on a particularly difficult section of Lucas's project when she'd heard a thump from the door to Stephen's office.

She'd thought of ignoring it, but that one thump had become many, and she could hear someone shouting.

As she walked into the loungeroom, the sound of the person's voice became clearer and she recognised it as Mark's.

Great, just what I need.

She stood on the other side of the door and considered allowing him to stand and thump and yell to his heart's content, until she realised he would probably keep it up for hours, and she wouldn't get any work done.

So she had unlocked it and thrown it open.

'You slut.' The words were spat at her. 'You'd just abandon your own son for sex? What kind of a mother are you?'

Ione narrowed her eyes. 'That's not what I did.'

'Oh, really? So it's just coincidence that you're here, with him.'

Ione took a deep breath and released it slowly, hoping it would bring her the patience she needed to deal with Mark. 'I'm here because there's something wrong with me.'

'I can't believe you'd risk Jack like this. That man is dangerous.'

'No, he's not.' She growled the words between gritted teeth. 'Stephen is a good man, one who has actually been quite kind to you, I think. I would've torn off your balls and roasted them for what you did.'

'So what, you get laid and now all you can think about is your pussy?' Mark's nose crinkled. 'You disgust me. If Patrick were alive —'

'For fuck's sake.' Ione stepped forward, and Mark actually backed away. She was vaguely aware of Maggie appearing next to her. 'He's not alive. When will you get that into your thick skull? Patrick's dead, and I am allowed to be happy.'

'Not at Jack's expense.'

293

'It's *not*.'

'Not any more.' Mark pulled his shoulders back. 'I'm going to be petitioning the bardria to hand Jack's guardianship over to me.'

Despite knowing that he wouldn't succeed, a chill ran through Ione's body at the thought of losing her son. 'No.'

'I wouldn't do that if I were you, Mark.' Maggie spoke very quietly, putting an arm around Ione's shoulder.

Mark, however, wasn't in the mood to listen to advice. 'I've warned you, Ione, but you've just blithely risked Jack for this obsession with O'Malley.'

Ione had reacted without thinking. She'd lifted her hands and thrust the push incantation at him, her time-honoured method of relieving frustration.

Her power flared, brilliant white, and she screeched and pulled her hands back to cover her eyes. She was bathed in a scorching heat that had sweat instantly popping out of her forehead.

Then it had gone, and she had slowly pulled her hands from her face and stared in horror at the hole in Stephen's office wall, and Mark's crumpled figure lying in the corridor beyond.

It was an image she couldn't shake from her mind. She closed her eyes and tried to think it away, but it wouldn't go. And over it was repeated the refrain — *I killed him*.

'Ione.' Her hands were shaken, and she forced herself to open her eyes and pay attention to Stephen, even though it was through the image of Mark.

'Ione, he's going to be all right.' Stephen squeezed her hands. 'The Heasimir's checked him out. He's injured, and it will be a week before he's up and about again, but you didn't kill him.'

'What?' His words didn't match the picture in her mind.

He shook her hands again. 'You didn't kill him. He's going to be fine.'

The impact of the words was like a shot going off in her head, shattering the thought of Mark's funeral, of trying to explain what she'd done to her parents, to Jack. 'Oh, star.' Ione pulled her hands free, put them over her eyes and began to sob.

Stephen pulled her against his chest and rocked her and crooned words — at first nonsense, then slowly they became clear.

'It's going to be OK, Ione. He's going to be fine. You're going to be fine.'

Slowly, Ione relaxed against him, the sobs subsiding. So, she wasn't a killer. But she was still dangerous. Someone who could use their power to hurt.

She became aware of other voices — Maggie, the rest of the guardians. She opened her eyes and pulled away a little from Stephen to pay attention to them.

'I'm not happy with how this is progressing.' The Sabhamir was pacing back and forth. 'That the power just blasted through my lock is a real worry.'

'Are you sure the lock was good enough?' the Heasimir said. The look he speared her would have chastened most people, but Sarah Hennessy wasn't most. 'Well?'

'Yes.' He spat the word out. 'And yet she cut through it easily.' His strides grew longer.

'It makes sense that this isn't ordinary power, Hampton,' the Firimir said. 'What I'm intrigued by is that Ione is so good at the push incantation, considering her lack of ability.'

'That's 'cause she uses it all the time,' Maggie said. Everyone swung round to face her. 'It's her way of letting off steam. Whenever someone really gives her the shits, she'll use the incantation, knowing full well it has no juice behind it. She's been doing it to Mark for years. There's no way she could have expected this would be the result.'

'Are there any other incantations that she knows?' the Garramir asked.

'I'm here,' Ione said, interrupting the conversation about her. 'And yes, it's not the only one.'

'Then might I suggest that we need to teach Ione how to control her power?' the Firimir said.

'I'll do that,' Stephen said. All eyes now swung to him. 'It is my job.'

The Sabhamir's lips twisted. 'I feel like I should try another lock on her, even though it seems a pointless proposition.'

'She probably used enough power against Mark that she's no longer a threat.' The Garramir walked over to her and held out his hand. Ione put her hand in his. He frowned. 'Now, that's interesting. Ione, when you cast the incantation, did you take back power at the same time?'

Ione shook her head. 'I don't know how to.'

'Then I'm intrigued by how it is that you still have the same amount of power as I felt in you last night.'

'What?' The Sabhamir almost elbowed the Garramir aside as he barged over and reached out to take Ione's other hand. 'Hmm.' He frowned for a moment, then nodded. 'Ione, I'm going to start taking power from you. You don't need to do anything, just relax and open yourself to me.'

Ione nodded and closed her eyes. She felt warmth wrap around her, then something poke at her power, before it began to stream from her. She noted dispassionately that her power was orange. The stream appeared in her mind about two centimetres thick, and it flowed steadily. She waited for the end to become clear. More power. No end.

The Sabhamir released her and she opened her eyes. 'Touch her,' he said to the Garramir.

The equaliser of the gadda leant forward and put a finger on Ione's forehead. 'It's the same. How much did you take?'

'Almost too much for me to handle.' Ione looked up at the Sabhamir and noted beads of sweat on his forehead. He held his hand out to the Garramir. 'Ken.'

The Garramir put his hand on the other man's and held it for a moment. 'There, does that feel better?'

'Much.' The Sabhamir tapped a long finger against his chin while he looked down at Ione. 'Do you know what I'm thinking?'

'Lodestone,' the Garramir said, looking at Ione.

'No.' The Heasimir stepped forward to join them and looked down at Ione. 'That's impossible.'

'Can you think of another explanation?'

'Right.' Ione held both her hands up. 'First, you lot, back off. I don't need you looming over me.' The three guardians all immediately stepped back, the Sabhamir and Garramir looking apologetic. 'Second, what is a lodestone?'

'An unending source of power,' the Sabhamir said. 'No matter what you take, they always retain the same amount.'

'But how is that possible? You know, balance and all that.' She looked at the Garramir.

'For every lodestone, there's a sink – a place of negative power,' he said. 'There've only been two lodestones ever found, and their location is known only to the Sabhamir, Garramir and Heasimir.'

'You'd make number three,' the Sabhamir said.

Ione started to shake. How could she have gone from having so little power that she couldn't pass first order to being an unending source of the stuff?

'So if Ione's been made a lodestone, somewhere a sink has been created,' Maggie said. 'Surely that's not a good thing.'

'Depends where it is,' the Garramir said. 'If it's in a sufficiently isolated spot, then it shouldn't pose any real danger.'

'But if the new lodestone is a person, doesn't it make sense the new sink would be too?' Stephen said.

'That's not the case with the existing ones — lodestones and their corresponding sinks are not usually made of identical matter. I don't see why it would be here,' the Garramir said.

'What does this mean for Ione? Does it put her in further danger?' Maggie reached over and squeezed her best friend's hand.

'We don't know.'

'Then find out,' Ione snapped. She sat bolt upright. 'You lot,' her fingers pointed at the four standing guardians, 'go and find out what the star is happening to me.' Then she turned to Maggie. 'You, go and fill Paddy and Susie in. Tell them that the moment I'm under control, I want Jack with me.' Then she swung to Stephen. 'You, teach me control.'

She didn't miss the look that passed between the six guardians, but as five of them left immediately, she decided to forgive them their obvious doubt in her sanity. Instead, she focussed on Stephen. 'What do I have to do?'

'Well, you should have gone through the control

exercise at training.' Stephen's words were hesitant, as though he didn't know what to say to her.

'What, all that meditation stuff?' He nodded. 'All right.'

She closed her eyes, took deep breaths until she had blocked out external stimuli, and then she looked inside herself. Her power was a glowing ball — orange in the centre, white on the edges. Even she could see that it was substantially bigger than when she'd last tried to control it.

She recalled her teacher's words — *approach your power slowly and calmly but don't hesitate. When you reach it, grab it, not hard but firmly. It will flare at your touch, but don't be put off by it or it will escape you.*

So she reached forward, slowly and calmly, and when she touched it she didn't hesitate but took a firm grasp. It did flare, but it remained within her and under control.

She opened her eyes and, for the first time in her life, was aware of both the world around her and her power within her. It was an awesome sensation.

'Shit.' She stared at Stephen, her eyes wide. 'So this is what I've been missing out on.'

He smiled, then leant forward and kissed her forehead. 'Welcome to the gadda, Ione Gorton.'

She sat, basking in the warmth of her power for a moment, then frowned at him. 'Right, what's next?'

He laughed. 'I think that's enough for today, don't you?'

She shook her head. 'No. Not if it means I can do what I did to Mark.' She shuddered and decided to turn her mind from such a horrible image to something more positive. 'Besides, there is the added point that I need all the control I can get in order to safely jump your bones.'

He frowned, then his eyes widened and she realised it had taken him a moment to understand what she was saying. 'Um, right.'

'So, you better keep teaching me, buster, 'cause it's been too long and I've an itch.'

'Well, that's the best incentive a teacher ever had,' Stephen said. Ione grinned and leant forward to kiss him, glad that she'd get something good out of all this, but then he pulled away.

'Sorry,' he said with a grimace. 'My next interview is here. I can't cry off, not —'

Ione held out her hand. 'Say no more. I understand, the Forbidden Texts, blah, blah, blah. Just promise that we'll do the rest of the exercises tonight.'

'That and more.' He kissed her quickly with barely enough contact for her to react, then he stood and marched into the office, closing the door behind him.

Ione sat on the lounge and stared down at her hands. She lifted them up to eye level, and turned them to look first at the palms, then at the back.

They looked the same. She looked the same. But she felt very, very different. And she was capable of incredible things ...

She closed her eyes and fought against the tears. Seeing Mark like that, knowing she'd done it, had torn away all the annoyance and rage of the past few days. She'd been taken back to when they were children. Of course they'd had their spats — every brother and sister did — but Mark had also been her protector, her inspiration and at times her only friend.

And she'd almost killed him.

She couldn't fight the tears any more. She lay down on the lounge, curled into a ball and cried.

TWENTY-SEVEN

'Do you really think threats help to instil knowledge?' Stephen stared at Frances Peate, his four o'clock interview, with astonishment.

For all the differing ideas on education he'd heard, it had never occurred to him he would meet someone who would advocate corporal punishment as a learning tool.

She nodded. She was in her late thirties — too young for his idea of a middle-aged woman. But when you looked at her stern demeanour and listened to her old-fashioned ideologies, it was clear why she could be considered more mature than she was.

'Indeed. Children can be extremely lazy and easily distracted, and the threat of pain is very good for keeping them focussed. I find I don't often have to actually follow through on my threats, and when I do the children generally deserve it.'

Stephen made a mental note that he would find a way to ensure that Frances never taught children again.

She'd just left the room when the Sabhamir's voice echoed in his head. 'Stephen, can you come over for a chat?'

He transferred to Hampton's office. The other guardians were there.

'Is Ione all right?' asked Hampton.

'Her power is under control. We're going to do some exercises to refine it tonight.' Stephen looked at Maggie. 'I'm guessing Jack will come stay with us in a day or two.'

'Instant family, huh?' Maggie grinned.

'So it seems.'

'Right, back to Blair Callaghan.' Hampton was pacing. 'Sarah, what did you find while you were there?'

The Heasimir sat upright, her posture perfect. 'Blair's power was very dull, which is normal in someone who is ill. There was no sign of darkness.'

Stephen felt hope drain away. So it wasn't Blair.

'As Stephen said, there was a dullness in the residue of power in the house, but to me it was too even for it to be about lack of residence.' The Heasimir looked at Stephen and Maggie. 'Normally over time, the areas of the house where power is used least dull first, so generally after a few months you might find, for example, that there's barely any power to be felt in the loungeroom, more in the bathroom and a lot residing in the laboratory.'

Stephen nodded. He knew most gadda eschewed electricity and used their power for things such as heating water to wash themselves. What the Heasimir was saying made sense.

The Heasimir continued. 'In Blair's home, the dullness was universal. I was able to walk into a few rooms, and it was at the same level in the loungeroom, the kitchen and the bathroom.'

'Which would suggest that it's not related to lack of living there, and therefore is artificial.' Owen scratched his chin.

'So we're back to having to consider Blair a suspect but not having proof enough to do anything,' Hampton said. 'And we need to find a way to keep an eye on her.'

'Spy on her with Oxlan's peepers,' Kenyon said.

'If she has the Forbidden Texts, it could be hard to place them without her finding and destroying them,' Owen said.

'There are six of us, with all our various skills and diversities, and one of her,' Kenyon said. 'There has to be a way we can outthink her.'

'Ken, I think you're right.' Hampton stopped in front of his desk and stared down at its top for a moment. Then he spun around. 'I think each of us should go away and think of our particular skills and how they could be used, then we'll meet back here in a couple of hours to compare notes and see what we can come up with.'

The Heasimir needed no more of an invitation to leave than that.

'Would it be better to work it out together?' Owen said.

'Not at first, I think, although Maggie and Stephen, I'd like you to stay so I can guide you,' Hampton said.

Kenyon and Owen left, and Stephen sat next to Maggie and watched the Sabhamir grab a chair and straddle it in front of them.

'Right,' he said. 'That was an out-and-out lie. I don't think the others have the skills to help, although Ken is right — there is one source of diversity we have that might just beat her. You two.'

Stephen looked at Maggie and saw she was as amazed as he felt. 'Us?'

Hampton nodded. 'We've been looking at outwitting her with power, but Owen's right about that being futile. We don't know what her power is doing, or what we're facing in that respect. So we need to outwit her from another point of view. Humanly.'

Maggie leant forward. 'Hampton Rourke, you sneaky son of a bitch.' She turned to Stephen. 'Hampton, Owen and I have been talking a lot about cop shows. That's how we should be thinking, like human cops.'

Stephen frowned. 'Can't say I've watched a lot of TV.'

'No, but you've lived in the human world,' Hampton said. 'You've experienced how they follow each other around, keep track of each other.'

'Newspapers. Television. Radio.' Thoughts started to pop into Stephen's head.

'It's the whole Big Brother thing,' Maggie said. Stephen stared at her, wondering what the hell she was talking about and could see Hampton was similarly confused. She sighed. 'George Orwell? *1984*? Modern technology has allowed humans to develop all sorts of systems for keeping track of each other. For example, surveillance cameras. There're so many of them around, particularly in the big cities, that it's quite possible to follow someone for an entire day. You can watch them on the traffic cameras, on the in-store security cameras — with the right technology, you can follow their movements via their mobile phones. A satellite can follow every step you make. And with so many computers having cameras built into them nowadays, there are concerns people can watch you even in your own home.'

'Ione said Blair was interested in getting a computer.' Stephen looked at Hampton.

'Could we put one of those cameras in a computer, and have it watch Blair without her knowing?' Hampton asked.

'I'm sure we could. Ione would know.'

Stephen grimaced. 'She's not going to be part of it. She's convinced it can't be Blair.'

'Then don't tell her it's for Blair. Say I want it to keep track of people in my office.'

Hampton's lips quirked. 'You'd lie to your best friend?'

'You don't want to know the depths I'll plumb to do the right thing.'

'You're probably right.' He looked at Stephen. 'What do you think?'

'Not a bad idea,' Stephen said.

'Ooh, here's a better one.' Maggie bounced in her seat. 'An award. Best teacher or something. You present it to her, Stephen, and she'll probably put something like that in her laboratory.'

'I think we may have created a monster,' Hampton murmured.

'Ooh, ooh, ooh! A traffic camera, on the road outside her house, only it happens to be trained on one of the windows and looking inside rather than the road. Or send her some flowers, and have the camera hidden in the vase.'

'That'll do, Agent Gibbs.' Hampton patted her knee.

'Huh, proves how much attention you pay. McGee's the geek, not Gibbs.'

'What?' Stephen looked from one to the other, wondering if this was a new code.

'*NCIS*. Great show. Don't worry,' Maggie grinned, 'Io will have you watching TV in no time.'

Yet again, Stephen found a conversation interrupted by a mental message. '*Coiremir? It's Kimberley Gaines. Are you able to make our meeting, or should I go?*'

'Do you guys ever get to finish a conversation?' Stephen said as he stood.

'You get really good at continuing them after long gaps,' Maggie said.

Stephen shook his head as he transferred. Kimberley Gaines was standing near the door of his office, facing the centre of the room. Stephen walked toward her with a smile.

'Kimberley, my apologies for my tardiness.'

'No need to apologise, Coiremir, I understand you have duties to fulfil.' She lifted her hand for the greeting and, as Stephen touched her, a chill ran through his body.

'*Hampton.*'

'*Yes?*'

'*Kimberley Gaines is here, and she's been in contact with the texts.*'

He felt a shimmer in the energy of the room and knew Hampton was appearing behind him. Kimberley looked over Stephen's shoulder with a surprised glance. 'Sabhamir, good —' She froze in a plume of Hampton's black power, and stood before Stephen like a statue.

Hampton strode forward and put his hand on Kimberley's shoulder. 'It's the texts,' he said. 'We need to secure her and then search her home. I'll take her down to the cells. Call the others here, and then transfer over to Kimberley's home.' Hampton and the teacher disappeared.

Kimberley lived in a small cottage on the edge of Sclossin, with an overgrown garden of flowers and a fabulous view over the peat bogs that stretched from this edge of town into the dim distance.

Stephen didn't immediately feel any darkness as he stood in her loungeroom. They all turned to Sarah, who was the most senior guardian present.

'Spread out,' she said. 'We need to scour every part of this place. I'll take the laboratory. Owen, you do the kitchen. Kenyon, search the garden. Maggie, the bedroom and Stephen, remain here.'

'I don't think it's a good idea to search individually,' Owen said. 'We are talking about the Forbidden Texts here. They could well be too dangerous for one of us to handle on our own.'

'I agree,' Maggie said.

'We don't have time to stand here arguing,' Sarah said. 'I am the Heasimir, do as I say.'

Stephen frowned and was about to say she didn't have the power to tell them what to do when Hampton appeared. 'Right, Kimberley's secured and the stillness resolution means she's no threat for now. We need to go over this place as carefully as possible. Don't just look for the Forbidden Texts — Ken's been quite clear he doesn't sense them working here in Sclossin. We might need instead the clue as to where she has been using them. In pairs. Owen, you go with Sarah. Ken, take Maggie. Stephen, come with me. We'll take the laboratory. Be careful, everyone, and use as little power as possible so we don't trigger the texts.'

Throughout Hampton's small speech, Sarah's expression had got darker and darker.

'Out into the garden, Sarah.' Owen smiled. 'It will take us hours to get through all that growth if we can't just blast it away.'

Stephen waited for Sarah to refuse, but instead she spun on her heel and stomped out of the house. Owen winked and followed.

Stephen and Hampton went into Kimberley's laboratory, which was just off the loungeroom and next to the bedroom. It was incredibly neat, and everything was in perfect rows and labelled.

'Now this isn't a surprise,' Hampton said, looking around. 'Kimberley's always struck me as being a bit anal.'

'That could make it harder for us to find anything, if she's cleaned it all up properly,' Stephen said.

'On the other hand, she might have recorded everything. Let's get cracking.' Hampton walked over to the shelves and started to pull books down.

Stephen shrugged and went over to the bench to start testing everything for the now-familiar darkness.

Ione stood at the door of the room, her hands clenched and pressed against her chest. She wanted to walk in, but she was scared. She couldn't see Mark's face — her mother was blocking the view.

She had hoped to see her brother, try to explain, before she had to face her parents as well. But in this, as in everything lately, she was destined to be thwarted.

She swallowed, and stepped into the room.

'Hi.'

Her parents spun around. Her mother's face was pale, her father's flushed. They didn't say a word, just stared at her as though she were a stranger.

It hurt.

'Is Mark OK?' Ione tilted her head to look at her brother.

He was awake, and his eyes were narrowed at her. 'Fat lot you care.'

Tears welled in her eyes and she fought them down. 'I do,' she whispered.

'Ione, Mark tells us you did this to him.'

Ione looked at her father and nodded. 'I'm sorry.'

'How?' Gerry shook his head. 'How could you do this? You don't have access to your power.'

'He's changed her,' Mark cut in. 'I told you he was bad news.'

'Not Stephen. The Forbidden Texts.'

Her mother gasped. 'Is this because of Brian Mochrie?'

'Actually, the guardians don't know. They don't think so. But something's working on me, and now I have power. A lot, actually.'

Her father held out his hand. Gratefully, Ione took it. He looked down at their clasped hands, then at her face with a frown. 'I can feel it. There's a lot there. I'd say you're now as powerful as a sixth order.'

Ione considered whether to tell them about being a lodestone, and decided against it. This was a difficult enough concept for them to deal with. 'That's what the Garramir thinks too. I'm staying with Stephen until they can work out what's happening to me, and what it means. He's helping me learn to control it.'

'I bet he is,' Mark snorted.

'Mark, be quiet,' their mother said. Then she looked at Ione. 'And how did you manage to throw Mark through a wall?'

Ione winced. 'I've known the push incantation since I was a teenager. I use it against Mark all the time, as a way of relieving frustration when he's being a dickhead. I just did it again, not thinking that with power ...' She closed her eyes and shuddered. 'I could have killed him.'

Gerry put his arms around her. 'You weren't to know you could do that, Ione.'

'Hang on, you're going to just forgive her?'

Ione hoped so, although she could understand Mark's annoyance with the idea.

'It was an innocent mistake, Mark, and you'll be fine. Although I daresay you've both learnt the importance of not taking power for granted,' Harriet said. Ione nodded her head against her father's chest.

'Innocent,' Mark snorted again. Ione felt her temper rise.

'If you weren't such a dick, I wouldn't have done it,' she muttered. Her father squeezed her gently, a sign to her to be quiet. She fully intended to, but then Mark spoke.

'Mam, can you do me a favour?'

'I'll try.' Harriet leant over and stroked a lock of dark hair from his forehead.

'Contact the caelleach and tell him I want to begin proceedings to have Jack put into my custody.'

'What?' Harriet and Gerry looked at each other.

'Can it, Mark,' Ione growled. 'The bardria will never take Jack from me to give to you. Especially when he's on the verge of living in a two-parent household.' She looked at her parents. 'Stephen and I are together now, and we're determined to create a stable family for Jack.'

Gerry frowned. 'Are you sure that's a good idea? With everything that's been going on, maybe you and Stephen should wait a while.'

She noted with relief that he didn't say she and Stephen shouldn't be together at all. 'I don't want to waste time, Dad. We've lost two guardians recently — I can't risk missing out on being with him.' Then she looked at Mark. 'And that's my heart talking, not my body.'

'Ione.' Her mother shook her head.

'Talk to Mark. He's the one who was threatening to take Jack away from me 'cause I was obsessed with sex.'

Both her parents frowned at Mark. 'Why would you do that?' Harriet said. 'Ione's a wonderful mother, and always puts Jack's needs first.'

'You haven't seen the way she sniffs around this Stephen.'

'Ione's entitled to happiness, like anyone is, and if

Stephen makes her happy and Jack's OK with it, why shouldn't we be?'

Mark looked at Ione and she saw the fear in his eyes. He thought she'd tell their parents the truth. She considered it for a moment then pushed it aside. She'd already hurt him enough. She shook her head. Mark's shoulders slumped. 'I guess,' he muttered.

Ione smiled. Maybe Mark would never understand, but she could see she had her parents' full support, and they'd help keep Mark under control. She leant over and kissed her father's cheek. 'Thank you.' Then she looked at Mark. 'I really am sorry I hurt you.'

Mark flushed but didn't refuse her apology. She took that as a sign that maybe they could reconcile.

Hampton spun around with a small notebook in his hand. 'Look what I found in the cover of a very well-used educational text.'

Stephen walked over and put his hand out toward it. 'I can't really sense darkness here.'

'It's not one of the texts, but notes that she's written.' Hampton flipped it open. 'Ah, interesting. This is theory, rather than any actual conjurations.'

'But it is about the Forbidden Texts?'

'Oh yes,' Hampton said softly as his eyes skimmed over the page. 'Yes, this is stuff that no one I know has ever thought of before.'

'Except someone did,' Stephen said. Hampton looked up with a grin.

'True. I'll have a look through it to see if there are any clues as to what she's been doing, or where. I'd suggest you keep searching the bookshelf.' Hampton walked over to a chair and sat down to read.

Stephen pulled every book off the shelf, flicked through it and gave it a shake to make sure nothing was hidden in it.

'*Nothing in the kitchen or bedroom,*' Kenyon said mentally. '*Maggie and I are in the loungeroom now, but I'm not confident of finding anything here either.*'

'*We've not found anything outside yet,*' Owen said.

'*We've found a notebook, but no sign of darkness,*' Stephen said.

Hampton snorted and then stood, closing the notebook with a snap. '*This isn't where she did most of the work, that's clear. The texts themselves certainly aren't here.*'

'*I'll tell you what is here,*' Owen said. '*Some lollies.*'

Hampton shook his head. '*It's time to question Kimberley herself. All guardians, to my office.*'

Everyone but Hampton arrived in the office. He appeared a few moments later with Kimberley. She was sitting on a chair, utterly still, her hands lying on her lap. Hampton placed her in the middle of the room and released the stillness resolution.

'What is this?' She looked around, her eyes wide. 'What are you all doing here?'

Hampton crouched down in front of her and smiled. Stephen found the protector's lack of obvious authority interesting.

'Kimberley, my apologies if our actions have scared you. However, we've got some concerns that we need to discuss with you. Now, I'm sure I'm right in saying that you're second order. Is that correct?'

Kimberley blinked and nodded. 'That's correct. I did attempt the third-order test, but I failed.'

'That was fifteen years ago?'

'That's right.'

'And you've not attempted to go any further, or do any training?'

She flushed, and Stephen saw the value in Hampton's approach. The truth of Kimberley would be slowly revealed without backing her into a corner that would force her to stop talking to defend herself.

'I've not resat the test, no.'

'But you've worked to develop your skills? I would imagine that as a teacher, you'd want to stay ahead of your students.' Hampton smiled.

'Of course,' Kimberley murmured.

'Tell me some of the texts that you've been using as part of your studies.'

Kimberley's eyes started to track around the room. She met Stephen's gaze and he could see the confusion and concern building.

'Have I done something wrong?' she said.

Stephen walked forward, shaking his head. 'We don't believe so, Kimberley, but we need to be clear on what's happening with gadda at the moment. Please, tell us some of the books you've been using.'

'The usual,' she said, looking back at Hampton. '*The Power Theory* and *Concentration and Growth* and I've done quite a bit of work with *Transference*.'

'With a tutor?' Hampton said.

'Yes.' Kimberley looked around again.

'Who?' Stephen said.

'Some of my fellow teachers.' Evasively.

'It's wonderful, isn't it, working with other teachers?' Maggie launched into the conversation. 'That was one of my favourite things, the professional development days. You get a lot of inspiration from just talking with other professionals.'

'Indeed.' Kimberley smiled at Maggie, obviously comfortable with this topic. 'There are ideas you can get from gadda in your field that you can't get from others. They don't understand the nuances.'

'So you've been working on your power with other teachers,' Hampton said.

Kimberley's eyes widened, and then she slammed her mouth shut. It was clear to Stephen they'd got as far as they could with the soft approach.

Obviously Hampton thought so as well. He stood and looked down at Kimberley. 'Kimberley, the guardians have searched your home and we have found evidence that you have been using the Forbidden Texts. This is your chance to reduce your sentence.'

Owen stepped forward and put his hands on either side of Kimberley's face. She fought him, staring at the other guardians with confusion, but eventually she succumbed.

'Tell us about the Forbidden Texts.'

'I don't know anything about the Forbidden Texts.'

'You have been using them. We can feel them on you.'

'No.' Her head was swinging from guardian to guardian, as if she had no control. 'I've not been using them. I swear.'

'We have been to your home. We've seen it, Kimberley. Tell us the truth, and we can help you.'

'I don't have the Forbidden Texts.' Tears began to stream down Kimberley's face. 'I don't know what you found, but it's not real. It's not right. I don't have them. I've never touched them. I never would. You have to believe me.'

'Kimberley.' Hampton's voice was quiet yet every person there turned to look at him. 'I don't want to hurt you by doing a mind-read on you while you're so emotional. Now, either you tell us the truth, or we'll keep you here until you're calm enough for us to read.'

Kimberley began to sob. 'I am telling you the truth. I am. Why won't you believe me?'

Owen's voice echoed in their minds. *'She believes what she's saying. For her, it is the truth.'*

'Is that because she convinced herself it would be, to survive this interview, or because it really is?' Hampton said.

'You know I can't tell you that sort of thing without a mind-read and you're right, she's too emotional for that right now. I will say that it takes a remarkable person to believe something that is false so completely that it reads as truth to me.'

'Are you asking the right questions?' The Heasimir cut in.

Stephen saw Hampton's back stiffen and his voice was curt as he said, *'I'll try another tack.'*

'Kimberley, tell me where you've been for the past forty-eight hours.'

Kimberley took a deep, shuddering breath. 'This morning I was teaching, until I came to see the Coiremir. Yesterday and the day before, I spent the entire day teaching. After each day, I went home and I didn't leave the house until I went to work again the following day.'

'Can Helen back up that you were home and you didn't leave?'

Kimberley nodded. 'She can.'

'Did you spend any time in your laboratory on either of those evenings?'

'On Tuesday night, yes. One of the children had asked a curly question about some of the tasks required to reach sixth order, and I did some research and practised a couple of them. The story of what our new Coiremir was doing has inspired lots of children to try to be the best gadda they can be.'

Stephen felt some reaction to the compliment was due, so he bowed his head to her. He tried not to feel too pleased about it. After all, it could be a ploy to gain his sympathy.

Hampton asked her more questions about what was in her lab, and she answered them calmly and with an air of accuracy.

Owen confirmed it. '*All truth,*' he said.

'*So, does she actually have the texts and is she trying to pull the wool over our eyes, or has someone set her up?*' Maggie said.

'*Do any of us know Kimberley well? Does she strike us as being the type who would take the texts?*' Kenyon asked.

'*I wouldn't have suspected her,*' Hampton said. '*I've never noted anything extraordinary about her in any way.*'

'*Her health and power have always been fine,*' Sarah said.

'*Until today.*' Stephen's mind went to another woman whose power had suddenly been affected. If Kimberley has been using the Forbidden Texts, would her power be affected like Ione's had been?

'*I feel darkness, but no increase of power in her,*' Hampton said.

'*So not like Sean either,*' Maggie said.

Hampton looked over his shoulder at her. '*No, not like Sean. More like Brian Mochrie.*' He looked back at Kimberley.

'Tell me about the group of teachers you've been working with,' he asked Kimberley.

The tears, which had stopped, began to flow again. 'We share ideas and experiments in order to develop our own power, so we can teach the children better.' She looked at Stephen. 'It's not that we're not worthy to be teachers. We want to be better ones.'

'A sound aim, I think,' he said. She smiled, a watery smile. 'Who are the teachers?'

She gave a list of a dozen men and women. Stephen had spoken to all the women, and none of them had been dark in any way.

'This isn't making sense,' Maggie said. *'With every passing moment, I'm becoming more convinced she isn't the one.'*

'The only way we'll know for certain is to mind-read her,' Hampton said. *'I'll put her in one of the bardria guest rooms tonight so she can calm down. The rest of us should rest.'*

Stephen didn't need to be told twice. He bowed to the rest of the guardians and then transferred to his apartment.

Ione wasn't in the loungeroom, although the smell of something cooking in the kitchen told him she'd been busy. He started down the hallway, and noticed the door to the laboratory was ajar.

He went over and pushed it open. Ione was sitting at the table against the far wall, bent over a laptop computer. She spun around and smiled. 'Hi.' She joined him, put her arms around his neck and kissed him.

Stephen wrapped his arms around her waist and crushed her against him. Her power flowed up and over him, and it was sweeter and more potent than anything he'd ever felt. Star, kissing her before had been wonderful, but now she had power ...

His own responded and touched Ione's and then passion exploded. Her arousal was instant and his body reacted, hardening, ready to push inside her.

Ione moaned and started to rub herself against him, and he realised that her new power was overwhelming her and she was losing control.

As incredible as this felt, it wasn't right for her. Stephen gathered his own power, his determination, and somehow he managed to pull away from her.

She frowned up at him. 'Well, I thought it was a nice way to greet you after what was probably a hard day.'

'Very nice, and when you've got better control over your power, I'll insist on being greeted that way.'

Her face paled. 'Star, I'd forgotten.' Tears started in her eyes.

He pulled her back against him, pushing her cheek to his chest and kissing the top of her head. 'I'm glad you did. You can't do anything about it right now, and so worrying all day would have been pointless.'

'But how could I forget that I almost killed my brother?' She began to shake. 'What kind of woman am I?'

'One who's had a hell of a lot to deal with lately and is coping the best she can with it.' Stephen rubbed his hand up and down her back. 'Don't be too hard on yourself, Ione. It happened because we misjudged your power. But you're going to get control over it and, once you do, that will never happen again, 'cause you won't let it.'

'Damn right I won't,' she sniffed.

Stephen smiled. 'Now, did I smell something fabulous cooking?'

'Maggie brought over some supplies earlier.'

'I hope you cooked a lot: I'm starving.' Stephen kissed her hair again, then started to guide her toward the kitchen. 'This has, in many ways, been a crap day.'

'Do you want to talk about it?' Ione said.

Stephen thought, and decided he really didn't. Ione had enough to cope with at the moment, and just being with her was all the comfort he now needed. 'No, but thanks for the offer.'

'Any time.'

So as they ate, they talked about other things, such as Ione's computer work and how they were going to decorate the apartment.

'We can just transfer Jack's room from my place,' Ione said, putting a forkful of sausage bake into her mouth.

It was time to talk practicalities. He put his fork down and looked at Ione. 'Exactly how is this going to work?' he said. 'Am I going to be Jack's father now?'

Ione put her fork down as well. 'Well, no, I guess not. I mean, this is a commitment, and Jack's part of it, but at the same time he's had no say in the relationship and I don't think we can force anything on him.'

'So take Jack's lead?'

'I guess so. Without letting him dictate entirely, of course.' She pulled her lower lip in between her teeth.

Stephen reached across and put his hand on hers. 'He's a good kid, Ione, and I'm looking forward to having him here.'

'Well, he's already comfortable with you, so it shouldn't be too hard.'

'Then we'll work on your control after dinner, and maybe we'll be able to fetch him first thing in the morning.' He grinned. 'Besides, I believe there were going to be incentives for me training you.'

She looked at him blankly for a moment, then her mouth spread in a wicked smile and her eyes began to twinkle. 'Oh, yes, there certainly will be. So eat up, Coiremir. You'll need your strength.'

Stephen saw the promise of pleasure in her eyes, gulped and the concerns of the day finally stripped away.

TWENTY-EIGHT

After the constant swing of emotions of the past few days, Ione wasn't surprised at how quickly she descended into irritation once she and Stephen started working on control.

She'd forgotten that her lack of skill had also played a part in her failures thus far, and had thought it would only take a few minutes to gain enough control to get Stephen into bed, where they both belonged.

By the time an hour had passed, and she hadn't successfully completed one of the tasks Stephen set her, she was a seething mass of frustrated desire and power.

'Damn it, why is it so bloody hard?' She kicked out at the leg of the table in the laboratory and barely missed it. 'Why can't I do this?'

'The more emotional you get, the harder it will be.' Stephen sat in a lounge chair at the end of the room, his hands resting on his thighs. His expression and his voice were calm. 'I've still got a number of activities to try. We just haven't found the right one to start you off on yet.'

'But I should be able to do these. They're basic.' She paced from one side of the room to the other.

'You haven't learnt to use your power yet. Once you do, I'm sure you'll be able to do those activities. Now,

I want you to stop and centre. Meditate on your power for a few minutes and control yourself. Then we'll try again.'

'Better bloody work,' Ione muttered as she stopped in the middle of the room and closed her eyes. She tried to blank out her thoughts, to focus on her power, but she couldn't. Why wasn't she able to do this? She wasn't stupid. She'd done a lot of study in her time, knew pretty well how power worked, how it should be working for her. But each time she tried to use it, either it wouldn't react or it would flare up and she'd stamp it back down before it could flood from her control again.

She clenched her fists. Every time she went near her power, she could see Mark lying on the floor of the corridor, all but dead. She was scared that it would happen again, and that this time it might be Stephen that she hurt.

Her stomach roiled, her heart thudded. She opened her eyes and looked at Stephen.

'I can't do it. I can't calm down. I'm scared.'

'Come here,' he said. She went over and curled up against his chest. Here, close to him, she felt safe.

'What are you scared of?' He stroked his hand up and down her back, an action that was both soothing and stimulating.

'That it will escape my control and I'll hurt someone again.'

'You've already got basic control, Ione. You've got a grip on it. It can't ever escape you like that again, not without you intending it to. And you can also shut it down as quickly as you need to.'

'What if I can't?' She hated the quiver in her voice. She hated feeling like this. It was so unlike her.

'I think we need to prove to you that you can.' Stephen shifted her and she had to stand. Then he turned her around to face the far wall and stood behind her. He put his hands on her shoulders and whispered in her ear.

'I want you to have a go at firing all the power you can at the wall, and then try to stop it. Don't hold back.'

Ione frowned. 'I'll damage the wall.'

'I doubt it. This is the laboratory of a guardian, it's stronger than just about any other room in the world. And if you do, then we'll just fix it. Go on.'

Ione wrung her hands. 'What if it bounces back and —'

Stephen leant close enough that she could feel his hot breath against her neck. It sent shivers down her spine. 'If you can't do this, then I don't see how we're ever going to be able to have sex again.' Then he pressed his lips just under her ear, and the simple touch sent her temperature soaring.

'Right.' She lifted her hands and held them palm out toward the wall.

'Give it everything you've got for two counts, and then stop it.' His voice was husky and his power moved against hers, just enough to announce his growing arousal.

Taking a deep breath, she grabbed hold of her power and shot it against the wall. It flamed out, a blazing orange trail that hit the plaster with such force she felt the floor under her feet shudder. That terrified her, and she slammed down on her power, cutting the stream short.

'Fuck.'

Stephen squeezed her shoulders. 'A little faster than I suggested, but still you did it. You released your power, and then you stopped it. You do have control.'

'I do.' She spun around and looked up at him, eyes shining. 'I do have control.'

He grinned down at her. 'Indeed you do. Now, let's

try this next exercise, and see if we can get onto the more pleasurable part of the evening.'

It was simple — he wanted her to send her power out in a stream that passed through a circle without touching it. The circle of brown power that he formed hung in the air a couple of metres in front of her, chest height. It was a metre wide.

Ione took hold of her power and sent it out in a stream that only measured about ten centimetres in width, right through the middle of the circle and to the wall on the other side.

'Good. Now, try to expand it, so it's only just a little smaller than the circle,' Stephen said.

Ione chewed on her lip and slowly thickened the stream until it was about ninety centimetres wide.

'Good. Now, I'm going to start making the circle smaller. Let's see how small you can go.'

Ione saw the circle shift and immediately drew her power down to half, so there was a huge gap between it and Stephen's.

'Try to finesse it,' he murmured, pulling his circle in until it was just a few centimetres from hers. 'Try to move it with mine.'

His shifted and she tried not to panic, but to make the circumference of her stream of power smaller in gradual increments. She watched them both decrease, Stephen's sometimes getting a little close to hers and causing her heartbeat to increase, but she just pulled her power back a step or two more without panicking.

Finally, Stephen's circle was just five centimetres, and her stream was sitting well inside it.

'Now, drop your power, count to ten, then try to recreate it within my smaller circle.'

Ione pulled back the orange stream and counted slowly to ten, her eyes never leaving Stephen's circle. Then she pulled on her power and sent it out again.

It passed neatly through the centre of the circle, and she smiled. 'I did it.'

'You certainly did. Now, let's try some of the other exercises that you failed earlier.'

Two of them she still couldn't do, but the other two she managed; although the piece of paper that she lifted up was a little crumpled when she put it back down.

Finally, Stephen nodded at her. 'Not bad. I think you're probably safe enough to let out into society.'

Ione turned around to thank him, but all thoughts were wiped from her mind when she saw the heat in his eyes. She smiled, and walked over to him, swinging her hips.

'I think I need a reward for all my hard work, don't you?' she purred, pressing herself against him and winding her arms around his neck.

'Absolutely.' He bent, put his arms under her thighs and swept her up against his chest. 'I think we both do.'

Ione kissed him and felt her power respond and decided that this was going to be a magical night.

As Ione swept her fingernails up Stephen's side and felt a corresponding flash of pleasure in his power, she wondered how the gadda weren't constantly in bed. If this was what having sex was like when you were in full control of your power, how could you resist it?

Being able to feel every nuance of Stephen's arousal and pleasure was the most powerful aphrodisiac she'd ever known. So much so, that she'd made him put his hands behind his head and forbade him from touching her so she could focus on how incredible it was to know exactly what she was doing to him.

She'd discovered that Stephen liked being touched. It didn't matter where she stroked him — arms, legs, face, chest — every touch was matched with a pulse of his power. He was particularly sensitive in the curves of his body — where his neck and shoulder joined; just above his armpit; the dip at the top of his thigh; the back of his knee.

Before, spending time touching a man anywhere but his penis had been about her pleasure. Now, it was solely about driving Stephen mad with delight.

So she was taking her time — even though her own body was tingling with need. There was a part of her mind begging her to give it up and just lift herself and sink down onto him and then ride him until she was fulfilled. She was keeping that part of her mind at bay, but every passing minute it was getting harder.

She stroked her finger back down his side, and at the same time leant forward and dragged her teeth across his distended nipple. The roar of his power was almost overpowering, and she barely heard his groaned, 'Ione.'

She lifted her head and looked at him and her control over her desire slipped. Every muscle in his face was drawn tight, his eyes were burning and he was panting.

'Are you trying to kill me?'

'Of course not.' She grazed her teeth over the edge of his chin. He liked that too. 'You being dead would quite ruin my plans.'

'Then have mercy.'

Her body clenched in agreement and she decided that as nice as this was, it was time for it to get even nicer. So she lifted herself and turned around. With one hand on his thigh, she used her other hand to hold his penis and then lowered herself onto him.

She'd thought over the past few days that she'd remembered how incredible it felt to have Stephen inside her, but this moment was far beyond her memories. He stretched her, filling her so completely that she couldn't imagine anything more perfect than this.

Then she started to move on him, squeezing with her internal muscles as she lifted and then lowered herself, and realised the perfection was only just beginning.

'Star above.' Stephen grabbed hold of her waist and began to guide her. 'Your power ...'

Ione put her hands on his thighs. 'I know,' she gasped.

Her power was rubbing against his with the same cadence as their bodies. Tiny shivers ran over Ione's skin, each signalling that breaking moment of ecstasy but not taking over. Instead, the intensity of her power mating with Stephen's lifted the pleasure to heights she'd never known before.

There was nothing but the slide of Stephen's penis, dragging sweet delight up and down the walls of her slick channel.

'Stephen.' The word came out as a choked sob. Star above but she wanted to come. Needed to.

His hands tightened on her hips and he thrust hard and her power broke into orgasm. It felt as though a star were exploding within her, sending her into a quiet part of space where for that second she knew nothing but the supreme satisfaction her body was experiencing.

It was almost a surprise to snap back to the moment and feel Stephen beneath and within her, still moving. His power swamped her and she arched her back, grinding herself down onto him.

He shouted and thrust his hips against hers and she felt him pour into her, and as their powers met and melded she came again.

She collapsed back against his chest, panting, shivers running through her body. She could feel the same reaction in Stephen. He was barely able to say the words to ensure she wasn't impregnated.

After a while, she was aware of a strange sense of satisfaction filling her. Not strange in that she'd never felt it before — this was to her mind almost the best part of sex — but strange because it wasn't coming from her alone.

She turned her head and looked at Stephen. So this was it — the much-vaunted gadda connection. The moment when sated lovers' power enabled them to sense each other's emotions.

Stephen opened one eye and looked at her lazily. 'Something surprising you?'

She blinked, then realised he was feeling her emotions. 'I've heard about it, but never felt it.'

'What?' He lifted her and turned her over so she was resting more comfortably on him.

'The way gadda can feel each other after sex.'

He opened both his eyes. 'I didn't realise that you couldn't.'

She shook her head. 'You know, all those years that I thought not having power didn't matter —' She stopped as a lump formed in her throat. 'Shit.'

Stephen wrapped his arms around her and hugged her to his chest. 'It's going to be OK.'

'I know.' She blinked her eyes to stop the tears welling. 'But when I think of the things I missed out on ...'

'Like with your husband?'

That brought the thought she was trying to hide from straight to the front of her mind, and Ione burst into tears.

Stephen rolled onto his side and cradled her against him, holding her face to his chest while Ione sobbed out her regret. It had been hard enough to say goodbye to Patrick when he'd died, but now knowing what they should have experienced and hadn't brought the pain back again.

'Why did he love me?' she sobbed. 'When he could have had this with another woman, why did he stay with me?'

'Because you are you,' Stephen crooned in her ear. 'Because you're strong, and smart, and passionate, and loving, and kind, and caring, and a mean cook.'

She laughed and then choked a bit as she tried to stop laughing. Stephen rubbed her back.

'There's no way Patrick could have not loved you, and not wanted to spend the rest of his life with you. Just like me.'

Ione lifted her head to look at him through her tears. He was smiling, but more than that she could feel his happiness and love. She pressed her hand against his cheek, wondering how she'd been lucky enough to find this twice in her life.

TWENTY-NINE

The siren clanging in his head shocked Stephen out of his doze. He looked down at Ione, whose head was resting on his chest, her body pressed against his. There was a moment of simple awe as he looked at her and recalled their time together — the intensity of their lovemaking, the pure joy of feeling her love afterward.

She was his.

Then he pulled his mind to the present. He'd been woken by Hampton, and that probably meant it was bad news. He kissed Ione on the forehead and started to ease her head from his shoulder to the pillow, hoping not to wake her.

Her eyes popped open. 'Where do you think you're going?' She smiled up at him, a wonderful mix of sleepiness and naughtiness.

'Sorry.' He kissed her lips. 'Much as I would probably really like what you're thinking, I have to go.' He got up and started gathering his clothes from their various spots on the floor around the bed.

Ione sat up. 'Something wrong?'

'The Sabhamir's called, and since he gave us the night off, he wouldn't have woken me if it wasn't big.' He started to pull his clothes on.

He felt a wave of fear wash over him and looked up. Ione smiled, but it wasn't quick enough to hide the initial concern on her face.

'Good luck,' she said.

He put a knee on the bed and leant forward to put his hands to her face. 'You don't have to hide your worries from me, Ione.'

'Worried? I'm not –' She screwed up her nose. 'Hmm, maybe this connection isn't so good after all.'

It occurred to Stephen that if something was going to happen, he didn't want Ione feeling it. But he had no idea how to stop it. 'I'm going to be fine.'

'I know.' Her feelings said she didn't.

He kissed her. 'I'll be back before you know it.' He pulled back, put on the rest of his clothes and transferred.

He followed the trail left by Hampton's summons, and was amazed to find that he didn't appear in the Sabhamir's office. Instead, he stood in the middle of a street on the edge of Sclossin. He recognised it as Howarth Lane, which led directly from the centre of town, past rows of houses and out into the country, eventually joining up with a road that led to Drumdart.

He stood just a block from where the houses ceased, and green paddocks dotted with cows and sheep began. Just half a kilometre out of town was the beginning of a series of bogs.

He was surprised to see that there were lights on in all the houses, and that people were milling around in their front yards.

Then a shrill, inhuman scream echoed through the night, sending a shiver down his spine. He spun around and started to march down the road toward the countryside. That scream had sounded like it came from just outside the village.

Another scream, and Stephen fancied it was a call to war, an invitation to attack. He started to run.

Over the roof of the last house, he saw a stream of white flash into the sky. The power of the Heasimir. Seconds later, Hampton's voice rang through his head. '*Stephen, hurry.*'

He ran past the last house, and stopped by the stone wall that marked the border between the town and the countryside. In the middle of the field stood the other five guardians, and looming over them was a dark shadow. Only the immense size and a vague sense of shape were discernible in the darkness.

There's something familiar about it, Stephen thought as he started across the grass. Its body was that of a horse, but there were three heads ...

Fatharr.

Stephen stared up at the incongruity of Ione's giant monster standing in a field on the outskirts of Sclossin. For a moment he couldn't move and was pinned to the spot by the question – how the hell had it got here?

As he watched his fellow guardians shoot their power up at the creature, the stench hit him – at first a strong watery smell, and then it became sour and mouldy and he felt unclean.

Fatharr reeled back from the blasts of power, roared and then kicked out at them. The guardians ducked, Kenyon flinging himself onto the ground to avoid a blow. Hoofs pounded into the dirt and the ground shook.

Stephen raced in behind the attack and stopped next to Maggie. 'What the fuck?'

'Fatharr,' she yelled back at him. 'Don't try the Wanton attack. It's just bouncing off him.'

'I meant what the fuck is it doing here?'

'Forbidden Texts.'

The monster screamed and then lashed out with a hoof toward them, but it missed. Stephen saw the others lift their hands and he did the same.

'Hextable Crusher,' Hampton shouted. 'Now.'

Stephen called the incantation to mind and then shot his power out at the monster, aiming for where he imagined the creature's heart would be, metres above his head. He felt his power hit, felt it absorb, but then he lost it.

'Damn.' He pulled back before he gave the creature too much.

'It just sucked that in,' Owen yelled. 'That one gives it power.'

They all ducked another kick and, by the time they'd regained their balance, saw the monster had taken a couple of steps and was now going past them and toward Sclossin. Every thud of a hoof on the ground shook Stephen's legs.

'Aim for the ground,' Hampton yelled. Six bolts of power flooded out and thumped into the dirt. The earth shuddered, and then a forest of grass and weeds rose fifty metres into the air in between Fatharr and the village.

The monster roared and the sound vibrated through Stephen's bones. It whipped out with its wiry horse's tail and again, the guardians were diving for cover, strands of wet-smelling hair flying over their heads. Stephen heard a deep thud and looked up to see the creature kicking their wall of plants. Leaves were flung several metres and fluttered down to the ground, a delicate response to a violent act.

'It's going to get through.' Stephen scrambled to his feet.

'Then we make it bigger and stronger,' Hampton said. 'Harder. Ready?'

Even as he spoke, the monster surged forward, broke through the hedge and placed a huge foot down on the Sclossin wall, crushing the metre-high, metre-wide stone construction as though it were made of paper.

'Fuck.' Hampton started to run, firing his power at the monster. Stephen and the others followed. The monster stopped and turned to face them, but in the process one hind hoof slammed a house, turning what had undoubtedly been a centuries-old stone and wood cottage into rubble.

'We need to get people out,' Maggie shouted.

'I've spoken to the caelleach. He's ordered all gadda in this part of Sclossin into the bardria building,' Hampton said.

'So as long as we can keep this from there, it will be fine,' Owen panted.

Stephen doubted that *fine* would ever be a word used to describe this night. He looked up at Fatharr, getting his first clear view as the moon shone on its faces. The two side heads were snakes — slits for eyes, forked tongues sliding out between pointed teeth. The middle face was a lizard's — it had a flat snout and a round, thick tongue. The eyes on this face were the strange part — round, yellow, more cat-like than lizard.

In Ione's movie, those eyes winked after dispatching a baddie. Stephen wondered if this Fatharr would wink if it killed one of them.

The monster lifted its foot and lunged forward to place it right on top of the guardians' heads. A quick transference got them out of the way of danger, but not before Stephen felt the rush of the hoof over his head. He felt Maggie grab hold of his arm as the earth shook from the impact of foot on ground.

'Try Jermanti,' Hampton shouted. This incantation was designed to smother the opponent by ridding the air around them of oxygen.

Stephen pulled the spell forward and fired it up at Fatharr's main head, and saw the others doing the same.

'Different heads,' screamed Maggie. Some of the power shifted.

It felt good, Stephen thought. It felt like it was working. But the monster simply tried to stamp them out of existence again and didn't appear to be struggling for breath at all.

'It's not alive.' Stephen looked at the Heasimir and was surprised to see even she looked worried. 'It's not like any other created monster I've seen.'

'That rules out most of the incantations we have available to us,' Hampton said.

'Now what? We have to protect the town.' As Maggie spoke, the monster turned, kicked left, then right, and two more homes were destroyed.

'I'm going to put a dome of protection over the first few blocks here,' Hampton yelled. 'That should give us time to work out what to do.' Then he darted forward, aiming for the space directly between the monster's legs.

'Shit.' Owen ran after him, a blue light playing from his hands and over the Sabhamir. Protecting him from the monster, Stephen hoped.

'Draw the monster's attention.' Sarah lifted her hands and shot a stream of white power up at Fatharr. He, Maggie and Kenyon did the same, but that only had the effect of having the monster start to duck and weave, moving his feet and putting Owen and Hampton at even more risk.

Dirt, plants, bits of wood and bricks flew into the air as Fatharr danced and his hoofs clattered around the two guardians. Hampton and Owen swayed and darted around, as if trying to avoid a ram while standing on a mound of jelly.

'*Stop that.*' Hampton's scream reverberated through Stephen's mind.

They pulled back their power; the monster let rip its ear-piercing shriek, and then spun around. Hampton and Owen weaved to avoid the feet, but it took their attention from the work and the monster stomped forward and flattened another couple of houses.

Hampton lifted his hands and streamed power out over the houses near them. Fatharr kicked forward at another house but its foot bounced off a shimmering black barrier. The monster screamed, shaking its heads from side to side while its body trembled. Stephen could hear the frustration in its cry.

Then it lifted a foot to stomp on the house in front of it. Stephen waited for the barrier to stop it, but instead the foot went down and turned the two-storey home to kindling.

Owen turned away as wood flew around Fatharr's legs. Hampton released more power. The monster aimed another kick, which was blocked, but then tried again and another two homes fell.

'*The dome will only hold for one strike,*' Hampton said. '*It must be sucking the power into itself with the first blow and then it's clear to strike again.*'

'Then stop,' Kenyon said. 'We don't want to give it any more power. We need to try to distract it, pull it away from the town.'

'How the hell do we do that?' Stephen said as the creature screamed and destroyed three more homes. It was now standing several hundred metres into the town.

'Another monster.' He looked at Maggie, whose eyes were shining. 'That's what happened in lots of the daikaiju movies.' Obviously Ione had made her watch them too.

'I have an idea.'

Stephen looked over, and saw Hampton and Owen appear in front of them.

'That close, it's easy to see that its made of peat bog,' Hampton said. 'So if we created a giant allphetine ...'

Stephen saw the logic. The allphetine was a creature of fire, and would dry out and maybe even start to burn the peat-bog Fatharr. 'Good idea.'

'But we're going to need a lot of power to do it.' Hampton looked at Stephen. 'We need Ione.'

Stephen shook his head. 'No.'

'Yes.' Maggie stepped forward. 'I know that you don't want to put her in danger and when this is all over, I'll hug and kiss you for it. But if Ione finds out she could have helped, and you didn't ask her, then I'll be hugging and kissing your corpse.'

Kenyon wrinkled his nose. 'Nice image, Mags.'

The ground shook and they all turned to see the monster stomp on another house.

'We don't have time,' Hampton said.

Stephen looked at the creature, silhouetted against the bright circle of the moon. It was going to require power beyond what they had to defeat this monster, and Ione could supply that. But if anything happened to her ...

He looked at Maggie, who put her hand on his arm and smiled at him. She was Ione's best friend — she wouldn't risk her life if there was any alternative.

'Fine, I'll get her.' He closed his eyes, sent up a silent prayer to anyone who might be watching that it would work out, and transferred.

Ione sat on the bed, her legs crossed, hugging the pillow to her chest and thinking that this being connected to someone sucked. She could feel Stephen's worry and terror, and wondered where the hell he was and what he was doing. And wished he'd stop it and come back to her.

She heard the knock at the apartment door like a hammer against her heart. Someone was in the office, wanting Stephen. She scrambled off the bed, pulled her clothes on and answered the door.

To her amazement, Lucas stood on the other side. He lifted his hand and she saw he was holding a bottle of honey bourbon.

'Sucks, doesn't it?' he said. 'I've come to offer my support.'

She realised Lucas was feeling the same things she was — Maggie's emotions during whatever evil it was the guardians were facing. 'I'll get the glasses. Don't have ice, I'm afraid.'

'Right now, getting the alcohol in is the most important part.'

Moments later they sat on the lounge, each holding a glass with about half a cup of bourbon in it. 'Ione, I welcome you to the life of the partner of a guardian. I hope you survive.' He took a huge mouthful.

'This bit is pretty awful.' She took a tentative sip and was surprised at how mellow the brown liquid tasted.

'And this is pretty good. Not a good whiskey, mind you, but still passable.'

'America thanks you for your vote.' He saluted her with his glass.

'So, have you got any idea what's actually going on?'

'Only that it's the texts, and it's something big, and Maggie's half out of her mind.'

'Stephen's not happy either.' She took another sip. 'I wonder if there's a way we can learn to shut this off, during these times. Not permanently, of course.'

'I'll ask Hampton if he knows of any tricks. Perhaps his parents taught him something.'

'Ooh, yeah.' Ione shuddered. 'I mean, think about how scary this must be for a child. You and I are adults, and we're connected, so we kinda know the state of things. But for a little boy or girl, wondering where mammy or daddy is and when they'll get home ...' Her voice petered off. It was a hell of a lot to ask of Jack. Should she reconsider this?

'I don't know. I think police officers' kids and that cope OK. Just tell them it's the job and don't let them in on how dangerous it really is until they can deal.'

'I have to say, the alcohol seems to be dulling things delightfully.' Ione had another sip. 'A genius idea of yours, Dr Valeroso.'

'I must look after the newest member of SuLoG.'

'SuLoG?'

'Surviving Loving a Guardian. I know, not the catchiest title, but I'm sure as the years progress we'll come up with a better one.'

Ione considered decades of feeling like this and shivered. She looked at Lucas and saw the same dread in his eyes. In one motion, they lifted their glasses and swallowed.

'So is being a member of SuLoG just about drinking, or can we distract ourselves as well?'

'I'm open to suggestions.'

'I've got the latest season of *True Blood* on DVD, if you're up for a bit of mystery and vampire porn.'

Lucas blinked. 'Vampire porn?'

Ione grinned. 'My friend, watch and be amazed.'

As they watched the DVD on her computer, Stephen's emotions became background noise and she'd almost relaxed when suddenly, he was standing in the middle of the room.

He looked from her to Lucas and back again with puzzlement on his face. 'What's going on?'

'Star, is it over?' She jumped up and ran to him. 'Is everyone all right?'

'No, not over.' He touched her cheek. 'Excuse me, Lucas, but I need to take Ione with me.'

Now it was Ione who was frowning. 'What?'

'You have to come with me. We need your power.' He looked at Lucas. 'Maggie's fine, but it will take a while. I'd wait for her at your place if I were you.'

'What's going on?'

Stephen put his hands on her shoulders. 'Fatharr is attacking Sclossin.'

'What?' The word echoed through her as they transferred. Then she could see for herself exactly what Stephen was talking about.

She was in a field on the outside of the town, the guardians standing alongside her. There, triumphant in the middle of the desolation that had once been homes just inside the Sclossin wall, was Fatharr. Real to life. Ten storeys tall, thick and greeny-brown, massive hoofs, thick thighs and back, two snake heads and one lizard visage, and a spiked horse's tail. As she watched, the creature lifted a truck-sized foot and slammed it down on another house, reducing it to rubble. Ione felt the ground beneath her tremble and realised this was no movie. Fatharr was real.

'Ione, I need to use you as a lodestone in order to create an allphetine large enough to distract and fight that thing.' The Sabhamir put a hand on her shoulder.

'Of course,' she said.

'Ione.' She looked over her shoulder to see Stephen frowning. 'We don't know what this new power means. If he takes too much ...'

'You'll stop before you get to that, right?' Ione lifted an eyebrow at the Sabhamir.

'You have my word.'

'Then let's do it.' She held out her hand and as she did so, glanced up at moonlit Fatharr. There was a fraction of her that was excited by the fact that she was just metres from a real, living daikaiju. Then she shook her head and put it aside. Excitement needed to be over. She had to help the guardians save the town and destroy the monster.

Then she looked at Sclossin. It seemed to her eye that more than a dozen homes had been destroyed in a path that led directly to the centre of the town. A terrible vision flashed before her and she looked at the Sabhamir.

'No one was in there, were they?'

He shook his head. 'Everyone has been evacuated. We shouldn't lose any lives tonight.'

'No, just homes,' Ione whispered, looking back at the mess. There was going to be heartbreak when the danger was over and the damage revealed.

He took her hand; she closed her eyes and opened up her power.

It flowed from her in a steady stream, and she relaxed

as she realised she wasn't going to feel any pain. Then she started to wait for the tiredness to come upon her.

Time moved on. Heartbeat to heartbeat, breath to breath. She tried to count, to keep track of the seconds, but grew tired of that somewhere in the two hundreds. Minutes passed, yawned out, and yet the tiredness didn't come. Her power continued to flow, and she continued to feel comfortable.

'*You're doing well.*' The Sabhamir's voice sifted into her mind.

'*How are you doing?*'

'*Open your eyes and see.*'

Ione opened her eyes and gasped. A tower of red and orange flame, several storeys high, streamed up from the paddock in front of them. As she watched, the flames wiggled as if alive, and then spread into arms, legs and head.

She'd never seen an allphetine before, but knew from her studies that they were usually no more than a metre high. This oversized version was in a strange way the most beautiful and impressive thing she'd ever seen.

'Mother star.'

'Fatharr hasn't noticed it yet,' Maggie said, standing just behind Ione.

'It needs a call,' Ione said. 'A good old-fashioned allphetine scream.'

'Something like this?' The Garramir opened his mouth and let out a bellowing screech that sent a sharp pain through Ione's ear and echoed across the paddock.

'Next time you do that, warn us,' Stephen said.

'It worked though.'

Ione looked and saw Fatharr had swung its head around to check out the sound. The creature screamed,

Ione shuddered. Fatharr turned and started to lumber toward the allphetine. As it got closer, the sour smell and ground-shaking made Ione regret she'd ever been excited by this. It wasn't fun at all. It was a disaster.

'Right, here goes,' the Sabhamir said. Ione looked at him and saw a fine layer of sweat across his forehead. She didn't think it was from the heat of the monster he had created. 'Fatharr versus fire monster.'

'Doesn't feel right without subtitles,' Maggie said. Ione barked out a laugh, and then blushed when the other guardians all looked at her.

'Now is not the time for joviality, Ceamir,' said the Heasimir.

'Speak for yourself. If I don't find something to laugh about in this, I'm going to cry.'

Fatharr stopped just out of the allphetine's reach and screamed again, then reared up, lashing out at the other creature with its hoofs. The allphetine attempted to catch it, rather than avoid it, and managed to do neither. Fatharr fell down, and a side head crashed into the allphetine, then swept right through it and out the other side, seeming not to damage its opponent at all. Dirt flew into the air, momentarily obscuring the fight.

'Did it work? Did it burn it?'

Ione looked at Fatharr as it staggered back to scream at the allphetine. 'It looks annoyed, not hurt.'

'It's still quite moist, so it's not going to burn straight away,' the Firimir said. 'It will have to dry out before it catches fire.' Ione looked at him with a frown. 'It's made out of peat bog.'

'Then we should have more fire.' Maggie stepped forward, and pointed her hands at the ground. The grass behind Fatharr burst into flames. The other guardians followed suit and soon the monster was surrounded by a ring of fire that lit up the darkness as if it were day.

It was obvious to Ione that Fatharr didn't like that at all. The creature bellowed and screamed and shook and waved its heads. It squeezed its yellow eyes shut and poked its tongue out. Meanwhile, the Sabhamir pressed the attack with the allphetine, rushing at the daikaiju and wrapping itself around the other monster.

Ione felt the drain on her power increase. 'You're taking too much.'

'Not me, the monster.' The Sabhamir pulled the allphetine back. 'I'm really starting to wish I had read the bloody texts, then I'd understand what we're facing and how to deal with it.'

The monsters fell into a dance. Fatharr didn't want to get too close to the flames, so the allphetine couldn't get close enough to inflict serious damage. Minutes crept by, each one dragging out until it felt like an hour.

Then Ione noticed one side of the ring of fire was starting to weaken. She looked at Maggie, and saw her friend's face was drawn and pale.

'Maggie, use me.' She held out her other hand.

Maggie shook her head. 'No, Io. Stephen's right, we don't know what the power will do to you and while I'm sure Ham — the Sabhamir can look after you, I don't think I can.'

'You've done well, Maggie.' The Sabhamir smiled at her.

Maggie nodded, and her fire winked out. Those of the Garramir and Firimir on either side joined up in order to fill the gap. Maggie collapsed onto the grass next to Ione.

'I might be the first, but I won't be the last,' she said. 'How long can we keep this up?'

'We've got several hours before daybreak and we can rely on the sun to help,' the Sabhamir said.

Maggie shook her head. 'We can't manage.' She scrambled to her feet and looked at Ione. 'Think of the movies. Is there something we can do?'

Ione had flashes of scenes from a variety of daikaiju eiga come into her mind, and one stood out. '*Mothra versus Godzilla*. Remember how the baby Mothra wrapped Godzilla up in silk until he couldn't move, and he eventually fell off a cliff into the sea and was defeated?'

'Until the next movie. Funny how many of these monsters did nothing until the next time there were movie cameras around.'

'I wouldn't say things like that when we've got real, live daikaiju thumping around the countryside.' Ione looked at the two giant monsters, lashing out at each other yet hesitating to go in for the kill. The physicality of it all — the way she could feel every thud of a foot on the ground, how the screams reverberated through her — was giving her a headache. 'So maybe we could do the same thing. Create silk rope to bind the creature, then when day dawns it can start drying out until we can burn it.'

'That's it.' Maggie clapped her hands. 'That's what we'll do. We can turn the grass into silk rope and use it to trap Fatharr, and then he can just lie here until the sun comes out and dries him.'

'Can you do that?'

'Absolutely. At least, I think I can. Hang on.' Maggie put her hands down on the ground and focussed her attention on them. Ione flicked her glance between Hampton and the battle between the giant beasts and her friend.

Slowly, a thin string of white appeared between

344

Maggie's fingers. She kept her left hand on the ground and held up the right, and Ione saw a bundle of thin string on it.

'That's not thick enough,' she said.

'I know,' Maggie hissed and Ione noted the strain on her friend's face. It seemed that Maggie was reaching the limits of what she could do, having had this level of power for just a few months.

'I've got an idea.' She looked across at her lover. 'Stephen?'

'Yes?'

'Maggie needs a hand. Can you help her?'

'We can handle this, Stephen.' Ione was surprised that the Sabhamir could follow their conversation while he was working the allphetine.

Stephen stepped away from the fire circle and ran over. 'What is it?'

'Maggie needs this spun into a thick rope. We're going to use it to trap Fatharr.'

'Onto it.' He knelt down next to Maggie. 'You just keep making the stuff, I'll worry about the rope.'

Ione looked up and saw Fatharr step backward and scream as the end of his tail sparked red. Were the flames starting to work?

'OK, let's give this a go.' Stephen stood up, several metres of rope as thick as his thumb looped around his hand. He walked over to the fire, held the rope up and then shot it forward at Fatharr.

The rope passed close to the allphetine and, instantly, it caught on fire. Flames started to dance down toward Stephen and he threw it on the ground so he wouldn't get burnt.

'Fuck,' Maggie said.

'Silk's obviously too flammable,' Ione said.

'Should have fucking known that,' Maggie muttered. 'You don't see the rural fire service running around in silk overalls.' Her face went blank and then she nodded. 'Grandpa says to use wool. And he's making up a synthetic mix to bring over.'

Ione smiled. John O'Hara was not just a sixth-order oman, but a leading chemist and the chancellor of his own university. She didn't doubt his solution would be perfect. 'So, we're going to turn all this grass into wool?'

'Why not go direct to the source?' Maggie said. 'This is Ireland, a farming mecca.' She disappeared.

Fatharr squealed and Ione put her hands over her ears. She looked at the monster and it seemed parts of his neck and tail looked different to the rest – lighter and duller.

'I think the fire's starting to work,' she said.

Stephen looked over his shoulder and nodded. 'We're getting there.'

'But we need that wool,' the Sabhamir said. 'This will take too long and wear us out. If it escaped us, and went back into the town, we might not have the energy to draw it back out again.'

Ione shook, rage growing within her. Damn whoever had the Forbidden Texts. Damn them to the darkest pits.

THIRTY

Maggie returned with a couple of sheep, her hands clenched in their fleece. The moment she released them the animals baaed and tried to run away, but Stephen used the soil to trap them in a pen.

'I'll go get a couple more,' she said and disappeared.

Stephen looked at Ione. 'She is asking for permission, right?'

Ione grinned. 'This is Maggie Shaunessy we're talking about here.'

'Less talk, more action,' Hampton said.

Stephen put his hand on one of the sheep and carried it over to the fire. The poor animal was trembling and he put a stillness resolution on it so it wasn't aware of its surroundings. Then he pushed his power into the wool, disconnecting it from the animal's skin and pulling it into a thick rope.

He threw it at Fatharr. This time, the rope made it past the fiery allphetine and started to wrap around the peat-bog daikaiju's leg.

It took Fatharr a moment to realise what was going on, and then one of the snake heads swooped down to try and get the wool off. That left one side of Fatharr's torso vulnerable, and Hampton focussed the attack of

347

the allphetine there. Fatharr's main face looked from fire beast to its wool-enclosed leg, unsure what to do.

'That's it, keep it up,' Ione cried.

Stephen looked at her. She was glowing, her face alive with wonder and excitement. He couldn't see anything in her that showed she was being tired out or hurt by the continual drain on her power.

Kenyon appeared next to him and approached the other sheep, which was lying on the ground. The Garramir followed Stephen's example and the woollen rope fired at the snake head that had come down to pull the rope from the leg Stephen had trapped, binding the thin part of the neck to the creature's thigh. Fatharr started to stagger around as it tried to get free.

Soon, Sarah and Owen had a sheep each and were firing at Fatharr's rear legs. The creature flung itself around, lashing out with hoofs and legs, trying to cut the rope while it also tried to avoid the circle of flames and the allphetine, now being controlled solo by Hampton.

Stephen spared a glance over his shoulder. Hampton looked calm, except for the trembling of his hands. Ione still seemed fine.

Maggie appeared with two more sheep. She dumped one in the pen and brought the other over to the fire to start working it herself.

'Good work, Mags.' Hampton released the fire and the allphetine winked out of sight. He turned and put a hand on Ione's shoulder, murmuring something in her ear. Then he took a sheep to use himself.

Stephen looked at Fatharr. One snake head was now strapped to a front leg and his legs were being pulled together. The daikaiju was moving its two remaining heads around, ferociously trying to cut the wool threads that ran through the air while not being captured themselves.

'Well, hello. This isn't something you see every day.'

Stephen looked up to see an elderly man with tufts of white hair and deep brown eyes. He was staring at the monster and clutching a large bowl to his chest.

Stephen frowned. 'Can I help you?'

The old man looked at him and grinned. 'John O'Hara, sixth-order oman. Pleasure to meet you, Coiremir. Maggie tells me that you need some artificial wool, and I can see why. I'll just get to work.' Stephen watched the old man put his bowl down and start to swirl his finger through the thick white liquid in the dish.

A string shot forward from it and started to plaster itself all over Fatharr's main head. Reinforcements, Stephen decided, and went back to shooting the last of his sheep's fleece out.

He was almost out of wool when Fatharr rocked, and then fell. It hit the ground with a thud that shook the area where Stephen was sitting, and sent a great plume of dirt and grass up into the air.

There was a moment of stillness, of silence, and then there were cheers.

'We did it, we did it.' Ione ran across the grass and threw herself at him. Before he had time to move, she was kissing him. Before he had time to respond, she had moved away.

'It's done. We've saved Sclossin.'

Stephen grinned. 'I think there's still a bit of work to do, Ione.'

'Bah. Dry him out, burn him up. He's going to smell lovely, which is some small recompense for the shit he's put everyone through.'

'We're not finished yet,' Hampton said, looking into the darkness, away from the town. 'Guardians, with me.' He disappeared.

Stephen transferred, following the thread of Hampton's essence. He found the Sabhamir standing over five supine forms, lying on the edge of a peat bog.

'What the hell?' Kenyon walked up next to him. 'What is this?'

'I think this may be the gang who gave us the monster.' Hampton bent down next to a young girl with short blonde hair. He put his hand on the girl's forehead and closed his eyes, shaking his head. 'The texts.'

'Are they all dead?' Maggie whispered.

As if in answer to her question, the woman on the end moaned. Shauna Connell. Sarah knelt down next to her and touched her throat, then looked up at the guardians. 'We might be able to save her. Kenyon?'

'Coming.' The two guardians and the woman disappeared.

'We've lost the rest,' Hampton said, rocking back on his heels. 'Shit.'

'It would seem that's where the beast came from.' Owen pointed to the bog, where there was a large hole.

'How did this happen?' Maggie whispered. 'How ...?'

The answer of course was the Forbidden Texts, but Stephen knew that wasn't the point to her question. Apart from one man, Lachy Ackland, the spirit of the Coiremir told him the other victims were all younger than he was. All of them had still had long, productive lives ahead of them, full of all sorts of possibilities. They'd chosen the path of the texts instead, and this was the result.

'Damn it.' Hampton thumped his fist into the ground. 'If only —'

'No.' Owen put his hand on the Sabhamir's shoulder. 'Don't do that to yourself. *They* decided to follow the texts. You are not responsible.'

Stephen looked into the bleakness of Hampton's eyes and knew the protector would blame himself for these deaths for the rest of his life.

'We need to take these poor sods to the bardria building, take the darkness from them and then tell their families,' Owen said. 'Hampton, you take Ellen, I'll take Glen. Maggie, Stephen, stay here with the others, please.'

Stephen nodded. The two older guardians disappeared with their loads. Maggie shuffled closer.

'How many more?' she whispered.

Stephen could do nothing but put his arm around her and offer her silent comfort.

Owen and Hampton returned after a few minutes. 'Stephen, you take Ione home, then meet us at the bardria. Maggie, arrange for some of the bardria guard to stay with the creature. I dare say you need to start preparing for the human fallout of this.'

Maggie shuddered. 'Explaining a giant peat-bog monster is going to take some doing.'

Stephen squeezed her shoulders, then transferred back to Ione. She was talking to John O'Hara and the two of them were standing closer to the fallen monster than Stephen liked.

'Ione.'

She turned, smiled and came toward him. As she got closer, she must have seen the expression on his face because her smile died. 'What's wrong?'

'I'm taking you home. Mr O'Hara.' Stephen nodded to the older man, took Ione's hand and transferred them back to their bedroom.

'Talk to me.' She wrapped her arms around his waist.

'I can't, not just now.' He kissed her forehead. 'There's a lot I still have to do. You should try to sleep.'

'Be careful,' she said. He smiled and transferred to the healers' wing. He went looking for Shauna and his attention was captured by the sound of raised voices.

He walked into an empty room and found Owen, Kenyon and Sarah standing on one side of the room and Caelleach Cormac on the other.

'We are aware that this is going to be a hard time for the families whose homes were destroyed, and that many people will feel unsafe for some time,' Owen was saying. 'We are here to help with all that.'

'It shouldn't be necessary.' The caelleach's hands were clenched fists, pressed against his thighs. His lips were thin and his eyebrows drawn together. 'This should never have happened.'

'We wish it hadn't.'

The caelleach looked around and glared at Stephen. 'Where is the Sabhamir?'

'Coming, I would imagine.' He went over to stand with his fellow guardians.

'The Ceamir?'

'Making preparations to deal with human questions and interference.'

Cormac shook his head. 'That you allowed the destruction of a huge part of Sclossin is unconscionable —'

'We didn't allow it.' Hampton's voice cut through the caelleach's diatribe. He strode forward, and stopped between the guardians and the caelleach. Stephen could feel the pulses of power radiating from him and realised Hampton was on the point of losing his cool. He hoped the caelleach would also recognise that and back down.

'And I find the implication that the guardians have not been doing their job insulting.'

His voice was as icy as even Sarah Hennessy could only dream of making hers.

The caelleach pulled back his shoulders. 'Nevertheless —'

'Nevertheless, we are dealing with the greatest danger to face the gadda in centuries, and if you thought we were going to get the texts back without some sort of collateral damage, you were sadly mistaken. In fact, you should be grateful to be facing this with the guardians that we have, because if it weren't for the particular skills and knowledge of the gadma standing before you, along with the Ceamir, it would have been more than houses that were lost tonight. Now, you need help in guiding the people through this nightmare, and we are ready to offer whatever assistance we can. And we will continue to fight for the gadda, and to search for the texts, because we are honour-bound to do so. But don't think for one moment that if you ever speak to us like this again, I won't come and make you regret it.'

Stephen watched Horatio Cormac, a man he'd admired for well over a decade, rendered speechless. The caelleach's mouth opened and shut as he sought the words to respond to the Sabhamir's speech.

'Now, Horatio.' As he continued, Hampton's voice softened a little. 'You are undoubtedly in shock, with what has happened here tonight. I think it would be best that you inform the gadda that the threat to Sclossin is over. Then take aside the families that have lost their homes, tell them what has happened and inform them that first thing in the morning, the Firimir and Garramir will be there to help them recover what they can. I, the Garramir, Coiremir and Firimir will go to the families of the people who died, and the Heasimir will hopefully be able to save Shauna so we can find out what happened. I will come see you first thing in the morning to report on our progress. I suggest you try to rest, if not sleep, between now and then. You will be a very busy man over the next few days.'

Cormac nodded, turned and walked from the room in a zombie-like fashion. Hampton turned to the guardians and appeared calm.

'Sarah, how is Shauna Connell going?'

'It is very delicate,' Sarah said. 'Not knowing exactly what she was doing is hampering the healing. Kenyon has removed the darkness, so now it is mostly a matter of whether her body is prepared to fight to survive. I will stay with her.'

'Thank you. The rest of you, come with me.' Hampton walked out the door. Stephen, Kenyon and Owen followed.

'We have to go to Blair Callaghan,' he said. Stephen frowned. 'Who was the last person you saw Shauna with?'

Crap. 'Let's go.'

Hampton held out his hands in front of him, palms pressed together. Then he slowly pulled them apart. The air shimmered between them, then it tore and the loungeroom Stephen had stood in just the day before was visible between them. Stephen stared at this example of the power of the Sabhamir. Gadda were always told that their homes could only be entered with their permission. If they knew the truth ...

They stepped through the fissure into Blair's home. The place felt as curiously blank as it had when Stephen visited. They went through every room but there was no sign of Blair.

'Her apartment in Sclossin,' Hampton said. Again, he tore them a path into it.

This place was furnished in much the same way as the country house. Blair wasn't there, but there was a pulse of power in this residence.

'Check for a sign of the Forbidden Texts,' Hampton said.

It took only a few moments to do so; the apartment was tiny. Kenyon summoned them all into the laboratory.

'This is strange,' he said, patting a spot on the bench. As Hampton went over to touch it, the Garramir continued. 'It doesn't have the chill that we've associated with the texts, but it doesn't feel, well, right.'

'Remember how Maggie found out that whoever had the texts moved them via a car to Carrick-on-Shannon and took the train?' Owen said. Hampton and Kenyon nodded. 'That was some time after they were stolen. What if she had them here but wasn't using them – just reading them and waiting for the right time to move them?'

'If she hadn't used them, there probably wouldn't be any of that darkness produced,' Kenyon said.

'Fuck.' Hampton slammed his fist onto the bench and the others all jumped. 'It was her. All along. And we were this close to getting her and the texts. Fuck.'

'That's probably what the beast was about,' Owen shook his head. 'A diversion, to keep us busy while she escaped. Kimberley too.'

'She could fucking be anywhere.' Hampton hit the bench again. 'She would have used human transportation again. How the fuck are we supposed to follow her?'

'We'll ask Maggie,' Owen said. 'In the meantime, we've got four dead gadda to deal with, and their families to inform.'

'We'll deliver the news in pairs,' Hampton said. 'Stephen, you're with me. At each site, we need to not only tell the family but also search their laboratory for signs of use of the texts.'

'Damn, that's a hard conversation,' Kenyon said. 'Sorry, your kid's dead; can I check out your lab 'cause they were betraying the gadda?'

'It must be done,' Hampton said. 'If they weren't thinking they would die, they may not have hidden things away before they left. The evidence could be sitting there, waiting for us.'

Stephen and Hampton went first to Lachy Ackland's home. Stephen was shocked when a small, stocky young woman greeted them, a baby pressed against her chest.

'Sabhamir, Coiremir.' She nodded. 'To what do I owe this honour?'

'I apologise for coming at such a late hour, Lauren.'

Lauren Ackland shook her head. 'I was up feeding. Lachy's not home, I'm afraid. He was —' She stopped and frowned. 'He was called into the bardria for an emergency. Is that what this is about? Has something happened?'

'Lauren, please, sit down.'

The young mother looked at Hampton, then Stephen, then sat down with a thud. 'What is it?'

'Lauren, I'm sorry, but Lachy wasn't called into the bardria for an emergency.' Hampton sat down in the chair next to hers. 'Lachy made the decision to undertake an action against the gadda and the bardria, and he's paid a heavy price for it.'

She frowned. 'I don't understand.'

'Lachy and a group of people conjured a monster to attack Sclossin. The attack failed, the incantation backfired and Lachy was killed.'

Stephen could hear a clock ticking. It was slow, sluggish, numbering the moments with dispassion.

'Lachy's dead?' Lauren's voice was hoarse.

'Yes.'

'Because he tried to attack Sclossin?'

'Yes.'

'I don't understand.' She shook her head. 'Yes, Lachy has some strange ideas. But to attack Sclossin?'

'I know it's hard to understand. I don't understand myself. I'd like to look through your laboratory, if you don't mind, to see if there's an explanation there.'

She looked at Stephen. 'He's really dead?'

'Yes, Lauren.'

She shuddered and squeezed the baby to her chest. The infant screamed, its little face glowing red. She started to bounce the child in her arms, cooing at it while the first tears washed down her cheeks.

'Lauren, who would you like us to bring here for you?'

'He's dead?' She bent over and kissed the baby's forehead. 'But we had corned beef for dinner, and he was planning to have it on sandwiches tomorrow.'

'Lauren, shall I contact your mother?'

She looked up and, for a moment, her eyes didn't focus. Then she looked at Hampton and said, 'Yes, please.' She bent her head to coo at the baby again.

Moments later, an older version of Lauren appeared in the middle of the room. 'What is this?' Alice demanded, rushing over to Lauren's side. 'What is going on?'

Hampton told her in a quiet voice. Stephen heard a sob, quickly swallowed. Then another.

Stephen stepped forward and reached for Lauren, but it was too late. The young woman melted into a puddle of tears and wailing, while the baby started a new cacophony.

Leaving Lauren to her mother's comfort with murmurs of support and distress, Hampton and Stephen went into the Acklands' laboratory. A notebook, much like the one they had found at Kimberley Gaines's home, sat open on the bench. Around it were piles of crushed leaves, containers of liquid and a dirty mortar and pestle.

'Like you said, he was expecting to return and hide it all,' Stephen said.

Hampton picked up the notebook and the equipment. 'Clean the rest of this up, will you? Lauren shouldn't have to deal with a mess on top of everything else.'

With a flick of his hand, Stephen set the laboratory to rights and followed Hampton out into the loungeroom.

Alice stood in the middle of the room with her hands on her hips. 'How dare you accuse Lachy of attacking Sclossin?'

'If the eyes of the guardians are not enough, the proof is here, Alice.' Hampton held up the notebook. 'I'm afraid Lachy was not the man we thought he was.' Lauren's sobs increased. 'Take good care of her, Alice, and anything you need, call me.'

Next they went to the family of Glen Flaherty, who was barely in his twenties. He'd still lived with his parents in a huge stone house in the centre of the village, and they refused to believe what Hampton said.

'My son would never do that,' Heath Flaherty roared. 'He was a good boy.'

'The best of boys. An ornament to the gadda.' Moira Flaherty sneered at the two guardians.

'I do not wish to destroy your memories of your son,' Hampton said. 'I do, however, need to look at your laboratory.'

'No.' Heath slammed to his feet. 'Why would you want to search my laboratory? I have done nothing wrong.'

Hampton straightened his back. 'I have asked. I do not have to.'

Heath's face purpled and Stephen wondered if he might actually see someone die of rage. 'Do as you must, Sabhamir.'

At first, the Flaherty laboratory looked clean. Stephen tried to put the glare from Heath, standing in the doorway, from his mind and pay attention to what his senses were telling him. Then cold washed over his skin as he walked down near the end of the room.

'Hampton.' He stopped in front of the end of the table. 'There's something here.'

Hampton walked over and put his hand on the table. 'I can feel the darkness, but I can't see where it might be coming from.'

'Isn't there some sort of secret Sabhamir incantation that you can use to bring the nasty stuff out to the open?'

Hampton grinned. 'There is, but I'm not game to use it where the texts are concerned. Let's think this through logically. This is the only place we can feel darkness. So it would seem this is the only part of the lab that Glen used.'

'So we're feeling the residue of use?' Stephen tapped the wood, and frowned. 'Interesting.' He moved up the table, tapped it, then back down to where Hampton stood. 'Hear that?'

Hampton crouched down. 'Well, look at this.' He tugged on the facing of the tabletop, and a piece of it pulled away, revealing a tray. He reached in and pulled out another of the notebooks.

'So, it wasn't residue but just the notes, and he didn't work here at all,' Stephen said.

'What's that? What have you got there?'

Stephen looked at Heath. 'The proof that Glen was doing all we have said.'

Heath's face paled. 'No,' he whispered. 'It's not possible.'

Owen and Kenyon were waiting in Hampton's office. They also had two of the notebooks.

'How did you go?' Stephen asked as Hampton sat down and began to flick through the notebooks.

'Ellen's partner went into immediate shock and we had to give her a calming draught. Grace's parents said they weren't surprised, she was a disgrace to them with purist sympathies and they hoped we'd left her to rot. Lovely family.' Owen grimaced.

'Grace was living by herself, so searching her laboratory was easy, and she hadn't cleaned up like Hampton said. Ellen and her partner didn't have a laboratory, but we found the notebook in the bedside cupboard.' Kenyon shook his head.

'So they were working with Blair somewhere, but where? Not any of her residences,' Stephen said.

'The laboratory where she killed Wilma,' Owen said.

Hampton nodded. 'Until it was discovered. I bet they've found another location. If we can find that, we might find Blair. Let's hope Shauna survives and can tell us.'

Stephen did just that.

THIRTY-ONE

Ione awoke feeling no less tired. She'd slept, but her night had been one of dreams and restlessness. She saw Stephen searching for the texts and would shudder from the sense of darkness around him. She saw the battle against Fatharr, over and over again, and they didn't always defeat it. She saw Jack, and he would be clear as day and then recede, moving away from her until he was just a speck in the distance and she knew that no matter what she did, she'd never get him back.

She got up, dressed, and then walked around to Maggie and Lucas's apartment. As she passed through the office of the Ceamir, she thought about what her friend had been doing last night and wondered what might be asked of her next.

She knocked on the door. There was a moment of silence, during which she thought there might not be anyone up. Then she heard a pop from behind her. She turned around to see a message ball peeling open.

'Hello, mysterious visitor. I'm afraid that I'm not available at the moment, but if you take a seat, I'll be with you as soon as I can. Ta.' Maggie's voice.

Ione turned back to the door and pounded on it. 'Lucas, it's me.'

She heard footsteps, and the door opened. Lucas looked no better than she felt. His hair was a tousled mess, his eyes bloodshot and his skin pale.

'Io. Thank Christ you're safe.'

She stepped forward and put her arms around him. 'Everyone's safe,' she said. 'They're all fine.'

Lucas pulled back to look at her. 'What the hell happened? Why did they need you? Maggie was here briefly, but she wouldn't say.'

Ione took his arm and led him over to the lounge to sit down. Then she told him about the fight with Fatharr and how they'd needed her ability as a lodestone to keep their power up.

By the end of it, he was slumped against the back of the chair, staring at her. 'Fuck.'

'Tell me about it.'

Lucas shook his head. 'I was just about to put some coffee on. I don't know about you, but I'm in desperate need of caffeine.'

'Alleluia.'

Lucas made the coffee and they both sat at the dining table. Lucas put some sugar in his and began stirring, staring down at the brown liquid.

'So, are they going to require you for all their little endeavours?'

'Star, I hope not. You know, for a while there it was exciting and all that, but I'd much rather spend my time here with you, drinking and watching vampire porn and waiting.'

'I wouldn't. I'd rather be out there doing something.'

'Then you'd better get your act together and move up those orders so you can propose yourself as some sort of wingman.'

She felt a warmth touch her mind, and then came Stephen's voice. '*Ione, where are you?*'

'*Maggie and Lucas's apartment.*'

She blinked, and he was standing in front of her. If she'd thought Lucas looked bad, then Stephen was worse. There were black rings around his eyes, his lips had thinned and his face was drawn.

'How are things?' Ione heard the desperation in Lucas's voice and felt bad about being happy that her partner was home safely.

'Fucked up, but they'll get better.' Stephen ran his hand through his hair. 'I'm going to go relieve Maggie in a little while so she can come home.'

Ione opened her mouth to tell him he needed to rest too, but Lucas said, 'Thanks.'

Stephen looked at her. 'I was thinking that since you've proven that you can control your power, maybe we should go get Jack.'

Ione walked over to him and took his hand. She loved the idea of having her son with her — she could do with one of his all-encompassing hugs right now — but she wasn't sure if Stephen was ready.

'You sure?'

He nodded. 'We could both do with the distraction, don't you think?'

Paddy and Susie looked up from the kitchen table with shy smiles as she and Stephen appeared. Jack whooped and threw himself off the chair and into Ione's arms.

Ione collapsed to the floor, pulled him onto her lap and pushed his head against her shoulder. She took a deep breath and the familiar scent of shampoo, sweets and Jack settled her nerves.

'Are you better?' His voice was muffled against her jumper. 'Really for real this time?'

She blinked. How the hell to answer that? Sure, she felt fine, but then she didn't know what effect the power would have on her long-term. Could she give Jack the reassurance he needed?

He wriggled, his signal that he needed her to loosen her grip. She did, and he pulled back to look up at her. 'You feel different, Mam. Like you have power.'

'Well, actually, Jack —'

His eyes widened. 'You do have power. How? Cool!'

His enthusiasm made her smile. 'We don't know how yet. The Sabhamir's investigating.'

'Is it for real? I mean, do you get to keep it?'

'I don't know.'

'Then you should do first order, right away, in case it goes again. Then you'll still be first order.'

Ione lifted her eyes to look at Stephen, stunned by the idea. If what the Sabhamir thought was true, she could not only finally pass first order, but maybe even go further — something she'd never thought possible.

'He's got a point,' Stephen said.

'Yeah, do it, Mam, do it.' Jack bounced on her lap.

'Ione?' She looked up at Paddy and Susie.

'It's true,' she said. 'Whatever was done to me has given me power. I've already started to learn to use it. Surprise, right?'

'Stunning.' Susie shook her head. 'You're sure you're all right?'

'I am.' She stood, pulling Jack close to her. 'This is why I'd like to take Jack back with me. I know you're all having a great time here, but I want my son at home.'

'Of course. There are times when you need a break

from your children, and times when you need to hold them so close you want to make them part of you.' Susie smiled. 'I'll go pack his things.'

Within half an hour Ione, Stephen and Jack were standing in the middle of the Coiremir's loungeroom.

Jack looked around. 'What's this?'

Ione gulped. It was time for the talk. 'Stephen's apartment. I thought we'd try living here for a while.'

'In America?' Jack's eyes were wide.

Stephen shook his head. 'In the bardria building.'

'Cool.' Jack looked around. 'Where are the dining chairs?'

'We need to do a bit of decorating,' Stephen said. 'But if you'll follow me ...' He started to walk down the hallway. Jack followed, skipping, and Ione trailed after them.

Stephen pushed open the door to the spare room. 'I think this is yours,' he said.

Jack went to the doorway and jumped up and down. 'My room. You brought my room over here. Thanks, Stephen.'

'Jack.' Ione crouched down and reached out to grab her son's hand, making him turn to look at her. 'Buddy, I need to know that you understand. You and I will be living here now, with Stephen.'

'Forever?'

'I hope so.'

Jack pulled his lower lip in between his teeth, as he always did when thinking. Ione wondered where his agile mind would go. 'If I'm going to live with the Coiremir, do I have to go to school?'

'Yes.' He wrinkled his nose and Ione began to smile. 'You'll still get to see your friends and all that, but you'll be living here in the bardria building.'

More thinking. 'Does this mean you and Stephen will get married?'

'We don't know that yet. We need to make sure we work together, all three of us, before we do that.'

'What if it doesn't work?'

'You and I will go back to the flat.'

'What about Grandma and Grandpa Gorton?'

'You'll still go to stay with them on holidays, and they'll still come down to visit you.'

By now, his little face was screwed up into a mask of concentration. 'Do I have to change my name? 'Cause that happened to a kid at school, when his mammy got a new boyfriend and they got married. 'Cause I like Jack Gorton. Jack Coiremir doesn't sound right.'

Ione bit the inside of her cheek so she wouldn't laugh. 'You can have whatever name you want.'

'Will you change your name?'

'I don't know.'

There was a pause, and she wondered what else he might think of. Then he blurted out, 'Can we have pancakes for breakfast?'

'Absolutely.'

'Good.' Jack grinned. 'I like pancakes. Where's the bathroom?'

Ione directed him, then stood and watched him skip away, seemingly unconcerned with anything. 'That went well, I think.'

'We'll make sure he's OK with it.' Stephen pulled her against his chest. Ione rested there and considered how nice it was going to be to have support in her efforts to raise Jack.

THIRTY-TWO

'Right.' Hampton paced from one end of his office to the other. 'How the hell do we find Blair Callaghan?'

Everyone looked to Maggie, who frowned. 'First things first. Let's tell everyone she's missing. Gadda will let us know when she's sighted.'

'We can't just let innocent gadda approach her, Maggie,' Owen said. 'Star knows what she'll do to them.'

'Are we all convinced it is Blair who has the texts?' Maggie looked around the room.

'I am,' Stephen said. It made perfect sense to him.

'I want the proof,' Hampton said, his feet thudding into the carpet. 'I want to find her and question her and work out exactly how she's involved in all this.'

'I think Maggie's right,' Sarah said. Now all eyes switched to her. Stephen saw that Hampton, Owen and Kenyon looked quite stunned. 'I'm not convinced myself that Blair has the texts, but if she does then we need to find her as soon as possible.'

'Thank you, Sarah.' Maggie gave her fellow guardian a wide smile. 'Now, as to how to follow her ourselves. We're sure she didn't transfer out of either of her homes?'

Hampton nodded. 'I've been back to search them carefully. There's no sign of use of power in either of them for several days. There's also none of her personal effects in either of them — handbag, money, nothing.' He stopped and frowned. 'That blankness in the country house is intriguing. It's not as blank as a human place, but it's definitely not a normal gadda home either.'

'She cleaned up after herself,' Stephen said. 'Got rid of the darkness of the texts before I got there.'

'But then why ask you to her home?' Owen said. 'Why not come here to you?'

'Because then how could she use Shauna to shield herself so I wouldn't touch her and feel the darkness?'

'Except Sarah did,' Hampton said.

Sarah nodded. 'There was no darkness. She was ill, as she said she was.'

'Then she's not the one with the texts?' Maggie looked around.

'This is why we need her, to find out for certain.' Hampton started pacing again. 'She didn't use gadda means to leave, so over to you, Mags.'

'Well, obviously she's used human means. Blair doesn't have a car, does she?'

'Not that I've ever noticed,' Owen said.

'Then she called a taxi.' Maggie's eyes widened. 'No, she caught a bus. There's a bus stop just outside the Gortons' place. She packed up, walked to the bus and got on it like any normal human would.'

'Perhaps the Gortons saw?' Stephen said.

'Stephen, go ask,' Hampton said.

Stephen nodded, asked permission to visit them and once it was granted, transferred to the Gortons' loungeroom.

Susie put down her knitting and stood. 'Coiremir.' She bowed her head. 'Paddy's out in the fields, I've asked him to come to the house as quickly as possible. What can we do for you?'

'Susie, my apologies for disturbing you. The guardians have just found out that Blair Callaghan is missing. No one has heard from her for several days.' Stephen hoped the semi-lie was delivered casually. 'Have you seen her recently?'

Susie shook her head. 'Not since Ione was here. She came over the night that Ione went back to Sclossin to see you. Ione went to have afternoon tea with her the next day, but that's all I know. We generally don't see much of her unless she comes to visit. Goodness, I hope she's not hurt.'

A door at the back of the house banged and moments later, Paddy Gorton appeared in the doorway. 'Coiremir.'

'Paddy.'

'Paddy, darling, the guardians are looking for Blair. They think she's gone missing. You haven't seen her, have you?'

'Not since yesterday.'

That was more recent than Susie. 'Tell me more, please, Paddy.'

'Well,' the older man scratched his chin. 'I was ploughing the far field and I saw Blair come out of her house with a couple of suitcases and a satchel slung over her shoulder. She gave me a wave and then walked up the road. I guess she was going to the bus stop.'

'Morning, afternoon, evening?'

'Morning. She musta been catching the nine-thirty bus into Ennis.'

'Thank you, Paddy. You've been a great help.' Stephen transferred back to Hampton's office. 'Paddy said he saw Blair yesterday morning, leaving home with suitcases. He thinks she was catching the bus to Ennis.'

'Right,' Maggie said. 'Ennis, that's in County Clare, right?'

'Right,' Kenyon said.

'Isn't there an international airport at Shannon? That's just near there.'

'Fuck.' Hampton sat on his desk. 'She could be anywhere.'

'Io might be able to hack into the airport computer systems and find out –'

'Hang on,' Stephen said. 'You can't just ask Ione to break the law.'

'Do we want to find Blair or not?' Maggie shot back.

'I think we can do it without breaking the law,' Owen said. 'On the cop shows, they go around showing pictures of people to see if anyone remembers them.'

'Of course.' Maggie grinned at Hampton. 'Wanna wear a uniform again?'

'We can be plain-clothes, thanks,' Hampton said. 'Owen, you come with me.'

'Before you dash off,' Kenyon said, leaning forward, 'I wanna run another idea past you. We tell the gadda the texts are missing.'

'No.' Sarah shook her head. 'It could cause panic.'

'It could also gain us valuable information,' Kenyon said. 'We tell people what to look out for and they dob in anything they see.'

'Be alert but not alarmed,' Maggie said.

'What?'

'It was something the Australian government did to respond to the threat of terrorism. Keep an eye out and ring this number if you spot anything, but don't worry, it's all OK. I'd have to look up the figures, but from memory most of the calls amounted to nothing, however, all had to be investigated. Do we want to spend time on that?'

'No,' Hampton said. 'For now, we keep the worst of all this to ourselves. Owen and I will let you know if we find anything. The rest of you might as well go home.'

It was the best idea Stephen had heard in a long time, and he transferred to his apartment. He could hear Ione's and Jack's voices coming from down the hall.

He found them in Jack's room. They were sitting on his bed, playing a game of checkers, in which all the pieces were in the shape of a star of gulagh.

'Stephen. Wanna play? Mam sucks.'

'Thank you, Jack.' Ione got up and walked over to Stephen. She wrapped her arms around his waist and lifted her face. It was the most natural thing in the world to kiss her.

'How are things?'

'Quiet. Right now, that's the best we can hope for.' It really did help to wash away the stress of the day, to be able to hold Ione and talk.

'Stephen? Wanna play?'

'You play with him. I'll get dinner ready.' Ione gave him another kiss. 'Then I'm thinking we'll get him bathed and into bed quickly, so we can get into bed ourselves.' A pulse of lust washed over him — Ione's power.

Stephen grinned. 'Sounds the perfect end to the day.' Ione released him and left the room. Stephen walked over and sat on the bed.

'Be ready, Jack,' he said as he set up the board. 'I don't take any prisoners.'

Ione stepped from the bardria building into a bright and sunny day. Jack danced on the end of her hand.

'And I wanna have my own telly, 'cause then I can watch what I wanna watch and you and Stephen can watch what you wanna watch, and then we'll all be happy,' he was saying.

'I think we'll do just fine with one television.' Ione stood at the edge of the street and looked both ways before she started across.

'Wow, look at the inn. That bomb really tore a hole in it. Mam, have a look at the inn.' Jack tugged at her hand, fighting the pull across the street in his attempt to turn around and stare at the building next to the bardria.

Once she had her son safely on the other side of the road, Ione turned to look at the inn. It was strange to see it now, knowing what it had meant for her. If not for that bombing, she'd never have met Stephen. She might never have been wherever it was she had been when she was touched with the Forbidden Texts.

She started to walk up the street, parallel to the inn. She was headed to see Hetty Barry, a very talented textile artist. While there was decorating material aplenty down at the main shops, Ione had decided the apartment of the Coiremir deserved a pattern of its own.

Directly opposite the inn's front door, she was shocked to a halt when a man erupted from the crab-apple bushes that hid a house from view. He stopped in the middle of the footpath in front of her and started to brush at his legs.

She recognised him as Hank O'Toole, one of Brian Mochrie's cronies at school.

He looked up and a flicker of disgust crossed his face. Then he went back to brushing dirt away.

Ione would have ignored him, except Jack piped up. 'What were you doing in those trees?'

Hank glared at Jack. 'None of your business.' He stood and almost barged right into Ione in his haste to get away.

'Prick,' Ione muttered, then she pulled on Jack's

hand. However, the little boy yanked his hand free and dove into the thick growth of the crab apples.

'Jack.' Ione put her hands on her hips. 'What the hell are you doing?'

'I thought I saw something.' The soles of his shoes were poking out from under the greenery.

'Get out of there — you'll get dirt all over yourself. Honestly, I can't take you anywhere.' She bent down and pulled on one ankle. 'Get out of there now.'

'It's a feather.' Jack started to wriggle out onto the footpath. Ione stood straight and put on her stern-mother face. Jack scrambled to his feet and stared at his prize, rendering her efforts useless. The feather was downy near the base of the stalk and then spread out into grey fronds with tips of black.

'Why's it cut like that?' Jack held the feather up to Ione's face. Ione took it. It had been split up the middle, as if to put it over something.

'I don't know.' She handed the feather back.

'I bet I've discovered a new bird. I'm gonna show Stephen when I get back.' Jack shoved it into the pocket of his jeans.

'Look at you. Covered in dirt.' Ione pulled a twig out of his hair. 'Why can't you be more careful?'

''Cause I'm not a girl,' Jack said. 'We going or what?'

Ione took his hand with a shake of her head.

The hour spent with Hetty was very productive and, as she walked back into the apartment, Ione felt confident that she would end up with a pattern that she could use with great effect throughout the rooms.

Stephen was waiting. He stood with a smile. 'All's quiet, so unless something else happens I could well have the rest of the day with you.'

'Excellent,' Ione said, immediately starting to make plans in her mind. They were scuppered by her son, who raced over to Stephen.

'Stephen, I found this really cool feather and I reckon I discovered a new bird and I want to call it the Jackbird.' He pulled the feather out of his pocket and waved it around.

'Can I look?' Stephen held his hand out and Jack handed the feather over. Stephen looked at it and Ione watched his face close over.

'Where did you get this?'

'I found it in the trees across the road from the inn. Cool, isn't it?'

'*Ione, is there some way I can get Jack to let me have this feather for a while? I think Hampton needs to look at it.*'

Icy fingers ran over Ione's scalp. 'Jack, how about we get you cleaned up while Stephen checks the feather out?'

'I reckon it's a big bird,' Jack said. 'I reckon it's like a million centimetres high, and eats other birds for breakfast.'

'*What is it?*' Ione asked Stephen as she led Jack to his bedroom.

'*I think this was used in a ritual. Jack finding it where the attack against the inn was launched has me worried. I'm going to see Hampton; won't be long.*'

Ione oversaw Jack getting cleaned up, then got him to help her with lunch. She had just about finished the sandwiches when she heard the door to Stephen's office open and close.

'Ione, Jack. I've brought company for lunch.'

Ione wasn't surprised to walk out into the loungeroom and see the Sabhamir standing there.

'Hey.' Jack danced up to the protector. 'I live here now.'

'So I see.'

'If I live in the bardria, does that mean you protect me?'

Hampton's lips twitched. 'I protect all gadda, Jack.'

'But if you live here, there's special protection, right?'

'Right.'

'Cool.'

'Jack, Stephen showed me the feather. It's very interesting. Where exactly did you find it?'

'Under the tree. I thought I saw something funny there, after the man came out.'

'The man?' Hampton looked at Ione.

'Jack and I were walking down the path when Hank O'Toole came out of the bushes. He was brushing dirt off himself. Jack asked what he'd been doing, he snarled at him and then stormed off. Jack turned and dived under the bushes and returned with the feather.'

'Hank O'Toole. Interesting, very interesting. Jack, I need to keep this feather for a while.'

'Oh, but —'

Ione stepped forward. 'That would be fine, Sabhamir.'

'Thank you, Ione. Jack. Have a great lunch.' He disappeared.

'I thought he was staying.'

'He's a busy man, Jack.' Ione ruffled her son's head while she looked at her lover. *'Is it important that Hank O'Toole was good mates with Brian Mochrie at school?'*

'Could be. I'll let Hampton know.'

'Now, sandwich time,' Ione said briskly. As Jack whooped and ran into the kitchen, Stephen leant in and kissed her forehead.

'All will be well,' he whispered.

THIRTY-THREE

Stephen ate the sandwich as quickly as possible, expecting the summons. Sure enough, Hampton's chime soon rang in his head.

'Have to dash,' he said, standing.

'I wanna play *Halo* with you,' Jack said.

'I'm sorry, buddy, but when I'm called I have to go, no matter what.' Stephen walked over and kissed Ione. 'I love you.'

'I love you too.'

The guardians were all gathered in Hampton's office. None looked particularly happy to be there.

'Sorry, but we've got the breakthrough in the bombing we've been looking for,' Hampton said. 'Jack Gorton found an artefact of summoning in the trees where the attack was launched. I daresay what they did was set the summoning spell, to bring them there and then send them back so they didn't have to use their own power, which is why they've been so hard to trace. Luckily, Ione and Jack gave me a possible name, so I was able to test the evidence easily. This was created by Hank O'Toole.'

'So when Ione and Jack saw him earlier ...'

'He was obviously there to retrieve the artefact, or maybe there was more than one. Luckily, he wasn't as good at looking as an eight-year-old boy. Now, when we were keeping an eye on Brian after his first contact with Ione, we saw him meet with both Shauna Connell and Hank O'Toole. It's probably not too much of a leap to assume those three were involved in the bombing, however I think they would have needed others. Neither of those three are powerful enough.'

'If Hank was looking for the artefact just a short time ago, it's possible he's with his accomplices right now,' Maggie said.

'So, shall we pay Mr O'Toole a visit?' Hampton said. All the guardians grinned.

'Then follow me. We'll just let ourselves in, shall we?' He tore a hole to Hank's apartment, stepped through the fissure, and the other guardians followed.

Hank O'Toole jumped up from his armchair, too shocked by the unapproved appearance of the guardians in his loungeroom to do anything but gape at them. Hampton waved his hand and the man froze.

'Search the house,' he said. 'There has to be evidence.'

Four more of the feathers were found in the laboratory, along with everything needed for a power punch. Hampton looked at them with a satisfied smile.

'I bet I'll get the essences I need from these,' he said. 'I'm willing to bet one will be Brian Mochrie and another Shauna Connell. I'll take O'Toole back to the bardria. Keep searching.' The protector and his charge disappeared.

It took an hour to search every bit of O'Toole's home. The only things of interest were the amount of bottles and remains of cakes and biscuits in his rubbish bin — more than a single man required.

'Like he had a party,' Maggie said.

'A celebration, maybe,' Stephen said.

They were about to leave when Hampton returned. 'I've identified the last two,' he said. 'Let's go get them.'

The first was a very pretty sylph of a girl who fainted on the appearance of the guardians in her home. The other was a middle-aged man who screamed for the few seconds it took Hampton to put him into stillness.

They also had the makings for a power punch in their laboratories.

'Enough evidence to go before the bardria,' Hampton said.

Within half an hour, the six guardians and the three offenders were facing the bardria.

Hampton put forward the case against the three of them — the way Jack found the feather which led them to O'Toole and how that led them to the remaining two.

'No.' Councillor Robert Yarrow, the father of the young girl, surged to his feet. 'Impossible. You lie, Sabhamir.'

'I do not,' Hampton said with what Stephen considered admirable calmness in the face of that provocation. 'I am sorry to bring you this news about your daughter, Councillor Yarrow, but there is evidence she was involved in the bombing of the inn.'

'Councillor, sit down,' the caelleach said. He leant forward. 'Let's hear from those accused. Hank O'Toole will speak first.'

Owen took his position and they waited until O'Toole was relaxed before the questioning began.

'Hank O'Toole, did you bomb the Sclossin Inn?' Cormac said.

'No.'

'Lie,' said Owen.

O'Toole flinched and the caelleach nodded. 'Do you see, Hank? You cannot lie to the Firimir. There is nothing you can do to hide the truth. Confess, and we will be merciful.'

'I've done nothing wrong,' O'Toole said. 'We need to get humans out of this town, to preserve the sanctity of the gadda way.'

'*I am so over this,*' Maggie said. '*Fucking purists.*'

'So you are saying that you did bomb the Sclossin Inn?'

There was a pause, then O'Toole hissed, 'Yes.'

'With no care or consideration for anyone you might have injured?'

'There are always innocent casualties of war. It's the price to be paid for doing what is right.'

Rage erupted as Stephen heard himself declared *an innocent casualty.*

'Who did this with you?' the caelleach said.

O'Toole started to frown. His nose twitched, his head swung from side to side. 'I ... I don't know.'

'Firimir?'

'He speaks the truth. Hank O'Toole knows there were others involved, but cannot name them.'

The councillors gasped. 'How is that possible?' Cormac said.

'I do not know, Caelleach. With your permission, I would like to mind-read him.'

Cormac turned his head to one side and then the other, seeming to look at his fellow councillors. Then he nodded. 'We will hear from Stephanie Yarrow and Will Stephens first, to see if it is necessary.'

However, while both Stephanie and Will eventually confessed to having used a power-punch incantation to attack the inn, neither of them could identify anyone else involved, not even their co-accused.

'This is very strange, Firimir,' Cormac said. 'How is it possible that they cannot remember these things?'

'It could be the Forbidden Texts,' Owen said.

'No.' Stephanie's father was on his feet again. 'My daughter would never deal with such a thing.'

'Nor would I,' O'Toole called out from his position in the front row. 'The texts are evil and to be abhorred.'

'*How very interesting,*' Owen mused.

'*Is this like last time?*' Maggie said. She touched Stephen's hand. '*When we tried to question some of Sean Flaherty's friends, we found their memories scrambled and they couldn't see who they'd been involved with.*'

'*It seems so, although I'd need to mind-read to be absolutely certain,*' Owen said. Then he addressed the councillors. 'Do I have the bardria's permission to mind-read these three?'

'No.' Robert Yarrow's face was so red that Stephen thought it must be painful. 'You have the feathers, you've gained the essence of those involved. These three have confessed, Brian Mochrie is dead, Shauna Connell sure to be soon. Leave it at that.'

Cormac stood. 'Councillors, we'll go to discuss this.' They all trooped out the door behind him.

'I'll take these three to the cells,' Hampton said. He shot a string of black power around the accused and they all disappeared.

'It can't be coincidence that we've found these three with tampered memories, and they were involved with Brian and Shauna, who we know worked with the texts,' Stephen said.

'Except there is no darkness in these three,' Kenyon said. 'They haven't been using the texts.'

'Then Blair chose who she wanted to work with, but they were still involved with their other activities,' Maggie said.

'It must have been Blair who tampered with their memories.' Owen walked over to join them. 'She's tried to cover her tracks by ensuring no one who worked with her can remember that they did so. I wonder whether, if we checked Kimberley Gaines, we'd find the same scrambled recollections.'

'We're convinced it's Blair?' Maggie said. 'No more doubts?'

'No more doubts,' Kenyon said.

'She's been in my apartment,' Maggie whispered, 'tutoring Lucas.'

'It would explain the feeling of betrayal we got from Wilma's spirit,' Sarah said. 'As the head of the school, Blair would have been a very close confidante of the Coiremir.'

'She was always one of my biggest supporters,' Stephen said.

They stood in silence, each dealing with their own sense of betrayal.

Stephen was nervous as the bardria returned to deliver their verdict. He was sure they'd find the three of them guilty, but if they didn't allow the mind-reads then Blair's plotting could continue unabated.

Hampton brought the accused back and the caelleach stood.

'Hank O'Toole, Stephanie Yarrow, Will Stephens. The bardria find the three of you guilty of bombing the Sclossin Inn. Your sentence is to be banished.'

Stephanie broke down into tears while Will screamed abuse and Hank fell to his knees, begging for mercy.

Stephen was glad for the severity of the sentence. Hopefully it would deter any other purists from doing something so dreadful.

'Councillors.' Hampton stepped forward. 'Are the guardians allowed to mind-read them before banishment?'

To Stephen's sorrow, the caelleach shook his head. 'No. We know who did this — these three, Brian Mochrie and Shauna Connell. There is no evidence that points to anyone else.'

'But Mochrie and Connell have both used the texts.'

'Have these three?'

'No, but they might have memories of those who have.'

Cormac looked at Robert Yarrow, who shook his head. 'Do the representatives of the clans of Hank O'Toole or Will Stephens object?'

'I do,' said Kenneth O'Meara, on behalf of Will. 'The boy has confessed, that is enough.' He glared at the guardians.

'*What's his problem?*' Stephen said.

'*He hates the whole world,*' Kenyon said.

'I have no problem with Hank being mind-read,' said Councillor Sheila Smyth. 'I want to know the truth of what is happening, as the guardians do.'

'Very well,' Cormac said. 'Guardians, you may mind-read Hank O'Toole. The banishment of all three is to take place in two days' time.' The councillors left.

'Take Hank to my office,' Hampton said and then he transferred away with Stephanie and Will.

Kenyon took control of Hank and soon they were in the Sabhamir's office, Hank confined to a chair in the middle of the room.

Hampton appeared and nodded at Owen, who took his position.

'Close your eyes and focus on your power,' he said. O'Toole stared up at him. 'The choice is yours.' Owen put his hands on either side of Hank's face, and closed his eyes.

Stephen watched Hank go rigid, obviously fighting Owen's presence in his mind. Then his body slackened, and Owen began to speak.

'Friends. Comrades. I trust them. Satisfied with plan, will leave little evidence. Must remember to tidy up. Nervous. Concerned. What if it doesn't work? What if we are caught? Greenery. Tension. Power building. Release. Safe. Satisfaction. Wish I could share this joy, but I don't dare meet up. Will wait. Will be worth it.'

'Can you identify anyone?' Hampton said.

'No face. Voices, but no recognition beyond feelings.'

'That doesn't sound very helpful,' Maggie said. Owen released Hank and opened his eyes.

'That's all we're going to get,' he said. 'His memories are too messed up to be of any use.'

Hampton sighed. 'I'll take him to the cells. You guys stay here.' He put his hand on Hank's shoulder and they were gone.

'How is she doing that?' Maggie said. 'Messing with their memories like that. And why would they agree to it?'

'Maybe they didn't,' Owen said as he sat down. 'Maybe they don't know they've been affected. As to how, it seems the texts contain some really interesting information.'

Hampton returned and was immediately pacing again. 'So now our only hope is Shauna lives and we can find something there.'

'I'll spend some time considering ways we might be able to get around the blockage,' Owen said. Hampton nodded.

'So, back to the story before this interrupted it,' Maggie said. 'Did you guys find anything at the airport?'

'The check-in staff remember Blair — they said she seemed very nervous and upset. But they wouldn't look at the passenger manifesto without a warrant, and I don't know what one looks like so I didn't feel confident to make it myself,' Hampton said.

'Should be able to find one online.' Maggie frowned then nodded. 'I've got Io looking for one. You can go back and demand they look.'

'Good. Otherwise, no one has any recollection of seeing her, so we know she did go to the airport but not where she went from there.'

'We'll find it,' Maggie said. 'We'll get the warrant, get her destination and then we'll know where to keep looking.'

'And hope she doesn't get up to too much in the meantime,' Kenyon added.

Stephen nodded. The sooner they found the texts and shut Blair down, the better.

THIRTY-FOUR

Ione stretched and then snuggled against Stephen's side. She laid her head on his chest, listened to his thudding heart and grinned. He was getting a crash course on the joys of living with someone, morning sex being one of the best aspects of it.

'Will you be free for lunch today?' She traced her finger over his chest, drawing idle squiggles.

'Could be. You know I can't promise anything.'

'I know. I was going to invite my parents over and I wanted you to meet them.'

'We're at that point of the relationship, are we?'

'Absolutely. Besides, I've met yours and it's not fair that you haven't met mine. In fact, let's invite your parents too. Might as well get the trauma of the first family get-together over and done with.'

She felt Stephen still beneath her hand. 'You don't need to do that.'

Ione lifted herself on her elbow to look down at him. 'Why don't you like your parents?'

He sighed. 'It's not that I don't like them. In fact, I think we'll probably see them often. I just —' He stopped and frowned.

'Just what?' She poked his chest. 'Tell me.'

'My father and I were fighting. We've patched things up, but I'm not ready to socialise with him yet.'

'If you're not ready to socialise with him then things are far from patched up. What were you fighting about?'

Stephen closed his eyes. 'You know how I was heavying the guys who hurt me while I waited to get them back? Well, one of them went running to my father, and Dad half believed his story and I went ballistic and we basically didn't talk for two years.'

'Why would your father believe him?'

'Aaron Lansing was one of his students. He thought he knew Lansing well and couldn't see how Aaron could have done what I said he did. When he questioned me, I got so angry that I wouldn't listen, and then he got so angry he wouldn't listen to me, and ...' Stephen shrugged.

'But you're OK now?'

'Hampton found out the whole thing from Maggie, went to arrest Aaron in front of my father and in the process, Aaron confessed.'

'So now your father believes you?' Stephen nodded. 'Must shit you, that it took that for him to believe.'

'It did, but there're more important things to worry about.'

Ione smiled. 'Like me, perhaps?'

'Perhaps.'

She slapped his chest and Stephen grinned. 'Just for that, I'm definitely inviting them for lunch.'

Stephen's eyes flew open. 'Ione.'

'No, look, what better way for you and your father to start to communicate than within a crowd? Or semi-crowd. Within family. I'll look after you.'

That heart-rending smile. 'You will, won't you?'

'Absolutely.' She leant forward and kissed him. 'And

if you're very good to your daddy, you might get a reward after.'

Stephen turned and she was lying on her back and he was looming over her. 'I think I might need a taste to keep me going,' he murmured, lowering himself onto her.

Just as she felt the delicious heaviness of his body on hers, Jack called out, 'Mam!'

'I hope his timing isn't always going to be so bad,' Stephen muttered.

Ione was smiling as she got out of bed to begin the day.

As midday approached, Ione had to admit that she was nervous. It was a good thing that Stephen was learning to shield his emotions from her — she didn't want to know how bad he was feeling.

She heard voices in Stephen's office, smoothed her tartan tunic over her black and white striped tights, and then opened the door.

'Hello.' She smiled at Stephen's parents who were by his desk, talking to him.

'Ione, you look wonderful.' Elizabeth came over to give her a kiss. 'I'm so pleased that you're feeling better.'

'Thank you. Won't you come in?' She turned and led the way into the flat.

Liam whistled as he walked in. 'Now, this is an improvement over last time we were here,' he said, looking around.

Ione smiled. Stephen had brought all her furniture from the apartment over and the place now looked very homey. 'Thank you. There was no way I was going to abide living in a furniture-less hole, I can assure you.'

A door slammed open. Footsteps, and Jack appeared. He skidded to a halt beside Ione. 'Hello.'

'Hello, you must be Jack.' Elizabeth held her hand out and Jack stepped forward to press his against it.

'Jack, this is Mr and Mrs O'Malley, Stephen's parents.'

'He can call us Liam and Elizabeth.' Liam held his hand out.

Jack touched it, then looked at the O'Malleys. 'Are you my kinda-grandparents?'

Elizabeth's eyes widened. Liam grinned. 'What do you mean?'

'Well, Stephen's my kinda-dad, so I guess that makes you my kinda-grandparents.'

'My word,' Elizabeth said softly.

'You're going to have to excuse my son,' Ione said, grabbing Jack's shoulder and pulling him against her. 'I try and try to beat tact into him, but I keep failing.'

Liam laughed. 'Reminds me of his father.'

Ione's jaw fell open and she slammed it shut. 'I beg your pardon?'

'I was working at the school when Patrick went through. He seemed to be missing the tact button as well, although he was a good kid for all that.' He looked at Ione. 'I was very sad to hear of his death.'

'Thank you,' she whispered, unsure what else to say.

Stephen walked over and put his arm around her shoulder. 'Can I get anyone a drink?'

'Yes,' Ione said. 'Whiskey.' Stephen gave her a gentle squeeze.

'Do you play *Rock Band*?' Jack piped up.

'No, but I'd like to,' Liam said.

'Come on.' Jack grabbed Liam's hand and pulled the older man down the hallway.

'He's delightful, Ione,' Elizabeth said.

'And unfortunately, he knows it.'

Elizabeth laughed, and then looked at Stephen. 'And how are you coping with the sudden elevation to kinda-fatherhood?'

'So far, so good,' he said. 'But Jack's not a teenager yet.'

'I wonder if he'll live to make it that far,' Ione mumbled as the strains of *Ballroom Blitz* began to echo from Jack's bedroom. She looked at Elizabeth. 'How often did you want to kill this one?' She jerked her head toward Stephen.

'At this age, I'd say once a week. By the time he was a teenager, daily.'

Stephen shook his head. 'I'll go get the drinks while you two trash your sons.' He headed into the kitchen.

'We only do it out of love,' Ione shouted. Then she linked her arms with Elizabeth and led her over to the lounge. 'Now, I want all the dirt you've got on Stephen. Every skerrick of it. I warn you, I won't be satisfied with anything less.'

'Then we'll be here for a long time,' Elizabeth said as they sat down and began to chat.

The lunch went much more smoothly than Stephen had expected. While he and his father weren't able to speak comfortably to each other, they were able to both join in the conversation and even tell a story of Stephen's childhood.

Things were starting to wind down when Hampton asked for admittance. Stephen gave his permission and shook his head when the Sabhamir appeared and Ione said, 'Sucked in.'

Hampton frowned. 'What?'

'You're too late. The food's all gone.'

'Ione.' Her father shook his head too.

Hampton grinned. 'I do come here for reasons other than your cooking, Ione.' She snorted and he winked at her before turning his attention to Stephen. 'I was about to deal with that little matter of yours and then thought that, as Coiremir, you're quite within your rights to ask to take over.'

Stephen grinned. He'd completely forgotten about Lansing and the crew. 'That's very kind of you, Sabhamir.'

'Stephen.' He looked at Ione. 'You said you weren't going to do anything to them.'

'They don't know that.'

'What's going on?' Gerry said, looking at them.

'Mark's story to tell, Dad, not mine,' Ione said.

Liam stood. 'Would you mind if I sat in on this? I've got something to say to Aaron myself.'

'Of course.' Stephen touched his hand and the three of them transferred to Hampton's loungeroom. Stephen noted the Sabhamir's apartment was almost as poorly furnished as his had been.

Hampton walked into the office first. Stephen took a moment to turn his brown jumper and jeans into the robe of the Coiremir then followed, Liam behind him. Aaron, John and Mark sat on one of the lounges. All three jumped to their feet, Aaron's face losing colour as he noted Liam's presence.

'Gentlemen.' Hampton folded his arms over his chest. 'I was going to take you before the bardria and try you for your actions, but the Coiremir has asked to have the privilege himself.' He looked over his shoulder. 'All yours.'

'Thank you, Sabhamir.' Stephen stepped forward. He pulled his shoulders back and looked down his nose at the three men who had caused him so much pain and directed his life for so many years. 'My initial consideration is to charge you with assault. If you're found guilty of that, you'll probably be banished.' The three men looked ill. 'However, I can probably be persuaded to agree to a lesser charge.'

'How? Tell us how and we'll do it.' John Scally began to sob, rivulets running from his nose. Mark and Aaron gave him a brief glance of derision.

Mark knew what Stephen wanted. 'I confess that I took part in drugging through drink and then tattooing Stephen O'Malley and leaving him to regain consciousness in the river park. It was a stupid, immature act and I deeply regret it.'

'Oh, yeah, me too, me too,' John said.

Stephen nodded, and then looked at Aaron. 'Well?'

Aaron looked at Liam and gulped, then whispered, 'I confess as well.'

Stephen fought not to smile. 'Thank you. I am inclined to think that I don't want to take this to the bardria.' All three men looked at him with shining eyes. 'I do, however, want you to pay recompense by spending the next six months assisting at the gadda school.'

'Sure,' Mark nodded. John smiled between blubbers. Aaron's shoulders slumped.

'Now, Mark and John, you can go. Mark, perhaps you'd call into the apartment and tell Ione. She'll be glad to hear we're no longer at odds.'

Mark nodded and the two men left. Stephen took a step back. 'Dad, I believe you have something to say to Lansing.'

'I do.' Liam O'Malley stepped forward. 'I trusted you, Aaron, and you betrayed that trust by lying and turning me against my own son. As of this moment, I am no longer your trainer. I will withhold your manuals until your six months of service to the Coiremir are over, after which you'll be free to take them to another trainer and continue your preparation for third order.'

'But, Liam —'

Liam turned his back. Stephen grinned. 'You heard the man, Lansing. On your way.'

Aaron dragged his feet like a recalcitrant schoolboy as he walked out of the office.

'Too easy on them,' Hampton said. 'Should have made them squirm longer.'

'I don't have the time, or the energy,' Stephen said. 'Let's save it for Blair.' Hampton nodded. 'Thanks.'

'My pleasure.'

Stephen turned to his father. 'Stephen, I'm so sorry.'

Stephen waved the apology away. It was over. He wasn't going to waste time on it any more.

THIRTY-FIVE

'*It's time.*'

The sound of the Heasimir's voice popped into and out of Stephen's head so quickly that it took a moment for it to register. Then he stood and transferred to the healers' wing. Moments later, he, Maggie, Kenyon and Sarah were gathered around Shauna Connell's bed.

Stephen's stomach churned and he pushed down the feelings that threatened to burst from him. This was it, then. They were going to find out what Blair was doing and why.

'Where are Hampton and Owen?' Maggie said.

Sarah frowned. 'They're at the airport at Shannon. Hampton said they'll get here as quickly as they can. I'll keep Shauna still until then.'

It was ten minutes before the Sabhamir and Firimir arrived and Sarah woke Shauna up.

As they watched, the girl's eyes fluttered and then opened. Her pupils widened as she scanned the room and saw the guardians looking down at her. Then she closed her eyes and her face relaxed.

'Shauna Connell, we need to speak to you about the monster and how you came to have the knowledge and power to create it,' Hampton said.

There was no reaction to his words — Shauna was still and calm.

'We also need to speak to you about your part in the bombing of the Sclossin Inn.'

A shadow passed over Shauna's face, but Stephen felt sure it wasn't in reaction to Hampton's words. Something else was bothering her.

'Shauna, open your eyes and look at me.'

Something moved in the corner of Stephen's eye. He looked down and saw that Shauna had gripped the cover of the bed. Something was really wrong.

'*Hampton? I don't think she's listening to you.*'

'Shauna. Open your eyes and look at me.' This time, Hampton's voice resonated with the power of the Sabhamir. With a gasp, Shauna's eyes flew open.

'You will tell me who you have been working with.'

'No.'

'We will mind-read you.'

Shauna smiled and Stephen felt his stomach sink. 'Go ahead. You will see nothing, hear nothing. I will not betray the teacher.'

'Firimir.'

Owen stepped forward and put his hands on either side of Shauna's face. They'd gained bardria permission to do this. 'Relax, Shauna, and this will not hurt.'

'Of course.' She closed her eyes, obviously at ease over what was going to happen.

'*Be careful,*' Sarah said. '*Remember what happened to Brian when we started to question him?*'

'*Ah, that's it,*' Stephen said and everyone but Owen looked at him. '*I thought she wasn't listening to Hampton. She was waiting for her teacher to kill her, like Brian was killed.*'

'*Yet she wasn't,*' Hampton said. '*I wonder why. Surely the teacher is in more danger now than she was when we had Brian.*'

'*Shauna is right.*' Owen's voice cut into the conversation.

'Just as with everyone else we've questioned over the past few weeks, her memory has been messed with. I can see ordinary details of her life, but nothing to do with either the texts or the League of Purification.'

'So unless she's prepared to talk, we've got nothing,' Hampton said.

Owen released his hold on the girl and stepped back. Hampton took his place, looming over Shauna. It wasn't often that he called on the might of the Sabhamir to intimidate someone, and Stephen was glad it would never happen to him.

'Shauna Connell. Know that you are to be banished for your actions, not only in conjuring the peat monster to attack Sclossin but in being one of the five responsible for damaging the inn. You will spend the rest of your life in a cell here in the bardria building. You have nothing left to you but your reputation, and now is your chance to save that. Tell me who your teacher is.'

'No.'

'Do you want to put this shame on your family? To let them live with the knowledge that you could have saved us and you didn't?'

Shauna smiled. 'They will know that by refusing you, I have saved us.'

'*Fuck.*' The mental explosion slammed into Stephen's brain. '*What the hell now?*'

'*I've got an idea,*' Owen said. He nodded to Hampton and the Sabhamir stepped out of the way.

'It occurred to me,' he said, '*that while the memories of the actual interactions have been wiped, the importance of that person remains. If Shauna sees her out socially – she may not approach her to avoid suspicion, but the person would be noticed, and would imprint on her memory.*'

'Owen Taggert, you're a genius,' Maggie said.

He again connected with Shauna's mind. '*Hmm, running through some of the minutiae of her life, and guess whose face seems to be jumping out of the crowds?*'

A shiver ran down Stephen's spine. '*Blair Callaghan's.*'

'*Correct.*'

'*We're not going to get anything else here,*' Hampton said. '*Guardians, back to my office.*'

Moments later they were in their customary positions – he, Maggie and Kenyon on one lounge; Owen and Sarah on the other; Hampton pacing up and down the room.

'Damn,' Hampton said. 'Fuck. We needed Shauna to know more.'

'Why? Haven't we found anything at the airport?' Stephen said.

Hampton shook his head. 'The warrant that Ione made up for us was perfect and they searched their records but couldn't find any instance of anyone called Blair Callaghan flying out of Shannon.'

'Damn.' Maggie slumped. 'She's either got a false passport, or she just went there to throw us off the trail and then got on another bus, or took a taxi. Either way, it's going to be almost impossible to find her.'

Stephen felt his heart sink. He'd been looking forward to seeing Blair and making her pay for the misery she'd put Ione through, even if Ione seemed to have adjusted well to her new-found power. After all, it was still unclear as to whether she would survive in the long term.

'Then we hope another gadda spots her and lets us know, before she uses the texts to hurt someone,' Hampton said.

The despondency in the Sabhamir's voice echoed the pain in Stephen's soul. When was this going to end?

***

The piece of paper hovered in the air, turned over, and then lightly drifted down to rest on the desk. Ione pushed an errant curl back from her forehead and looked at Horatio Cormac with a grin. She was sure that, this time, she'd done it.

The caelleach shook his head. 'I cannot believe that I'm saying this, but Ione Hammond Gorton, it is my pleasure to announce that you have passed the first-order test.'

'Yay, Mam!'

Ione looked over her shoulder and smiled at Jack, who was sitting between her parents. Their faces were a picture of pride and admiration.

She looked to her right, to where the guardians stood, people she now considered friends. Well, all but Sarah Hennessy, who wouldn't be friendly if her life depended on it.

Hampton was grinning widely, Owen bowed his head and Kenyon gave her a thumbs-up. Maggie's hands were pressed tight together, no doubt in order to stop herself from jumping on the spot and shouting, which would be a very undignified response from the Ceamir.

Last, Ione looked at Stephen. The glow of pride on his face sent warmth through her. It seemed remarkable that just a few short weeks ago, she hadn't even known he existed. Now, he had joined Jack as the focus of her life — everything that was good and right.

'I believe this calls for a special celebration.' Ione swung back to see the caelleach stand. 'Everyone's invited to the bardria restaurant. My treat.'

'Yay, free food,' Jack shouted.

Ione rubbed her forehead. She was looking forward to the day Jack learnt discretion.

She walked over to the guardians. She wanted to put her arms around Stephen, but the bardria chamber was not the place for public displays of affection.

'Well done, Ione.' Hampton held out his hand and she touched it. 'I suppose now we have to say that at least one good thing has come out of the Forbidden Texts.'

'Yes, the bizarre situation of a Hammond being crap with power is over,' Maggie said. 'And I happen to think now that you not only have power, but are actually a lodestone, there's no need to cling so determinedly to the recipe for Hammond Stew. You don't need it to make you interesting any more.'

Ione decided that while hugging the Coiremir might not be appropriate in the bardria chamber, hitting the Ceamir was warranted at any time and so she thumped Maggie on the arm.

'Rules are rules. To get the recipe, you must marry a Hammond. Not my fault you dumped Mark and chose Lucas instead.'

Maggie spun around to face Stephen. 'You'll tell me, won't you?'

'Sorry, Maggie.'

Maggie pouted. 'Fine, be a bitch. See if I care.'

'Mam!' Jack called out across the chamber. Ione turned to see him standing, holding her mother's hand. 'Are you coming?'

'Tact. One day, he'll have tact,' Ione murmured.

Stephen grinned, then, to her delight and the amazement of gadda watching, kissed her. 'Not sure we'd love him as much if he did.'

Ione smiled as she walked from the room holding Stephen's hand.

ASARLAI

The library was impressive — floor-to-ceiling bookshelves covered all the walls, as well as the door she'd just walked through. The room was divided into two sections by two beautifully woven carpets. On one sat a couple of wing chairs, with footstools and a table between — a comfortable reading environment. On the other was a huge wooden desk and a leather chair.

Asarlai tried to make a mental calculation of the worth of the items in the room, and soon gave up. Wealth had been obvious the moment her taxi pulled up outside the Boston brownstone. The windows gleamed, every wooden surface was freshly painted and the brass doorknob was polished. The plants were clipped and neat. The entrance hall to the home was decorated on the floor by a Turkish runner and on the ceiling by three miniature chandeliers.

She stood in the middle of the library and turned her mind from the beauty around her to the interview that was about to take place. On the flight over, she'd run through her plan again and again. Truth be told, she still wasn't completely sure this was what she wanted to do. There was an element of risk here, but she didn't feel she had any choice.

Experimenting on Ione Gorton had been a mistake. There was no doubt in her mind that in giving Ione the power she'd always deserved, Asarlai had destroyed her own. If she was to see her dream for the gadda come to fruition, she needed someone to work for her, and that needed to be someone outside the structures of the bardria.

She was going to unleash the monster, and hope that he didn't devour her first.

She heard the door behind her open, and swung around. She recognised him instantly — after having spent the past few months with his son, those features were very familiar to her. She was surprised at how well he had aged; there was a sheen of silver in his dark hair and his jawline had softened a little, but there was no denying that even in his late fifties, Rogan Connor was still an attractive man.

He was dressed in neatly pressed trousers, a collared shirt and a navy blue jumper, with tasselled loafers. Asarlai guessed that the outfit had probably cost more than her entire wardrobe.

He closed the door behind him, then turned and regarded her calmly, his hands clasped behind his back. Time began to drag, and Asarlai found herself remembering what he'd done to get himself banished — strangle a woman to death.

She felt a frisson of fear, but told herself to stop being dramatic. Right now, Connor needed her. That would stay his hand.

'It's been a long time since I heard that name.' Despite the decades in America, his voice still had an Irish lilt.

Asarlai smiled. She'd known asking to discuss Connor with the man now called Patrick Dublin would get her this meeting faster than anything else she could have said. 'It is your true name.'

He tipped his head to one side and studied her. 'And your true name?'

'Lisa Booker.' Asarlai hoped he couldn't see the lie in her eyes. 'I've wanted to meet you for a long time.'

'Really? Why would any gadda want to meet me?'

'Because I think you and I can help each other.'

'In what way?'

'I need someone to help me bring the gadda out of the darkness and into the light. You need someone to help you unlock your power. Help me, and I'll help you.'

His forehead creased as his eyebrows drew low over his eyes. 'You know how to break the banishing?'

'I do.'

He stepped forward, and she could see the excitement lighting his eyes. 'How?'

'I'm not ready to tell you that.'

'So I'm to just trust you when you say you can do this?'

She smiled. 'Can you afford not to?' His fists clenched and unclenched. 'It's been more than thirty-five years since you were last able to use your power. Do you still dream of it, see it every night in the shadowlands, or have you forgotten?'

'Do you think anyone can forget what it feels like to use their power?' His lips drew back from his teeth in a snarl. 'You have no comprehension of how it feels to go day and night, knowing the power you had and now being useless.'

Asarlai knew very well what that felt like. She reached within, for her power, and almost cried when she couldn't find it. 'Then what have you to lose in trusting me?'

He lifted his chin and looked down his nose at her, and she was reminded of the Flaherty half of his ancestry. 'And what do I have to do for you, for this boundless gift?'

'To begin, shelter me. Help me to live as a human, to blend in. The guardians must not find me. The Sabhamir in particular.'

Connor's mouth twisted. 'There's a man I look forward to seeing again.'

Asarlai opened her mouth to tell him his dream of revenge was over — the Sabhamir who had banished him had managed to get himself killed by an insignificant little goblin — but decided against it. Information was her only remaining weapon. 'The time will come.'

'Then, Miss Booker, welcome to my home.' He bowed, waving his hand before him in a flourish. 'First things first — we must give you a new name. You'll also need documentation.'

Asarlai smiled. 'I knew I was right to come to you.'

Connor walked toward her and Asarlai forced herself to remain where she was. Even with his power locked, there was an arrogance in his posture and a determination in his gait that said Rogan Connor was dangerous.

'How did you get here?'

'I flew. Human transport.' She shuddered. That had been a soul-dampening experience that she hoped never to repeat. 'I have all the usual human documentation.'

'Show me.' He reached out and his hand briefly touched hers.

She staggered back as the shock of power jumped from him to her. Damn, she thought. Damn, he's already got his power. I've misjudged. I'm doomed.

It sank into her, filled her for a terrifying moment and then it disappeared. She gasped and tried to grab hold of it — any power was better than none. But it disappeared into the yawning blackness that was now her centre and she knew it was gone for good.

She glared at Connor, and then realised he didn't look the way she expected. She would have thought he would be triumphant over tricking her. Disappointed, perhaps, that whatever that incantation was hadn't worked.

Instead, he was — stunned. He stared at her with wide eyes, his skin pale.

'What did you do?'

She shook her head. 'I did nothing.'

His eyes flicked around the room, and then he closed them. Slowly, a smile spread across his face. 'Star be praised.'

'What is it?'

In answer, he turned to face one of the walls and lifted his hands. A bolt of deep blue power burst out and slammed into the wall, sending books, wood and pieces of plaster flying. Asarlai ducked, and watched between her fingers as fire roared up the exposed beams and began to lick at the ceiling.

Rogan Connor tipped back his head and laughed. 'My power. My power is back.'

Asarlai stared at him, dumbfounded. It was an honest reaction — he hadn't had power when he touched her, and now he did.

Star above, what had she become?

'You wonderful, wonderful woman.' Connor moved forward to put his arms around her, but the moment he touched her she felt his power drain into her and disappear into the blackness. He jumped back and snarled, 'What are you doing? Why are you stealing my power?'

'I don't know.' Asarlai lifted her hands, terrified by what was happening. 'It was not my intention to lift your banishment, nor to just take your power now. It just happened.'

Connor took a couple of steps backward and frowned at her. 'You said you knew how to lift my banishment.'

Asarlai pushed away her fear to think calmly about how to maintain her hold over him.

'The information I have works in amazing ways, Connor. This is just the least of what it can do. Did I take all your power?' He'd be useless to her without it.

He shook his head. 'What information?'

She smiled. All was not lost. 'Not yet, Connor. You have to prove yourself to me, before I tell you what it is that I have.'

His eyes went blank, and Asarlai wondered what he was thinking. She knew that Connor's skill and intelligence had once been so well regarded there'd been talk that he might become a guardian, perhaps even the Sabhamir.

She must never underestimate him.

'Very well, Lisa. I'll help you look human, and in return you'll trust me and tell me the information you have.'

To Asarlai's ears, it sounded as though he were commanding her to trust him.

'Prove yourself worthy and I just might,' she said.

He smiled. 'Then we have a deal. I would shake on it, but ...'

'For now, your word is enough.' Exhaustion began to sweep over her. She needed time by herself, to try and fathom what was happening to her.

'Then let me show you to your room.' Connor nodded his head.

Asarlai followed him, hoping that this gamble would pay off.

ACKNOWLEDGEMENTS

Thanks to my family and friends for their love and support, particularly my husband. To my beta readers Kaaren Sutcliffe, Donna Maree Hanson and Annette Dunkley — your honest appraisal of the strengths and weaknesses meant the world to me. To my experts — my husband, Tim, for helping with the computer stuff and Rob Hood for introducing me to giant monsters and doing what he could to make Fatharr worthy of the title 'daikaiju'. To the members of FWOR — Cat Sparks, Donna, Kylie Seluka, Matthew Farrer, Russell Kirkpatrick and Trudi Canavan — for the hand-holding, the claps on the back, the smacks to the forehead and generally helping me survive this journey. Finally to the team at HarperCollins, particularly Stephanie and Kate — you've made me a better writer. Thank you.

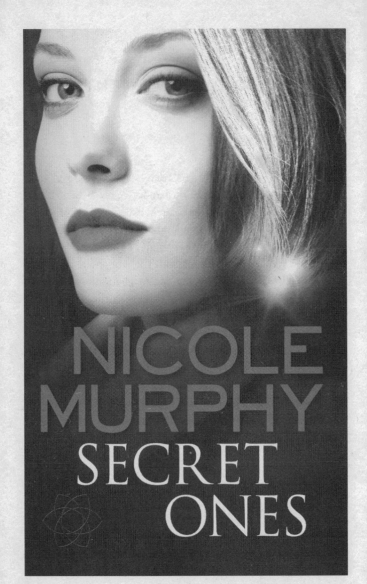

NICOLE
MURPHY

SECRET
ONES

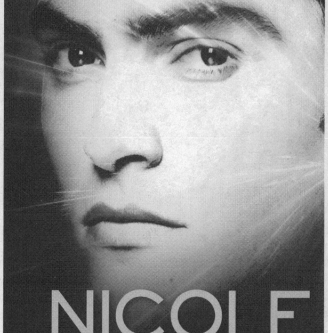

NICOLE
MURPHY
ROGUE
GADDA

Voyager Online

FOR TRAVELLERS OF THE IMAGINATION

MAKE VOYAGER ONLINE YOUR NEXT DESTINATION

VOYAGER ONLINE has the latest science fiction and fantasy releases, book extracts, author interviews, downloadable wallpapers and monthly competitions. It also features exclusive contributions from some of the world's top science fiction and fantasy authors.

DROP BY the message board where you can discuss books, authors, conventions and more with other fans.

DISCUSS SF/F in depth: take part in the Voyager Book Club which runs every two months, or look up some of the available reading guides to your favourite books.

KEEP IN TOUCH with authors via the Voyager blog, which is updated every week with guest posts from authors and all the latest news and events on sf/f in Australia and around the world.

FOLLOW US on Twitter and Facebook.

ENJOY the journey and feel at home with friends at www.voyageronline.com.au

HARPER
Voyager

www.voyageronline.com.au